MONEY GAMES III
The Gold Standard

Kimberly Barnes

Urban House Publishing
P.O. Box 1826
Montclair, N.J.
07042

Email: urbanhousepublishing@yahoo.com
Telephone: (973) 744- 7122
 Fax: (973) 744- 5067
See us at Face book: Urban House publishing
 Instagram: Urban House Publishing

More Books by Urban House publishing coming to print soon!!!

ACKNOWLEDGEMENTS

Writing this novel would not have been possible without the advice and insight of several former Marines I've come to know and love. For me, the most difficult part of writing this adventure had to do with the military. I have to thank my friends for talking me through so many aspects and allowing me to use artistic license when dealing with the elements I adopted from our conversations. Thankfully, they were kind enough to accommodate me and my unending questions.

George, this would have been an impossible endeavor if you had not helped me. Your descriptions of tactics and weapons are awesome. Also, I can't thank you enough for your editing suggestions. Patrick, as always, you helped me move the story along with all of your great advice. There are no words to show my appreciation. To Bill, my legal advisor, thank you for all of your hard work

Special thanks go out to Rasool Jacobs for believing in me and helping me embark on this endeavor. Without his encouragement and business mind, this could not have become a reality.

I would also like to thank my family, especially my husband Celester for allowing me the time to work on this trilogy. Of course my heartfelt gratitude goes out to my granddaughter, Khalia, for helping me with the computer formats.

Any mistakes, omissions, or errors dealing with the military, weapons, tactics, high finance, or locations are purely my own. This is a novel and the characters, along with the events described in this story, are purely fiction.

DEDICATIONS

I would like to dedicate this work to the men and women of the armed forces. It is only you who stands between the citizenry and the ascendancy of a tyrannizing class of elitists.

Prologue

The first television station to come back on the air and retain a steady signal was FOX out of New York. They were only able to display their logo, but it was a start. Shortly thereafter, other major broadcast networks lit up and every radio station in the city came back on the air. It took a little longer, but soon the cable channels returned and the internet started to show signs of life. Minutes later, all of the cell phone towers started the process of rebooting their systems and clearing the buffers of disconnected calls. Although unable to place calls immediately, the mobile devices and smart phones across the city started to be pinged with signals.

It would be the first time in days anyone had access to news, the ability to find out about the welfare of family, or to reach out for help. They weren't all that disappointed about the delay because everyone realized getting things up and running would take some time. They found hope in their screens that displayed the same singular line of text: PLEASE STAND BY FOR A SPECIAL REPORT.

Word spread fast among the various groups of protesters, rioters, and looters. Night was falling, and the ability to once again hear what was going on in the world, or maybe communicate with family, did what the police could not do. The return of radio waves, satellite signals, and streams of digital broadcasts cleared the streets of Manhattan and eventually every other city in the nation. The only ones left behind were the drunks, the injured, the mad, and the dead.

As soon as people got off of the streets and went home, most of them turned on the television sets or sat down to log onto Face book or Twitter. It seemed like ages had passed since the world went mad and the people were tired, exhausted to the point of passivity. The restoration of media and return home was a much-needed respite from the stress and anxiety of what had become a chaotic situation. Settling in and waiting for the news, it gave families much needed time to come together to take measure of what had happened and what they had lost. Then, the Emergency Broadcasting System started to sound its buzzing tone.

Gathered around television screens all around the country, families and neighbors as well as strangers and travelers listened to the uncanny beeps and watched the text start to scroll across the screen: "THIS IS NOT A TEST. PLEASE STAND BY FOR A SPECIAL REPORT...THIS IS NOT A TEST..."

On every station and on every device able to process streaming video, Andrew Stevens appeared on screen. There was only one camera and it was zoomed in to focus on his handsome face and perfectly manicured dark hair. He was standing at a plain wooden podium lacking insignia of any kind. As the camera panned back, the audience could see a line of men and women seated in chairs several feet behind the dais. They were sullen and still, not talking to each other, and they all wore morose expressions. The camera zoomed back in, moving from one face to another, so everyone watching could see those in attendance.

In the center was the President of the United States. To his right was the Vice President and to his left was Secretary of State. Also on the stage was the Secretary of Defense, the Speaker of the House, and both the majority and minority leaders of both houses. Standing along the stage were senior members of the Cabinet and the nine Supreme Court Justices.

No one outside of D.C. knew about the explosions that had rocked the Capitol, the Supreme Court, and the Old Executive Office building. Few beyond the President's inner circle knew about the secret meetings at Camp David or the rapid dispatch of messages delivered by heavily armed Secret Service agents. No one but a very select few had heard the offers, counter offers, or rejections concerning the fate of the federal government. And, only the President himself heard the threats that resulted in the explosions that caused three federal buildings enough damage as to be near collapse.

The President had been threatened, but he had not given in--and then he had to be shown the truth. Only after Andrew Steven's men had put on a display of power did he relent. The President was no longer in control. No one but Andrew Stevens saw him break under pressure and agree to all of the terms for fear of many more explosions and a violent coup the President of the United States did not have the power to stop.

It was impossible to determine the venue of the powerful gathering, but the caption on the screen read, "Washington, D.C." The camera operator panned back over to the tall man standing at the podium and held it steady. He looked directly at the camera and spoke in a deep, clear voice:

My name is Andrew Stevens and I am speaking to you tonight at the direction of the President of the United States and with unanimous consent of Congress. As of twelve noon today, the United States of America has been placed under Martial Law.

Until further notice, no one, I repeat, no one is to be on the streets or out of their homes after sundown. Units from the National Guard have been dispatched with orders to kill on sight. This order will stay in effect until law and order is restored.

Furthermore, I am calling upon all civil authorities and public employees to go back to work tomorrow morning. Police, fire fighters, anyone involved and contracted under law to protect, serve, or administer to the needs of the people must return to work or face severe consequences. Believe me, I understand the complex reasons why many of you felt the need to walk away, to go home and protect your families, and leave the streets at a critical juncture in this great nation's history.

I understand your lack of faith and trust in the system. Nevertheless, to all the policemen and women, to all the fire fighters and other public employees--I promise you this, you will all be made whole. If you go back to work, you will be given amnesty and, eventually, you will be able to live the American dream once again--but first we need your help. The National Guard and federal authorities need your help to restore order.

The reason why I am speaking with you, and not the President, is this: I, along with other concerned Americans, have the means to offer you a new social contract, one where you will no longer be burdened by debt, where you can save for your retirement and earn a decent living. All I...we...are asking is for you to give us a chance to correct the wrongs that have been done to you. The consortium I represent is willing to do what the politicians weren't willing to--we are going to offer you, the American people, a bail out.

To all of the public union members, we are simply asking you to return to work and return law, order, and justice to our streets. You will be the first ones rewarded. Through your unions, the twelve Federal Reserve Banks will renegotiate the terms of your mortgages, reduce the amount due, interest rates, and extended the time to repay the debt.

Once order has restored, the banks in the Federal Reserve System will be working with us to do the same thing for all Americans. Imagine a future with manageable student loans, mortgages based on the actual value of your home, and more years to pay off your car loan or credit cards at much lower interest rates. Yes, the future can be yours if you just give us a chance.

Now, in order to do this, we need your help. The consortium I represent has to take steps to stabilize the monetary system. To do so, we will also have to guarantee the principle and interest on all government debt, foreign and domestic. In short, a the bankers and industrialists who have pledged their fortunes to save this nation will have to bail out the United States of America because this country, the greatest nation on earth, deserves to be saved.

To enable us to make the changes we must make, I am asking you, the American people, to temporarily suspend the Constitution of the United States. This will only last until order is restored and a vote cast to reinstate it. The second thing I asks of you is to grant me, Andrew Stevens, temporary authority to administer the legal and financial affairs of this nation. Acting as a Special Master, with the advice and consent of the President of the United States, we can restore this country to stability.

To get on the path of a secure financial future, I am asking every American of voting age to register online with the newly created Federal Election Registry and vote. After you read the plans we have proposed, vote your conscience and give me the authority to act. What we shall see is a successful experiment in direct democracy. Directly after this broadcast, more details and information will be provided to you. The voting begins immediately and ends at noon tomorrow.

Unless you show your support through the democratic process by temporarily suspending the Constitution and granting me the authority I seek, I will have no choice but to step aside and retract the generous offer the consortium I represent has made.

I thank you for your time and goodnight.

He had gotten the attention of some Americas and inspired them. In a few towns cops started to return to their stations and organize patrols. With the permission and assistance of the National Guard, fire fighters returned to their firehouses and started pulling out the engines to look for and extinguish fires that were still burning. Many Americans felt a sense of relief and hope that things would not just return to normal but be better than it was.

At the same time, a sizable percentage of the population was vehemently against both propositions. Some vowed to fight tooth and nail if the Constitution fell while others did not know who Andrew Stevens was and did not trust him. A small group of patriots was sure that the President had been hoodwinked and swore to find out the truth behind the conspiracy. As upset and vocal as the dissidents were, very few of them bothered to read the lengthy, arcane language of the bills that authorized the vote.

By the next day, both question had been answered by majorities that could not be overcome. A slim majority voted to suspend the Constitution of the United States of America. By an even narrower margin, Andrew Stevens was democratically appointed to the position of Special

Master of the United States.

A "Special Master" was usually a person appointed by a court of law to administer to the estate of Bankrupt Corporation. Stevens had assumed the title because it was so appropriate for what he planned to do--disburse the assets of the United States to his associates. He would have all but dictatorial authority over the banking system, the military, as well as every department in the executive branch.

The bloodless coup was over. Andrew Stevens was in charge and would stay in charge. The only people who did not realize it were the citizens of the United States of America who had voted to support him.

Chapter One

If General Smythe didn't know better, just watching the news would have made him want to pack up the station wagon and head for the hills.

Several hours before, MSNBC had gone live to a burned out Sacramento gas station where the owner and his family were slaughtered. The customers had been waiting in line for hours, some for days, and had just watched a tanker truck deliver a much-needed supply of gasoline. Apparently, the owner refused to accept old money, Federal Reserve Notes, as payment. Instead, he demanded payment in something tangible--gold, silver, diamonds, or other precious gems was all he would take in trade for fuel. The people were so furious at the greed; they armed themselves and attacked the station. At the exact same time the cops arrived, the customers, desperate to fill up their tanks mobbed the pumps and then started attacking each other. What MSNBC was showing was the aftermath of the ensuing riot.

Smythe knew that same type of scene had been playing out all across the country. It was the havoc of post-revolutionary Tunisia, Egypt, and Libya all rolled up into one. What he feared most of all, though, were scenes that were similar to Syria. He did not want to see troops, his soldiers, gunning down unarmed civilians. One incident, like what happened at Kent State on May 4, 1970, was enough.

In the major cities all across the country, the people were clearly out of control and everyone seemed to be losing their minds. That insanity, he knew, was a symptom of the disease of desperation. Once the flood gates of anarchy had opened up, it would be an almost impossible job to still the waters--but that was exactly what he had been ordered to do.

Sitting high up in his secluded office, Smythe had to fight the urge to pour himself another drink. With a full division under his command, the Joint Commission Task Force on Terrorism had taken center stage in what appeared to be the last line between civilized society and total anarchy. At the same time, he knew he was right in the middle of the biggest power play in American history.

It was audacious move but the riskiest part was over and Smythe no longer pondered the ramifications of the transfer of power. Instead, he wondered how things would have gone if Andrew Stevens hadn't been able to get the rest of the military on board--or at least get the other services to sit on the sidelines. It was a lot to take in but Smythe accepted it with a sigh of relief.

*****

The peaceful view overlooking Central Park belied what was going on all around it. Although there wasn't a cloud for miles, the air was thick, dark even, fouled by the fumes from burning tires and other debris that had been set on fire in the streets.

Michelle looked out of the double-paned windows on the park side of the penthouse suite. She was leaning on one of two matching Victorian chairs situated to get the best view of the great lawn below. A faint, musky smell of disuse was all around her. No one ever bothered to use the place; she mused, let alone air it out or restore the ancient furniture. Still, the exquisitely decorated penthouse retained the elegance and charm of the Gilded Age. None of that mattered now. That age had long passed and would never return.

She took a long sip of wine, knowing it was not a good idea bury her sorrows in alcohol. But, she had been trying everything in her power to suppress the hurt she felt from the loss of Tommy. Running her long fingers through her raven-black hair, she pushed several loose strands back away from her caramel-toned cheek. The gray had started to show at the roots, giving away her true age, but that was the least of her concerns.

Thinking about Tommy, about never being able to see him again, was what had been dominating her thoughts. Every time she thought about him, about the wonderful man they had all lost, her eyes filled with tears. Even though he had been married to Darla, Michelle had loved him. His murder felt like a dull knife slowly slicing through her tender heart--the deeper it went, the more it hurt.

As much as she wanted to think about Tommy, to morn for him, or to go on a mental holiday and forget about the insanity of the past year, she couldn't. Too many things were happening around her and she had to figure out a way to get out of the city.

It was only several weeks before when the lawyers and investment bankers from Goldman had left the penthouse in a rush. On any other day, if she had disclosed the discovery of a massive amount of gold to the same group, they would have found a way to excuse themselves so they could pass off the inside information to their friends. The initial public offering of a company possessing $100 billion dollars in recoverable gold was big enough to have made international headlines. However, after the lead lawyer had taken what he said was an emergency call, the visitors had scattered like roaches.

In hindsight, Michele understood why--the fact the city was on the cusp of burning must have curbed the vultures' capitalistic appetites. When they left, they were picked up by heavily armed, private security details. That was an obvious warning sign she had missed, a dire prediction about how dangerous the situation had become. She figured they had been tipped off about the crisis and not one of them had bothered to warn her. Since then, because of the way the oil shock and financial crisis played out, it had not been possible to leave the city.

Michelle stepped closer to the window, pulling a Channel serape tighter around her shoulders to keep out the chill. The stress of the past several weeks had taken its toll on her, as had the shortage of food. Her busty, hourglass figure was not as curvaceous as it had been, and the loss of weight seemed to have made her feel like she was always cold. Looking down at the scores of leafless trees in the park, she found it impossible to remember how long ago the trouble had started...how many weeks had passed since the world fell apart.

As she thought back on the series of events leading up to the collapse of the markets and the descent of Manhattan, Michelle was still having a difficult time wrapping her brain around everything she had witnessed. More than anything, though, she was shocked how quickly the city had fallen apart and sickened by some of what she had seen.

No one was sure exactly what triggered the initial chaos in the states; but clearly, the people of New York had had enough. After the Straight of Hormuz was reportedly mined, in short order, the stock market had crashed and the price of gasoline doubled. Then, stores all over the city tacked on delivery surcharges, more than doubling the prices for everything. That rapid, unexpected price increase caused a run on the banks and that seemed to have been the trigger.

At the start of the financial panic, before the civil service workers abandoned their posts, the mayor of New York City retained what could be considered his own private army 40,000 strong. The men and women of the NYPD were armed with weapons and technology developed for and passed down by the military and they thought they would be able to handle the crisis. Yet, despite their best efforts, they had no answer for what was happening in the streets. It was clear, though, once the banking system froze up, everything spiraled downward.

The glass, concrete, and steel cathedrals of the world's biggest financial institutions were almost immediately placed under siege. The situation had quickly gone from marches and protests, to demands for the banks to return money, to window smashing and looting. Thousands of cops dressed in riot gear and armed to the teeth had been no match for the hundreds of thousands of the city's denizens who, over the course of days, increasingly took to the streets demanding remuneration, justice, and a whole host of other unattainable concession. With no singular voice, the collective wants, needs, and demands of the people were drowned out by the melee and impossible to answer.

As the rioting continued, the NYPD had been able to scatter the crowds around the cluster of Midtown bank headquarters and the multitudes besieging Wall Street. The marauding groups quickly reassembled and either went after another target or attacked again from another direction. It was then that the Mayor made the biggest mistake of conflict. He ordered the NYPD to use the untested, military-grade, crowd control equipment to stop the rioting. Using the gear, the police had unintentionally killed several protesters using microwave blasts that made their skin bubble and fried their brains.

That disastrous experiment had been recorded and the results broadcast globally. The airing of the gruesome footage was a major turning point--not just in New York, but around the world. Almost immediately after the killings, the Mayor's mansion and many police precinct houses were attacked by large crowds. The disturbances spilled over into residential neighborhoods and other commercial districts. From that day on, citizens all over the world had taken up arms and revolted against the authorities. If such atrocities could happen in the United States, they could happen anywhere.

The further the civil uproar spread, the more force the police used, the harder the crowds struck back. The amount of property damage cause by the rioting citizens increased with the level of force used against them. That had gone on for weeks, weeks Michelle thought would never end. The vicious cycle of attack, counterattack, and escalation on both sides of the struggle rapidly turned into a free-for-all and the city showed the scars of the battle. The entire time, though, she never left the security of the penthouse.

Eventually, there had been no way to watch or listen to the news. The radio and television stations went off the air. Every once in a while a few local stations would reappear--but the broadcasts were inconsistent and spotty. It looked like someone somewhere was trying to get things up and running again but just falling short. Then, the internet went down and so did the cell phone networks. For what seemed like an eternity, only the basic utilities continued to function.

Holed up in her protective nest, Michelle could only hope the electricity and water would hold out or else she'd soon have to find another place to hide. Being so many floors above street level made her feel safe, but without water, it wouldn't matter. As a precaution, she filled the tub and every container she could find. Luckily, over the prior few days, the local broadcast stations, as well as cell phones and the internet, had come back on line. What she saw and heard over the government controlled media outlets, however, had not put her at ease.

Pondering the situation, Michelle wondered how long it would be before she would feel safe enough to leave. There was no way to know or find out about the circumstances at street level. But, if the smoke staining the sky and the smell of burning rubber was any indication, things had not gotten much better. She did hear from a neighbor that federal troops were supposed to come in and make good on Special Master Steven's promise to get the economy back on track. To do that, though, they had to secure the exchanges and try to jump-start commerce.

In New York and Chicago, where the concentration of dissidents was highest, the National Guard was trying to establish buffer zones. The financial district and Midtown had been cleared out and locked down. Thousands of people had either been killed or arrested and there was now a secure corridor patrolled by heavily armed soldiers, armored vehicles, and even unmanned aerial vehicles. Although the rioting and looting continued in other parts of the city, the buffer zones made reopening the exchanges possible.

She had followed the developments with great concern--the reopening of the exchanges had led to nothing but more losses, more confusion, and an even larger economic disaster. As if on cue, in the days after Andrew Stevens's speech, all hell had broken loose all over again and the country had become even more deeply divided. Across the globe, individuals, companies, and even nations, did everything they could to dump dollars and it was happening so fast there wasn't even enough time for a period of hyperinflation. The U.S. currency was finished.

Michelle Alvarez-Rivera, a woman who had struggled her entire life to attain credibility in a world dominated by stuffy old white men with outdated ideas, felt it was up to her to figure out how to take advantage of the critical failures of the old-boy network. She wasn't in a position to change the world--but she controlled enough gold to make sure the people she loved were safe and secure. She had the means and she had a plan. If she could pull it off was another question all together.

A loud knock on the door startled her out of her thoughts. Not expecting anyone, she had no idea who it could be. The elevator only came to the top floor if a special key was used, but with the world gone mad,

Michelle couldn't be sure who had found their way up. Thinking her friends could not possibly make it through the treacherous streets, she had no idea who could be pounding on her door.

She walked quickly to the kitchen counter and picked up a snub-nose .38. As she slowly made her way down the hall toward the front door, the bell rang and it startled her into a complete stop. Without realizing it, she had raised the barrel of the weapon and was pointing it at the door.

"Whoever it is, I'm armed--just go away!"

"Michelle, don't shoot! It's me, Carlos."

"And me Darla. Hurry up and open the door, Carlos is hurt."

Michelle pushed the cabinet she had blocking the door out of the way and fumbled with the locks and chains. As quickly as she could, she pulled the door open. Standing with an arm around Darla, Carlos leaned against her and held a blood-covered rag to his head. Darla's shirt was ripped and where the skin showed, the grip of a large handgun poked out of the waistline of her pants.

"Oh, my God, Carlos! What happened to you? How did you get here?"

"It's nothing, Dona Michelle," Carlos answered weakly, his usually mild Spanish accent slightly more pronounced. "I got hit in the head with a bottle."

Thin but wiry, Carlos was much stronger than he looked. Although the gash on his head throbbed, he somehow maintained a passive, unaffected expression. His dark features were only mildly distorted by a slightly curled lip and some blood that had dried around his eye.

After she secured the door, Michelle reached out and took his arm, leading him and Darla down the hallway to the kitchen table.

"How did you get here? I mean, I thought the streets were--"

19

"It was a nightmare, let me tell you," Darla responded.

Turning to catch a glimpse of her friends as they all but collapsed into chairs, Michelle couldn't help but admire Darla. The woman had been on the run and under attack, and yet everything about her was perfect. Even the beads of nervous sweat on her chocolate skin made her glisten like a model. There was no other way to say it--Darla, Tommy's widow, was an amazing looking creature. Listening as she went, Michelle walked to the freezer and got out a tray of ice.

"We flew from Teeterboro to the heliport," Darla explained, "but there was nowhere to land. So, Carlos flew us over to Brooklyn saw a place on top of a parking garage. After he landed, we've been trying to make our way here ever since."

"Oh, my God. How long ago was that?"

"I don't know, Michelle. We lost track of what day it is, do you know what day it is?"

"Tuesday, the 14th,"

"Oh, my God! You're kidding me?"

"No, sweetie, this mess started weeks ago."

Darla shook her head in disbelief and went on, "After we crossed the East River, we've been working our way here, and it's almost like we've been able to move block by block. You wouldn't believe what happened' down there."

"From up here, it's looked like a war zone." Michelle mentally pictured the scenes of the rioters and protesters being all but mowed down on the street below her. She had to shake her head to get the vision out of her head.

"Yes, a war zone. That is exactly what it is," Carlos chimed in weakly.

"Well, we got some help along the way and a guy took us to his place so we could hide out. It's not far from here, just a few blocks, but as soon as we were spotted, a whole bunch of people stormed the building looking for us. Luckily, they ran up the stairs while we rode down the elevator."

Carlos added, "We would have gotten away, but someone saw us and threw bottles."

Although Carlos was alert, it was clear the blow to his head was having an impact on him. His usually slow, clipped style of speaking was even slower and he was drawing out his words. Darla made sure he kept the rag pressed against his head to stop the bleeding, and then hushed him to get him to stop talking.

"It was just a lucky shot. The bottle bounced off a sign and straight down onto his head. After that, it was easy. Child, we ran here like two baby gazelles on the Sahara bein' chased by a hungry pride of lions."

"Oh, God, Darla!" As Michelle wrapped cubes into a towel, she asked, "How the hell did you get a helicopter, I mean..."

Michelle handed the ice pack to Carlos and pulled his hand away from the wound to check it. "Yeah, you're going to need stitches. That's a nice gash." She turned back to Darla for the answer."

"It was easy. When we flew into Teeterboro, Dan and Susan had already picked--"

"Susan? You saw Susan?"

"Oh, my goodness. Yes. Yes! Oh, Michelle, I'm sorry, Susan's doing just fine, and she's in good hands."

"Where is she, Darla? Why isn't she with you?"

"Her and that guy she's with have to go find Donny's brother, Richard."

"What guy, and what do they want with Crazy Richard?"

"Michelle, sweetie, you'd better sit down for this one--have I got one heck of a story to tell, and you're gonna have a hard time swallowing' this one...But first, let's talk

21

about Tommy. Where's my husband's body?"

Chapter Two

The Remington 700 sniper rifle was sitting straight and level on its bipod. The top of the hill not only provided a flat, solid surface but also kept her downwind from the target.

Seven hundred yards away, the mark lowered his head and tore at a small patch of dry brown grass. His lips and tongue extended out from the end of a narrow, brown snout. A majestic 12-point rack tilted down and then up as the white tail deer, a big old buck, chewed on the snack with his grinding teeth. Usually, he wouldn't be out at that time of the day and should have been bedded down in his hide until nightfall. But, the smell in the air meant snow was coming and would make such a simple meal more difficult to obtain. Besides, the plentiful dry grass provided him some camouflage.

Lying prone, looking through the scope, Susan saw it all and watched the graceful beast pause and huff, trying to detect the scent of any predators in the area. When he looked up, she put the crosshairs directly on the white patch between the protruding muscles of his forelegs. Slowly, steadily, she exhaled and squeezed the trigger.

The report echoed through the valley at the exact same time as the buck dropped. Susan DiGiovanni had scored her second kill.

"Woo-Wee! I got him!"

"Nice shot," Sampson's voice was filled with pride. "Let's get down there and carve us up some steak."

"You're not gonna make me eat the heart, are you?"

"Only if you want to."

Susan let go of the rifle and shifted her body so she could grab onto her instructor. Although she was diminutive compared to the former Marine, the weeks of hiding in the Ramapo Mountains had changed her. She looked a little scruffy, a little more rugged, and more than ready for a wrestling match. She dug the toes of her hiking boots into the ground, pulled up her knees, and lunged. As she launched herself toward Daniel Sampson, the locks of her frazzled brown hair fell away from her gorgeous, angelic face.

Sampson had been lying beside her with a small spotting scope trained on the target. Instinctively, the second she lunged in his direction, he turned to his back and took up a defensive posture. Still, he was unable to stop her from landing right on top of him.

"Whoa, whoa, what are you doing?"

"I figured, since I'm the hunter and you're the gatherer, I was gonna drag you to my cave and have my way with you."

"Feeling a bit aggressive, huh, Susan?" he couldn't help but grin at her child-like excitement.

He dropped the scope and grabbed her by the wrists. With an upward lift of his hips and a quick spin, he had her on her back and was hovering directly over her. The move shocked her but when she realized he had taken away her advantage, she started to squirm and squealed in delight.

A second later, with he knees pressed up against her butt and her legs spread, Sampson buried his head into the nape of her neck and bit her gently. A master of hand-to-hand combat, he had to hold back quite a bit so he did not hurt her. The little nip on her flesh did not even leave a mark.

"Sampson, oh! You bastard, you're going to pay for that!"

"Am I? You promise?"

Having no choice, because he had immobilized her by pressing his body weight against her with her arms pinned above her head, she surrendered to him completely.

"Yeah, I promise...since you got me to submit, what are you gonna do with me?"

"Eat."

"Mmmm. Sounds delicious."

Sampson stood up and helped Susan off her feet. He brushed the dead, dry leaves off her back and reached down to pick up the rifle. "As much as I'd love to taste you right now, we've got a body down there that's getting cold. We should get down there, bleed him, and clean him before the meat spoils."

"Party pooper!"

He smiled at her puerile response. Even though she was nearly forty, Susan's youthful disposition made him think of everything he missed as a kid. It had been a complete surprise to him how much he was enjoying her company and their time together.

Several weeks had passed since they had hiked into the Ramapo Mountains. A professional at tracking, scouting, eluding, and evading, being in the forest was Sampson's comfort zone. He knew the terrain and knew exactly where to go to keep them away from civilization.

His initial plan was to camp out for a few days and then return to find out if the situation had settled down. But, as it turned out, there had been no need to return and many reasons to stay out of sight.

From several of the vantage points along the higher ridges, he had spotted warplanes flying overhead. Even more revealing than seeing the fast-movers leave their contrails across the sky were the blimps.

It hadn't been hard to observe several LEMV's-- Long Endurance Multi-Intelligence Vehicles flying toward Manhattan. The military hadn't even bothered to disguise their movements. Most Americans did not even know the blimps existed, but the highly classified airships were specifically designed for war zones. Only because of Sampson's involvement in the planning of several clandestine strikes inside of Pakistan was he made aware of them.

The blimps were designed to do the work of dozens of drones and loiter over combat zone for weeks at a time. They were outfitted with high-tech sensors that could intercept phone calls, shoot full motion video or track movement. The equipment was so sensitive that the blimp's operators could even pick up on a phone call, detect its location, and point an assault team or attack drone in the right direction. The fact that the blimps were being set up and sent to New York City meant that things were even more serious than he initially believed.

It wasn't just the jets and blimps that had spooked Sampson. When on recon and able to get a closer look at the highway, occasionally he would see Army trucks heading south. An active military on American soil meant only one thing--Martial Law was still in effect. As long as they were imposing Martial Law, it made no sense to try to find Richard Clearmont. Just moving around could subject them to detention, or worse, and that would not be a good thing.

Staying with Susan in the mountains had turned out to be a new kind of adventure for him. He taught her how to set up camp, fish, and make a fire. He also showed her how to track game and how to preserve as much meat as possible. To his surprise, Susan had turned out to be a quick study, anxious to learn and to try new things. At the same time, he found himself thinking she was funny, charming, and she brought out feelings in him he had never experienced. To Sampson's delight, she had been as capable as any recruit he had ever trained. She was also the only person he ever trained who he wanted to screw--but he kept those thoughts and feelings to himself.

For her part, Susan found herself teaching Sampson the most valuable lessons he had ever learned. It wasn't something she thought of or intended to do. Actually, she had no idea how damaged Daniel Sampson really was. Instead, everything she did came naturally to her and was done with absolutely no forethought.

From the way they met, him knocking her out and bringing her along with him to Cape Cod, to the uneasy way he carried himself, Susan knew the man had issues. His mannerisms were reserved and his emotions obviously stilted; but she thought that was because of his decades of military service. Even though she had noticed how awkward he looked trying to comport himself like a normal human, she had no way of knowing how icily cold, almost inhuman, Sampson really was.

When they first trekked into the mountains, Susan had not allowed him to get any closer than to keep her warm at night in the cold mountain air. But, by being kind and tender, open and honest, little by little she started to show Sampson how to care, and eventually how to feel. Without realizing it, she was doing more than opening his eyes to a different kind of relationship, one he had never experienced before; but as the days passed and she allowed him to get closer, she could sense his heart was opening up to her.

For the first time in his life, Sampson actually cared about someone more than he cared about himself. Oddly, within a few days of being together, he found himself wanting to protect her and keep her happy. When those feelings started to take root and grow in him, and she noticed it, Susan had decided it was time to take things to the next level. She made the conscious decision to let the man who was guiding her, teaching her, and protecting her into her heart--and into her bed.

A week after they made camp, Sampson started to instruct Susan how to shoot and how to hunt. It was the first time he reassembled the Remington 700, took her down into a ravine, and let her shoot. That night, lying beside the fire pit, Susan taught Sampson how to love.

It came as no surprise to her, but after that long, passionate night, she could feel and see the transition in him. Consciously or not, Sampson's entire demeanor had changed.

Down in the valley, they located the buck Susan had just shot. Together, they cleaned and dressed the venison, returning to camp with more meat than they could eat in a week, but plenty to last them for a long time after they cured it.

The sun had gone down, but both of them continued to work and clean, making sure the strips of flesh over the fire were properly salted and cooked. The heat of the fire and the activity kept them warm even as the temperature dropped and it started to snow.

Sampson's deep voice broke the silence between them, "So, what do you think about heading back?"

"What, now Sampson? What about all of this?" Susan stretched her arms, indicating all of the work they had done.

"No, not now. I mean when we're done. We can take some meat with us and see if we can find your sister. If we can't find her, we'll try to locate Richard or come back here, depending on the circumstances."

"I don't know. It sounds dangerous, but Liz might be in trouble and, who knows, she may even need food."

"Exactly. Once we're in town, we can find out what's going on and then go from there."

"Sounds like a plan to me."

Susan was touched. The fact Sampson thought of taking her sister food showed, at least in her mind, what kind of a man he really was. As distant and cold as he seemed when they first met, she figured she had probably read him all wrong. Deep down, she believed he was really kind, sensitive, and thoughtful not the cold soldier he had made himself out to be.

Lucky for her, she thought, all of those attributes were wrapped up in a package that was to die for. Somewhere in his mid to late fifties, Sampson looked exactly like the aged warrior he was. Swarthy, rugged, with a taught muscular body, he obviously took very good care of himself and it showed. It didn't hurt that somewhere along the line he had some sort of surgery that tightened the skin around his face. Although he looked Asiatic, his lips and nose revealed a European heritage that was handsomely highlighted with Mediterranean hued skin.

As much as she hated herself it, especially so soon after losing Donny, Susan believed she was really starting to fall for the former Marine and hit man.

Thinking they were done with the conversation, Sampson turned his back to her and the fire, hanging strips of meat to cool off the branch of a nearby tree. Susan walked up behind him and wrapped her arms around his waist.

She leaned up on her tiptoes to whisper in his ear, "Hey, caveman, before we leave, why don't you drag me into your den and do whatever you want to me?"

"I thought you were the hunter now and you were gonna do that to me."

He turned to face her put his hands on her hips as she draped her arms over his shoulders.

"Yeah, but since you won our wrestling match, I thought it'd be fun to submit to you--"

She was unable to finish her sentence. He picked her up in his arms and carried her to a warm, dry spot next to the raging fire. That night, they made love for hours and fell asleep in each other's arms.

Chapter Three

Almost every nation in the world had seen unrest ranging from minor flare-ups to all-out civil war. Even if there was relative peace in one country, troubles would spill over from bordering nations. Across Europe, Africa and parts of Asia, some cities were literally burning. Elected officials had come under fire to the point where some had been executed, while others were fleeing for the lives.

The governments of Portugal, Italy, and Spain had been the first to fall, joining Greece in tearing down the remains of the European Union. Switzerland was the country with the most stability. But, they too fell victim to the turmoil spreading from England to the member nations of the European Common Union, and as Far East as Turkey.

Most nations in Africa, save several mineral-rich states on the west coast of the continent, either had seen their governments fall or were in the midst of a revolution. Oddly, the natural resources themselves, particularly the gold mines, had been left unmolested. Groups of soldiers from diverse nations had quickly taken up posts at the most mineral-rich locations. To those mercenaries, there was no such thing as borders. They were the only law that mattered. No one knew whom the soldiers were sent by or who controlled them. Nevertheless, they were unified, well armed, and highly disciplined.

In Central and South America, except for some heavily contested territories and large population centers, there was relative peace and calm. The battles that did flare up were mostly between decades old warring factions and ideological lines. But, ultimately, it was the people caught in between who suffered the most.

Because of the lack of resources and abject poverty,

Southeast Asia had not been as tumultuous. Although there were clashes from Pakistan to Vietnam and signs of growing insurrection from Sri Lanka to the Philippines, it was not as severe as it was elsewhere. Shortages of food and fuel in provinces in many nations of Southeast Asia was commonplace and most people saw only a little more suffering than usual, thus the governments were able to maintain security.

In India, the people had little faith in the banking system, and because it had long been a cultural practice to store personal wealth in gold, the people seemed least affected. With their wealth preserved, the most influential people kept the masses calm during the crisis.

China, however, was in complete turmoil. A dissident political faction had caused the Communist Party to lose control of the internet. As information spread, so did the violent protests against all authority. Soon after, the burgeoning middle class was in full revolt against the Party and all that was left to be seen was which faction the Chinese Army would support. Uncharacteristically, up until that point, the military had stayed on the sidelines.

Japan had been unable to import the much-needed commodities to sustain the population, and there was rioting in the streets of Tokyo. When the military was called in to quell the disturbances, the completely unexpected happened. Several commanders forced out the Prime Minister and immediately installed ministers to what was called the Ruling Cabinet. The men selected to take over and run the country were extremely wealthy and powerful in their own right. The conversion from a parliamentary democracy to plutocracy was complete with extraordinary efficiency. What had been accomplished in Japan was a pattern the world's most powerful men hoped to emulate and spread across the globe.

Russia, Canada, and Australia were not immune from the crisis. In short, order, oligarchs, and mineral barons had taken almost complete control of all three countries. The people tried to fight back against what everyone saw as an illegitimate grab for power and land, but it was useless. The elected officials of all three nations simply caved in because; unbeknownst to the public at large, the men associated with the neo-feudalist movement had been the ones in control all along.

Unlike every other developed nation, in those three nations, the oligarchs were prepared. Almost immediately, they launched a massive media blitz to explain what they had planned. They would nationalize all critical natural resources so they would have the capacity to defend their currency with hard assets. They would be the only nations in the world able to back up their money would become an islands of safety for all of the world's finances. Canada, Russia, and Australia would be the bankers for the entire world.

By any measure, the big cities of the United State of America had fared the worst. The richest neighborhoods in cities from New York to LA were still red-hot with looting and violence. The loss of civic trust had started with the banks and had led the people to go after who they considered responsible for the collapse of the nation. Based on the level of violence and the growth of the movement to destroy those who had stolen the American dream, a large number of people believed that the United States would never survive.

Although the major population centers were in distress, there were remnants of social order in the suburban and rural areas. And, while the larger cities quickly became places where only the brave would dare to travel, the rural farmlands and small towns had become havens for those who were able to make it out of the cities in one piece.

With all of the insanity going on, Major General Adam Smythe had little time for distractions. However, meeting with the Andrew Stevens was important so that as the situation developed, they would all be on the same page.

On top of the problems with delivering food, protecting fuel supplies, and the orders he had been given for deployment, Smythe was also trying to make sense of the other developments around the world. Unfortunately for him, he was only vaguely aware of some of the details of what was supposed to happen. He felt like he was flying blind.

Since Stevens had taken over, the chain of command was not nearly as concrete as it should have been and, no matter whom he dealt with, Smythe was smart enough to be cautious.

What was once called the Joint Commission Antiterrorism Taskforce under the command of General Adam Smythe had been reassigned to the National Guard. It was supposed to be an autonomous command group with only the Commander-in-Chief to answer to--but now they only answered to Andrew Stevens. The general wasn't a stupid man, but the political maneuvers made little sense to him. There was no way for any one man to cogently put it all together with so many variables. Deep down, though, he knew he was simply a soldier and was good at doing one thing, following orders.

A young man's voice announced from the intercom on the large mahogany desk, "General, the Special Master and Senator O'Connell are here to see you."

Smythe pressed a button and responded tersely in his gruff voice, "Escort them in." Up until that point, Butch O'Connell had been the liaison between the general and the Special Master, so it would be good to have a confab with the big man himself.

An Air Force Second Lieutenant escorted Senator O'Connell and Andrew Stevens into the general's suite of offices. Behind them, the Special Master's advance team and staffers shuffled in.

The main office in the suite overlooked the newly constructed Command Center of the Task Force's Rapid Response Team in Fort Bragg. Adam stood and walked out from behind his desk to receive the visitors.

Butch O'Connell, a swaggering, obese man, took the lead. He had the booming voice and condemning spirit of an overzealous Southern Baptist minister. Independently wealthy from his days in the oil services industry, the Big Butch was a powerful force in the Senate.

As the senator approached General Smythe, he extended his hand, "Glad you could see us on such short notice, Adam, I know you're a busy man."

"It's no problem, Butch. Actually, I'm glad you could make it." Smythe turned to face Andrew and started to salute.

Extending his hand, Stevens smiled and said in a cordial tone, "No need for such formality, General. I'm Andrew Stevens."

Smythe introduced himself and shook hands with the man who controlled his destiny. "It's great to finally meet you, Mr. Stevens,"

"Call me Andrew, please."

"Okay, Andrew. Anyway, seems I've been hunkered down here so long, it's been impossible to keep up with everything that's happened. It'll be terrific to find out more about what's going on from the big man himself."

"Wow, this place is quite impressive," Stevens commented while looking through the glass-paned windows to the operations floor below.

"It should--we paid enough for it," Butch commented snidely.

The operations center and Joint Taskforce Headquarters was quite impressive. Because quantifying electronic intelligence was their primary function, the building located in an obscure corner was made specifically for that purpose.

The top-secret intelligence system relied on a multitude of other sources for data. It also had the most advanced artificial intelligence for analysis; and that was the key to tracking the movements of anyone who posed a threat to the nation. Although the cloud of computers making up the network was widely dispersed around the world, the core of the system was concentrated right below General Smythe's office.

MIN-OPS, the computer network and silicon brain behind the intelligence gathering, was used to monitor all internet traffic, voice and data, in the United States. The system had also been wired into the financial transaction markets, enabling the storage and analysis of every credit card purchase and business transaction. MIN-OPS even had its tentacles wired into to every camera on every city block, the network of stoplight cameras, and the E-Z Pass toll collection system. The system's facial recognition algorithms had even improved to an accuracy confidence level topping 95%.

Used in tandem with the cities and states, the agents and soldiers at the Task Force's headquarters had the ability to track people's electronic fingerprints as well as their physical movement anywhere in the nation.

To help conduct surveillance, more than 250,000 government positions had been created to specifically monitor and investigate any possible internal security threat. After all hell broke loose, those employed by the FBI, Homeland Security, ATF, DEA, ICE, and many other domestic agencies were easily absorbed by Smythe's Intelligence Section. The ability to do so had been put in place before the Constitution was suspended and Andrew Stevens named Special Master

In addition to the human resources, billions of dollars had been spent on designing and building systems to digitally sort, organize, and correlate data from banks, credit cards, internet usage, or any other contacts each and every American had with commerce. Every American with a Social Security Number had been assigned a coded profile and method for tracking, tracing, and even predicting their behavior. When Stevens did take over, the personal data collected was the most valuable resource they had to determine who their enemies were and where they might be and it was the Rapid Response Team's Intelligence Section that had the responsibility of subverting the insurrection by Americans on American soil.

Besides locating and arresting the rebels, the other big task for General Adam Smythe and his men was to try to bring order to the streets. Under Martial Law, Special Master Andrew Stevens had the full capabilities of the United States Armed Forces at his disposal. He and his advisers were reluctant to fully activate the regular forces because doing so was filled with potential pitfalls; the worst of which was potentially having brother fighting against brother. Instead, under the guise of only using the National Guard to restore peace, Stevens had given the task to the Special Forces operatives who had come under the command of Smythe.

The combat division under Smythe's command had been divided into battalions and sent to four different regions. There was no other way they could manage all the assignments they had been given in such diverse locations. Unfortunately, judging by the reports, he had been getting and how ass-backwards the country had become, he wasn't so sure he could accomplish much of anything at all without killing a heck of a lot of people. But, if necessary, he would do it.

Being in control of so much firepower came with a huge dose of temptation, and thinking about having so much power made General Smythe's head swim. Not for the first time, it made him wonder why he was answering to anyone. He had no idea what Andrew Stevens stood for and he really didn't care. However, Smythe was hopeful that his internal conflicts could be dissipated if Stevens would fill in some of the gaps and better explain how events were supposed to play out.

They moved to a private room in the general's suite and settled into a smaller, glass enclosed conference area. After they were served drinks, they kicked everyone else out so they could talk in private. Smythe remained standing near the wet bar while Butch sat in the corner of a big leather couch with his legs spread and a big, hairy-knuckled hand rested on his belly. Andrew sat regally to the senator's left in a stately, high-backed recliner.

"It's safe to talk freely in here, right?" Stevens asked.

"Sure is, this entire suite is rated SCIF."

"What's that?"

"Special Intelligence Classified Facility. It's bug-proof."

"Oh."

"So, how's everything going on the civilian front? Being on base all the time, I'm sort of isolated."

"Well, that's exactly why I'm here, Adam," Andrew said with a flourish, "to give our future military commander the inside scoop." He turned to Senator O'Connell and asked, using a feigned inquisitive tone, "Butch, could you excuse us? I'd like to talk to Adam in private." The question was not a very well disguised order and could only be answered in one way.

O'Connell did not respond immediately. Having done so much, and being involved from the beginning, the theatrics made his pasty white face turn red with anger. He didn't dare speak for fear of what may come out of his mouth. Stevens did not take his eyes off the senator. The cold, silent stare he displayed was a clear indication for Butch to keep his mouth shut and leave.

Filling the uncomfortable silence, O'Connell took a

quick sip of whisky and laughed. "Okay, a man who likes to get right down to business. I like that! Let me leave you two alone to talk. Besides, I wanna check out the rest of the facility myself, if that's okay with you General."

Sensing the tension, Smythe was a little taken aback and simply indicated with his hand for O'Connell that it would be okay.

Big Butch left with the airs of prince, as if leaving had been his idea all along. When the door closed and sealed behind him, Stevens smiled and directed his attention to the general.

"So, tell me General, what would you like to know?"

Expecting a briefing instead of being served an open-ended question, Smythe was flustered. "Well, what I'd like to know is when all of this is gonna be over."

"As you know, things have calmed down quite a bit these past few weeks and I believe we're on the right track." Steven's oration sounded as smooth as or smoother than that of Bill Clinton or Barack Obama. He went on, never answering the question directly, "It was just a matter of days after my call for civil authorities to go back to work that state, and local governments started to get their act together. The emergency response personnel and other functionaries of local and state governments starting trickling in and making plans how to restore a semblance of order."

Smythe cut in, "How exactly did you get the public employees to go back to work?"

"I just gave them exactly what I promised them in my first speech. General, I am a man of my word. Ah, but the first thing I had to do was recruit a few hundred thousand bankers and lawyers to help the cops and firefighters straighten out the legal and financial details. For example, every cop who came back to work was granted amnesty."

"Why was that?" Smythe asked with a raised eyebrow and genuine curiosity.

"We had to do it because so many public safety workers left their post and joined in the riots."

"Oh?" Smythe was not surprised by the pronouncement, but acted as if was something he would never expect. Unlike the military, the civilians who were supposed to maintain order had become unhinged rather quickly, which was exactly what Smythe thought they would do.

"Our legal teams fanned out all over the country and offered the public sector what we like to call, 'personal service contracts.' Anyone who wanted to alter the terms of their loans and mortgages, or go back to work earning real money instead of dollars, had to sign it."

"Similar to the contracts given to the military?" General Smythe asked.

Both men knew the military had remained intact because of the special financial terms the soldiers had been granted. The rapidly implemented pay provisions allowed the Special Master to declare Martial Law while keeping the warrior class loyal.

"Yes, but there was more to the contracts signed by the public service unions."

"If I may ask--"

Stevens nodded as a gesture for Smythe to continue.

"What exactly did you give to the cops to get their support?" Smythe could not conceal the resentment in his voice. He expected that, like usual, he and the rest of the military would be the ones getting the short end of the stick.

Andrew answered in a demeaning voice of his own, as if the terms were distasteful to him as well. "They had the balances of their outstanding debts consolidated, reduced; and then they were issued new, longer repayment schedules with much lower interest rates. The terms were so sweet, I heard a lot of folks laughed, danced, or cried with joy," he added derisively.

Stevens went on to explain how the public workers believed they had been set free from insurmountable burdens so there was little to no resistance. Also, the state and municipal employees who did sign the contracts would retain their jobs, work in the same locations, but be paid by the federal government. In addition, they were promised their salary would be paid in Ameros.

The men and women under Smythe's command, as well as under the jurisdiction of the other most important federal agencies, had stayed on the job and had stayed loyal. That had been a very critical component in the way everything had shaken down. Even before the shit first hit the fan, almost all of the critical employees and nearly every member of the military had signed a special service contract that required confidentiality. The special federal contracts, unlike the ones signed by the other public employees, stipulated that payment for services would be made in special gold certificates, not Ameros.

Paying for a military force with hard assets was history repeating itself. Just like the King of England paid his soldiers in gold to fight Napoleon Bonaparte, so too did the collective headed by Andrew Stevens arrange to buy the loyalty of the troops with precious metal. The only difference was the English mercenaries actual received gold, not promises of it.

General Smythe listened with great interest as Stevens went on to explain the downside for all of the public employees who had signed on the dotted line, features that were not part of what the warrior class had signed.

"There are several clauses in the contracts that would have been very provocative if more than just a few people had bothered to read and decipher the arcane language."

"Like what?"

"Well, in return for the considerations they received, what those folks agreed to was, they and their offspring were beholden to the Corporation of the United States of America for a term of fifty-years; conscripts, actually, regardless of whether their parents are able to pay the outstanding loans back or not."

"What the hell does it mean to be beholden to the Corporation of the United States of America?"

Andrew chuckled. "Very few seemed to ask or care as long as their loans were made manageable and they're paid in Ameros." He knew exactly what the phrase meant but manipulatively withheld the information. He went on, "More than ninety-five percent of civil employees signed the contract without batting an eye, ecstatic with what they got. Since then, they've been doing their best to clean up the streets, get the rest of the riff-raff to start conforming, and get themselves to one of our many roving medical vans for DNA testing. Now, we're all in this together and we have to get the rest of the population to go along."

"DNA testing? For what?" All soldiers were already mandated to give DNA samples, so it came as a complete shock to the general that civilians were being ordered to give up something so personal and revealing.

"For the new I.D.'s everyone's required to have."

"And everyone's going along with it?"

"Everyone but the Religious Right. Those fanatics say that's the Mark of the Beast. Not even Butch O'Connell could get his core constituency to go along. The funny thing is he thought they were the flock, and he was their shepherd. Funny thing, he never played by the same rules as his sheep. They showed him, though."

Smythe could not miss the derisive tone in Steven's voice. The disdain the Special Master felt toward the senator was obvious. He tried to ignore what was probably no more than a pissing contest between two politicians, but then it hit him. If Stevens could so easily dismiss someone he had to have trusted, it meant that there was no true loyalty, no honor between them. It was a fact Smythe locked away and would have to remember--Andrew Stevens was not a man to be trusted and he'd have to be careful.

Stevens was powerful enough to bring down the President without even a shot being fired. There was no way of knowing exactly what was said, what threats were made, or how Stevens got all three branches of government to all but bend over and kiss his ass. Nevertheless, it had happened. Knowing that, Smythe never wanted to be painted as an adversary.

Stevens asked, "Is there anything else you want to know?"

"No, sir. As long as you tell me what you need from me, you've told me everything that I need to know." With his brows squeezed together and a dire look on his face, there was no way to tell he was lying through his teeth.

"Good, I'm glad to hear it. All that's required of you, General Smythe, is to keep doing what you're doing.

*****

By the time Hellbender, a big blue former Coast Guard cutter, was near enough to shore to be boarded, all of the military hardware they peddled had been stowed away. The United States was in complete chaos and the harbors were probably not secured, yet the captain of the ship did not want to take any chances. Everything on deck looked exactly like it was supposed to. It was packed with scientific equipment, and that matched perfectly with Hellbender's registration as a research vessel.

Before they had passed the western tip of Fire Island, an encrypted ship to shore radio call had gone out to make sure everything was coordinated and there would be no delays. Getting close enough to Bayonne for a drop under the cover of night was infinitely easier because of the lack of security. The harbormaster and customs agents were gone when Hellbender set anchor less than 1,000 feet from the piers. Even if the port had been fully staffed and routine security checks performed, the large ship would have cleared scrutiny without a problem. Coming in covertly was not about hiding the ship, but to make sure they were able to get Maxwell York ashore with no one knowing.

A G6 jet was waiting on the tarmac near the executive terminal at Newark-Liberty International Airport. Maxwell York's driver, a former NSA agent, along with his security detail and pilot, all former CIA operatives, were still on duty and still loyal. The team had taken all necessary steps to make sure the plane was fueled up and ready to go as soon as the black Suburban entered the gate to the private terminal. The second York and his men boarded the jet, and the hatch was sealed, the plane taxied down the runway and took off.

York was pushing 90-years-old and it showed. His skin looked translucent with blue veins forming spider web patterns all over his hands and legs. His thin gray hair, just weeks before a thick mane he could be proud of, was falling out. The liver spots had also become more pronounced. Even though he had access to the best of everything and unimaginable wealth, there were no treatments he could buy that would turn back time. But, the fact that his one-time protégé had turned on him gave York a new purpose in life. When Andrew had left him for dead, it was actually the best thing that had happened to York in decades.

Maxwell York, the originator and architect of the neo-feudalist movement, knew all was not lost. Although he was weak from the chemotherapy and devastated by the complete loss of his Cape Cod estate, the rage he felt towards the impudent, contemptuous fool, Andrew Stevens, gave him the strength to do whatever it took to make things right. If that meant chewing Andrew to pieces and spitting him out, so be it.

The plane leveled off and set a westerly course. They were headed for what everyone in the nation thought was a restricted Air force base. Instead, it was top-secret national defense research facility in Utah. Since York and his associates owned it, he knew he would be safe there.

Chapter Four

It had taken time to maintain enough stability to reopen the financial markets, but once the reinforcements arrived from Fort Bragg, they were able to regain control of the buffer zones around the major trading facilities. Once the streets were calm, the markets did manage to reopen.

Ironically, the resumption of trading on the exchanges corresponded perfectly with the reactivation of the internet. Not only were people once again free to communicate and gather news, but they were also able to try to trade stocks, bonds and commodities.

The trading activity got off to a rocky start under the newly imposed rules. Because the value of the American dollar had collapsed and no one had any faith in it, trading became more literal than it had been in centuries. Using a barter system instead of currency, there were many hurdles to overcome, but eventually the trading was able to commence.

For hours, the values of commodities whipsawed back and forth, gold and oil futures moving wildly as traders attempted to find rational price points markets could sustain. Adding to the confusion, because no one wanted to hold dollars, gold and oil were also being used as money, making the market's vicissitudes even more pronounced. It was all but impossible to manage what had become the most raucous trading environment ever seen.

As wild as the markets had been, suddenly, everything started to stabilize. Without warning and for no obvious reason, the prices of many stocks started to level off and then rise. With no centralized clearing of trades and absolutely no transparency, no one had any idea what was happening or who was behind the buying that was driving the market back up. Instead of jumping on the rising tide by buying into the rally, traders across the globe felt relief that they could bail out and move whatever funds they had left into hard assets with actual value.

Not even the relatively rich or the seemingly well connected had the ability to protect their wealth or sit on the sidelines. With everything in turmoil, it was impossible to sit back, watch, and hope that when all was said and done they would have something, anything, left. The only ones who were free from concern, the ones who had nothing to fear, were the family, friends, and associates of Maxwell York--the ones behind all of the buying.

At the Manhattan headquarters of York's firm, MYB, Ltd., Andrew Stevens, and his cohorts were busy buying up anything and everything of material value at huge discounts. If Federal Reserve Notes had still existed, they were picking up assets for pennies on the dollar. Using their previously accumulated stockpiles of hard assets, the brokers, and traders under Andrew Stevens completed the quickest, most massive redistribution of paper wealth and property ownership the world had ever known.

It was the culmination of years of work and decades of planning, but the destruction of the old social order had been necessary in order to get legal ownership of everything under their control. When they were ready and finally restored order, they would once again enforce the rule of law. By that point though, an elite group, the associates and partners of Maxwell York, would legally be in possession of everything and no one would have the authority to dispute any of their claims.

Even though things had not gone as smooth as it would have under Maxwell York's plan, Andrew Stevens was proud of himself. He had accomplished in days what would have otherwise taken years. Instead of being a calm, peaceful transition of power, it had been violent with many lives lost. But, Andrew thought to himself, that couldn't be helped. The creative destruction had started, leaving its victims drowning in sea of tears. Andrew believed that no

46

matter where York, his teacher and mentor, was hiding, he too would be proud.

*****

One of the Metropolitan Correctional Center's high security units was designated Nine-South. Wang Kai, a young Asian, was being escorted out of cell 38-L by a trio of uniformed men in the lead and another team protecting the flank. The six soldiers who surrounded him were dressed in battle fatigues and carrying assault rifles, something that was previously unheard of inside the facility's secure perimeter.

The men escorting Kai were not the usual guards. Even in his hazy, scrambled mind, he somehow knew they weren't FBI, U.S. Marshals, or even N.Y.P.D., but he had no idea who they were, who sent them, or what they wanted. Actually, he didn't care about any of that. All he cared about was leaving Nine-South.

Earlier in the year, Kai had been working as the head of computer information systems at Troth Capital Associates. He was responsible for setting maintaining the servers for the infamous money manager Roland Troth in downtown Greenwich.

Not only was Kai a savant in the realm of computer science, he was also wildly ambitious and working for Troth had allowed him to capitalize on his passions. Beyond his regular duties, he had been paid quite handsomely to do what he loved most--break into other people's computers. He had made millions hacking other systems and guiding Troth's funds with information garnered off of others' servers. Kai had been arrested along with Roland Troth at Troth's firm and detained in the MCC with no bail ever since.

For many months, he had been locked away and all but forgotten in the god-forsaken steel and concrete jungle.

47

At his lowest point, when he thought he could no longer take the filth, noise, and horrid food, when he believed things couldn't get any worse, they did. One day, the regular guards simply disappeared and the inmates took over the asylum. That was the day the Metropolitan Correctional Center became a level of hell that would have made Dante blush.

The inmates who had somehow gotten out of their cells did try to break out when the regular officers bugged out, but they quickly learned they were sealed in. The National Guard had posted up with automatic weapons at every possible exit. The news did, however, make it in and the inmates were able to follow developments in the United States. They knew the Constitution had been suspended and it wasn't long before they realized they had lost all protections. Starving, filthy, some of them in fear for their lives, many lost all hope of ever getting out of there alive. And, since they had no hope and no rights, they also had no restraints and acted accordingly.

Kai did not know how long ago that had been. He hadn't even noticed when the National Guard raided the facility to fully restore order. Left semiconscious in his cell, he wasn't even sure when the regular corrections staff had come back to work. Battered, beaten, and broken, it was only after the heavily armed escort came to get him did he start to comprehend some of what was going on around him.

The camouflage-garbed soldiers led him to an elevator and took him to the Medical Unit. They hadn't told him a thing but, because he was out of that disgusting chamber of horrors, Kai's mind had started to clear and he started reconnecting with reality. The Medical Unit was cleaner, quieter, and he felt safe because he was alone and behind a locked door. Eventually, a soldier came to give him some medical attention.

The medic had helped him clean up and gave him a

shot for the pain, but the morphine only went so far. Despite the broken ribs, missing teeth, and sore jaw, the worst pain of all was the type of ache no medication could ease. The fact Kai had been raped repeatedly had done much more damage than what the eyes could see--and there was no cure for that.

Finally able to relax, Kai laid back and tried to rest on the clean bunk on the medical unit. No matter how hard he tried, sleep eluded him. The fear of being sent back, of being taken back upstairs and thrown in with the wolves, was overwhelming. He knew no one really cared about him--or what he had gone through--or else they wouldn't have left him up there for so long in the first place. Even in his befuddled and battered head, he realized there had to be something else they wanted from him--another reason they decided to save him. As hard as he tried, he couldn't think of what they wanted from him or why they had come to get him and no one else.

Unable to figure the out the puzzle causing him so much distress, bile rose in Kai's throat and he vomited. As the sour taste of fear spewed out of him mouth, another big chunk of his sanity went down the drain as well. Absolutely convinced he would be taken back to his own personal hell, he once again lost touch with reality.

Kai woke up when another squad came to get him. The men quickly secured him in leg irons and a waist chain, tools to prepare him for transport. Cuffed up like he was Charles Manson, and escorted by heavily armed soldiers, Kai was led through several passages and taken deeper into the complex.

To Kai, it was like a bad dream. None of it seemed real and everything he saw seem to jump from one scene to another. In his mind's eye, it looked like an old, scary home movie with frames cut out--a strobe-light effect with longer delays between frames. Instead of allowing the visual mishmash overwhelm him, he focused on the gloomy sound of gates clanging and keys jingling, hoping it would be the last time he heard the disheartening clamor.

Breaking through the routine metallic sounds of confinement, the echo of gunshots made Kai jump.

"What the hell was that?" he asked. It was the first time he had spoken in days, maybe weeks. His throat was dry and he words almost imperceptible.

The soldier to his left didn't respond. Instead, he grabbed Kai tighter around the arm and led him even more quickly down a brightly lit stone and tile walkway. More shots rang out causing Kai to flinch.

"What the hell is that? What's going on?" The first thing that ran through Kai's mind was that they were not leading him out of the building, but leading him to a firing squad and he started to panic.

A sergeant, obviously the squad's ranking NCO, responded in an emotionless tone, "They're icing your boyfriends. You should be happy, son."

More and more gunshots rang out but the later ones were accompanied by cries and screams of terror. The inmates in their cells who saw what was going on knew it was only a matter of time. They were next. They could be heard pleading for their lives. But, it was of no use, their fate had been sealed.

Kai did not understand. The idea that the United States of America would summarily execute all of its prisoners was beyond his comprehension. He could not have understood how Andrew Stevens had gained the power to order the execution of everyone who was incarcerated.

There was no easy or quick way to explain how a man who called himself a "Special Master" could do whatever he wanted to protect the nation from potential enemies of the state. Kai would also never understand how or why inmates became enemies of the state, and he would never find out. It was not something he would have been able to cope with, even if he was sane.

The soldiers took him down to the catacombs and put him in the back of what looked like a vehicle out of some futuristic war movie. Leaving the musty, dark basement, the armored personnel carrier drove out onto the streets of Manhattan between the escorts: a Buffalo MRAP in the lead and two Hummers with manned machine guns, one in front and one following closely behind.

There were no windows allowing Kai to see the high-rises or street signs as they passed, so he was unable to determine what direction they were heading. Too mentally lost and too damaged to care, he just closed his eyes and rode in silence. The small caravan drove slowly, taking several turns and not stopping for anything. Soon, the massive vehicle drove down some sort of ramp. They came to a halt and the soldiers unloaded Kai out of the back.

Because of the darkness and concrete support columns, it appeared as if they were in a basement of another building. Kai tried to wet his dry, split lips but was unable to get any saliva into his parched mouth. However, away from MCC-and the torture that place represented--a new sense of calm overtook his mind. To his conscious mind, it was like waking up from some sort of extended nightmare.

In a hoarse, cracked, whisper of a voice, he asked, "Where are we?"

The soldier to his left responded, "It don't matter where we are, son, but there's a gathering being held in your honor. I'm just here to make sure you make it."

The soldier had answered in a thick Virginia accent. If Kai had been in a better frame of mind, he would have known that the soldiers were not part of the Nation Guard, at least not part of the New York National Guard. But, he was in no condition to notice or understand the ramifications.

Slowly, they led him to a bank of elevators. He took baby-steps--the maximum length of the chain between his shackled legs--onto and off of the elevator and then down a long hallway. The opulence of the facility had absolutely no effect on Kai, at least not in any conventional sense. Instead, all he could think of was that he had escaped from Hell.

Wang Kai looked up as they walked through a set of double doors of a huge office. Uncomfortable in an ill-fitting orange jumpsuit, he stood in front of a group of strangers. Warily, he looked around while the people who were already in the room went quiet and gawked at him.

The room itself was intimidating. The shag carpeting was a luscious, dark red. There were two crystal chandeliers hanging down from a vaulted ceiling. An oval mahogany table took up the center of the room. Two finely dressed men and a woman were seated around the table on thickly padded black leather chairs. On smaller chairs along the walls of the room, more people were staring at him.

In Kai's mind, new thoughts manifested and took root, giving him the absolute conviction that he was there to be tortured. With nothing being said to him, he just knew they were going to interrogate him and beat him for information. The thought made his stomach churn and his testicles recede into his abdomen.

One of the massive soldiers started to unlock the chains and then bent over to unlock the shackles. Kai was stunned. He had a hard time believing it; after all of those long months, he was actually outside of the MCC and unchained. The urge to run was thrust into his head. The first chance he got, the first mistake they made, he would bolt.

Then, as the cuffs and shackles were stripped away and he was free from restraints, he recognized the rifles and the gigantic side arms holstered to the soldiers' sides and that quelled the almost irresistible urge to run.

Someone was speaking to him, addressing him by name, but Kai did not connect the sounds to the meanings. Instead, like the remnants of staring at a bright light, he could not clear the image of the soldiers' guns from his eyes or out of his head. The close proximity to weapons had mesmerized him.

Peace, blissful peace, was just one bullet away. The knowledge it would soon be over pulled him back from the brink and returned him to some semblance of lucidity.

"Mr. Kai, please have a seat." A man sitting to the side gestured to the vacant spot at the table. "My name is Raymond Behn."

"Where's my lawyer?" Kai asked sternly and then tightened his lips, as if to signal he would not speak again.

An attractive woman on his right answered, "You won't need him."

Kai noticed her blonde hair was up in a neat bun and her skin looked clear--but it was obviously covered by layers of makeup. She didn't seem real to him. Her perfect blonde hair and pasty, wax-like skin made her look like a mannequin or robot. Kai watched in awe as she slid a neatly organized multi-form document over in front of him.

"This grants you immunity from prosecution as long as you cooperate with us."

They all knew what Kai did not know; the document was nothing but a prop, a pretense to put him at ease. They wanted to give him a sense of security; so, they made it look like what they were doing was under the color of law. They were in full control of the situation and could do whatever they wanted--but they wanted Kai to join them on his own accord. That way, he'd be less likely to hold back information from them.

"Who are you, what do you want from me?"

"I'm sorry Mr. Kai, I'm Becky Longo, and these are my associates Sir Philip Gross and Mr. Behn already introduced himself. We represent the Special Master

Andrew Stevens in--"

"What the hell is a Special Master?" Battered, bruised, and on the edge of insanity, Kai retained some of the irreverence of youth.

"We'll get to that in a moment," Sir Philip responded in a waspish, British accent. "But first, tell me, Mr. Kai, do you want to be a free man, someone put in a substantial position beyond the reach of authority?"

"What do you think, princess? Do you have any fuckin' idea what I've been through in your dungeon? Look at me; do you know what they did to me?" The missing teeth and bruises were obvious, still, Kai titled his face up to give them a better look.

Acting like their guest was talking about a bad trip on the subway instead of being raped and having his face bashed in, Raymond looked away but continued, "We need your skills and your expertise, Wang--

"Call me Kai. No one calls me Wang."

"Okay, Kai," Raymond raised his eyebrows, intrigued by the display of attitude. "We know you worked for Roland Troth and we also know that you're an accomplished hacker."

Kai looked skeptical. "I don't have a clue what the fuck you're talking about."

"Listen, Kai, there's no need to be defensive. Roland Troth is dead and to prove we're on the up and up, that document grants you full immunity. In addition, I can guarantee that you'll have everything you've ever dreamed of and then some."

"Would I have to go back to the MCC?"

Becky and Raymond cackled with nervous laughter while Sir Philip covered his mouth with a silk handkerchief and cleared his throat.

No, Kai," Becky said, "If you help us, you'll never have to go back there again."

Kai was more confused than ever and he did not

know what to do. Roland Troth had many people working for him and was willing to do just about anything. And, after the previous court appearances, Kai knew he was going to be convicted for all the shit Troth had done. They had to blame what happened on someone. Troth was probably still alive, and since he had no idea who the people talking to him were, it was possible they worked for him.

However, there was one thing that overwhelmed Kai's mind, something that drove him to agree to whatever terms they were offering in the hope that they were being honest. All it took was one shred of hope for him to throw caution to the wind. He couldn't go back to the MCC; he just couldn't go back to the ninth floor. A future, money, a career; none of that mattered in the least if he had to go back to that hell.

"You promise you'll keep me out of the MCC?"

Raymond smiled a knowing smile. "I promise, all you have to do is help us."

Kai remained silent, sitting at the table with a blank stare on his face. To the others, it simply looked like he was being difficult, defiant.

The fact that Kai was so concerned about having to go back to jail gave Sir Philip the advantage he needed. At the mention of the MCC, he noticed Kai start to shake, so he pressed the issue.

"You do realize, sir, it is in your best interest to cooperate and stop acting like a bloody child. This is very important--and I don't want to have to send you back to your cell. Mr. Kai, think carefully about what you say. And what you do."

Kai picked up a pen from the table and signed the document without reading it. All that mattered to him was that he would be safe at night--not wondering if he'd be beaten and raped. "Okay, so what do you want me to do?"

"Do you know of a company by the name of MYB,

55

Limited?" Becky asked.

Kai shook his head no.

"You never heard of it?"

"No."

"How about a man named Maxwell York?"

"No. Never heard of him."

"There is a very powerful man behind LeStaro Bank. His name is Michael J. Papa. Do you know who that is, Kai? Have you ever accessed his private computer networks or his trading platform?"

Raymond chimed in, "We know he's communicating with the states through his proprietary network. Can you access it?"

Kai nodded acknowledgment.

Becky and Raymond looked at each other and exchanged knowing glances.

"And what about Karl Hensch?"

"I remember Troth's VPs talking about him."

Becky then asked, "Do you know where they did business, or the access points to their banks' networks off the internet?"

"Yes." Kai went back to his monosyllabic responses, the vision of the gun in his head, knowing relief was near.

"I know you've been kept incommunicado for a long time and you don't know what's happened, but you'll be getting a full briefing shortly. All we need you to do is track these men down."

Raymond cut in, "We need you to electronically hunt down these men using any means necessary. We're going to need you to intercept and block everything they try to do. Whatever equipment you need, we'll get it, no questions asked."

Mustering up a reserve of strength to articulate his growing unease, Kai spat out, "What, I do my dirt while you watch so you can charge me with more crimes? Fuck that and fuck you!"

Sir Philip stood and walked toward one of the large leaden windows. "Mr. Kai, the document in front of you grants you full immunity from prosecution. However, if you do not hold up your end of the bargain, we'll have no choice but to return everything to its previous condition."

While speaking, the Duke never raised his voice. His eerie calm and innate command of the room was very unsettling. "Just think about it old chap. Who brought you here? How did they get you out of the hoosegow? Focus, chap, focus. We could have had you taken to an alley and shot if that's what we desired. That's how much power we have. Why would we waste time setting you up when we could simply kill you? Now, let's move on and enough of these bloody games."

Just the mention of being taken back to hell made Kai's memories of the experience flash through his head and triggered a massive wave of stress hormones. Somewhere deep down, from the seat of his adrenal glands, a circuit breaker was tripped. The response to his panic went well beyond the sour, pungent adrenaline induced sweat and a racing heart. His brain went into overdrive, seeking a way to escape. It pushed him right over the edge and ripped right through the last few threads of sanity.

In his head, he saw himself being dragged off and put back into the same chamber of horrors, Nine-South, to endure the same abuse he just survived.

Swinging his head around wildly, his eyes once again landed on the soldiers and their guns. He concentrated on the large soldier standing a few feet to his left. The grip of the soldier's sidearm protruded out several inches and, for what seemed like hours but was actually less than a second, Kai could only see the weapon; everything else simply disappeared.

It was as if the weapon was beckoning to him, the safety strap that should have been secured over the pistol's rear groove was unsnapped. Kai sprung to his feet and got to the soldier's hip before anyone else could react. Stumbling as he reached out, his weight landed on the grip of the gun, enabling him to squeeze it as he pushed forward.

With all of his strength, Kai pulled his arm back and the gun came out cleanly in his hand while he was falling. He tucked his chin and twisted his body into a roll as he hit the floor.

The massive soldier was stunned to stillness. He was unable to react, let alone bend over fast enough to either retrieve the weapon or at least disable the prisoner.

Kai was intent on making sure he would not be going back to MCC's Nine-South. Familiar with guns from his troubled youth, he flipped the safety off with his thumb, put the gun in his mouth, and blew his brains out.

*****

Inside the gold-tinted mirrored glass building, security was on full alert, not just because of the possibility of an attempted assassination, but because Wang Kai had been able to shoot himself.

Right after it had happened, Sir Philip had made a hasty exit, getting an escort to JFK for a private flight back to London. There, he would try to disrupt whatever moves Carl Hensch and Michael Papa may try to make, or, if necessary, arrange for their elimination.

Andrew Stevens had received intelligence that Maxwell York was, in fact, alive. Up until that point, all of the other members of the consortium had been working with Andrew under the assumption York was dead. Hearing he was alive, and how Stevens had set him up to be killed, could change everything. But, as far as they knew, neither Hensch nor Papa had disclosed the fact that Maxwell York was still alive to anyone on the African

Counsel or any of the other boards who had taken control all over the world. Yet, the fact York hadn't popped up somewhere and hadn't said anything did raise more questions than it answered.

Becky Longo's condition could only be described with one word, disturbed. The way Kai had shot himself allowed her to see and feel what it was like to have someone's brains splattered all over a room. It was an image she would never forget and it had shaken her to her core.

The stress and anxiety had been building inside of her, even before witnessing a man kill himself, even before plotting with Andrew to try to take control of America and take it out of the hands of Maxwell York. She had been so competent, no one could ever question her ability. Yet, the whole idea of having almost limitless power, having so many responsibilities, having the fate of the most powerful nation on earth in her hands would have been a lot for anyone to swallow.

On top of it all, things were happening much too fast, seemingly spinning out of control with no obvious direction and no way to slow it down. What Maxwell York had planned was a much slower transition with many fewer potential pitfalls over the course of years. But, Andrew had taken a different route, pushing things at a hyper pace. Such haste required them all to think on their feet. What they had done would compress the time for transition but was loaded with potentially fatal hurdles they had to overcome.

After she had showered and scrubbed herself clean, unable to remove the psychological taint of witnessing such a gruesome death, she took some sedatives to try and get some sleep. With the shades drawn over the big windows, the bedroom in the residential penthouse suite was pitch black. The door to the hallway opened and a small wedge of light beamed in and slowly grew in size.

"Beck, are you awake?"

"Andrew?"

"I heard what happened. Are you okay?"

"Not really, but I will be."

"Can I come in so we can talk?"

"Of course."

Becky sat up and let the covers fall to her waist. All she had on was a lace and silk bra but she did not bother to cover herself.

Andrew walked in with slow, measured steps. He looked at her on the bed and thought to himself that she looked small, taking up only one tiny segment of the queen-sized bed. Usually, her hair was up in a tight bun and it made her look cold, solemn, detached. But, on this night, she had allowed her hair to flow freely, draping down over her shoulders.

In the faint light coming from the hallway, she looked heavy-hearted but still amazing--and Andrew sighed at her beauty. At another time, he may even have admitted he loved her: smart, determined, and as trustworthy as she was, but this was not the right time. They had a lot of work to do and no time to waste it on love.

"Beck, do you want something to drink? Cocoa, warm milk maybe?" he asked tenderly.

"No, I'm fine. Just come and hold me."

She held her arms open as Andrew approached. Deftly, he sat down on the edge of the mattress and wrapped his arms around her. He held her close and then reached and starting caressing her head, whispering in her ear that everything was going to be all right.

Becky sobbed. All her life she had worked and struggled, trying to prove herself to men. She always had to keep her emotions bottled up inside so she would never appear weak, and that was especially true since she had been working with Andrew and Maxwell York, two of the most powerful men in the world. By keeping her emotions in check, she had managed to prove she belonged, that she could handle anything they threw at her. But, after the crush of the past few weeks, finally letting out a display of her true vulnerability was a huge

She swallowed hard and lifted her head off Andrew's shoulder. Wiping the tears from her eyes, she forced herself to smile.

"Are you okay?" Andrew reached out and further dried her cheeks with delicate caresses.

"Yeah, I will be." Becky forced herself to swallow hard once again, this time entombing the memory of a horrible suicide, and the doubts about what they were doing, deep in her belly. "I'll be a lot better as soon as you make love to me."

Chapter Five

Susan DiGiovanni and Daniel Sampson, with their slightly soiled clothes and tussled hair, looked like they had been camping. Dressed in plaid lumberjack shirts, worn jeans and boots, with Sampson carrying a large canvas bag, they perfectly fit the part of two harmless hikers.

Even with her hair tied back and no makeup on, Susan looked stunning. The walking, climbing, and constant motion had tightened her body considerably. At the same time, being outdoors in the fresh, cold air made her Mediterranean skin glow radiantly. Despite the emotional hardship of being away from her children, the past several weeks of strenuous activity had made her more physically fit than she had been in years.

Sampson was always in great shape, and hiding out in the mountains had been a lot less strenuous than what he was used to doing. However, deeper, more significant changes had come over him. For the first time in his life, he had found an emotional connection, a bond with someone he legitimately cared about--and it showed.

Although not a stranger to human interaction on the superficial level, it was a unique experience for him to feel what he was feeling. He was even having a hard time reining in some of the base, pathological urges that were starting to creep into his head. He instinctively knew that if he wasn't careful, the growing need to protect and care for Susan was going to develop into something ugly, compulsive, maybe even obsessive. That was a sensation he did not like, but he was powerless to control the peculiar emotions ripening inside of him. All he had to do was turn and look at Susan's face or body and he would do something he rarely did, smile.

"Okay, okay. I'll give you an example. This is the best one I can remember--probably because so many people were burned and it was in the news. Do you remember that fund the former senator from New Jersey took over?"

"The one that when bankrupt? Yeah, I remember, Senator Corstien and XG Global were in the news all the time. I never understood what they did or what happened."

They dealt with farmers, mostly, and they were supposed to make sue the farmers got the best prices for their crops."

"Ok, I get that, go on."

There are men who wanted the farmers to fail, to get burned so they'd be forced to sell their land. So, they call Senator Corstien up and ask him to play along."

"You mean help them destroy the farmers?"

"Exactly. The Senator declined and that's when it got ugly. There was a meeting at the Royal Thames Yacht Club by The American Institute for Strategic Planning.

"Who was at the meeting?"

"A group of super-rich financiers. Anyway, they decided it wasn't a good thing for an outsider to refuse to help them."

"What do you mean by outsider?" Susan asked.

"I mean people who weren't with them. They wanted to punish Senator Corstien, so they laid out a plan to bring down the firm."

"This really happened?"

"Yup. The files York gave me had a copy of the policy paper and copies of articles when what they planned went down."

"So what happened?"

Sampson paused, trying to recall the details. "These other rich men knew exactly what Senator Corstien had invested in. He had borrowed a lot of money and all but bet the house on Italian bonds. To make sure the bet failed the men at that meeting intervened in the Italian bond market to make sure the value of the bonds would drop and XG Global would get a margin call they couldn't meet."

Susan chimed in, "So that's when Corstien used the customer's money, to cover the losses?"

Sampson gave her a sideways glance, shocked that she knew the details. Then, he remembered her telling him both her deceased husband and last boyfriend had been in the finance industry. Still, it surprised him how interested she was in high finance.

"Yeah, this one-time Wall Street darling farmers trusted went belly-up. They were forced to file for bankruptcy."

"And the bonds, selling at huge discounts from their face value, were bought up by these hedge funds and private equity firms, you know, vultures."

"Like Roland Troth?"

"Yeah, exactly like him. Anyway, those funds cut a deal with the bankruptcy court and carved up ownership of the bonds. According to what I read in those files, the vultures are still laughing all the way to the bank."

"And that's how those people got so rich and powerful?"

Sampson looked at Susan and nodded, knowing she was following him perfectly. "Yeah, and how they punish people who don't play along."

Susan was disgusted by what she heard, "I guess if they apply that same strategy across almost every industry-- the small investors get shit on and the big boys keep all the goodies for themselves." Sampson didn't respond. Instead, he simply gave her a knowing glance.

"How do they sleep at night?"

They made their way beyond the barrier blocking the dirt road onto state property and past the sign warning visitors the land was protected. They were making good time and thought they would be able to make it to Liz's house in Wyckoff before noon. Since they did not hear any explosions and didn't smell anything burning as they came out of the mountains, they were confident and not too concerned. They walked at a brisk pace, still holding hands.

"You know what?" Susan interjected, "now that I think about it, I remember stuff like that happening a lot. Merrill Lynch, Lehman, my sister's pension fund got burned--I don't even wanna talk about when the housing bubble burst."

"That's right--a lot of people were hurt and people like Troth made a killing. It's people like him and Maxwell York who were actually picking winners and losers--and betting on the outcome."

They walked on a west, southwestern vector through Bergen County, New Jersey, toward Wyckoff. They kept off the major thoroughfares while maintaining a slightly cautious watch for any threats. Only a few cars were on the roads and everything seemed relatively peaceful. The people they did cross paths with paid little to no attention to them, simply keeping a weary eye on their movements but nothing more.

A few times, when others engaged them or waved, Sampson made an attempt at gathering some intelligence. It was not difficult to learn some very important details about what had transpired while they were in the mountains. The more news they picked up, the more the conversation between Susan and Sampson turned to the factors that had caused the United States to descend into anarchy.

Susan asked, "So, when do you think all of this started?"

"How far back do you want to go?" Sampson asked. "I've known for years that we were heading for this."

Susan tilted her ahead at him and asked, "How?"

"When the government really started getting involved in business. If you study Nazi Germany, there are many similarities to what's been happening here. Combine that with white-collar criminals stealing billions and only getting a slap on the wrist, and I knew this country was headed for shit. I just didn't know it would get this bad this fast."

"What do you think was the straw that broke the camel's back?"

"The Occupy Wall Street protesters. They gave the real people who run this country the impetus to do what they had planned for so long." Sampson turned and looked at Susan, trying to detect if she had any reaction to what he said. Seeing a confused look on her face, he continued, "When the riots and demonstrations started to expand, you saw it, right?"

"Yeah, I watched some."

"The media really came out against the protesters, claiming they were a threat to democracy--"

Susan cut in, "Yeah, I followed the Arab Spring and the news said how great that was, you know, democracy spreading. When the Occupy Wall Street thing started, though, it was a totally different story--then everything seemed to fizzle out."

"A lot of that was propaganda. Those riots on the streets of Oakland, California, and police violence on college campuses gave cover for the politicians to enact laws to be used against the protesters."

"That's the part I don't get," Susan exclaimed with her thickening eyebrows pushed together. "We elect these jerks, why do they take sides against us?"

"Because, their real masters are corporations and their lifeblood is corporate donations."

"The same group of rich people we've been talking about?"

"Yeah. They don't just control the wealth, they control the corporations and the corporations control the politicians. It's fascism, pure and simple, and it's been that way for a long time. Actually, it was probably pretty easy to get the lawmakers to pass legislation the corporations wanted."

"Like what?"

"Like redefining resisting arrest to include passive resistance and increasing fines for civil disobedience tenfold."

Susan looked more confused than ever. "This was all in their plans? To make criminals out of protesters? That doesn't make any sense to me."

Sampson displayed a sardonic grin before answering. "I guess they did it so that any protest could be met with force and jail time. That scared the hell out of a lot of people. At the same time, it made a bunch of others mad as hell, or, I should say, even angrier. Think about it, Susan, right under our noses they've built hundreds of privately run internment camps."

"You don't know that for sure, you just read about that in those files, right Sampson? I mean, come on, you haven't seen internment camps, have you?"

"Well, yeah, I know for a fact prisons have been springing up all around the country, except they've been calling 'em detention centers for illegal immigrants. You remember all of those 'shovel ready' projects funded by the two stimulus bills passed during the 2008, 2009 recession?"

"Yeah?"

"Billions of dollars went toward erecting these facilities all over the country. All they did was slap on signs saying they were being run by the Immigration and Customs Enforcement and everyone was okay with that."

"Okay, so the politicians pass the laws, the police start cracking down, but so what? I mean come on, that isn't enough to make everyone go off. There has to be more to it."

"What, beyond the 20% unemployment and the price of gasoline going through the roof right up to the point it ran out?" Sampson asked sarcastically.

"Yeah?"

"I can only guess, but maybe combined, it made everyone say, 'I'm mad as hell and I'm not going to take it anymore.'" While quoting Peter Finch's famous line from the movie Network, Sampson couldn't help but smirk. "What can I say?"

Susan was amused, having rarely seen his playful side come out so much. She played right along by shooting a wrathful glare in his direction and playfully slapping him on the ass.

"Ouch! Okay, Okay!" Sampson took her hand again and continued, "What York and his kind thought was that after the civic manipulation and then economic collapse, it'd be easy to convince everyone that the best thing to do was to suspend the Constitution and install a dictator. I don't know for sure, but I'm guessing that's what happened. We'll have to find out more when we get to your sister's house."

Without knowing more about what had taken place while they were in hiding, Susan went back to the subject that interested her the most, the people who were behind the economic collapse and how Sampson was connected to them.

"What do you know about Maxwell York?" Susan asked, "Ripping people off in the stock and bond market, was that how he made his money?"

"Some of it. He was a major weapons dealer and he was born rich. But, the way he made his mark was financing things like weapons development and wars. For example, I know that he was the brains behind the Iran Contra affair back in the '80's. When I did a little digging, I found out the CIA has been protecting him for decades. I don't know if you know this but, people like him play a huge part in arming the world, guaranteeing there are always wars, making sure there's always funding for national defense."

"Sampson, is that how you ended up working for him, because you were in the Marines?"

Over the past several weeks, spending so much time

together, they had gotten to know each other quite well. Yet, when it came to Daniel Sampson talking about his past, somehow, he always found a way to avoid going into details.

"Yeah, I was a Marine, but that was another life."

"Well, did you being a Marine have to do with you hooking up with York?"

"Yeah, Susan, I guess you could say that."

"Can you please elaborate? I mean, come on!" she prodded and whined, pushing him to tell her more about how the association had started.

"Okay, I already told you how I got into a jam in Iraq and had to fight my way out to survive, my handlers left me hanging."

"Yeah."

Sampson paused and lowered his head. Having collected his thoughts, he continued. "Well, when I got my discharge, I had to find a way to live the kind of life I wanted. The war in Iraq was still going on with no end in sight, and the action in Afghanistan just started getting hot, so the government switched tactics. They needed to increase the number of soldiers with specialized skills and training. I cut my teeth on training military men to be super-predators, you know, reconnaissance operatives, snipers, stuff like that. So, I was asked to join a private outfit that paid $1,500 a day to train others to do what I was the best at doing."

What he was telling her was the truth, and even though it really had nothing to do with how he became associated with Maxwell York, he found it much easier to lie to Susan if what he told her had some basis in fact. Ever since they started sleeping together, he had an almost eerie feeling that she could see right though him.

He went on, "I was a private contractor, a mercenary hired to provide security. Instead, I trained our men in Iraqi how to use special military tactics. Maxwell

York and guys like him provided financing for the type of firms I worked for and they hired a lot of former Special Forces guys. I just happened to be one of 'em."

Susan felt deep in her soul he was not telling her the full story. She hesitated, and then decided to let the moment of doubt pass.

*****

The men surrounding Maxwell York were all, at one time or another, part of the CIA's Clandestine Service, and they had sworn an oath of service few men could understand.

The agents and former agents all had families to support, and when they were in the field doing the covert work for the United States of America, or York himself, they knew exactly whom they could count on if they ever got in trouble.

It had always been Maxwell York working behind the scenes to make sure they were released from foreign prisons. It was York who would fund rescue attempts in third world countries. Before the Soviet Union fell, it was always Mr. York making deals behind the Iron Curtain to arrange the release of a captured spy. As far as the United States bureaucrats were concerned, in many cases, those men, the most patriotic of Americans, didn't even exist. But, to Maxwell York, they were the lifeblood of his work.

The men who had sworn their oath of allegiance to their country, the Constitution, and Maxwell York, felt they were serving their duty to their country as long as they were working for York. In their mind, the two were synonymous. When Congress tried to audit the CIA or the funding it was York's company, MYB, Ltd. who creatively conceal appropriations. Or, if funds to topple a dictator ran short, it had been York who paid the bills. Swearing an oath of loyalty to the man, therefore, was a lot more meaningful than pledging allegiance to the flag--the man helped them in the field, gave them a life insurance policy like no other in existence, and all but signed their paychecks.

The Clandestine Service was a secret society of its own. The men and women who were part of it had been recruited from Ivy League college campuses and other exclusive institutions across the country. They were of the breed who weren't the richest, but from upper middle class families. They weren't the smartest, but in the top quartile of their college classes. They were the athletes who were a few inches too short or one-step too slow to turn pro, but exceptional enough to receive scholarship offers from top tier programs. Their breeding, smarts, and athletic ability combined made them a group of special individuals.

The men and women who were accepted and trained to be the most secret of secret agents were expected to do what they were told using any means necessary. More times than not, those orders had come from Maxwell York. To them, following those orders came as naturally as breathing.

Through the Clandestine Service, York and the rest of his most senior and powerful affiliates had been able to get the people they wanted in the positions where they were needed in almost every country in the world.

It was actually York and his associates' policies being dictated by the policy makers, their missions being thrust on the military, and their ultimate goals being fulfilled by the might of the greatest nation on earth. The trusted members of the Clandestine Service knew they were just the point of the spear, doing whatever their superiors demanded. They also knew their superiors were not who everyone thought they were.

It was simply accepted by the spies, agents, and counter-intelligence operatives that their elite directors were of a higher caste. They were individuals of extreme wealth, power, and breeding, and they were the only ones the spies followed.

For decades, Maxwell York and his partners worked hard to transform the world into what they wanted. To do so required the enlistment of a select group of like-minded compatriots with the appropriate heritage and breeding. They did not call themselves by any formal name, nor did they aspire to become known. However, it was not all that difficult to identify who they were.

They had been born into extreme wealth and were educated at the most exclusive institutions. Most had been members of secret societies such as Skull and Bones. After they graduated from college, most went on to become masters of their own domain, obtaining more degrees, powerful positions, more wealth, and excelling in all they did. Only then were they recruited to be a potential partner.

As the elite group got older, they were the ones who became CEOs of Fortune 500 companies, board members of the twelve regional Federal Reserve Banks, the directors of financial institutions and managing partners of law firms all over the world. They took positions at the International Monetary Fund, and were members of The Council of Foreign Relations. They were the power behind the American Legislative Exchange Council, a group able to have their will enacted as law. For years, the Council had spread the dictates of the senior partners throughout the States, bypassing the bureaucrats in D.C.

In addition to the status, titles, and wealth, the chosen were also put through many trials and tests of loyalty. In time, they were the ones who became the choice members of the Illuminati, The Bilderberg Group, The Thule Society, and the Bohemian Group. Some went on to important posts in the United Nations or had gone on to be presidents, prime ministers, or other heads of state. But, for the ones who remained in the background, with no need to have their egos stroked, their paths led them in another direction. They were in the upper echelon and the defacto leaders of the exclusive group.

To be a member of the highest of the high, there was one additional precondition for inclusion. The most important requirement for entry was heredity. They had to have a demonstrable genetic link to only one of a handful of families. The upper council, headed by Maxwell York, they were the ones who plotted, planned, and conspired to get the others in position to change the world.

This principal group, the elite of the elites, a group who referred to themselves simply as "Senior Partners," always stayed out of the spotlight. Just like the spies who were secretly ushering Maxwell York around the country, they were not known to the outside world.

Gathered in the NSA's two billion dollar, one million square foot Utah Data Center, Maxwell York was holding court with men and woman he considered to be his equals. Like him, they had flown in from all over the world to take refuge in one of the most secure facilities that had ever existed. It was York's final decision, but the body gathered in Utah to partition the world. They also agreed that, outside of their clique, no one should be told that Maxwell was still alive--at least not at that juncture.

Chapter Six

Sitting in the modest, modern kitchen of Liz's house, Susan and Sampson listened with rapt attention. Their retreat into the Ramapo Mountains had lasted a lot longer than they had expected, and by the time they came out of the woods, many things had changed. Only the hugging, tears, and Liz's demand for Susan to explain where she had been since dropping off the face of the earth prevented Sampson from hearing the news he was so hungry to get.

Liz, Susan's older sister, was a little taller and a little pudgier that Susan, but her beautiful Italian skin retained a healthy glow and she maintained the appearance of a much younger woman. Liz was a bit of a hippie and it showed in her style of dress. She also wore her hair long and straight letting the streaks of gray serve as a natural highlight.

The Wyckoff home, just a few blocks from Liz's specialty chocolate shop, had been in her family for decades. From the second they had opened the front door and walked right in, Susan felt right at home.

Despite the stores starting to restock and reopen, the cupboards were almost empty. Just like Sampson had suspected, she had been running low on food. As she prepared the venison they had brought along, Liz tried to fill them in on the pertinent events, as she knew them to be.

"From what I've heard, people have been splitting up into different factions. It's crazy, we used to be divided between Democrats and Republicans, but now it's like the country is split up into pro-government and anti-government sects. Lots-a people are against Andrew Stevens and what he's done and they're spitting mad about the Constitution being suspended."

"How do you know?" Sampson asked sternly.

Liz was not taken aback by the way Sampson

74

spoke. Even without Susan telling her, she would have pegged him as being a military man. "That's one of the only things people around here talk about. You have to understand what the last few weeks have been like. We've seen troops coming in and grab people out of their houses.

"Where'd they take them?" Susan asked.

"I don't know, but people are just disappearing and no one knows where they've gone. It's made everyone kind of paranoid--so you have to know who you're talking to and where they stand."

"Is it really that bad?" Susan inquired.

"Hell, yeah, it's that bad. You've got your activists and your pacifists and then the ultraconservatives are on board to do the pacification and prosecute everyone else. The country isn't just split up on ideological or racial lines, Susan, around here, we've got neighbor turning against neighbor."

Susan cut in, "So, what you're saying is, this drama isn't all about politics and money?"

"I guess not," Liz answered, not convinced her conclusion was right. "I do know it goes a lot deeper than liberal against conservative or rich against poor. People are divided by their careers, where they live, and a bunch of other crazy shit no one can make sense of."

"That's happening around here?" Susan asked, wondering how the friendly people in such a typical New Jersey town could turn against each other so quickly.

"Not so much here, but, damn--all you have to do is go down to Fort Lee and there's still a bunch of people from New York City camping out on people's lawns like its okay. If you dared to drive there, one of 'em just might mug you and take your car because you got gas and they don't. That would make you part of the one-percenters. To them, we're the rich folks who stole everything. I mean, it's not as bad as it was, but things aren't even close to being back to normal."

"Sun Tzu would have been proud." Sampson said to no one in particular as thoughts of strategy coursed through his head.

"Who?" Susan asked.

"Sun Tzu, he wrote a treatise on warfare about 2,400 years ago, 'The Art of War,' and that's where 'Divide and conquer,' comes from. From what she's saying, the riots in the cities and the destruction of property, that's the kind of thing someone would want to happen if they were trying to hide what they were really doing."

"Trying to hide, my ass," Liz said bluntly, as was her way. "Everything they're doing is right out in the open and they've got most of us scared to death."

"And that's exactly how they were able to pull off this stunt with the Constitution and everyone bowing down to Andrew Stevens." Susan added.

At the mention of Andrew's name, Sampson had to consciously force himself not to react and bite his tongue so as not to let Susan in on the fact that he knew the man. Without letting his expression or eyes give him away, he remembered taking Andrew down with a few well-placed jabs and slicing off a piece of his ear. It also made Sampson wonder if had been able to take anyone out with the truck bomb he set off on Cape Cod. If Stevens got away, maybe Maxwell York got away as well.

Liz went on, "I think some people are just looking for vengeance against the activists. But, you know what, I can't help but thinking a big part of those troublemakers just don't give a damn about anyone but themselves. As long as they can rob and steal, they're good to go-- Goddamn savages."

"Like modern day pirates, but on a mass scale." Sampson commented.

"Exactly like pirates, but what they're not thinking about is who's gonna feed 'em if they don't act civilized and let food into the cities? How will their kids be educated if they don't calm down and get things running again? Everyone wants something, but no one's talking about the future--shit, most of 'em can't even see as far as tomorrow."

"The splinter groups can't see the other's point of view, that we're basically all in the same boat."

"Nope. They're not even close to connecting, which is pretty sad if you ask me. You two have no idea how many people have died or disappeared already. People just don't know what's going on or what they should do." Liz's voice showed how despondent she was.

"And that, I think, is the entire point of this exercise." Sampson concluded.

*****

The lower floors of MYB's old headquarters on West 97th Street in Manhattan had been transformed into the center of the new government. With its own security staff and direct, encrypted links to the seven worldwide boards appointed to oversee the transfiguration, efficiency demanded that they convene closer to where the real power was located.

Initiating a new currency backed by a fractional reserve of gold was a necessity, and that was what Becky and Raymond were trying to accomplish. Surrounded by teams of traders, economists, and programmers, they were actively negotiating with other dignitaries around the globe. Some were resistant, upset that they were no longer dealing with Maxwell York. But, they continued to trade and work towards a resolution of outstanding debts. They all knew it had to be done as quickly as possible--for their own sake.

Establishing some form of money that people all over the world would accept was a daunting task, so they had broken their plans down to incrementally advance what they hoped would be a one-world currency, the Amero. After all that had happened, instituting a system of fraction reserve was the only way to restore faith in any form of currency. The idea of using a reserve-backed currency was not new, but to do it required the infrastructure to handle transactions and the commodities, especially gold, to back it up.

Ameros were being issued as credits and tracked and monitored by a computer network. Any American citizen or corporation, if they could prove they held dollars or dollar-based assets in legitimate accounts as of the day before the dollar collapsed, they would have the value of those balances converted to the new dollars. Federal Reserve Notes, the actual cash used to transact business, were worthless. For people who hoarded cash at home, or small businesses who held a lot of cash, they were left with nothing but stacks of worthless paper.

The federal government had some of the necessary gold reserves in bullion, enough to handle the immediate needs of the country and back the Amero with a reserve ratio of three percent. Those acting as trustees for the failed United States government had complete access to the reserves at the New York Fed, Forth Knox, and West Point, but that wasn't enough. Provisions would have to be made to raise the reserve ratio to ten percent or more. Any less and the public would balk at accepting it.

If nothing else, the consortium being led by Andrew Stevens his confederates had to make it seem like they were trying to build up the necessary reserves. Any hint or perception that the new government was trying to pull a fast one so early on in the game would be disastrous.

Another major task was to resolve the outstanding national debt with their partners--the other ruling councils around the world. That was Raymond Behn's responsibility, while restarting commerce had been charged to Becky Longo and her staff. The game plan had been laid out, the other players around the world were in place, and all they had to do was negotiate hard and follow through.

"Becky, where do we stand on the domestic front?" Raymond inquired as he brushed his graying brown hair back with his palm.

"Same as yesterday. People should be trading their money in for Amero Credits by now, but they're still not doing it. I don't know why--"

"We've got to do better. The lack of money is one of the problems fueling the riots." Along with the lack of food, fuel, and other basic necessities, Raymond wanted to add, but he held his tongue. "Bartering is too inefficient and until we get price stability, we're fighting an uphill battle."

"You think I don't know that, Ray?" she responded tersely. "The banks already have the software set up to handle the transactions; and, we've convinced most of the major retailers to change their pricing to Ameros. I don't know what else you expect me to do."

In order to quickly implement the country's networking and transaction processing needs, Andrew Stevens had ordered the seizure of the system that was already being used by several banks in Pennsylvania. Those banks were owned by the Seven Rams Gold Trust. There were other holdings of that trust that had caught the eye of Stevens, which would also be in play before long.

"If being able to buy what they need doesn't convince people to get the new ID's and access to money, I don't know what else we can do."

Becky moved past Raymond to another computer terminal. As she checked the data, she went on, "Andrew's cranked up the hype machine, and sending out the President and Vice President to do some cheerleading for Ameros has helped a bit."

The mention of the President made Raymond smile. He had become nothing but a puppet.

"Right after those two hit the airwaves touting Ameros, transactions increased and the level of commerce started to pick up again."

He leaned over her shoulder to inspect what she was reading, putting a comforting hand on her shoulder. "When companies start bringing people back to work, we'll see the level of activity skyrocket." Raymond smiled and tried to end on an encouraging note. "Don't worry, Becky, we're not out of ammunition yet. Eventually, everyone will go along, or they'll be left behind, you just watch."

"I sure hope so."

*****

When they finished eating, Sampson and Susan both took long, hot, showers while Liz ran their clothes through the washer. By the time they were clean, dry and dressed, night had fallen.

They were exhausted after expending so much energy, and, because they had indulged themselves on too much meat, their fatigue was redoubled. The idea of comfort in a big, soft, clean bed was too much to pass up. Not long after laying down, Susan and Liz were fast asleep.

Sampson was ill at ease. At first, he was upset because he had been aching to make love to Susan, but Liz hadn't given them one second alone. Then, when they went to bed, Susan said she was too tired--and that was the first time she had ever rejected or refused him anything. That bothered him, but as he thought about it, Samson realized he had been troubled ever since they set foot in the house. His unease was not about being in a strange home, nor about feeling exposed where they were. Instead, the more he thought about the sisters, Liz and Susan, the more disturbed he became.

Lying in bed, he found himself experiencing the unfamiliar pangs of jealousy. He had not had to share Susan with anyone until they met up with Liz, and the more attention Susan paid to Liz, the more he saw her as a threat. That was something he would have to resolve because feeling those emotions was distracting and taking him off his game.

Several hours after the women fell asleep, Sampson stealthy crept out of bed and looked around the neat, cozily decorated home. Without making a sound, he checked every room except for the master suite where Liz slept. Even while going up and down the old wooden stairs to the basement, he never made a sound.

Scoping out the residence, Sampson noticed many pictures hanging on the walls and several more sitting on the fireplace's mantle. His keen eyes picked up images of Liz and Susan as much younger women along with their parents. The rest of the pictures were of Susan, a man, and two kids. He surmised they had to be her children and deceased husband.

When he was finished with what he had to do, Sampson was able to sneak back into bed without waking Susan. She was sleeping so hard she didn't even react when curled his body around hers, feeling her warm body, and smelling her clean hair.

The following morning, after eating, they sat with Liz and talked while the sun came up. A fire was burning in the family room's fireplace. They sat near its warmth, and, holding big, steaming mugs of coffee, they could have been any other normal family chatting about their plans for the day. Having Sampson in the house, armed, capable, and fit, Liz felt secure for the first time in weeks.

Liz was sitting in her favorite recliner while Sampson sat to the far side of the sofa with Susan sitting sideways, leaning on his chest and with her legs up on the cushions.

"So, what about the shops, the stores, how come your cabinets are almost empty?"

"When the state and local police forces went back to work, that's when some of the stores started opening up, but still, there's lots of shortages. All that stuff I told you about

81

changing dollars for Amero Credits, you first have to give them a DNA sample so they can make you an I.D."

"You didn't do that, did you?" Susan asked, incredulous.

"No."

"And that's why you haven't gone shopping?" Sampson asked rhetorically.

Liz just lowered her head, not in shame but so as not to seem overly proud of herself for not caving in to the authorities.

"Oh, about the cops, that's something I forgot to tell you," Susan said. "When we hiked from Teeterboro to the Ramapo Reservoir, we didn't see one cop. But when we hiked back here, they were patrolling again, how did that happen?"

Liz went on to explain what she knew about the contracts, the new currency, and how the new government persuaded the cops to go back on the job. When she mentioned the loan modifications the government was offering to those who went along with the new regime, Susan cut her off.

She asked, "Wait, what was that about the banks and the mortgages?" She remembered how mortgages and mortgage backed securities were the instruments Roland Troth had used to try to take over the land in Pennsylvania and she wondered if this was connected.

Liz crinkled her eyebrows in deep thought. "Well, from what I understand, the banks who issued the mortgages were forced to transfer them all to the Federal Reserve, but the big banks are supposed to continue to service the loans."

"So who exactly is doing the loan modifications? You said that was how they got the cops to go back to work, what about everyone else?"

"The bigger banks, you know, the too big to fail ones, they're handling things--and word's gotten out that they're working through everyone, adjusting rates and lowering the principle."

"So people can make the payments and stay in their homes? The surprise in Susan's voice was evident.

"Yeah, go figure. The bankers who live around here were called back to work even before it was safe."

"How the hell is anyone going to make payments when no one knows if they still have a job--or how they'll be paid for that matter?" Sampson asked.

"That's the thing, if someone can't pay their mortgage, or refuses the new terms, the property reverts to the Fed and it turns into a rental property."

"With Federal Reserve as landlords?" Susan interjected.

Sampson thought to himself that offering the cops a sweet deal if they went back to work was a brilliant move. Using them as examples, the new government could let everyone see how kind and generous they were. He had used the same type of tactics in Columbia and Thailand, buying allies he'd otherwise have to fight. Liz didn't know anything about the military, but Sampson supposed they must have received the same type of deal or else they wouldn't have stuck around.

Susan shot a questioning look at her sister, "How do you know all of this?"

"I didn't have anything else to do, so I read the documents online. Besides, a lot of bankers live around here and they're all hip to what's going on."

All Sampson wanted to know was about the military's maneuvers since the crisis started. It did not take long for Liz to tell him everything she knew about the military, which wasn't much.

"As far as I could tell, we were being invaded. I mean, my God, there were planes and helicopters and Mr. Goodson from down the street said that he saw a convoy of Army trucks clearing and moving south on Route 17."

"Where were they going?" Susan asked with her head leaned lazily against Sampson's chest. She looked like she was exhausted and having trouble keeping her eyes open.

"The GWB, Manhattan, I guess."

"Did they make it?"

"I don't know, well, yeah, they must have because it's been on Twitter. They've been talking about clearing the streets of New York and how the National Guard was having such a hard time expanding beyond the secured sectors."

"Liz," Sampson cut her off as a select few of her words finally registered in his head. "When we first got here, you said after they declared Martial Law, the internet went down--"

"And the cable and the phones, but they're back on now." Liz responded.

Sampson jumped his feet, completely forgetting about Susan and allowing her head to plop down into the sofa cushion. "The internet is working?"

"Dan, what's wrong?" Susan asked as she pushed herself up and stood beside him, alarmed.

"Yeah, I thought I told you that."

"Do you have a computer I can use?" Sampson had a look of determination on his face, but it appeared like he was angry. He forced himself to relax and lower his voice. "I'm sorry, it's just, I think we may be able to get all the information we need--if I'm able to log-on to this, ah, site."

"What site? The internet is not the same as it was. They've got all kinds of filters and censors and most queries lead you right back to the same stupid government sites."

"He says he can get into this secret government system where you can find just about anything, CIA stuff, alien abductions, adoption records, even cloning, right Sampson?" Susan teased.

Susan's barb was an inside joke between them. Sampson had explained how he learned he was put up for adoption through the MIN-OPS network. She didn't buy what he told her about it--a computer system run by military agency she never heard of was too much to believe. So, she had let the idea of MIN-OPS go, along with the rest of what he had told her, except to tease him.

"Susan, do you think you can help me?" he asked, not even picking up on her not-so-subtle attempt at an insult.

Stunned, she responded, "How can I help you?"

"You told me about the tricks you learned so you can talk to your kids in Costa Rica--maybe you can get me onto one of those non-commercial trunk lines you told me about."

Susan's eyes lit up in a way Sampson had never seen before, making her look absolutely ravishing. "You think I'll be able to talk to my babies?" The first thing that popped into her mind was the welfare of her children.

Sampson bit his cheek, trying to keep his cool. He was falling in love with Susan, but not her kids. To him, they were a part of her he could do without. He also knew, though, that if he was going to get her best effort, he'd have to dangle a carrot in front of her face. For Susan, there was no bigger reward than the possibility of speaking to her children.

"Yes, of course! If you can get us onto those black networks, anything's possible."

Susan looked at he big sister with pleading eyes.

"Go! It's all hooked up in the study."

Grabbing Sampson by the hand, Susan led him out of the living room, up the narrow staircase of the split-level home, and through a door on the far side of a posh, formal dining room.

The study was a small room with a dark desk and dark wooden shelves lined with leather bound, first edition novels. It was obvious by the clutter that the office was little used. On the desk, looking completely out of place, was a relatively new computer system, router, and Wi-Fi station.

Quickly sitting down in the swivel chair, Susan reached out and woke the system from sleep mode. Once the screen was on, she starting clicking and typing away.

"What are you doing?" he asked.

"I'm trying to remotely log on to the system at my friend's house in Pennsylvania--that's where the utilities and applications are that'll let me find a secure line to Costa Rica."

"Won't your friend mind you hijacking his computer?"

With no emotion in her voice, Susan replied, "He won't mind. He's dead." After a few more clicks, a typed in password, she announced, "Okay, phase one is done."

She clicked on a few icons that Sampson did not recognize and started an application that immediately kicked the computer into text mode. Long strings of numbers started popping up on the screen as the system autonomously started navigating through one link after another, trying to locate a backdoor at first one and then another ISP.

Once the precise pathway was establish, thousands of URL addresses, TCP/IP instructions, and routing tables neither one of them could understand continuously scrolled up the screen.

"This reminds me of the movie, War Games," Sampson commented as he stood behind Susan, leaning forward and watching the screen. "It's kind of like a remote dialing program for the internet, huh?"

"That's exactly what it is, or at least that's what I was told...I have no idea what most of this shit is. If we're lucky, I won't have to try the other way to do this, which is really complicated."

Finally, the numbers stopped scrolling up the screen and the screen went blank. Dots started to appear behind the slow moving, blinking cursor on the text screen and then a series of execution codes flashed on and then off. Strange digital sounds beeped and chirped through the computer's speakers. Suddenly, the screen went back to graphics mode and they were both looking at the typical Windows screen as if nothing had happened.

Susan turned and looked at Sampson. "I think we're in."

Chapter Seven

Across every telecommunications network in North America, if anything came up in conversations, e-mail, or text messages that sounded even closely related to subversive or criminal activities, the communication was flagged. Then, information about the communicating parties, and the exchanged message, was further scrutinized by an agent who had the primary authority to decide if it was worth investigating. If even the slightest possibility of nefarious activity existed, the flagged data would be reclassified and kicked up to a higher level of command in that agency--one step below gaining nation-wide attention from the Joint Commission Task Force.

From there, if found to possibly be a legitimate threat, more data would be gathered and entered into the MIN-OPS network for further analysis. All communications between the parties--previously recorded and stored in massive databases--would be retrieved and checked for proof of criminal intent. Images from every city and every transportation hub were scoured. Even the databases of pictures from every single red light camera in the nation were searched for cars and license plates matching the target. Anything of interest that was found was then added to the investigation.

If the targets of the flagged data had made it to the point where background checks were required, the closest of the thousands upon thousands of Homeland Security facilities, covert satellite units located in strip malls and office buildings across the country, would send out agents to compile profiles, obtain photos, and conduct surveillance. All the while, the gathered intelligence would be logged into the system so that all other agencies with the proper security access codes could see the details.

Networked workstations then used the data to try to

link the suspects with other suspects, known terrorist locations, or suspicious bank accounts. If the computers could not find direct proof of associations to others--using machine learning algorithms and artificial intelligence--the system made its best supposition. In a matter of just a few years since the system had come online, almost every resident of the United States had a file or entry relating to them on the MIN-OPS network.

A node off a trunk line leased by Verizon had generated an alarm. An optical traffic server had been pinged several thousand times in what appeared to be some type of an attempt to hack the system. The system had traced the attack back through the West Branch node to Williamsport, Pennsylvania. From there, an automated system initiated a search that cross-referenced the source's computer chip identification number with the know residents and residences of that city.

It was quickly ascertained that the owner of the system was a man named Mario Mezzara whose residence was in a small suburb of Williamsport called Loyalsock Township. The system also recognized that Mr. Mezzara had been killed earlier that year. An attempt to probe the system's hard drive was thwarted by a non-commercial firewall.

The probing application automatically switched to data packet retrieval and inspection. When the data packet header was deciphered, it became obvious that the user had encrypted the data making the deep packet inspection routines impossible. That sent immediate alert to a human operator signaling that intervention was necessary.

Joshua Harger was the duty officer and the first to see the alert. As an experienced network administrator, his eyes and brain immediately parsed the data the automated computer alert system had sent him.

With no hesitation, he picked up the phone on his desk and hit a speed dial button for his Joint Commission

Task Force liaison.

"Billy? This is Josh Harger, Senior Monitor for trunk line ZA228760. We've got a live one, 128-bit encryption to and from Costa Rica on a non-com thread. It looks like someone hijacked some dead guy's system and is using it as a remote server for the attacks. You guys should try to trace it back to the source."

Joshua signed off and hung up the phone. He knew that whoever was free-riding one of Verizon's private lines to send encrypted messages was in for a world of shit, that was, if the Rapid Response Team's jackboot thugs were able to track them down.

*****

Two men wearing Navy Blue suits and white shirts came barging through the double doors of the conference room.

"What?" Raymond yelled, "Can't you see we're busy?"

"Mr. Stevens, sir," the taller of the two announced, "I'm sorry to interrupt you, but you've got an urgent call from General Smythe on the encrypted line."

The second of the two agents strode forward with purpose and extended a phone-like device out to Andrew.

"Adam, this is Stevens, what can I do for you?"

"I wanted to call you personally to let you know we've got a bead on Daniel Sampson. What do you want us to do?"

"I don't want you to do anything but tell me where he is."

"He's at a private residence in Wyckoff, New Jersey."

"Put the house under surveillance right away."

"That's already taken care of, sir. We've got three eyes in the sky as we speak."

90

"And he won't pick up on that?"

"These are the latest and greatest UAV's, sir, drones. They're small and cruising at an altitude over 10,000 feet. He can't see 'em or hear 'em."

"General, I want your best men on the ground to make sure he does not get away--but I don't want him engaged until I get there. Do you understand me?"

"But, Mr. Stevens, sir, we could take out that house and everyone in it right now. All we need is your order."

Having Sampson taken out by an air strike or a squad of Special Forces was too easy. Andrew reached up and touched his ear, feeling the scar and lump where the segment Sampson had slashed in their first encounter had been sewn together. When Sampson was taken out, Andrew wanted to be sure it was as painful as possible and absolutely positive Sampson knew exactly who ordered it.

"No! I want to take care of this myself; do you understand me, general?"

"Yes, sir."

"Now pass on the exact location to my men and make sure your men are in place by the time I get to New Jersey."

"I'll do exactly as you say, sir, but I must express my objection. Major Sampson is a very dangerous man."

"Your objection is duly noted." Andrew handed the phone back to the agent and started walking toward the door. "Call down and get my escorts ready, we're moving out."

*****

Looking around the penthouse suite, the rich decor, and through the clear windowpanes, it wall all too much. It was too rich, too luxurious, and way too calm. Even the puffy clouds lazily moving across the sky belied the turmoil that had been taking place several floors below.

Michelle did not have to look down to Central Park to remind her of the battles for territory between mobs of rioters and the National Guard soldiers that had taken place. She could still smell the acrid smoke and occasionally hear the roar of military vehicles racing past the building. What had been going on at street level was war--an all out war against the citizens of the United States.

With all forms of media functioning again, it had not taken long for Carlos and Darla to catch up on what they had missed while en route to the United States and then Manhattan. Michelle had been of little help because she was so stunned by what they had told her. The news about Susan and some man named Daniel Sampson was shocking and she had been unable to focus on much besides digesting the details Darla and Carlos had gathered at the Teeterboro Airport.

The news about the population being exposed to a man-made virus was what really threw Michelle for a loop. The details were scant beyond the suggestion that the virus was made to thin the population. Lacking any verifiable facts, and not knowing the potential effects it would have on them, frightened her more than she cared to admit. Just a few weeks before, she would never have believed the story of a man funding and unleashing a man-made virus. However, if it was possible some group was trying to take over the world, it made perfect sense, she thought to herself, that they would also try to eliminate the competition. Wasn't that what Hitler tried to do? And Stalin? Weren't they trying to eliminate any alternative culture, or way of living, other than their own? Some sort of biological virus would be a quick way to accomplish what other megalomaniacs had tried and failed to do.

While thinking about the virus, Michelle reached the conclusion that Susan had done the right thing to try to find Richard. Yes, Richard Clearmont was a bit loony, an aloof scientist obsessed with fighting the drug companies after his wife died from Lyme Disease. But, he was still a molecular biologist who had spent every last minute and every last dollar trying to learn all he could about infections. If anyone could help them figure out what a man named Maxwell York and a company called Hamilton Genomics was up to, it was Crazy Richard.

"The media outlets are all putting out the same exact stories," Carlos complained. "It's like they're following a script."

Carlos had been unable to get the much-needed medical treatment at a hospital so the gash on his head had been sewn up by Darla. She had handled the blood and delicate sewing of skin with strength and detachment, as if she were simply patching a pair of jeans.

His comment brought Michelle out of her contemplative state. "The networks ceded control to Andrew Steven's media commission."

"Why would they do that?"

"Because the Special Master deemed media a national security issue," Michelle responded with obvious cynicism. "That includes the internet, television, radio, and all newspapers."

Darla was sitting passively at the computer terminal, clicking keys. Almost every search query she entered brought up a red flashing bar that read, "CENSORED" and linked her to a government-approved site. She turned to Michelle and asked, "Why didn't they put up a fight, Michelle? The rights to the airwaves are worth billions."

"I don't know--but I suspect they're all in cahoots with Stevens. The cable executives are a big deal in the business world, and most of them are on the boards of several other companies. If anyone had the power and the resources to stop Stevens it would have been them."

"The fact they didn't shows whose side their on, huh?" Darla asked rhetorically.

"But what they're letting everyone see on TV isn't hiding how bad things are." Carlos interjected. "Wouldn't Stevens want to at least make it seem like the situation is improving?"

"Yeah, that's the conventional way of thinking, Carlos, but there's nothing conventional about what's going on. I think they want everyone scared to death so when their storm troopers come knocking on our doors, we'll see them as coming to our rescue. Keeping everyone scared will make it seem like whatever they have to offer is a huge step forward."

Darla chimed in, "But this is anarchy! As far as I can tell, no one's in charge. What are we supposed to do?"

"I don't know, Darla. I just don't know."

Michelle paused, running her chipped fingernails through her hair and across her scalp. Then, it dawned on her that all was not what it seemed. What they were seeing on the news couldn't be the whole story. She suddenly had a sickening feeling, a feeling she would get when she sensed someone was trying to get over on her.

With resolve in her voice, she went on, "You know, all along, we've been letting the politicians and media control us with fear. They've been manipulating us for decades--and this, everything that's going on right now-- this is all just another big con game."

"Michelle, what the hell are you talking about?"

"What I'm talking about is Stevens, Andrew Stevens. He's the one behind the fake mining of the Straight of Hormuz. He, or the people who're behind him, they're the ones behind the bombing of Iran's oil terminals, the Chinese dumping treasuries, and the collapse of the dollar!"

"How could you possibly know that?" Carlos asked.

"Because they were the ones behind the price stability once the markets reopened. Come on, you know I was watching all of that, trying to protect the trust's interests, our interests."

94

"Yeah, I know, but--"

"It had to be them, they were ready for it and no one else was." Michelle's cafe au lait skin was flush red with excitement and the pitch of her voice went up as she further elaborated on her epiphany. "Those greedy motherfuckers manipulated the world so they could buy up everything!"

"Are you sure?"

"Yes, I'm sure! When the exchanges reopened, they were the ones who were buying up what everyone else was dumping for Ameros, as if they were doing everyone a favor by taking junk assets off their hands. There're doing the same thing the Federal Reserve was doing, buying assets with money they're creating out of thin air."

"I thought the Ameros were gonna be backed by gold, right?" Darla's face revealed her confusion.

Carlos was disgusted. He knew exactly what Michelle was saying and what Stevens and his partners had done.

Michele answered, "That's just a confidence game. Darla, I don't think they ever intended on doing it--but they have to make it look like that's what their doing or no one will believe them."

Darla stood up and took two strides on her long, thin legs over toward Michelle. "I don't understand why the government let this happen. Destroying the dollar made everything worse!"

"To say things are worse, Darla, depends on your perspective. I mean, worse for whom? For most, yeah, it's a lot worse, but for people like us--people who have property, resources, gold, we're in better shape than ever. In a world without fiat currency, material assets are king."

As if to make a point, Michelle reached out and slid several thick, gold bangle bracelets up the smooth, beautiful black skin of Darla's arm. When she let go, the dense gold clapped together and produced a rich sound.

"But why would they go to the trouble?" Carlos

asked. "Why not just overthrow the government and take over by force?"

"Because they're not a country, they didn't have an army. The only power they had was the power to destabilize the currency. Before they took over, they had to blur the lines, get everyone distracted; and sliding in like Stevens did not only kept the public off balance but retains a government structure--"

"You're saying that the riots, the looting, that was all cover ups for when they stepped in and took over--and they did all right under our noses?" Darla interjected.

"Exactly. Think about it, we seem to have the same elected officials, but they're powerless. There's no Constitution, so, under what authority are they supposedly ruling? Now, we've got this guy, Stevens, running the country with dictatorial power. And, because everyone was so scared, he can legitimately claim he was duly elected. How the hell did that happen?"

Carlos recognized the implications immediately.

Michelle was on a roll and as she spoke the rate of her words increased dramatically. "You read what their planning, they're busy getting these sham laws passed that'll consolidate their power and get the people behind him. He's even got the President acting like a huckster, trying to convince the world that everything is okay and they're going to back their Ameros with gold. What we have to do is protect what we have and what Andrew Stevens wants."

"What you're saying is that this all about a bunch of rich people getting richer?"

"That and grabbing political, economic, and legal control of everything and everyone."

"Like the monarchies of the past? The big empires?"

"Exactly like that--and once they take all of the power and property, only they will have the means to pay for a military."

"And they become the new lords of us all."

"So, what do we do? How do we stop them?"

Michelle thought about it for a second before answering, "We stop them by not letting them stay in power when they try to adopt a new constitution. We can't let them impose the rule of law on us. Until we can tell the world what they have done, we can't let things calm down."

"Well, everything we've read about Stevens is about restoring some kind of order." Darla chimed in as she started fiddling with a long tress of black hair that had fallen in front of her face.

"Yeah," Michelle answered gloomily, "but it's not the kind of order we want."

Carlos chimed in, "Michelle, you know, I think they're doing the same things they've always done, but now it's completely out in the open. I didn't understand how the National Guard could bring troops in here from other states but now I get it."

"What do you mean?"

"The National Guard is made up of people from their home states. On the way here, we heard men talking, one soldier was from Ohio and another from Alabama. If that's true, what are they doing here in New York?"

"Besides, the fact they came here means things where they're from can't be that bad."

Michelle nodded in agreement and then added, "Okay, okay, let's slow down. If we're going to figure out what to do, we have to filter out the noise and try to see beyond all the lies we're being fed. We have to think ahead of Stevens and try to figure out what he's going to do next."

"You think he's going to make a play for our gold reserves in Pittsfield, don't you?"

"Not only that, Carlos, I think he's gonna go after the mines as well. They're going to need all they gold they can get to prop up the new currency their pushing."

"Even if they get our mines, they won't have enough

to back their currency--"

Michelle knew exactly where Carlos was going and cut him off. "Your right, and that's why when they talk about backing Ameros with other assets, they always stress that it will be a fraction reserve."

Darla asked, "So, what you're saying is the reserve requirement is bogus?"

"Yeah, for now it's simply another number they can manipulate." Carlos added decisively, "It's the same thing all over again except that this time to get the faith of the people; they're going to pretend to have the currency backed by something."

"Don't forget, Carlos, the way they're doing it is also deflationary, by taking foreign owned national debt off the table, there's going to be a lot less Ameros floating around than there were dollars."

"Which is going to increase the spread between the people who already have assets and those who don't. Money will be harder to get and workers, small businesses will be squeezed even more."

Thinking about what Carlos said, Michelle thought she had hit on an important point and the tone of her voice rose. "I think I've got it--switching to Ameros, they plan on deflating everything, causing a stasis where there is little to no growth."

"For what purpose?" Carlos asked.

"So everyone will be dependent on them for everything. They've been posting these documents on the internet talking about loan modifications and there's a lot of crazy language in them."

"Like what?"

"Well, to get out of debt, people have to basically sign away their lives. It's pretty vague, but there are clauses in the documents about turning DNA over to get an ID card, conscripting kids to military service, things like that."

"You're kidding me?" Darla's shock was evidenced

by her big eyes and gaping mouth. "I didn't see that!"

Michelle ignored the comment, "I'm not a lawyer, but I'm sure there's more."

Once again, Carlos caught on to Michelle's train of thought and ran with it. "It makes perfect sense. The less work there is, the more people who can't repay their loans, the better for Stevens and his side."

"Why?" Darla asked.

"Because the people who default will become like vassals."

"Vassals, like the people under feudal lords?"

"Exactly like that. Part of the contract people have to sign to get their money changed talks about some sort of pledge to protect the country and loyalty to the government, or party, or whatever they're calling themselves--"

Carlos cut off Michelle's words, "Actually, that's pretty smart. I can't think of a better way to prey on some of the rubes in this country."

That was something Darla, an African-American transplant from the south understood better than others. "Yup, that's exactly right. They play up some sort of patriotic angle and all of a sudden the rednecks and right-wingers sign on the dotted line because they feel like they're doing it for their country."

"What it comes down to is this, Darla, we've got to expose these people for who they really are, and even the rednecks down south will fight tooth and nail against them."

Carlos added, "As long as we keep our gold out of their hands and keep fighting until we figure out how to let the world know what we know."

"Then what? You think we'll be able to hit some sort of reset button and start over?" Darla asked. Not waiting for a response, she went on, "You know what I think? I think we should just forget about it and move on like you told me to do--you know, forget about my Tommy and move on."

Neither Michelle nor Carlos had a response for her. All they could do was look at each other, searching each other's eyes for help.

Darla walked stiffly to the large windows overlooking Central Park. She stood there like a statue, letting some time pass before she broke the uncomfortable silence. "We have to find ourselves a way outta here, lay low until the dust settles, and then go live our lives. Why are we sitting here thinking about this anyway? To take on Andrew Stevens? I mean, come on, we're billionaires; we're some of the richest people on the planet. Most of what we own is gold, so we're good, right? We're sitting pretty and to hell with everyone else."

Michelle immediately recognized Darla's words as that of a grieving woman with a bottomless pit of pain. Isolating herself, withdrawing, and catering to her own egocentric needs was the exact opposite of the woman she knew.

"Darla..."

The peace and quiet of the penthouse apartment was broken by the sound of helicopter rotors cutting through the air. Flying over the building at a very low altitude and swooping down to land in the open spaces of Central Park was one Blackhawk helicopter after another.

"Oh, oh my God!" Darla's words were all but swallowed up by the continuous droning of helicopter engines and the powerful chopping of their rotors.

Michelle and Carlos hurried over to the window to see what was happening. They leaned forward, their faces against the windows as they watched the completely black helicopters swoop in and land closely together in the open spaces of Central Park.

Heavily armed men jumped out of the landing airships and started run for the cover of trees. As soon as a copter had unloaded its cargo of Special Forces warriors

100

dispatched from the Rapid Response Task Force, it would take off. Not a minute would pass before another helicopter would swoop in and land. In less than ten minutes, there were hundreds of men in full battle gear securing a clearing near the north edge of Central Park West.

An old pair of binoculars was sitting on the table next to the large window. Carlos grabbed them so he could get a closer look at the squads as they took up defensive positions around the park.

When the double rotor Chinook came over the penthouse apartment it made the glass panes of the windows shake and shudder. Much slower than the agile Blackhawks, the Chinook lingered over the center of the clearing and came down landing softly on the grass. As soon as the massive helicopter touched down, a hatch at the rear started to open and slowly come down like a huge ramp.

Three officers, who were barking orders into headsets, and one civilian, surrounded by several ranks of soldiers, made their way down the ramp.

"Here," Carlos said as he handed the binoculars over to Michelle.

In the newfound peace and quiet of the penthouse, Michelle shook her head in wonderment, "Looks like the Special Master decided to put his foot down on the dissenters, huh?"

"Yeah, it sure does." Darla agreed, "And it looks like he's gonna crush us all like little bugs. You two still sure you wanna stick around?"

Chapter Eight

Susan, Liz, and Sampson were walking south along the service road of Route 17. Looking up the embankment, the carcasses of burned out or destroyed automobiles had been pushed up against the guardrail. They could hear the engines and smell the diesel fumes from the wreckers towing away the disabled automobiles blocking the road above them.

There were others walking along Route 17, but the level of fear and tension between strangers had been reduced to a respectful caution and awareness. The ever-present canvas duffel bag carrying all of his and Susan's possessions was draped over Sampson's shoulder and resting on his back. Liz and Susan were several yards behind the long-strided former Marine and looked harried trying to keep pace. Liz was carrying a bag of her own but seemed to be struggling uncomfortably with its weight.

Susan was in a world of her own. She had been able to reach out to her kids, see for herself they were safe, and tell them she loved them. Seeing them and hearing them, even though it was on a computer screen, had done wonders for her spirits. She missed them like crazy, but the fact that they looked happy and healthy made her feel a lot better. They meant the world to her.

Helena, Carlos's wife, was doing an excellent job caring for them and keeping them safe. Knowing they were in no danger, safely tucked away in Costa Rica, and that the situation there had been relatively stable, made all the difference in the world. Susan felt like a new woman and was ready to take on the world.

"Dan, I mean, Sampson." Liz was still trying to get used to calling the man by his preferred name instead of his given name. "Sampson!" she yelled out because he hadn't acknowledged her the first time.

He stopped and turned, waiting for them to catch up.

"I still don't understand why you made us leave and why you've moving so fast. Will you please slow down?"

Seeing she was sweating, even in the cold air, and realizing the bag she was carrying was giving her trouble, he waited for her to catch up. "I'd like to get as far away from your house as possible." They were the first words he had spoken to Liz in some time. Without warning, Sampson pulled open her heavy jacket, lifted up her sweatshirt and grabbed the t-shirt underneath.

"What the hell are you doing?" Liz protested as he exposed her milky-white belly.

With a harsh grip and a quick tug, he tore off a strip of cloth about a foot long and six inches wide.

The sight made Susan snap back from the warm, loving place her mind had taken her. "Sampson, what are you doing to her?"

He didn't answer. He was focused on putting distance between himself and the house they had just left. Little else mattered. He grabbed the long strap of Liz's bag and took it away from her. Then, he wrapped the soft cotton from her t-shirt around the strap and draped it around Liz's head. "Let the weight rest against your back and just use your head to keep it stable."

The cotton padded the strap enough so that there was very little pressure or friction on her forehead. With the mass distributed between her neck, shoulders and back, the bag's weight all but disappeared.

"Didn't you ever wonder why African women have been balancing things on their head for thousands of years?" Sampson turned and started walking again.

Following behind, Liz seemed satisfied by the reduced burden but was not pleased about her question being ignored. "What is your rush? I don't understand why you made me leave my house, I thought we were safe!"

The sound of chopper blades cutting through the air drowned out all other sounds. Sampson knew better than to look up for too long, or seem like he was too interested. He knew exactly where they were going and why. Sampson slowed his pace once again so Susan and Liz could catch up.

Sampson knew exactly where they were going and why. "Those helicopters are heading towards Wyckoff. There's five of them and they'll each land about a mile away from your house. Four squads will fan out and converge on your block, making sure no one gets in or out. Then, it's my guess that they'll raid the house looking to take out you, Susan, and me--but especially me."

"How do you know that?" Susan asked.

"Because after you talked to your kids and I tried to log onto the military network, the connection slowed down--I'm guessing they probably traced the connection back to your house." He lied.

He had not noticed the connection slowing down but knew they would back-trace to locate him the second he logged onto the MIN-OPS network. The lie--meant to get the women to trust him--was also a cover for what he had done.

Sampson knew better than to spend much time on the network and instead simply downloaded onto a thumb drive what he knew were the classified text documents that summarized the activities of every clandestine agency. As soon as he had time to himself, he'd read all about what the military had done and how Andrew Stevens had divvied up the world.

The panicked way he rushed Liz and Susan out of the house, though, was not an act. He knew some sort of government agency would be on their way and it would take only a matter of minutes to reprogram a drone to do fly-over surveillance. When they bolted from the house, he had scared the women enough with his feigned anxiety that hadn't bothered to question him.

Getting them out of that house was part of a plan Sampson was formulating in his head. He did not like Liz and he especially didn't like the influence she seemed to have over Susan. If Susan had not been there the whole time, he could have disposed of Liz. But, because the sisters had been inseparable, he knew he'd have to be a bit craftier about eliminating the distraction.

"So, if you knew they could do that, why did you use the computer at my house?" Liz asked, angry hearing her house was about to be violated.

"Because your sister's been dying to talk to her kids--I couldn't stand to see her hurt anymore--besides, I've been out of the game for a long time, how the hell was I supposed to know they could trace the connection so fast?"

"Oh, come on!" Liz did not buy the claim of ignorance for one second.

So touched by Sampson's concern for her emotional well-being, Susan didn't hear a word he said after he expressed exactly why he took such a big risk. Not wanting to argue, Susan quickly changed the subject. "So, where are we going now?"

Sampson reached into his pocket and handed her the disposable cell phone he'd bought and kept disabled since Cape Cod. He reached into his other pocket and pulled out the SIMM module and battery that were neatly wrapped in separate plastic baggies.

"Here, you said you transferred your data into this phone--put it together and tell me exactly where your friend Michelle is staying. If she's still there, we're going to go find her and make sure she's okay."

"But what about Richard Clearmont? I mean, that's why we're here, isn't it? If we don't find him, how are we going to figure out what that virus is?"

"While you two were sleeping last night, I looked Richard up on the internet and then called him. He wasn't at the Hohokus house, or if he was there, he wasn't answering. I also found out about a place he's got in Rochester."

"Where his lab is, right?"

"Yeah. I left him a message there as well."

"You told me he went nuts when his wife died from some disease, right?" Liz asked.

Ignoring Liz's question to Susan, Sampson went on, "The e-mail I sent said that I was a friend of his brother's and told him that if he wanted to find out what happened to his wife, he'd have to meet me at the Bronx Zoo in exactly one week."

"That was cryptic enough, I guess." Susan said as she looked back down at the restored and refreshed phone. "Here it is, the penthouse where Michelle was staying is on Central Park West."

"So, that's where we're going." Sampson looked at Susan, smiled and turned south, completely avoiding Liz's gaze.

*****

The area around Liz's Wyckoff home was buzzing with activity. The Special Forces units had rapidly closed in on the target from four directions and had the house surrounded long before Andrew Stevens and his five-helicopter escort flew into the neighborhood.

The first attempt to breach the front door resulted in the burglar alarms going off, which caught the attention of the neighbors, who came out to see what was going on. A minute later, the soldiers heard, saw, and smelled a small explosion in the basement of the house. There was just enough time for them to escape before the house exploded into a huge ball of flames, shooting burning wood and glass all over the area and setting nearby houses on fire.

When Andrew Stevens's chopper landed, the fire trucks had already started putting out the flames and the home owners in the area were looking over their property to make sure their houses were not damaged or on fire. Besides the pile of debris that was once Liz's house, there were many broken windows but, fortunate for all, no casualties.

"Who's in charge here?"

"I am sir," The man saluted, "Lieutenant Colonel Lee H. Szaravchek at your service, sir."

"What happened here?"

"It's pretty clear; the house was wired to blow, but we're trying to figure out if it was a trap, or if--"

"Or if what, soldier?"

"If whoever set the heating oil tank to explode sent us a warning, sir, so everyone could get out."

"Were there any casualties?"

"Besides a few blown eardrums and some scrapes, no."

"So, please, tell me Colonel, what makes you think Sampson gave you a warning."

At the mention of Major Daniel Sampson's name, Szaravchek cringed. "Besides the burglar alarm going off as soon as the house was breached and a fireworks display prior to the tank blowing, I have nothing, sir."

"Maybe he screwed up? Maybe Sampson set it up wrong and your men just got lucky?"

"No, sir. If Major Sampson wanted us dead, I wouldn't be taking to you right now."

"Fuck this!" Stevens turned to the commander of his escort detail and barked out, "Come on, let's get the hell out of here and get some work done."

As soon as Stevens was ushered out of the area and out of hearing range, Lieutenant Colonel Szaravchek called out to his communications specialist. "Sergeant Johnson, get General Smythe on the horn, level two encryption, ASAP."

"Right away, sir."

Standing in the center of the street, looking at the remains of what must have been a million dollar home; Szaravchek couldn't help but wonder if what they were doing was a mistake. Everything he had seen and was ordered to do was wrong. Military operations on American soil, people being rounded up and displaced from their own homes; and now he was hunting a legend, someone the Special Forces community considered a hero.

He knew in his gut that Sampson had spared him and his team a world of hurt. Instead of maximizing the death and destruction, the retired Marine Major had minimized them. Knowing the way Special Forces commandos were trained, it could only mean one thing-- Daniel Sampson was sending them a signal. As far as Szaravchek was concerned, the seed had been planted that they were on the wrong side of the conflict.

Sergeant Johnson extended his arm and handed Szaravchek a phone. "General Smythe, Lieutenant Colonel Szaravchek here. Yes, sir, everyone is safe and Sampson got away, but there's something I have to tell you..."

*****

As they walked toward Fort Lee, signs of turmoil from the prior few weeks were all around. Remnants from makeshift tent cities littered lawns and parking lots. There were thousands of abandoned cars, all with New York license plates. Some homeowners were in the process of boarding up broken windows or trying to fix unhinged doors.

Oddly, there were no cars driving on the streets. Instead, hoards of foot traffic, all heading east, converged to form a sea of humanity. The news was spreading fast. The streets of New York had been calmed and that had created a reverse exodus. The hundreds of thousands of people who had fled Manhattan and the Bronx were finally going home.

Another odd thing they noticed as they joined and walked with the masses was that very few people were using phones or any type of cellular devices. With so many people trying to access the cell towers at once, the nodes were well beyond overloaded. But, the few people who were able to connect and get updates were quick to share the information they gathered.

The George Washington Bridge had been open to foot traffic only, while the Lincoln and Holland Tunnels were restricted to military use. The Tappan Zee Bridge, along with the southern crossings into New York, had been reserved for commercial traffic. The major arteries and other bridges around the city alternately designated for specific purposes. It was the first time in weeks that there seemed to be any kind of order.

In order to establish and maintain the free flow of people as well as goods, the ramps and intersections were actively monitored and guarded by troops from the National Guard. Air traffic had resumed on a limited basis and the mass transit system, although functioning, had not yet resumed service.

Sampson led Susan and Liz down the concrete ramp and past the cameras of the Easy Pass toll collecting gates and booths. Lost in the crowd, they believed they were all but anonymous and they were not the least bit concerned about being seen by anyone who may have been looking for them.

Susan made an effort to steer her sister and Sampson toward the south side of the bridge, so she could look over the rail and down the Hudson River. Reluctantly, they followed, pressing their way through the droves walking toward the city.

The view from the rail showed something they did not expect, an abundance of traffic moving up the Hudson River. Boats of all shapes and sizes were working their way towards the landings and piers along the west side of the Isle of Manhattan. Since very few people could be seen on the crafts working their way upriver, they surmised the cargo must have been the supplies the residents of the city so badly needed.

Word was going out amongst the crowd that Special Master Andrew Stevens had ordered the military to provide free food. Distribution centers were being set up around the city with the central hub being the abandoned West Side rail yards. There was no way to separate the many rumors from the news, but as word spread, cheers went up and the mood of the walking caravan collectively improved.

Sampson heard it over the din of voices and shuffling feet. His survival instincts somehow allowed him to hone in on the sound before anyone else around him. He stopped, turned his head and then looked up to the northwest. Flying low, coming right at the bridge, were several Blackhawk helicopters. They were painted all black and rigged out for full combat. Once the booming sounds of the slicing rotors passed followed the trajectory of the helicopters with his eyes and saw them swoop down to the south and east of their location. The choppers took a semi-spiral approach to a landing zone near the center of the island. The helicopters disappeared behind several tall buildings.

Pointing in the direction where the military airships appeared to land, Sampson caught Susan's attention and told her, "Ya see where those helicopters landed, that has to be near Central Park."

"So?" Susan asked as Liz leaned in to hear the conversation.

"You see any other choppers in the air, any other military activity?"

"Besides the soldiers guarding the bridges, no."

"Do you see any fires or any signs of trouble in the city?"

Looking up and down the island across the Hudson, Susan didn't see any billowing smoke. And, in the distance, she thought she saw an undisturbed procession of vehicles meandering down the West Side Highway. "No, just like everyone has been saying, things look calm."

Sampson leaned a little closer, "Those helicopters were carrying someone important and they landed near where we're going."

Liz butted in, "How do you know that?"

Testily, he replied, "Number one, there's no action. Number two, the men leaning out of the hatches had their sighting visors on and their weapons locked and loaded, protecting the occupants. Three, the formation they were in was to give cover to the middle chopper. That tells me someone really big was along for the ride."

Liz looked at Susan and squinted. "Who the hell is this guy?"

"Shut up, Liz. Sampson, why's that important?" Susan asked.

"Because we may be walking into a hornets nest and have to be extra careful. Plus, knowing where the big shots are may give us an advantage."

"How, what are you going to do?" Liz asked rudely.

Susan grabbed her arm and pulled her aside. "Liz, I'm telling you, leave it alone. If Sampson's going to do something, the only reason he's thinking about it is for our protection."

"What? What's he gonna do, kill 'em?"

Despite Susan's attempt to keep her voice low, Sampson overheard their discussion. Coldly, he stared into Liz's eyes and told her, "Yes, if I can kill them I will. Whoever that was helped steal my country."

He did not believe one word of what he was saying. However, using his mono-toned voice and frightening gaze, Daniel Sampson was very convincing and made himself out to be the most loyal patriot in the world. While Susan was touched, maybe even a bit excited by his bravado, Liz was not fooled for a second.

Chapter Nine

Andrew Stevens was wearing a tan trench coat made of bulletproof fibers that were more protective than Kevlar. Underneath the coat, he wore another anti-shock vest, and he was armed with a USP, the 9mm version of the Heckler & Koch universal self-loading pistol.

As he walked down the helicopter ramp, the wash from the helicopter rotors managed to mess up his usually perfect, fine, brown hair and he was forced to secure his stylish sunglasses from blowing off his face. The new black Army boots he had on looked strangely out of place.

Despite the ring of security, he was still nervous and felt exposed out in the open. Walking across the grass, Andrew repeatedly looked over his shoulder and continuously scanned the perimeter of the defensive ring for potential threats.

After learning about the destruction of Maxwell York's mansion on Cape Cod earlier that year, Stevens had made it a point to read all of the highly classified files on Major Daniel Sampson, U.S.M.C. (Ret.). Remembering the last encounter with the assassin, Stevens unconsciously reached up and touched his right earlobe.

He knew Sampson was out there, somewhere, and if anyone was angling to take a shot at an assassination from 1,000 yards, Sampson was one of the few who could actually make the shot.

Finally reaching the cover of a copse of trees, Andrew moved quickly after the colonel with his security detail in tow. "Colonel Turney! Colonel Turney!"

James Turney spun on his heal, "Yes, sir, what can I do for you?"

"Any news, Colonel?"

"Yes, sir, Mr. Stevens, We located the Hellbender. She's anchored at Bayonne."

"Son of a bitch! And when were you planning on telling me this?"

"I'm telling you now, sir. I just got confirmation." The tone of Colonel Turney's voice barely hid the contempt he felt. "They didn't have the identification beacon activated and must of slipped in during the night."

"What night?"

"That I don't know. The Harbor Master has been trying to get shit straightened out for a week, she could have come in at any time within the last ten days, and men at Langley and Fort Bragg are checking the electronic surveillance as we speak."

Stevens was clearly agitated. "So you have no idea if Maxwell York was on board or if he disembarked?"

"No sir, too many gaps in port security coverage when the, uh, transition took place." Turney didn't know how else to put what had happened, but he knew better than to speak the word "coup" out loud.

"Fuck!" The frustration on Andrew's face displayed how anxious he was about having to deal with Maxwell York face to face. If things had gone as he had hoped, York, would have been at the estate when Sampson turned the place into a hole in the ground. If York had left early for his cancer treatment on board of Hellbender, the best opportunity to take him out had been lost.

Taking York out of the game had not been part of the original plan hatched with Becky, Steven, and Raymond, the other elements of York's staff who had teamed up with Andrew. But, when the hit on Daniel Sampson failed, Stevens just knew York would become a target of Sampson's revenge. Then, when the Cape Cod estate was bombed and no survivors found, Andrew simply acted as if York, his mentor and the architect of a neo-feudalistic future, was dead. He mourned appropriately but then quickly ordered Becky to pass the word that he was in charge.

Since Stevens was charting his own course, the death of Maxwell York would have made his goals that much easier to achieve. Even without proof of his demise, Stevens continued to act as if there was no one to answer to because he had already pushed things well beyond the point of no return. If York survived the blast at his estate, he'd just have to be dealt with in another way.

Not wanting to let on how badly he hoped York was dead, Andrew changed the subject. "Have you heard from your men in Cape Cod?"

"Yes, Mr. Stevens, sir, I have."

"And?"

"No change Mr. Stevens. There were no survivors and no one has seen or heard from Mr. York. Forensics did come back and did confirm what we already knew--that the IED was an ammonium nitrate truck bomb. If there was anything new or different, I would have advised you."

Andrew tried to soften up his tone, "I know, I know, I'm sorry James, it's just that I lost some good, loyal people up there and, well, I know you understand how that feels." Steven's insincere display didn't sound real, not even to himself.

Colonel Turney scowled, looking away from the man he knew was both full of shit and, ironically, acting as the most powerful man in the world. If Stevens knew the thoughts running through the colonel's mind at that moment--such as putting a 9mm slug right between the creep's eyes--the so-called Special Master would have shit his pants.

As if unable to settle his nerves, and reacting to the negative vibes coming from Colonel Turney, Stevens once again changed topics and demeanor, "Any news on Daniel Sampson?"

"No, sir. There's nothing to indicate he's in the area."

"How the hell could you possibly know that? The

man could run circles around any one of your flunkies and he's probably looking down at us right now from the top of one of those buildings--and you wouldn't even know it."

Colonel Turney was disgusted that he had been given baby-sitting duties with a civilian puke--even if it was the Special Master himself. He had no idea why the man had insisted on coming along for the round-up. With several hundred primary agitators to locate, subdue, and transport to the Bloomsburg Internment Camp, the mission was going to be a cluster-fuck mass of confusion as it was. Having a paranoid big shot getting in the way was not Turney's idea of fun.

"Listen, Mr. Stevens, we've got LEMV's--blimps--circling overhead with infrared detectors looking for people on and around the buildings." The thick chested, ghostly white colonel crudely nudged Stevens with undue familiarity and pointed to what looked like a two piles of green and brown leaves with a black, narrow tubes projecting out toward the west. "Those snipers and teams like them all over the park have been here for hours scoping out everything on the ground and the surrounding buildings just to make sure you're safe. We've got Lacrosse and KH-11 satellites looking down at us from Heaven above, searching for any threats with the men at both Fort Bragg and the NRO watching over the whole shebang. Now, if Major Sampson has the balls to try and take on three companies of the nastiest S.O.B.'s who've ever walked the face of the God's green Earth, then maybe, just maybe, he'd be willing to take a pot-shot at you. But I know Major Sampson, sir, I know him personally and he's too smart to try something that dumb."

With those final words, meant more as a chastisement than for comfort, Colonel Turney walked away in disgust.

Stevens, internally fuming from the colonel's disdainful attitude, shook his head to help snap him out of a paranoid train of thought and tried to focus on what had to be done. Just several blocks away was the secret headquarters of MYB, Ltd., and the security detail assigned to him had been sworn to secrecy to safely escort him to the building with minimum exposure from prying eyes.

The deep growl of huge, powerful engines coming closer drew his attention and the immediate response of his security detail. Gently, they grabbed onto his arms and led him forward to where the armored personnel carriers were headed. As if he were a delicate package with no physical capabilities of his own, the men of the operational security detail lifted and guided him into the second of two APC's. Special Master Andrew Stevens was safely tucked away and on his way towards MYB, Ltd.'s Manhattan base of operations where Becky, Stephen, and Raymond were waiting for him on the top floor.

Colonel Turney watched the vehicles pull away and hoped nothing happened to the little puke. As much as Turney would have loved to take Stevens off the roster, he was under the protection of Major General Adam Smythe. The order had come directly from Smythe that the Special Master was to be protected at all costs. If what was going around the rumor mill was true, Smythe had set himself up to be the head honcho in charge of all military operations and Turney was not going to do anything to mess with that connection or screw up the mission he had been assigned.

Using two APC's as a means of transport was overkill, to be sure, but he did not dare take any chances. There'd always be time for a military junta later.

It was just minutes after Stevens was driven away that the first returns were starting to come in. Surrounded by a squad of Rapid Response Team personnel, seven men and three women with their arms zip-tied behind their backs and black bags pulled over their heads came into the clearing.

A senior chief from signal intelligence and the

squad's staff sergeant approached the colonel and snapped to attention with a salute. The man was also a Navy SEAL and was well-trained in electronics warfare. He was holding a rectangular tracking device not much bigger than an e-book. The only function of the device was to detect and pinpoint the locations of cell phones and other wireless electronic gadgets.

"Senior Chief Bradley Baker reporting, sir."

"Staff Sergeant Ron Goode, reporting, sir."

"How did the device work, Mr. Baker?" Turney asked.

"Perfectly, sir. We were able to take down the entire cell minus one and they never even saw us coming. Squad two was right behind us and they bagged their targets as well."

"Good. Very good. How many more agitators do you have on your list?"

"About forty PA's, sir," the staff sergeant replied.

"Well, get to it, men."

"Yes, sir!" both men said in tandem, saluted and rushed off to rejoin their squad and head out to subdue more prey hiding out all over Manhattan."

"Captain Devos!" Colonel Turney yelled across the clearing. All around him, squads were coming into the clearing with subdued captives in tow. "Call in the Chinooks to transport these insurgents to Bloomsburg, we've got a bunch here already and a shitload more coming!" To himself he added, "This is going to be a lot easier than I thought."

Chapter Ten

Becky Longo was standing in the washroom, checking her makeup in the gilt-framed mirror while letting warm water wash over her hands. She turned the water off and grabbed a towel to dry off her hands when the door swung open.

"Andrew, what are you doing?"

He pushed the door closed and stepped closer to her as she turned to face him. "I just wanted to tell you how much I've missed you."

"You missed me? Why?"

"Why do you think?" He stepped forward and placed his hands against the sink on opposite sides of her hips, trapping her as he leaned in close. They were face to face, their lips almost touching.

"I think you missed me because of my incredible mind, my wonderful sense of humor, and, of course, my womanly charms."

"No, Becky, I missed you because of your gorgeous ass and because you give great head."

She reached up to slap him, yelling, "Fuck you, you pig," as she swung.

Andrew let the slap connect and then he lifted a hand to his hot, red cheek. "Mmmm, I like it when you get rough."

She tried to slap him again but he grabbed her wrists and twisted her arms behind her back. Unable to escape his tight grip, she twisted and thought seriously about lifting a knee to his groin--but then he leaned forward and started to kiss her neck, sucking and nibbling his way up to that secret spot of hers right behind her ear.

"You fucking bastard, you bastard! Oh, Andrew, Andrew, you bastard. Oh, please...please, don't stop. Please, don't stop."

Because he was sucking on her earlobe, breathing slow, deep, hot breaths in her ear, her legs simply melted from under her and she felt her tender nipples grow erect. "Oh, my God, you don't play fair." Her breathless voice was but a whisper.

He stopped kissing and licking her salty skin just long enough to answer, "When have I ever played fair?" He let go of her wrists and felt her hands go up to his head, pulling him roughly into the bow of her neck.

Although Andrew was tall and somewhat thin, he was strong, wiry, and covered with defined, striated muscles. Reaching his well-manicured hand down and around to the back of her thighs, he had no problem lifting her up and placing her gently on the sink's marble countertop. He gripped her luxuriant white thighs, one in each hand, spreading her legs open. Her skirt hiked up on its own, revealing her rapidly dampening panties. Andrew slowly, gently traced his fingertips down the back of her thighs until his soft hands were on her buxom bottom.

Becky could no longer speak. She had been in this position before, quite often, actually, at the Cape Cod estate. She and Andrew had been screwing right under Maxwell York's nose for years. Even though she knew, as far as Andrew was concerned, she was just a release, a way for him to get all of his stress and aggression out and that was just peachy with her. She was not interested in any type of relationship and those stress-relieving trysts were always quite pleasurable. Andrew would have his way with her exactly the way she preferred it; and the rougher he was, the harder she would cum.

Recognizing he was probably more stressed than ever and fully expecting him to take her roughly, Becky arched her neck, letting her head fall back, and spread her legs even wider, waiting for him to enter her.

Andrew's hands worked their way around her hips and thighs as he caressed her, felt her soft skin, and allowed his fingers to just barely brush against her most delicate areas. He slowly worked his way to the sides of Becky's thong. With a quick, strong pull, he ripped her panties right off of her body.

"Oh, shit! Oh, my God Andrew. Don't tease me, pleaaase! Take me! Fuck me now, please!"

He grinned impishly and started to lower his head down between her legs. Still holding her thighs, he pushed her legs open even more, making her completely exposed to him and completely vulnerable. He slowly moved his face toward her womanhood, blowing delicate currents of air toward her glistening wetness. She moaned, acknowledging the wondrous sensations, and then she gasped as he delicately, gently, with a tongue touch as light as a feather, tasted her.

"Oh, my God, Andrew!"

$$*****$$

The Special Master strode into the conference room on the top floor of MYB's 97th Street headquarters. Flanked by an identically dressed security detail, and with his head held high, Andrew Stevens had a pompous air about him.

The room, located across from the residential side of the building, was decorated in a contemporary fashion with lots of glass, chrome, and mirrors. There were large windows spaced closely together on two walls, making the room look even bigger than it was.

Becky, Raymond, and Steven, Andrew's three co-conspirators, were already seated with their tablet computers in front of them. They were dressed neatly but looked frazzled, even haggard, from constant work. Even though they were several floors above where most of the activity had been taking pace, there were sill important matters to tend to, events to monitor, and even a meeting called by Andrew could not pull them away from their responsibilities.

While Andrew walked across the plush white pile carpeting toward where they were seated, their fingers were flying over keyboards and the displays of multiple devices flickered and changed with constant updates. When the Special Master got closer to the oval, glass-topped table and stopped, the others stopped what they were doing and stood to their feet.

In that more formal setting, Becky immediately sensed something about Andrew that was different, something she hadn't noticed during their private encounter. His aura, his countenance, or maybe his demeanor, whatever it was, she couldn't put her finger on it, but something had changed. She thought to herself that he wore power well and blushed. Even though their tryst had ended a while before, she was still on fire for him and, sensing her Alpha-male near, could feel a renewed wetness between her thighs.

As Becky looked at him and remembered what they had done, she couldn't help but think that maybe she was wrong. Maybe a relationship with Andrew wouldn't be such a bad thing after all. She had no aspiration to be a First Lady, or the wife of a mogul, but a queen or maybe the powerful mistress behind the most powerful man in the world--that was something she could live with.

Unlike his three underlings, Andrew looked like he had just stepped out of a Macy's catalog. Every lock of his wispy brown hair was in place and his smooth, white skin blazed as if he had just shaved. The only sign that gave away he had been traveling were the mud splatters on his pants' legs of his dark blue slacks.

There was no politeness or hesitation in his manner. He motioned for everyone to sit and asked, "Updates, people?"

As Andrew's number two, Becky went first,

"Domestically, we've got the support of every major network and took over the independent stations who wouldn't play along. The military is completely on board and we've got no problems with any of the federal agencies."

"What about the cities, Becky? Any improvement?"

"Yeah, well, we're fighting on a lot of fronts and General Smythe's teams are spread pretty thin, but the good news is that most of the cities in the Midwest and South have been subdued. The strategy to round up the primary agitators, you know, the most outspoken, most closely followed agitators, and detaining them is working. Making a public spectacle out of the arrests and detention has been a very effective way to get others to capitulate and the faster the anti-government agitators are pacified."

Andrew raised a questioning eyebrow. "Are we using this strategy all over?"

"No, not yet," Becky responded. "We weren't sure how the public would react to seeing mass arrests and the detention centers, but it seems to scare them into compliance more than anything."

"Is that all that's different?"

"No, Andrew. In the Midwest and South, it wasn't as hard to get the supply chain for food and other necessities up and running. In New York, Philly, Chicago, and L.A., it's been a lot more difficult to get provisions in. What it comes down to is this, if we give people a choice between food or arrest, they choose food. But, if there is nothing to eat, they just keep on running rampant. Plus, lots of people have been hesitant about giving up their DNA for the I.D.'s. Without the new identification cards, there's no way for them to buy food."

"Okay, this is what we're going to do. I met with General Smythe and he's been pushed to the limit--we've got to take some pressure off of him. I want you to call the Secretary of Defense and have him activate the 82nd

Airborne. Tell him he's to handle all the logistics--the entire supply chain--"

As he was speaking, Becky was busy typing notes into her notebook, occasionally looking up and listening.

"They're not to engage in any tactical operations because I don't want to have to bring in the regular Army unless it's absolutely necessary. The last thing we need is soldiers defecting because we're conducting operations in their own neighborhoods. This is PR 101, people; I want the military seen as the good guys, not an occupying force. We've got to get out in front of this right now--so make sure they make a big deal out of it."

"For example?" Becky asked.

"Damn it, do I have to think of everything? Have them make food drops in Central Park, for God's sake, set up food lines in Lincoln Park in Chicago or on goddamn Sunset Boulevard for all I care, and start giving everything away; and make sure every reporter in the country is covering it. Make it a shining example of how far we'll go to make their lives better. Have them do it in every major city, and project the soldiers as heroes, passing out food to the hungry. Now, let's be smart about this, people can get their free food, but then they're going to have to submit and give up their DNA."

"I got it, Andrew." Becky declared as she typed in several more lines.

The discussion continued on internal security matters, the situation with the fuel, the implementation of the Amero, and other issues within the continental United States. The deepest deliberation centered on demonstrating that the new currency was backed by a fractional reserve of gold or other commodities.

Even after the rest of the nations fell under their complete control, and the conversion of national debt for territory was complete, they were still going to be hard pressed to maintain the huge amounts of reserves necessary. They considered everything from the seizure of all gold, like they were implementing in Canada, to attaching a percentage of the production of all raw materials.

Andrew silenced the discussion with a slap of his hand on the table, "Listen. I've got it under control. As soon as I'm done here, I'm going to call General Smythe and have him start making plans to take down the reserves being held in Pittsfield--"

He did not have to explain any further as they all knew what he was talking about.

Steve interrupted, "Andrew, I thought that was a last resort."

"I know, I know, but we've got to buy some time and if Smythe can pull it off, we'll have the time we need to get everything settled." Closing out the topic, he shared with them something Maxwell York had taught to him, "Listen, when it comes to people's money, the only thing that matters is the perception--all they have to do is believe in a form of currency for it to work. People are stupid, gullible sheep, and as long as we're able to convince them that the Amero is secured with commodities and they believe it's stable, it'll work."

"But we can't do that with everyone." Raymond chimed in.

"No, we can't. Our partners and the military--they're going to demand real gold, so let them go get it. With the media on our side, covering up whatever mistakes Smythe's troops make when they hit Pittsfield, how could we go wrong?"

Andrew quickly moved onto the other nations in the Western Hemisphere, and Raymond was pleased to report that Canada, Mexico, and Brazil, their three biggest concerns, had all made a relatively peaceful transition to new regimes with all of the right people in place for the next phase. There were some trouble spots, but, for the

125

most part, Central and South America were being peacefully assimilated.

The attention then turned to Steven, "Okay, Steve, what have you got?"

The partners had divided the globe into seven realms, roughly based on the continents. In each realm, a council of seven men were to maintain control over every nation within their territory creating forty-two council deputies and one chairman of each council. However, because of the population and relative strength of China and India, Asia had been divided into smaller spheres.

"Europe is the domain of Sir Philip--"

"Where is he, by the way?" Andrew inquired.

"He's still recovering from his flight, he said it was pretty hairy, but he'll be joining us shortly on a closed circuit video feed from London."

"Very well, go on."

"He's very optimistic about the situation, even though he was initially troubled by the fact that Mr. York is no longer calling the shots. Anyway, the only issue he's having is settling some of the accounts between the big boys, France, Germany, and Italy."

"Is their support that important? I mean, can't we just tell 'em to eat their losses?"

"I wish we could, but they're the ones who've helped keep the peace in Europe--and Sir Philip says they're the ones holding up the progress with the other governing boards in Europe. I honestly don't know how they'd react if we told them to blow, war maybe? Whatever the case, you know that's not something York would do."

"Fuck what York would do--he's not here, I'm here!" Andrew caught himself before he went further into a tirade. After taking a deep breath, he continued, "Okay, so what do you suggest?"

Steven wasn't fazed by Andrew's outburst. They had been working together for years and he was used to it.

Besides, if he cowered in the corner every time the boss went off, there'd be no way to tell him the truth and they'd never get anything done. It was one thing Andrew appreciated about all three of his compatriots, they were all ballsy and, although they respected him, they were not so afraid of him as to hide the truth.

"Don't worry about it, Andrew." Steven said confidently. "I'll mollify our European partners."

Andrew liked the positive, take-charge attitude and nodded. "Good."

"As far as Africa goes, we've heard from the African Council and both Hensch and Papa survived."

"For sure?"

"For sure."

"Shit!" Stevens intoned. "That means York probably survived the bombing in Cape Cod and he's in hiding. Do we have any idea where Maxwell may have gone?"

"Possibly to Europe or Africa with Papa and Hensch?" Becky asked.

"No," Steven said. "Sir Philip would have said something if York made it to Europe. Our people did pick up on a flight out west we can't account for, but they lost track of it."

"How?" Andrew asked.

"They went invisible, military technology."

"That was him. Shit! Okay, let me think about that for a while and I'll get back to you. We know York's going to make a move by making contact with his old networks, so be ready for any sign of a counter-measures inside the federal employees--especially the spooks." Andrew paused for a moment, trying to think like Maxwell York and predict what he would do.

"I'm on it," Steven replied.

Unable to channel York, Andrew moved on, "Tell me about Asia."

"I'm not going to bullshit you, Andrew, the China Domain is a big concern." Included in the China Domain were the nations of Taiwan, North and South Korea, Mongolia and Japan.

"I thought you told me things were falling into place?"

"In China proper, yeah, once the military stepped in and took control by executing the members of the Communist Central Committee, the people partied for days--as a matter of fact, I think they're still partying. The problem is the North Asia Counsel. The seven partners aren't satisfied with the transfer of territory, and they think the cancellation of two trillion in debt warrants more than what they got."

Andrew Stevens felt his face turn red. "I talked to Ti Kwei Fong myself. If he had issues with the arrangements, he should have said something before now."

Becky inquired, "Fong is Chairman for that counsel, right?"

"Right. What the hell's your point, Beck?" Andrew inquired, using her pet name, a signal to her that he was only acting harsh toward her so the others did not catch on to how he really felt.

"Well, he was personally selected by Maxwell York, not because his wealth or influence, but because they had some kind of connection."

"So, you think he's pulling the others along to get more of what? Control, territory, power? What's he asking for, Steve?"

"Vietnam and Cambodia as well as permission to act on Taiwan now, before originally planned."

"What do you think? Suggestions?" Andrew's stance made it obvious he was posing the question to the group.

Becky chimed in with her opinion first. "Get rid of him and replace him as soon as possible. If you make an example out of Fong, the other forty-eight council members will fall into line."

"She's right," Raymond agreed. "I mean, come on, Andrew, if you're going to lead them all, you can't let any one of 'em try to push you around or pressure you into anything."

Steve disagreed. Shaking his head, he cut in, "I don't know. I think trading a few counties with hardly any natural resources is a small price to pay for the settlement of a few trillion in debt. Shit, I'd throw in Hawaii for good measure just to shut them up. Besides, twenty, thirty years from now, there won't be any borders and none of it will matter. It's not like they're asking for anything substantial--I mean, if they wanted Afghanistan with all of the mineral resources we found, that would be another story. It'd be just a conciliatory gesture."

"Conciliatory gesture?" Andrew spat out. "Why do we have to appease anyone?"

"Well, for one thing, Ti Kwei Fong was expecting to be dealing with Maxwell York, not us and not this way--"

Andrew cut off his subordinate. "Fuck him! I want him eliminated and replaced with someone who's completely loyal to me. Now, someone get Sir Philip up on the conference screen. I want more details about how he plans to deal with the Blue Bloods."

*****

The Gold Credit System, the brainchild of Michelle Alvarez-Rivera, CEO of the Seven Rams Trust, was an experiment they had watched with interest since it was made public. Trying to rush and take the trust's gold mining operation public, Stevens thought, had been a huge tactical error. He would never had known how much gold they had in reserve if she had not disclosed it. Unfortunately for her,

129

the assets they had, including a discovery they had made in the frozen tundra of Canada, were disclosed to people who were allied with him.

Utilizing the executive authority as Special Master, Stevens had simply declared a national emergency and seized the Gold Credit System's computers and software from the trust's banks. The proprietary software handling the transactions was altered and immediately put to use to handle Ameros. Taking what he wanted and what the country needed had been as simple as signing a few papers.

But, now it was time to go after the rest of the Seven Rams' assets, and that, he knew, would be a much more difficult task. The trust retained a large, well-protected supply of gold bullion, a documented reserve large enough to make a dent filling up the gigantic hole they were in. The trust was also in possession of some very important mineral rights--not just for gold but for massive amounts of natural gas right in their own back yard. The natural gas was another commodity Stevens coveted and wanted to take from the trust.

Because the consortium of senior partners had to retain the property and commercial rights, simply seizing the land and the gold was only thought of as a last resort but it was also the easiest way to dig them out of the hole they were in. The tricky part was getting Smythe to make a play for the gold without making the old man suspicious. Before he had the video conference set up, he had come up with a plan.

Andrew was in his office, pacing. There was a secure video link to Fort Bragg and he could see the General sitting at his opulent mahogany desk.

"Listen, Adam, there is one more thing we have to discuss. As you know, you and your soldiers are not being paid in Ameros but with gold certificates."

"Yes, sir, I'm aware of that."

"Do you know where that gold is being held?"

130

"No, sir, I don't."

"You see, General, in order to create a special class of currency just for, let's say, important individuals, special steps had to be taken. I assure you that the gold to back up the currency being issued to you exists, but there is one condition."

"A condition, sir?"

"Yes, you have to go get it." Andrew's little sales pitch wasn't coming out as he hoped and the insecurity was revealed by a slight quiver in his voice.

The statement made Adam's jaw drop. "I don't understand, sir, what are you saying?"

"I'm saying that all the gold we need to pay everyone is being held at a facility in Pittsfield, Pennsylvania, and it's ours for the taking."

Andrew spent the next hour getting the general up to speed on the logistics. Like a good manager, Smythe took notes and asked important questions to get a better idea what he was dealing with. He already had it in his mind that his G-2 staff and satellites could do a better job than Stevens in providing intelligence, and he already knew exactly where Pittsfield was, but Smythe was wise enough to use the session as both a way to gather more information on Stevens, and put himself further in the good graces of the Special Master.

"Up until this point, the foundry and smelting plant in Pittsfield have been left untouched. But, I have to tell you, Adam, the facility has been built up like a fortress and is well guarded."

"Guarded by whom, sir?"

"By an entire town of locals."

Smythe had to bite the inside of his cheek to prevent himself from laughing out loud. The idea of townsfolk guarding anything conjured up an image in his mind of the Hatfields and McCoys guarding their respective stills.

Andrew continued, "You have to understand,

General Smythe, this has to be done with the utmost skill and with minimum collateral damage. Unlike seizing software, stealing a huge pile of gold reserves and killing a lot of people is something that could turn the public against the new regime. It's a situation that has to be handled delicately."

"I completely understand, sir. You just leave the details up to me. I'll get that gold in a way no one will even see us coming--or going."

Smythe and Stevens spent the next several minutes hashing out more details, discussing other pressing events and developments before the Special Master signed off.

Alone in his suite, General Smythe tried to go back to work but he couldn't concentrate. Instead, he turned on off the large flat-screen monitor and stared at the blank screen, trying to figure out what he had to do.

The fact that he had been recruited into a very special, select group of individuals and chosen as a military leader for a future government was all the motivation he needed to stay the course he was on. Actually, the future he was making for his kids was more than enough to push him beyond the misguided loyalty and passive obedience to a corrupt, ineffective government he once had. That he would be taking the best and the brightest men the military had ever produced with him was simply icing on the cake.

Given the job of leading his men into the future also erased the doubts he had about the methodology being deployed to further subjugate the masses. As long as he was going along for the ride, Stevens and his associates could do whatever they wanted. Besides, he had just been given the go-ahead to take down one of the largest hoards of gold in the world. That fact made him smile.

Chapter Eleven

Nagimoso Yoo stood shoulder to shoulder with Maxwell York. Facing an almost completely electronic wall, they were watching a streaming video image being projected onto 64" LED screen. The highly detailed images were obviously coming from a source flying over the high desert of the western Americas.

The secured computer room they were in was located right next to a plain, industrial conference room somewhere deep within the bowels of a nondescript building complex. The installation was conveniently hidden between Hill Air Force Base and several highly classified shops run by Raytheon, Lockheed Martin, and General Dynamics. The complex did not appear on any maps and had no address. As far as anyone was concerned, the facility were off limits and operated by the NSA, NRO or some other agency that no one was supposed to know existed.

Nagimoso Yoo was one of very few individuals outside of the inner circle who could identify York as a big player in the military industrial complex and one of the richest men in the world. Years before, Yoo's company was bought out by a subsidiary of MYB, Ltd., York's main vehicle of commerce. An expert in robotics, automation, and system design, Yoo became the main engineer behind the most advanced projects in MYB's portfolio. Although many universities and private companies had contributed quite a bit to robotics, getting the complex systems working together autonomously was Yoo's specialty.

In the world York and his compatriots imagined, advanced robotics and automation was what would allow the world to continue on as they wanted it. The primary goal was to eliminate the need for manual labor. With no need to support a massive workforce, they could maintain their lifestyles and still reduce the population to a more favorable level.

The types of plants and products planned spanned everything from cars to jeans to televisions and even included the assembly of the robots themselves. Anything a human could build, Yoo's systems could replicate, making everything faster, cheaper, and more efficiently. Even though York knew most of the background, it helped to hear it all again as he inspected the sites chosen to test their construction methods, automated systems, and efficiency.

The man directing the drone's camera announced, "This is the view from 5,000 feet above us."

Using a pointer, Yoo tried to sound confident as he spoke, "The first building you see takes in raw materials: iron ore, coke coal, copper, bauxite, silicone, petrol, and such. The commodities are then distributed to one of the next three structures where they are separated, processed, refined, and made into steel, plastics, wires, silicon wafers, carbon fiber and so forth. We make whatever we need and there is very little waste."

York interrupted, "Who brings in the raw materials?"

Pointing to a map of the United States on another terminal, Yoo indicated three places. "There are terminals here, here, and here. Raw materials shipped in from Australia are brought in from the west coast by train. Other things such as coal and rare earth metals are mined at these locations and we truck them in here. This final depot holds crude oil and liquefied natural gas. The liquids are also being trucked in right now, but a pipeline is under construction. As soon as the trucks arrive here," Yoo pointed to the location of the plant's main entry on another screen, "then it is all downloaded automatically."

"So, from the terminals to the plant requires trucks, drivers, manual labor, correct?"

With the disruptions in trade and transportation,

York knew raw material would be a concern, but at least they were not dependent on subcontractors for any parts. He already knew they had stockpiled a massive amount of the materials they would need in the short-term, so he did not concern himself at that moment with the issues related to the supply chain. There would be time for that later.

"For now, correct, but as you will see--soon, that will change."

York was very pleased by everything but very anxious to see the actual end products. If the factory to construct the UAV's wasn't ready for full production, then nothing else he was seeing--or planning--would matter.

"It's good to see everything working so smoothly, Mr. Yoo, but I want to see the drones."

Yoo silently nodded to his assistant who was sitting quietly at a computer terminal. The assistant typed in the instructions and the UAV's camera shifted again and focused on several hangars. The usually unemotional Yoo was obviously proud to give the presentation on how far the project had come. Because of the developments around the world, he knew the meeting with Mr. York would establish the final approvals and the timelines.

The scene on the large screen focused on the most expensive and most complicated of all the factories; the one that made military-grade UAV's--drones. Several displays from multiple drones lit up. The complex was vast. From far above the site, it looked like rows of warehouses and airplane hangers with corrugated steel roofs.

York tucked his hand into the pocket of his camelhair sports jacket. Calmly, but with malevolence in his steely, cold eyes, he addressed his subordinate in a way that could only be perceived as a threat. "The way things have turned out, Mr. Yoo, we need those drones fully functional right now. I can only hope for your sake that you've done what you promised."

Beads of sweat started to form over Yoo's top lip

and on his forehead. He had kept his boss updated on what they had been doing, and hoped to soften York's anger by showing off how far they had come. He said in a less than confident tone. "I offer my most humble apologies and meant no disrespect Mr. York." He bowed his head, lifted it and then continued, "The plant to construct the drones is 99% on line."

Yoo turned back to face the clear image, which had zoomed in to a tighter view. Indicating the fourth and fifth buildings that branched off from the other buildings, he explained, "Here and here are where much of the most delicate, technical work takes place. The silicon chips are etched, assembled, and packaged into ICs, CPUs, SIMMs, SIMPS, whatever we need. Even the EPROM modules are assembled into the necessary packaging, tested, and loaded with instructions in that facility."

"How are you handling the temperature variations, changes in humidity, variables like that?"

Yoo answered, "High pressure natural gas induction fuel cells assisted by wind and solar when practicable. Our laboratory and every building is programmed to stay within our parameters or else the plant shuts down."

York perked up, "You said every building is programmed?"

"Yes, the buildings themselves rely on smart designs, artificial intelligence, and machine learning. If anything goes wrong, everything stops until the problem is fixed or can be worked around."

"How important is the natural gas?"

"Very. We do so much with it from running our own power station off the grid to using it to make plastics."

Yoo's words made Maxwell think of Roland Troth and the monopoly he was trying to create in Pennsylvania. He wondered if the people who had taken up finishing the pipelines knew how important their task was. With Andrew Stevens in charge, probably not.

"Nice, very nice," York said absently.

Yoo walked Maxwell York through other stages of the process including engine construction, wiring, assembly and final programming. Everything was done by assembly line robots with no direct human intervention.

The final building was, he explained, quality control. Every drone built at the factory went through a series of tests to make sure it was operating at the optimum level. A machine at that stage could only leave the facility if it was rated at 99.9% functional--otherwise it was rejected.

Along the back of the last building, there was a series of rows of drones of various types. With only slight variations, the stingray-shaped planes contained only enough internal space for avionics, weapons and fuel. The thrust of the engines varied from subsonic to supersonic, depending on the type of drone and the maximum payload of armaments. The most agile of drones, the Hunter-fighters were made specifically to defeat fifth generation of American-made fighters, especially the Lockheed Martin F-22 Raptor. The Hunter drones easily surpassed the speed, ceiling, and G-force capabilities of the manned jets.

York hid the internal pleasure he was feeling. The pioneering stages of development, matters he had helped plan, were moving along at a pace he would never have thought possible. "So, how many men do you having working inside the plant."

"As it stands, we have three shifts of five technicians monitoring the robotics and two shifts of ten handling the movement of raw materials, everything else is automated. The functions of the materials personnel are currently being mapped into the system. They will be the next group replaced by robots."

"What about the technicians, the ones monitoring the robots? When can we replace them?"

Yoo knew that was the ultimate goal, to have the

plant as self-sufficient as possible--with absolutely no need for human intervention or monitoring. But, mapping the executive functions with incredibly complex decision trees--even with computer learning--was very time consuming. Simply double-checking a robot's response to likely catastrophic failures had been a huge undertaking. Every possible failure had to be accounted for and every reaction checked and rechecked. It was a task they had been working at for years.

After the contemplative pause, Yoo responded, "I don't know sir. If we extrapolate out from our prior failure rate, I'd say within the next five years. Maybe then it would be safe--you know, reducing it down by about one human supervisor per year."

Maxwell York was expecting to see several more demonstrations and he prodded. "So, what happens if one of our drones goes out of fault-tolerance? How do you arm them, refuel them?"

"As you know, sir, we have made provisions for defective units and have also automated the maintenance and resupply of our vehicles." Yoo turned to the man sitting at the other terminal. "Mr. Koizumi can you please pan over to the Seeker-bomber drone by the service door?"

The sound of keystrokes on a keyboard echoed in the room and the image on the large monitor moved over to the side of one of the buildings. As the streaming image continued to display the scene, Koizumi turned and waited for a signal from Yoo. As soon as Mr. Yoo nodded, the man turned back and hit several keystrokes on another terminal.

"What you are seeing is a machine recognizing a preprogrammed failure of its hydraulic system. We intentionally put that in for this demonstration--since major failures are rare and we don't have time for the typical wear and tear to accumulate."

Everyone kept their eyes on the monitor and the

view switched to a remote camera inside the warehouse. A steel device automatically went forward and locked on the wheels of the drone. Two robotic arms shot out from the sides and started to remove the wheels. In quick succession, the defective mechanical components were unbolted and lifted from the frame of the plane while other robotic hands attached wires and hoses. As the fuel was being loaded, two racks rose up underneath the wings of the drone and several heat-seeking missiles along with two cannon pods were attached to the bottom of the flying wing.

"Everything will go to a testing track. If a part fails, it is recycled or destroyed. If it passes, it will be used for the next vehicle. Every machine is designed to be interchangeable with the other designs and the hard-wired computer parts can be stored and swapped as needed if the same component fails on another machine. The refueling will be complete shortly and the weapons package is fully armed and ready to go."

"How many drone factories are ready to start production?" York asked, hoping the one they were in was not the only one ready to come on line.

"We have five operational factories of the new design but the final instructions for the plant must be incorporated before the master plan is finalized. Those principal instructions are contained within the machines and computers first sent to any new site to insure all of the planes are built to the same specifications."

York nodded. "It's the chicken--egg thing. You set up a proverbial egg and that turns into the chicken that lays more eggs, or, in our case, drones, but the chicken has to be perfected first."

"Ahh, yes! Very good. That is exactly correct sir. Put in those terms, we have thirty 'eggs' or, as I like to call them, 'seed plants' currently under development capable of autonomously building a variety of products and the robots to build more plants, five of those plants are for UAV production. Those will begin full operation as soon as we get your approval. However, with all respect, in building and programming the drones, we are not yet done feeding in the necessary data."

York nodded. "I approved the start of the drone program because I thought you had all the information you needed--so, what are you waiting for exactly?"

"I'm waiting for the rest of the CIA-operated flight recorders to be encoded and added to the decision tree matrix. We already have most of the digital records of most of the aerial missions flown by the CIA and the Air Force out of Nevada loaded."

"Such as?" York asked gruffly.

"We have the data for all different kinds of weather conditions, flight routes, flight times, attack angles, and so forth from the pilot-directed drones--but we need more data to make sure we have every eventuality covered. The computer modules on our drones learn to fly through the experiences and operation of the piloted versions. We need to program in what the human pilots ordered the drones to do during events such as when one was hacked and brought down over Iran--if we don't know what the Iranians did, the United States, or any nation for that matter, can use those same techniques and tactics against us, against the drones we make."

"The flight data recorders. I thought you had all you needed."

"I'm sorry, Mr. York, they do, yes, but my team, they need more time to finish the programming and insure the computers can fly autonomously under any conditions."

"Do we need anything else to bring those drones up to snuff? Tell me now or forever hold your peace."

"No, sir, Mr. York, that's all we're waiting for."

"Can you program in updates and software patches or does everything have to be fixed in ROM?"

Yoo was absolutely stunned by the old man's

technical acuity. Taken aback by the question, he asked, "Well, of course we can do patches or updates, why?"

"Then get the process rolling! We need squadrons of these babies in the air and ready for war--not now, but yesterday. I'm usually a very patient man, but things are moving quickly, my friend. This is what you're going to do, Mr. Yoo, once you get the logic programmed into the decision matrix, update the software on the fly. You have your own private frequencies for in-flight updates, don't you?"

"Well, yes--"

Then do it, man! I need at least five wings, half of each composed of combat groups. We've got to shift away from surveillance, can you handle that?"

Mr. York, our plants can handle anything you order, but how are you going to manage the munitions, the operations?"

"Don't worry about that, Yoo. You just build my planes and make sure they can fly and I'll take care of the rest."

Chapter Twelve

The elegant lamps lining the streets, along with the decorative fixtures illuminating each houses' walkway, provided the neighborhood with an affluent ambiance. Several saplings, all recent additions to the yard, stood meekly in front of the stately five bedroom, four bathroom, red-brick Colonial. It was a custom home built in the relatively new development outside of Arlington, Virginia. Lucky for Stanton Frazier, the development was far enough away from the city to have been spared from the riots and turmoil that had rocked D.C. and other big cities.

There were only a few dim lights on inside the large house. The far left windows of the attached garage, the ones closest to the house, had the unnatural, bright glow of florescent lamps that illuminated square patches in front of the garage. That section of the garage was what Stanton Frazier called his Therapy Room.

Even though he was not a proficient mechanic, he found the hobby of restoring older cars very relaxing. The hood of a 1984 Porsche 928S was propped open and Frazier was leaning down, his thin forearms resting on the candy apple red side panel. With a confused look on his face, he peered down at the engine.

Standing ten feet away, leaning against the wall, was a short, waxy-skinned man. He was wearing faded jeans and a plaid shirt--looking very uncomfortable in casual attire. His flesh was so white and plump it looked like he would melt like butter if heat was applied. James LeCroix, an Assistant Attorney General at the Department of Justice, always appeared wet and greasy.

In many ways, Stanton Frazier and James LeCroix were opposites. Frazier was tall, skinny and black. His refined look and thin wire-framed glasses belied his tough upbringing on the streets of Newark. LeCroix, born to a well-to-do Rhode Island family, had a law degree from Yale, but his slovenly appearance made him look like a dim-witted slob.

Beyond their physical differences, their politics and perspectives on life were polar opposites. The only thing that had brought them together was that they had both had worked for Roland Troth as part of his illicit expert network. Before Troth was killed, LeCroix had been Frazier's contact point with the DOJ's operations staff and had been tasked to handle issues dealing with Roland Troth's illegitimate forays into the criminal justice system.

The meeting at Frazier's house was highly unusual. There had been standing rules about interaction between Troth's contacts so that everything could be compartmentalized. With Troth dead, though, many of rules and protocols had gone by the wayside. Meeting face-to-face no longer posed the same type of risk. But, they both understood there were other significant risks to their well-being. Instead of being happy about the death of Roland Troth, Stanton knew that without the old man's patronage, he was expendable.

Both Frazier and LeCroix knew the stories about a bloodless coup were true. Inside the Beltway, it was no secret that, under duress, the President had capitulated and handed over the reins of government to the man occupying the newly created office of Special Master. With the Constitution suspended and Andrew Stevens given the authority to remake the nation, there was little need to hide the truth, at least from those within the government.

The new administration had already started take an ax to the dead wood in D.C. and they had already fired the President's most critical political appointees, replacing them with S.M. Stevens's supporters. It was just a matter of time before the so-called Special Master and his cronies would fire them as well. The old ways of getting ahead no longer applied and Andrew Stevens was busy stacking the

143

deck to make sure the people he personally selected retained all of the power. Retaining the President and Congress was nothing more than a sham to keep the majority of the 310 million-plus Americans on the sidelines.

The last thing Frazier wanted to do was bow down to the likes of Andrew Stevens. However, in order to gain power he needed to secure his future, Frazier was going after the only lead he had left to regain access to the insiders. That meant somehow discovering the connection between Roland Troth and Andrew Stevens--and to do that he had to trust James LeCroix.

Still, he had to be cautious. Floating around D.C., a number of people retained the hope that they would be assimilated into the Stevens regime, With the prospect of being one of the select few kept around to rule the masses dangled in front of them, they were the ones who followed orders faithfully, pushed Steven's agenda, and handled the rest with threats to do what they were told--or else.

Andrew Steven's snitches, LeCroix possibly being one of them was not the only danger. The brigade of Special Forces troops concentrated around the Capitol, units that were under the control of Special Master Stevens, were there to deter him and everyone else from taking any type of contrary action. The troops had been busy rounding up people they called "Primary Agitators" and shipping them off to internment camps. That same exercise could easily be extended to the past authorities if they dared oppose the commands of their handlers.

"Hand me the feeler gauges."

"The what?"

Pointing to the workbench, Stanton indicated a stainless steel object at the end, "The metal thing with the fan of prongs sticking out."

LeCroix waddled over and grabbed the device off the bench, gasping for air as he walked over to Frazier.

"Here," he said when he handed the object off.

Pulling out one feeler and reaching down into the engine compartment, Frazier asked, "So what haven't you told me? I know, I know, we've gone over this ten times-- Thomas Jones was clean, he had no skeletons besides his reputation as a ladies-man...but I got the feelin' you're not telling me everything you know."

Stanton stopped poking around in the engine compartment and gazed over to the chubby man. "As a matter of fact, that's why you're here, so I can look you in the eye and see if you're telling me the truth."

LeCroix couldn't stop the nervous twitches or keep himself from shifting his weight from foot to foot as if he had to urinate. "Why would I lie to you, Stanton? We're on the same side aren't we?"

"Yeah, LeCroix, we were on the same side--but what I'm trying to figure out is exactly what side that is."

What Frazier was looking for was some sort of angle, some leverage, to make sure he would either be safe from or part of the new government.

Frazier continued, "The last time I saw Troth, he was putting the heat on me to bring down both Tommy Jones and that woman, Susan DiGiovanni. Now she's missing and both Troth and Jones are worm food. Can you bring some light to this situation for me?"

James answered as if he were puzzled, "DiGiovanni...Susan DiGiovanni?"

"Right! Right." Frazier was annoyed by the act. "Come on, man, what can you give me that you haven't told me before...which, up until now, has been nothing."

"Does it really matter at this point? We're never gonna be able to get back what we lost."

"It matters because I'm asking you, I don't know about you, but I'm not just going to sit back and do nothing. If you want any kind of future, man, you got to get off your fat ass and do something for God's sake."

145

Frazier's ridiculing tone cut deeply. Even though he knew the sweating man was probably the only one who could help him track down Susan DiGiovanni, Stanton did not like him. Frazier's distaste was obvious and the gruff, pushiness seemed to discomfort the sleazy little man even more--which was the way Frazier wanted it.

LeCroix involuntarily shook his head and his eye twitched. Stressful situations got to him and that was one reason he never went into private practice. A law degree, even one from Yale, would do him no good if every time he went in front of a judge or jury he'd start to twitch, sweat, and feel like passing out. Hiding himself as a cog in the vast machine of the federal government, and being on Roland Troth's payroll, had helped him to avoid real work and real stress while making a substantial living. Having to occasionally associate with an asshole like Frazier--still a thug despite his degrees and title--was a small price to pay for the rapid career advancement and easy money.

With his easy life and security gone, he decided to throw caution to the wind and fall in with Frazier. "Fuck it," LeCroix spat out in an outburst of resignation. "Okay, Stanton, but you didn't get this from me."

LeCroix waited for some indication of agreement from Frazier but didn't get any. Uneasily, he went on, "You know the field agents' reports, everything they collected about the bombing in Williamsport? Well, you remember how we had to turn all of it over to that special unit from the military, right?"

"Yeah...the shit we spent so much time on--trying make sure nothing linked Troth in and pinning it on that other guy...Josephs, Paul Josephs, right?"

"Yeah," LeCroix agreed, nodding. "Well, when I was going through the reports the Pennsylvania State Police sent us, there were documents out of the Western Pennsylvania District offices, I'm talking a whole file-folder full about that farm outside of Pittsfield. A lot of it was redacted but there were detailed reports about a man being killed in the house and two other men who were found wounded in the barn, shot actually."

"How's that connected?" Frazier recalled putting the squeeze on Pittsfield's Sheriff, Randy Babcock, and according to the Sheriff, it had been Thomas Jones who shot the two men in the barn and Susan DiGiovanni who killed the man in the house. There was nothing official about it because everything was kept hush-hush under some national security shit. All he knew was the men who were shot were once with some rogue special-ops team. Frazier had been unable to find out more and he had dropped it once he knew both Jones and Troth were found dead.

LeCroix couldn't help but sound smug, "All of that was covered up pretty deeply, you know that, right?"

Frazier simply nodded in response.

"Well, whoever they had cover up that part of the mess forgot to purge a few significant details."

"Such as?"

"Such as the fact that Susan DiGiovanni was in Pittsfield at the exact same time, and that she was intimately familiar with some people who died in Williamsport."

"All of that should be entered into that new Homeland Security database, or part of the MIN-OPS system, right?"

LeCroix eyed Frazier suspiciously and then continued, "Yeah, it was but almost everything that went down at that farm was purged by someone above my pay grade before I got to it." Seeing the look of doubt on Stanton's face, he went on, "After you called me and set up this meeting, I logged onto the network to refresh my memory and check things out. I hadn't looked at that case in a while, but it's been changed."

"Changed how?"

"It was altered."

Frazier caught the implications immediately, "And if Troth wanted something like that altered, he would have gone through us to do it."

"My point exactly."

Stanton Frazier whistled. "They were all connected, huh? The gold and this shooting at the farm?"

"And the building being blown up in Williamsport," LeCroix cut in, "as well as both Troth and Jones being murdered."

"Why the hell didn't we know all of this before, why didn't we put all of this together? Do we know for sure that DiGiovanni was in Greenwich when Troth and Jones were killed?"

"I'm not sure, but we can find out--and based on the dates of the entries, someone altered those files after Troth was killed."

"Oh, you're a fucking genius!"

"Yeah, I am, but you don't think we're the only ones who worked for Troth?"

"Or maybe Troth worked for someone else, like Andrew Stevens? Who else has the power to do what you're saying was done?"

"I don't know. Actually, after all the shit that's been happening, I don't know much of anything anymore." LeCroix looked down at his feet, unable to hide his self-doubt.

"We've gotta find a way to link Troth to Andrew Stevens and the only one who's still alive to help us is Susan DiGiovanni. So, how do we find her?"

"You're asking me?" LeCroix said with derision. "You're the one who used to be a cop and a hot-shot special agent! I mean, damn it, Stanton, a whole fucking revolution is taking place around us and you're hung up on this old shit."

"Old shit? That woman may be the only one who can help us figure out what the hell's been goin' on!"

148

"Yeah, the woman was probably at Troth's estate when Troth and Jones were killed. Yeah, no one knows where the hell she is--but, how the hell does that help us?"

"What if she's missing and needs our help? We don't even know if she's okay."

"If you haven't noticed, lots of people have gone missing lately. I think we better start finding a better way to secure our future, and not chase some stupid bitch who doesn't mean shit to anybody."

Stanton stood up to his full height and wiped his dirty hands on the thin material of his stained workpants. "Yeah, well, that stupid bitch you're referring to happens to be worth a few billion dollars in gold, and, if you've been listening to Special Master Stevens, the Amero Credits they're paying us with is backed by gold. If you think Susan DiGiovanni isn't connected, that makes you a fool."

Hoping to satisfy Frazier and get out of there as quickly as possible, LeCroix responded, "Okay, so what do you want me to do?"

"I want you to help me find this woman so I can find out what she knows about Stevens...if he was connected to Troth. If he was, that could give us the in we need. But, you why I really want to find her?"

LeCroix stared blankly at Frazier, waiting for the punch line.

"My gut is telling me she's the queen bee behind everything that's happened going back to a bunch of shit before Troth being iced."

"And you're basing that on what?" LeCroix asked.

"I'm basing on the fact that her name just happens to turn up on my last three major investigations--the bombing of a building in PA, protecting a shipment of a shitload of gold, and the death of Roland Troth--and now you're telling me about her being at the spot where more of Troth's men were shot. Why is it that she's the only one left standing? I want to know how and I wanna know why."

149

"Then what are you going to do? What if I do help you find her?"

"I don't know." Frazier answered honestly. "Maybe I can get closer to the truth about this Stevens character and the people behind him. Maybe I can, I don't know...make things right."

LeCroix couldn't help but laugh. "Are you fucking kidding me?" The laughing quickly turned in to a coughing fit and then a brief bout of choking. It took a few minutes for him to recover, but when he did, he continued the ridicule. "You're insane, Stanton. You, a one time Assistant Director who was actively passing on inside information to a hedge fund manager? Shit, you're worse than Robert Hanson and got a lot of fucking nerve talking about making anything right."

Frazier just stood there and took the insults. He knew LeCroix was right, he had been a dirty agent and then a crooked, politically appointed insider. But, in this case, the United States was being torn apart by the seams and that was something he just wasn't willing to accept. "I love my country, LeCroix! I want my country back the way it was."

The statement made James burst out into laugher again, leading to another coughing fit. "Okay, okay. I'll help you--but this goes no further than us."

*****

The conference room at the Rapid Response Team's new Fort Bragg headquarters was a digital wonderland. Almost every wall was covered with crystal-clear display screens either showing locations or data relevant to the mission at hand. Sitting around the oval, mahogany table that was covered with laptops and other digital devices were the members of General Smythe's Executive Staff. Every man and woman in the room had more than two decades of service under their belts dealing with logistics, personnel, supply chains, and intelligence. They had worked together for years and Smythe had the utmost respect for their abilities and loyalty.

"Someone give me an update on the Pittsfield Foundry. Where are we at?"

Lieutenant Colonel Andrea Campbell spoke up, "Sir, we're still in the planning stages, but we're making progress."

"Progress? How exactly, and why aren't we moving units into position now?" Smythe asked dryly.

Campbell responded by clicking on several icons on her computer screen. With a delay of only a few seconds, images from satellites and other aerial surveillance assets populated the dominant displays in the room.

"According to the parameters of the mission, you've asked us to covertly find a way in and take over this facility with minimal collateral damage. Along with the aerials that you're looking at now, we've had teams on the ground and we've even been able to infiltrate the facility."

"And?" Smythe's eyes flashed back and forth from the images of what looked like a heavily guarded concrete bunker on the main screen to the masculine-looking intelligence officer in her ill-fitting uniform. He already knew what she was going to say but relished the idea of putting the she-man on the spot and knocking her down a few pegs. That, he knew, would motivate her to work even harder.

"And, we've come to the conclusion there's no way in without taking out lots of civilians."

"What's your best estimate of a body count?"

"High teens up to thirty. They've got armed guards posted on the perimeter and two-foot thick concrete walls around an underground storage facility. Our ground-penetrating radar has picked up multiple levels of rebar and steel hatches. We can only assume those caverns are

151

guarded as well. Going in without raising a ruckus is basically a non-starter."

"Great work, Andrea," a full bird colonel shot across the table.

"Shut up Tony! You can't expect me to make chicken salad out of chicken shit!"

Smythe cut them off, "Knock it off! We don't have time for that. Does anyone have any ideas to help out Lieutenant Colonel Campbell?"

"How about Stevens and his crew buy out the owners, make a deal with them to sell out or else." Colonel Franklin suggested.

"Sell out for what? General, it simply can't be a one-for-one trade that would defeat the purpose of taking the gold they have stored there." Campbell shot back in a derisive tone.

"She's right, Franklin, but what about the owners? If the owners dropped off the face of the earth, who would be left to stop us from taking over, saying we bought them out?"

"So, you're suggesting we take out the trustees and use the media to convince everyone they sold out? With all due respect, general, that won't work."

"And why's that?"

Campbell blew a few loose strands of hair out of her face in frustration before responding, "Because that entire town, hell, the entire valley is involved in that operation. They're all owners, beneficiaries in one way or another. How are we going to convince them that the trustees simply bailed out on them and left them all hangin'? Besides, we don't even know where these people, the trustees, are."

As if he had not heard the first part of Campbell's argument, Smythe commanded, "Well, get on it! Why the hell do you think we spent billions of dollars and millions of man-hours building MIN-OPS? Damn it, people! Andrea, do you even know who the trustees are?"

"Right before all hell broke loose, the trusts were converting to a public corporation." Campbell sent around copies of a document.

The pages of the document were from an amendment to a SEC listing application summary. Michelle Alvarez-Rivera was named as the CEO and had just disclosed updated estimates of recoverable gold reserves in Canada. The value, an enormous number, was calculated in old American dollars at the price of gold before the world fell into chaos. If the world was planning on basing currency on gold, the price of the metal would soar even higher than it already had, magnifying the holdings of the Seven Rams Gold Trust and the Clearmont Geology and Mining Trust.

General Smythe could only whistle at what he read. "Okay, this is what we're going to do, we're going to track down Ms. Alvarez-Rivera and monitor her movements. After I talk with Stevens, if we decide to do a snatch and grab, I want people in place to do it with no delay. Do you understand me?"

"Yes, sir!" several officers answered in unison.

"What about Pittsfield? What do we do about the foundry and the gold they're hoarding?" Campbell inquired.

"Don't touch it--as a matter of fact, protect it, don't let anyone or anything near that place who could be a potential threat." Smythe shook the documents he was holding in the air. "These billions of dollars of gold bullion they're sitting on belong to us--as a matter of fact, maybe it'd be a good idea to let the public know, so they can be sure their Ameros are even more secure."

"How would we do that?"

"Simple, just add it to the balance of Federal gold reserves and publicize it. When the time comes, we'll deal with explaining where it came from."

"And if that doesn't fly?" another colonel asked.

"Then Stevens will stop pussy-footing around and

153

he'll be forced into letting us take down that town our way. Let me get him on the horn and get the ball rolling."

Chapter Thirteen

Carlos walked out of the elevator and made his way down the wide passage to the door of the penthouse. He didn't get the chance to knock. The door swung open inwardly and Michelle reached out to grab him.

"Where've you been? We've been so worried about you!"

With a quick tug, she pulled him inside and slammed the door shut, she tucked the snub-nose .38 inside the waist of her jeans and secured the door by engaging several locks and sliding a cabinet up against it.

"When you say you're going to be gone for a while, Carlos, you just can't disappear for hours. What if you were caught by the police or the military? How would we know, what would we do?"

Carlos turned and starting walking down the hallway towards the kitchen. "I'm sorry, I should have come back sooner, but I had to find out where Stevens goes when he comes into the city. I guess I lost track of how long I was gone."

When they entered the kitchen, Michelle put the gun on the counter and they both went to sit down at the table. Darla was at the stove, stirring something in a pot.

Plainly not caring about the ongoing discussion, Darla announced, "This is the last of the rice. I ain't got no idea what we're gonna do after this is gone."

Michelle and Carlos looked at each other. They had heard Darla slip into that same Southern affectation when she was angry or upset, but to hear her sound and talk so different when all she was doing was cooking disturbed them. They also wanted to take issue with the fact that no matter where she went, Darla always kept the two Berettas with her--or at least within arm's reach. But, neither had the guts to speak up about the curious way she handled the deadly weapons.

In a tender voice, Michelle asked, "You want me to go ask Ms. McGinty if we can get some from her, honey?"

"Nah, I was just sayin' we should move on from here and go someplace where it's safe. It'd be best if we went home."

Darla had not been very stable since she heard Tommy was killed. The fact that they had no idea where his body was and she could not give him a proper burial had caused her to sink a little deeper into her own little world. The tipping point, though, seemed to have been what they had endured over the past few days. The constant racket of military helicopters coming and going at all hours, using Central Part as a staging area, had caused even more damage.

She had regressed, acting and talking more and more like a little girl. Michelle was disturbed by the change and had no idea what to do. Before Carlos had left the penthouse, he pointed out that other than the two 9mm weapons she babied as if they were China dolls, Darla seemed harmless enough--so they left it at that.

Instead of answering Michelle's question, Darla filled two small bowls with steaming piles of rice and carried the dishes over to the table. "They ain't no butter, so I used mayonnaise to keep the rice from stickin' and there ain't no proper seasoning, so I used flavor from Ramen Noodles. I hope you like it." She reached back and grabbed two forks, putting them on the table next to the bowls of rice.

"Darla, it's quiet now and Carlos is back. Why don't you go lie down and try to get some rest? I know you haven't been able to sleep the past few days."

"I can't get no rest, Miss Michelle, not while my Tommy can't get no rest."

"Please try?" Michelle asked with pleading in her eyes. If you can't fall asleep I have some Valium in the medicine cabinet."

"Hmmm," was all Darla was able to get out as she turned to leave and walked straight for the bathroom.

"Michelle, listen," Carlos interrupted, "I think we should get her some help."

"No. She's going to be okay, she just needs some sleep. Besides, who would we get help from? I don't think psychiatrists are taking appointments right now."

"You're right."

Hungry from consuming significantly fewer calories than their bodies were used to, both Michelle and Carlos dug into the strange rice concoction. They both ate with gusto and nodded, enjoying an unexpectedly delicious flavor combination.

"Can you believe it's come to this?"

"To what?" Michelle asked.

"Eating like this and being thankful for it."

"That's nothing, Carlos, we've had it easy so far and who knows, it may start to get a lot worse from here." Eating another forkful and swallowing, Michelle asked, "So where the hell were you?"

"For a while, I was just walking the streets. Over the past few days, a lot has changed since Darla and I came into the city."

"How do you mean?"

"The streets are clear, well not clear of people, but there were no rioters, no mobs of people, and people are starting to clean up. I even saw some stores taking measurements for new windows."

Michelle listened intently. She had been able to watch the news reports and every station had the same scripted report showing people being rounded up and detained, explaining the zero-tolerance policy against sedition. They had shown what was called, "revolutionary tactics against the peace of the people" and the internment camps where those who violated the laws were taken.

"Michelle, the people I talked to are scared, they're hungry, and everyone seems to know someone who was hauled away. They told me that the first people to go were the organizers, the one's setting up protests. As soon as someone stepped up to take over, they were taken as well."

"How are they finding these people, I mean, hunting individuals in Manhattan?"

One man who said that the government is using the internet and cell phones to track and monitor everything. I know this sounds paranoid, but he thought they had the ability to turn on the phones, turn on the cameras and listen in. And, if they want, they can track down any computer or phone. We did see those soldiers carrying electronic equipment, so I'm assuming that at least part of that is true."

"So, that means we can't use the internet and we can't use the phones?"

"Not for anything you don't want anyone else to hear--and not from where we're staying if we want to stay hidden. The man I talked to said that hackers were trying to figure out a work-around to bypass the government monitors, but they were the next group to be rounded up and arrested."

"Shit, Carlos! So that's why everything has settled down so quickly."

Michelle couldn't believe the American people could be intimidated and beaten. She always thought that the collective will was too strong. Yet, as he went on to describe what he saw on the streets, which seemed to be exactly what was happening. The people had been cowed into submission.

"Seeing troops conducting operations in the streets, breaking down doors, raiding houses, and dragging people away, it's a nightmare."

"No, things are settling down into a new normal and no one's going to confront the new government--I just can't believe this is happening. What are we going to do,

Carlos?"

"I don't know. But I was able to find out where Andrew Stevens goes when he comes into the city."

"How did you manage that?"

"I walked in the same direction his caravan went and kept on asking people if they had seen the vehicles and they pointed me in the right direction until I saw those big trucks."

"Where?"

"Just a few blocks from here on West 97th Street. The street is cordoned off with security, but I was able to get close enough to see the building the soldiers were protecting. I saw Stevens come out of the same building and get back into one of the big military vehicles. I don't know where he was going, but they were in some kind of a hurry."

"So, you know where he is when he comes here. Now what?"

"I don't know, Michelle. I don't know."

Carlos fell silent, his thoughts were scattered and he could not cogently put together any course of action, let alone a logical, reasonable one.

Michelle sat quietly as well, looking at him and trying to figure out what he was thinking. The idea of following Stevens sounded good a few hours before, but now that they had the information, it seemed useless. What were they supposed to do, launch a counter-revolution? Chop off the head of the snake by killing Stevens and then try to restore the country to the way it used to be? Then, she thought maybe they should do what everyone else seemed to be doing, just let it all go and try to make the best out of the situation--what Darla had suggested days before.

Unable to decide, Michelle moved onto the other matters swimming around in her head. If they did not have the strength to take on the new regime, at least they could protect their own interest and get themselves in the best position they could. With no segue, she launched into what had been percolating in her mind. "Right before you got back, I was watching a world news update."

Knowing how Michelle's mind worked, Carlos was aware that she had moved onto the next topic. He acknowledged her with a nod.

"And, the Canadian's are voting next week to nationalize all the operations to obtain natural resources: gold, oil, gas and uranium."

"You've got to be kidding me?"

"No, Carlos, I'm not kidding you. If the Canadians fall for that ploy, almost everything we have will be lost, the gold mine, the new vein we found, everything."

"Why would they do that, I don't understand--the people in Canada can't be that stupid, can they?"

"I never thought the Americans would be stupid enough to suspend the constitution, but they did it, didn't they? Anyway, it's being sold to the public as a way to be the bankers of the world, and they're doing it in tandem with Australia and Russia."

Carlos put his fork down and started rubbing his stubble-covered chin. "So, what's on your mind, I can tell you've been thinking about this."

"I think we should destroy and abandon our site. Blow the rigs, collapse the boreholes we've drilled, and erase all the records we have of what we found and how we found it. To hell with them if they want to take what's ours."

The fact that government agents had seized the Seven Ram's Gold Credit System was a sore spot. What made it even worse was that, under the guise of national security, they had also hauled away their computer programmers and taken them to an undisclosed location. It didn't matter to Michelle that they had stolen her brainchild, or that the government was using the underlying software for Ameros. What had made her mad as hell was

160

that the people the agents had seized were people she cared about, many she had worked so closely with to perfect the Gold Credit System. No one had any idea where they were taken or if they were safe and there was no way to find out. She had never felt so helpless in her life.

Only because Carlos had been there to calm her down and counsel her not to fight back, lest they come and snatch her up, did she force herself to let the issue go. After that, they were all smart enough not to broach the subject so as to ire Michelle or draw the attention of the authorities.

Carlos was taken aback by Michelle's proposition that they demolish the site. The last thing he would have considered was to destroying everything so that no one could seize it. But, because of what had already happened, and the pain that situation had caused her, he fully understood why Michelle wanted to destroy it all. If it was a war against the people and their property the new government wanted, it was war they were going to get.

Carlos smiled and looked her admiringly. "Michelle, I think that's an absolutely brilliant idea. But how?"

"Zeke."

"Old man Zeke?"

"Yes, All we have to do is let Zeke know what we want done and he can get word to our people in Canada."

"Why go through Zeke? Why can't we contact them ourselves?"

"Because of what you just told me about the phones and the internet. Zeke can send someone to tell them what we want done without anyone else figuring out what they are saying to each other--that odd way of talking of theirs."

"Yes!" Carlos agreed enthusiastically. We can also tell them to grab all the unprocessed cores they can and bring whatever production they have down to Pittsfield."

"After they blow the site?"

"Agreed, after they blow it."

They knew they had plenty of gold stockpiled as long as Andrew Stevens did not try to seize the gold in America the way Roosevelt had done in 1933. Plus, if things changed, they knew the details about where the gold mine was, how to get to it, and only they possessed the technical expertise to make it profitable to mine.

Michelle grabbed a notepad and pen out of a drawer and started to write down what she wanted to tell Zeke.

"How is he doing? Are things okay in Pittsfield?"

"You must be joking," Michelle retorted with a smile. "Zeke is doing better than ever. He's got the whole county organized. They take turns guarding the gold reserves, hunting deer in the Allegheny Mountains, and taking tanker trucks up to the Oil City refineries to get fuel. At the same time, he's got crews working around the clock converting vehicles to run on natural gas. He's got people from Pittsburgh to Harrisburg building pipelines so they can have natural gas running everything."

"That man is simply amazing." Carlos shook his head with amazement. "Sounds like they're doing a lot better than we are."

"That's because it is a different world. They don't have to rely on anyone for anything and that makes all the difference." Speaking as she wrote in her own form of shorthand, she wrote, "Okay, so we're going to tell Zeke to blow all the holes they've dug, destroy the rigs, destroy coring bits and GPR sensors."

"In Pittsfield and Canada."

"Right! Delete the computer files and schematics for rigs and bits. Can you think of anything else?"

Carlos smiled, "Yeah, bring the gold with them when they leave."

"Oh, yeah! Right, I almost forgot that one."

"Okay, I'm going to send an encrypted e-mail to Zeke."

"No you're not, not unless you want Steven's storm

162

troopers coming in here to take us away and then raiding the foundry in Pittsfield. That may happen anyway, but why push the matter."

"So what do you suggest?"

"Do you still have a Blackberry?"

"Recharge it and send an encrypted message using it."

"Why the Blackberry?"

"That guy I was talking to on my way here--"

"Yeah?"

"He said hackers have been able to keep some private network, private. Blackberry is one of them where the 'watchers' are having a hard time snooping. Besides, Zeke's still addicted to his Blackberry-it's the only form of communication we can get him to use."

They laughed. It seemed like the first time in days they had anything to laugh about.

"What the hell is so funny?" Susan asked from the entrance leading to the kitchen. The Jersey accent she put on was thick, and her voice was high and nasal, not meant to scare as much as amuse. If they thought they were under attack, Susan wanted them to think it was Snooky who had broken in.

Sampson, a man they did not know, was standing right beside her, holding Michelle's .38.

"Oh, my God! Susan! How the fuck did you get in here?" Michelle screamed. She held a hand to her chest to try to calm her palpitating heart.

*****

Even as more and more units were being committed to pacify the trouble spots around the nation, additional operatives had to be devoted to monitoring and tracking all forms of communication.

In order to hunt down the most vocal, most

163

dangerous opponents of the new government, extreme steps had been taken to retain the best and brightest computer scientists in the world. Because of the necessary ramp-up, the number of analyst and programmers crowding into the Rapid Response Team's Headquarters had increased to the point of near chaos.

Along with the huge increase in manpower, each and every hour there seemed to be a new crisis. Endless hours were spent trying to choke off the biggest threat to national security, the hackers. The organization between the widely dispersed code writers was growing and the unmonitored electronic traffic between regions was expanding. Because the net was such a valuable propaganda tool, and critical to the communication between the governing councils, the only sure-fire way of ending the unauthorized, unmonitored internet traffic had been taken off the table. Shutting down the net was not an option.

The nameless, faceless digital cowboys corrupting the system seemed to never give up in their attempts to get around surveillance through encryption or by devising alternate methods of linking computers. They had left behind the well-known browsers and preloaded software packages. Anyone with even a basic knowledge of computer security knew that every computer was hard-wired to give up data to the authorities and the FBI had every software company write a "backdoor" into their product so the users could be snooped on. That had happened long before the world had even heard of Andrew Stevens.

Facing thousands upon thousands of coders and programmers who were hell-bent on disrupting the new government, the men and woman working for General Adam Smythe had their work cut out for them. It had become an electronic battlefield where the powerful forces had to commit increasingly more resources to try to stomp out what seemed like endless battalions of army ants before their defenses were overwhelmed.

It was only because of the level of activity that the encrypted message from New York City made it to western Pennsylvania without being intercepted and cracked.

*****

As soon as Zeke read what Michelle had written, he laughed. Destroying the Canadian gold mines--mines he had worked his entire life to conquer--would have been like destroyed himself. But, under the circumstances, where they stood to lose everything to a bunch of elitists who had taken over the world, denying them access to the ore would be a pleasure.

Zeke knew, no matter what it took--even if he had to walk to the Arctic Circle himself, he would not let Michelle down.

Chapter Fourteen

Establishing seven world regions and governing councils under the control of Andrew Stevens and his partners made way for American military personnel stationed overseas to return home. The pronouncement of an all-encompassing world government did not cause the stir they expected, at least not in the less developed nations. Instead, the details concerning regional government councils working together brought on an unexpected unifying peace and stability.

Military bases all over the world were being close and ships were actively steaming towards their homeports. The beginning of the end of one superpower policing, occupying, and dominating the world had started. With what the new feudal lords were attempting to put into place, there would be no need for such wasteful endeavors.

The military forces of the United States were engaged in retrenching; not only reducing their global footprint, but also preparing for a new mission. Many long serving units returning home were given the opportunity to join their home state's Reserves or National Guard units. But, instead, seeing how the world had changed, many men and women took advantage of a one-time employment offer and buyout bonus. For those who took the offer, they left the military behind and returned to civilian life with a hefty Amero Credit account, no debt, and a secure job with a federal, state, or local agency.

With a signed contract and their new Federal ID in hand, many soldiers, sailors, marines, and airmen were quickly returning home to be with their families and start their new careers as part of the North American security apparatus. For those who had no desire to leave the military, they were granted some much needed R&R and provided with whatever they needed to get home on leave.

The career soldiers, many officers, and specialists, whom the military still needed, however, were sent back to their duty station to be reassigned according to the needs of the nation. Large bonuses, in Amero Credits, were offered to some of the Special Forces units to re-up with the Rapid Response Team. Of the several hundred thousand soldiers and sailors returning from their overseas duties, only a small minority actually qualified to become part of Adam Smythe's elite corps, but still, the influx of men was difficult to absorb.

Getting everything under control as quickly as they did was a team effort by the new aristocracy. It had to be or else they would all have been brought to their knees, probably slaughtered by the masses. The monopolists, oligarchs, the true power behind the prior ruling class, had come out of the shadows and had taken control. In most instances, they had not used force, nor had they threatened violence. Instead, they had seized it by offering a helping hand in terms of a new currency, better terms on outstanding loans, and promises of a secure future.

Using the media to their advantage, members of the ruling councils made speeches and explained their intentions in the best possible light. The world's population was sold on the idea they would finally have the ability to live in prosperity and soon be able to elect the leaders of their choosing. As soon as the economic crisis was resolved and fair elections were held, they were told, the regionally appointed board members would step aside. No one had reason to doubt their veracity.

It was not long before people were able to recognize the names and faces of their new leaders. The sense of familiarity made them feel a more secure that their welfare was in the hands of people they could blame, criticize, or support as they saw fit. Coming out of the shadows gave the unelected administrative councils infinitely more credibility.

The men and women of the new aristocracy had replaced the puppet dictators and elected officials around the globe. In addition, the dollar and the euro had been supplanted by the digital Amero Credits and New Euros. What the people did not know, and what they could never find out, was that an environment where the playing field was level for all was only a temporary condition. What was being constructed was simply another house of cards that would come crumbling down in another few decades. By then, though, it would be too late to change the trajectory of the world or reverse the decline of the world's population.

In the future, everyone who was still alive, still procreating, would have a defined purpose and would have been selected to be born. By that point, what people thought of as a government or currency would no longer matter.

No hint of that plan, that grand design, was ever revealed beyond the highest levels of the senior partners. It was kept better hidden than the most critical of state secrets because the lives of those in such an elite group depended on it. All the people were told, and what they were convinced would bring them the great benefits, was that they had to have faith in the changes to come. And, in order to participate, all they had to do was submit a sample of their blood or skin and get an identification card.

Because of a dearth of organized resistance and rapid compliance with new mandates, there seemed to be an overwhelming, profound desire for the type of life being promised. The pronouncements of the governing councils, backed by and endorsed by every news station and broadcaster publicizing the transformation, made many people believers. They believed in a better future, and they believed it was right around the corner.

The rapid transformation from anarchy to passivity had not taken as long as Andrew Stevens and the other senior partners expected. Witnessing the vast majority of the world capitulate based upon lies piled on top of lies was an enlightening process to observe.

Unfortunately for all it had been Andrew Stevens, not Maxwell York, who had grasped the reins of power in America and obtained control over the most capable military force known to man. The people at the very top, the ones behind the transformation, knew things were not supposed to have transpired the way they did, but no one dared to question Steven's authority.

Only the oldest, most connected of the partners-- ones who had been with Maxwell York from the beginning--knew that York had survived the attempt on his life and was in hiding. But, they had to hold their tongues and make accommodations every time the most powerful man in the world deviated from the plans, biding their time until York made his move to regain control.

Because of the absence of Maxwell York, and the rise of Andrew Stevens, the other senior partners had another major issue to face. If Stevens chose not to eliminate the military gap between the seven regions and refused to disarm the American nuclear arsenal, he would eventually rule over them all. For those unaware that York was still alive, that was their greatest fear. They knew exactly who Andrew Stevens was and that he had been trained by York. What scared them the most, though, was that York's ruthlessness had rubbed off on Stevens but not his sense of duty, loyalty, or honesty. If Stevens did not disarm as the plan demanded, he would be impossible to stop--an unacceptable situation the other partners would have to confront. In the mean time, the partners and members of the governing councils were busy overseeing and handling situations in their own sphere of influence.

In the former United States, it did seem that Andrew Stevens had been good to his word and that ratification of a new constitution would be achieved by means of a true democratic process. In his daily speeches, Stevens repeated the same themes over and over again like a mantra; asking the people to participate and give his handpicked Council of Seven the opportunity to respond to their wants and needs.

There were still many protesters and many who were antagonistic to the new regime. However, most activists had learned the hard way to keep off the streets. Instead or rioting and causing havoc, the rebellious types put most of their time and effort into convincing others to join with them; to support or attack one issue or another. That, in turn, split their attention and divided the disgruntled insurgents and self-proclaimed patriots into camps along old moral and ideological lines.

What was taking place looked like a defining moment for the nation. People were becoming more and more engaged, participating in the process, and keeping the government controlled computer networks inundated with ideas and suggestions to make a perfect union.

However, it was all to no avail. With Stevens controlling the data centers, hence the debate, any major changes to the proposed new constitution never stood a chance. He had been a very good student of Maxwell York and everything he did was a calculated move to impose his will on others, getting them to believe they were in charge while getting them to do exactly as he wanted. Paul Joseph Goebbels would have been proud.

The region of North America, besides a few troublesome regions along the Rust Belt and the Bible Belt, were quickly put completely under his control.

For Andrew Stevens, Becky Longo, Raymond Behn, and the others who had taken control of the United States, Canada, and Mexico, very little had gone as planned. Getting the people in the developed world to capitulate had been and continued to be a challenge. They were more astute, better educated, and highly suspicious. Succeeding to the extent they had, had taken a lot more than promises and free food. He had known all along that variable approaches would have to be used to get the hardheaded Americans to come around.

Report after report came in claimed that regions, states, and cities were being brought under control. It was true; a segment of the public had fallen in line. They were the ones who bought the premise of a new social contract and new social order. What they did not realize was that their dependence on the elitists, and signing onto their program, brought them one-step closer to conscripting themselves to bondage.

Despite what Stevens himself considered a successful transition with minimal violence, even he realized things were not as rosy as they seemed. There was still a sizable portion of the population against what he was trying to do. They were the ones who were unwilling to turn over their DNA for food or refused to sign contracts that would reduce them to nothing but vassals fought on. They were ones, the senior partners knew, who would either have to be detained or eliminated.

The drastic measures of Martial Law imposed on the cities were intentionally designed to keep people off balance and in fear. Public displays of force had been the only way to regain control, especially in the inner cities. From his point of view, Stevens found it ironic that so many people in such a highly educated populace only understood one thing when it came to complying with his directives, violence.

Because of the use of the more extreme but most efficient tactics, the truth of what was happening was much more evident in the cities of America than anywhere else. From Los Angeles to Boston all one had to do was look out of their windows to witness the truth--they were all but prisoners. Although some progress had been made toward the promised political resolution, the reality on the ground felt much different.

The people of Manhattan, for the most part, simply did not want to be involved with the authorities. Mostly, they just wanted to get their lives back. But, before that could happen, the citizens, many of whom were returning from an exodus, had to have their basic necessities met.

Providing shelter was not that big of a problem since the majority of the apartments and co-ops were left intact. After a period of cleaning and assessing if anything had been damaged or stolen, most settled back into their own homes. The water situation, luckily, was fine. The main pipelines from the reservoirs into the city, as well as the pumping stations, had gone unmolested. The biggest problem was food.

It had taken some drastic measures to finally get the people the resources they so badly needed. But, once the 82nd Airborne dropped in, parachuting in tons upon tons of supplies sponsored by Wal-Mart, Target, and other large retailers, the state of panic and anxiety that had the city in a stranglehold finally started to dissipate.

Distribution centers were set up all around the city and people could come and get necessities at will, free of charge. Unlike the strange Nation Guard troops who seemed so hard-core and disaffected, the soldiers from the 82nd put up their weapons and put on big smiles as they handed out food to the hungry and desperate citizens. The sincere, but well-planned show lasted for three days. Then, the 82nd pulled out--leaving the distribution of food to the newly hired, well-armed, and militaristically trained public service employees.

The availability of food was one of many changes that had overtaken the city. At the direction of Special Master Andrew Stevens, every city under military administration was to be put back under civilian control within weeks.

The first decree that had been made by the newly selected Mayor and City Council banned the use of personal vehicles in the city. Then, they mandated commercial deliveries take place after midnight, except for the case of an emergency. The ban on automobiles was not just intended to make it much easier to protect against rioters and protesters--people who were tagged as terrorists and deemed enemies of the state--but it would simplify maintaining surveillance.

In all five boroughs, in order to go anywhere, everyone not in uniform would be walking, using the subway, or riding busses, in clear view of any one of thousands upon thousands of newly installed cameras.

Despite the initial moaning and complaining as people were yet again being forced into another disruption of their lives, the new leaders believed the measures had worked. Forcing people to use mass transit had an immediate calming effect. With no traffic jams and many more trains and busses operating, they were able to clear the streets to the point where people could more easily go to work or go out to look for a job.

Within days, the situation had stabilized to the point where the National Guard was able to pull back. Although they maintained a heavy presence, supported by forces from the Rapid Response Team, they no longer needed to have a designated safety zone and were able to stop providing extra security for the big Wall Street firms and Midtown banks.

The involuntarily imposed alterations of the way people traveled, although providing an immediate improvement in some aspects of life, did not bring an end all dissent. Instead, the inability to move without coming under scrutiny of newly installed cameras or sensors on every street corner drove the rebellious types further underground. For the inhabitants of The Big Apple, the missing voice of the opposition and the large reduction in violence failed to ease their minds. To them, it felt like going to a Yankees game and instead of experiencing the

Bronx cheer, hearing golf-claps.

The atypical quiet only served to add to the fear and mistrust of the new leaders. It made everyone realize that dissent was still actively being crushed; that those who did not go with the program were still being rounded up and put into internment camps. The reality of the situation, that they were under siege in their own city, was right under the surface.

The day after the 82nd pulled out and city employees took over, anyone coming for food had to first wait in line for a new national ID card. The new valid ID everyone was required to carry at all times not only had their picture, but also a memory chip embedded that contained a decoded exemplar of their DNA, their genetic profile.

The most common and fastest method to obtain an identification card was from an automated van. Hundreds of vans equipped to take specimens and rapidly produce ID's were parked all over the city. Slots in each van would accept a hand or a bare limb and take a painless scraping of skin. At the same time, a picture was taken. Less than two minutes later, a new Federal ID Card would come out of another slot. Some people grumbled, but the majority chose to go along because they, or their children, needed to eat.

Once new identification was obtained, people were required to go to a financial counseling station to convert their Federal Reserve Note balances to Amero Credits. Thousands upon thousands of clerks stationed outside of the food distribution centers handled the conversions on specially made IData tablets.

It was the financial part of the process that seemed to make everyone feel better about the future. Since all banks, brokerages, and other financial institutions were linked by the networks, the identification of assets and liabilities only took seconds. Everything was connected and the process of consolidation was a breeze and, of the hundreds of thousands of New Yorkers who participated, most of them were overjoyed with the result.

Details of the conversion, loan modifications, and how well people were making out spread like wildfire. Despite the initial hesitation, the program was quickly overwhelmed by people not only willing, but quite anxious to give up their DNA and participate in the new system.

The new ID's were not just for obtaining food. In order to work, use transportation, get paid, or buy anything, a Federal ID was required. Many people went ahead and got their identification cards because they had nothing left to lose and a lot to gain, or so they believed.

The final step, after signing the necessary contracts almost no one bothered to read, was shopping. With the identification and financial matters settled, people could go to the food distribution centers and buy whatever they needed. It made no difference if they didn't have enough Amero Credits in their account. It was decreed that because of the economic disaster, no one would be denied provisions and the accumulated expenses would simply be added to the outstanding debt account. When commerce started again and everyone was fully employed, then they could think about paying back the government of Andrew Stevens.

Getting 350 million Americans processed was a logistical nightmare. It required more people to be hired for government jobs, which made the formerly unemployed even more dependent on the new regime. The people who took the jobs did not consider it as a negative or traitorous to work for the new government. Instead, most saw it as both doing something to help their country and as a safe, secure way to survive. If, along the way, they were able to get ahead, as they had been promised, all the better.

The sudden increase in jobs meant people were getting paid. The starting salaries were above a living wage and with the newfound income came demand for goods and services. That had a direct impact on the private sector who started to bring back more workers to produce more goods. There was still a lot of work to do for the streets to be safe and clean, but that provided the opportunity for everyone to have a secure, well-paying job.

Stevens and the others managing the country knew that the more people and businesses that came on board, the more everyone else would be forced to conform to the new system, and the better off people would be. At the same time, accumulating the data the new ID's provided--knowing exactly where everyone was and what they were doing with their earnings--was invaluable. But, there was a lot more to the identification process than just security.

The more people's DNA they collected, the better their scientists would be able to determine how quickly the Hamilton virus had spread through the population. Just as important as the virus's progression were the millions upon millions of genetic profiles available for analysis. Correlating the data generated from financial activity, hospital visits, and eating habits with the genetic profiles would help inform the scientific teams and statisticians who should be allowed to procreate.

Matching earnings and spending habits to genetics simplified the process of deducing who the smartest people were, who had the best athletic pedigree, who was the most attractive, who had the most artistic talent, and who had the fewest health problems. The sampling of the genetic code and identifying specific genotypes could not have been accomplished without the data a mandated system of identification and commerce provided. With precise details of each person's, using the computer models, the process of genetic selection could begin.

It was all part of the plan thought up and devised by Maxwell York and people of his ilk. As initiated by Andrew Stevens, even though things were not going like clockwork, the evolution of the North American economy, government, and identification system were moving faster than anyone had dreamed possible.

Chapter Fifteen

The Department of Justice headquarters on Constitution Avenue and 10th Street in Washington, D.C. was frothing with activity. However, the inner offices of the upper floors were only sparsely populated. Andrew Steven's minions had been busy carving up the ranks of Assistant and Deputy United States Attorneys to be replaced by a hand-selected staff friendly to the new regime.

Access to the executive suites was highly restricted and James LeCroix only retained access because inside of the DOJ, he was a relative nobody. Many of the old names and faces in the department were gone. The fact he had been able to remain all but invisible as a career staffer allowed him to escape the purging of potentially disloyal holdovers. He was spared only because the new Attorney General needed the career staff around to help keep the machine running and give the appearance of continuity. Since LeCroix occupied the space between essential and non-essential employees, his new masters allowed him to keep his keys and his access codes.

Standing behind LeCroix in a small, well-lit office, Stanton Frazier watched as the pudgy man's thick, pasty fingers raced over and clicked on the wireless keyboard and mouse. Besides a large flat screen with a port for a communications/encryption card to securely connect the workstation to a network, no other hardware was necessary. Through the restricted card, the vast cloud of computer networks beyond the LAN was opened up to him.

The screen flickered for a second and the opening page for the MIN-OPS network appeared. In a red box that covered the lower quarter of the screen, a dire warning flashed ominously about restricted access and the penalties for unauthorized use.

"Okay, here we go." LeCroix announced as he lifted

his head so the small camera above the screen could zoom in and focus on his eye.

A schematic of his ocular veins came up on the screen as the system verified a match. A pulse monitor and the heat signature from his face checked and confirmed that the user attempting to gain access was alive and well. In a little more than a second, access was granted up to Level-Four on the powerful MIN-OPS system.

"What kind of search do we start with?" Frazier asked.

"I don't know, how far back do you want to go?"

"Let's start with a log of prior search requests, see if anyone else is looking for our little lady."

"Okay, I'll start with that." LeCroix typed in Susan DiGiovanni's name and clicked on the correct search parameters. "Here goes nothin'."

They both watched the screen clear and a picture of Susan flash up onto the upper left hand side. On the right were her vital statistics and a brief summary of her financial status. Below were details about her prior residences, occupations, and family. Each entry had links to other pages that would provide many more details and break down each and every element of information the government knew about Susan DiGiovanni's life.

"Whew, she's definitely a MILF."

"Cool your jets, son, a woman like that is way outta your league."

LeCroix responded by turning his fat head and giving Stanton a dirty look.

On the bottom half of the screen, a short list appeared in columns of text. Each row listed the name of a requesting agent or official, the agency or department, and the date and time of the request. They both recognized the first few queries that had been entered by LeCroix as part of his earlier searches. Below those, one particular entry was obviously different. The text for the agent and agency

179

making the request was a series of characters that looked like hieroglyphs.

"Hmm, I wonder what the hell that is." LeCroix clicked on the link to view the details of that search.

"Shit, that was done on the same day Roland Troth was killed," Frazier commented, shocked. "Who initiated the search?"

"The DCI himself, strangely enough, from Cape Cod."

"Why the hell would the Director of Central Intelligence want to know about this woman? You see, I told you she was connected to all of this. What did he want to know?"

"Not much. It was just a level-one background check, but at least we know she's on someone's radar besides ours." LeCroix paused, scrolled down the page and clicked on several icons. "That's strange."

"What?"

"The access point in Cape Cod used to do that search no longer exists."

"Do you think it was a remote?"

"No. Wait a minute, wait a minute, do you remember hearing about that estate blowing up on the east coast of the Cape?"

"Barely. There was so much going on," Frazier related, his eyes tightening as he reflected. "Wasn't it just an accident, a heating oil tank exploded or something like that?"

"Yeah, something like that. Let me crank it up to a Level-Four and see if we can find out what she's been up to."

"That's gonna take a while, isn't it?"

"Not really, the AI has probably already started searching for her, trying to link her with others." LeCroix boasted as if he had thought up and developed the entire concept himself. "Let's see who else has been spying on our mystery woman." LeCroix clicked on several icons to initiate the detailed search and then returned back to the previous page. "Son of a bitch."

"What?"

"I missed that before, same day, just a few hours before the Cape Cod query, there was another one by J.T. Snyder, ex-special ops, deceased."

Leaning over LeCroix's shoulder to read from the screen, Frazier's eyes opened wide. "I'll be damned; this was a remote connection from Greenwich, Connecticut."

"Sure was, and look, it was flagged as unauthorized because Snyder died before this request was made."

"How do you know?"

"Don't you remember? How the hell were you a cop? Snyder was the head honcho behind all that shit in PA, you know, Troth's security team gone wild. The men who were killed on that highway were part of his company."

"Oh, yeah, I remember now. He was one of the confirmed kills on the highway--"

"Yup, made into a smear on the road by those A-10's."

"So, the person using his code must have been part of Snyder's team."

"Wow, you're quick," LeCroix said sarcastically. "Whoever accessed MIN-OPS using Snyder's name must be one who got away."

"Which one, who isn't accounted for?" Frazier asked.

"A few, but that was only because the site where they were taken out was such a bloody mess. But, we can ask the computer."

"Go ahead, do it."

The search for the men on Troth's security detail and possible survivors ended in a dead end. There were several names and faces of men who were listed as presumptively deceased but unconfirmed. Among those men, one was Daniel Sampson, the man Andrew Stevens was so desperate to find.

There were only three people alive who knew who Daniel Sampson was and that he had been with Roland Troth in Greenwich: Maxwell York, Andrew Stevens, and Susan DiGiovanni. Only two people knew he was the one who assassinated Troth and neither York nor Stevens had any desire to share that information with law enforcement or enter it in the MIN-OPS system. Besides them, no one else knew both who Daniel Sampson was and what he looked like since the surgical procedures that altered his appearance.

Neither LeCroix nor Frazier had a reason to know or hear of Sampson before--but the Special Master's insistence that he was a threat to the country had made him a marked man. However, what MIN-OPS had found based on the Sampson's unaltered likeness and potential paper trail was absolutely nothing.

Frazier stood to his full height and briefly turned away. Looking around, he commented, "This is a waste of time, man. I think Stevens is just chasing ghosts. How the hell does he know this guy Sampson is still alive anyway?"

"I have no idea, but from what this says, Stevens has lots of people burning up the midnight oil looking for that ghost. I mean, there has to be something to it, look at this report from Wyckoff."

Frazier turned back and scanned over the text summary about the raid and the house being destroyed. "That doesn't prove anything, does it?"

Seconds after LeCroix and Frazier finished analyzing the search results for Daniel Sampson, an icon popped up announcing the level-four search request they had submitted was done.

"That was fast." Frazier straightened up to stretch his long, lanky back. Looking back down at the screen, he whistled. "Holy shit, man, we hit pay dirt!"

The computer had somehow come up with an answer to the question, "Where is Susan DiGiovanni?"

MIN-OPS Had gone into the past and worked forward to chronologically piece everything else together. The technology for digital facial recognition had advanced to the point where it could pick up even the smallest details that were impossible for people to hide. After the system had found and confirmed several images of DiGiovanni from different angles, it was off to the races. The network simultaneously scanned multiple databases of images and video from the most probable zones of the country. It began with the latest images and then connected them by route and time to the earlier matches it had found. It then used backtracking methods to further narrow the search and eliminate impossible locations.

A map appeared on the computer screen which coordinated all of the times and places the system thought Susan DiGiovanni, or a vehicle she was spotted in, had been captured in a picture or on video. Distances, rates of travel, and times were all calculated to a very high probability of confidence.

Stanton Frazier and James LeCroix were able to pick up Susan's trail when they saw pictures of her leaving the country using a false passport and then returning from Costa Rica after altering her appearance. She had made that same trip one more time using her real name and traveling alone, leaving her kids in Costa Rica.

From that point, there was a huge time gap and little photographic evidence to demonstrate where she had been because the databases being searched only had a few images of her captured by surveillance cameras. The small town where she had been staying, Williamsport, Pennsylvania, was not safeguarded like the larger cities. Nevertheless, there was a paper trail demonstrating she was there that included credit card receipts, phone bills, and a series of legal filings in Federal and State courts.

The petitions accessed by MIN-OPS clearly connected Susan DiGiovanni to Thomas Jones, Mario Mezzara, Michelle Alvarez-Rivera, Donald Jeremy Clearmont, a trust formed in the Bahamas called the Seven Rams Trust, and the Clearmont Geology and Mining Trust based in Williamsport.

Moving forward from what was in the public and private records, the network created a timeline and connecting dots between the bombing of the building in Williamsport, the attempted hijacking of a gold shipment in Pittsfield, Pennsylvania, and the murders of more than a handful of people. The deaths of Jones, Clearmont, and Mezzara were further connected to the slaughter that took place in Troth's estate. A web of people had been killed and, at the center of it all, only a few people had been left standing. One of them was Susan DiGiovanni.

Frazier had been trained to follow the money. The person who had the most to gain from any criminal enterprise was usually the one who was guilty; and, in this situation, it was no different. All he had to do was look at the net worth of Susan DiGiovanni before and after all of the killing and a crystal clear picture emerged. That woman, along with Michelle Alvarez-Rivera, had become billionaires almost overnight, and that had red lights flashing in front of his eyes. He knew that if he got to them, he would be able to control his own destiny. Moreover, he was surer than ever, they were the key to his future.

As they went over the connections and events that, in one way or another, centered on Susan DiGiovanni, they were clicking on map points on the display. Frazier and LeCroix went from sighting to sighting to confirm with their own eyes what the computer had based her projected path on. There were some questionable images, and a few insignificant gaps in time when there was no photographic or paper evidence of her location. The MIN-OPS network had retraced every move she had made, so they went to the point where her trail was picked up in Greenwich. That was where she and Thomas Jones had rented a Range Rover at the airport. From the time of Troth's murder forward was all they needed to see.

By following her movements and the events taking place around her, they quickly determined DiGiovanni was not alone. From the images taken by red-light cameras, Frazier and LeCroix were able to repeatedly see the face of an unknown man she was traveling with, and probably the man who had been creating so much havoc everywhere they went. They couldn't be sure who the man was, but the MIN-OPS system was looking.

Snippets from security cameras, tollbooths, ATM machines, and even from a gas station restroom, created an accurate timeline detailing exactly where she had been and when. Several cameras had captured her on Cape Cod before and after she switched vehicles. The last image from Cape Cod was from the airport, right after the mansion was blown up and right before a private plane was stolen. The next time her likeness was captured was outside of a customs warehouse at an airport in Teeterboro, New Jersey, where a helicopter had been stolen. But, they knew she had not been on that helicopter.

The last marker on the map displayed on the screen was where the computer had last detected Susan's image. The camera was part of the rebuilt surveillance systems around the city of New York. When LeCroix clicked on the icon near the Manhattan side of the George Washington Bridge, a clear image of Susan DiGiovanni walking down the ramp for the West Side Highway popped up. The date and the time of the picture revealed that the picture was just a few days old. The odds were, based on further searching and connections made by the computer network, she was heading for a building owned by the Seven Rams Trust located in the Upper West Side on Central Park West.

Seeing the video image of the man walking beside DiGiovanni left no doubt in Frazier's mind--the mystery man was Daniel Sampson, the ex-Marine and the man Andrew Stevens was hunting. Even though his face was different, the way he walked, the way he carried himself, screamed military. Using the seasoned eye of a long-time law enforcement agent, even with the facial alterations, Frazier could see the resemblance. In addition, his gut told him the destructive events surrounding that man's movements and what they knew about Sampson's capabilities could not be a coincidence.

"Move!" Frazier all but shoved LeCroix out of the way to take control of the computer terminal.

"What the hell are you doing?"

Frazier used the mouse to highlight and then tag a clear shot of the man's face. He clicked on the command to attach a name to the face and then instructed the MIN-OPS network to rescan for matches.

It took only seconds for the results to come up, since the man's movements paralleled those of Susan DiGiovanni right back to the killing of Roland Troth in Greenwich. Before that, the computer picked up Sampson's trail on Cape Cod, where he was driving a Rolls Royce with Roland Troth in the back. Based on what they already knew, it was not hard to link Sampson to the house that was destroyed on the Cape or the fact that Andrew Stevens, the Special Master, was on the Cape at the same time.

"Holy shit!" was all LeCroix could say as everything fell into place.

*****

It was dark outside by the time James LeCroix escorted Stanton Frazier out of the building. What they had stumbled on had taken hours to go over and digest. Despite the copious amount of time they spent painstakingly doing

186

research, all of a sudden, Frazier seemed to be in some sort of rush. It was like he was possessed, driven to try and get to New York so he could find DiGiovanni.

Stanton walked double time on his long, thin legs toward his gray Chrysler 300. "Come on, LeCroix, let's get a move on."

Gasping and trying to keep up, James responded, "What, you think flashing that badge is going to get you up the New Jersey Turnpike any quicker, that is, if we can even get out of the Loop!" LeCroix shouted breathlessly, "Every highway up and down the coast is like a parking lot--"

Frazier cut him off, "The sooner we leave, the sooner we get there."

They were on the second underground level of the parking garage, getting ever closer to Frazier's car. He reached into his pocket and pulled out the remote without slowing. When he pushed the button and heard the chirp signaling the door was unlocked, he looked over and saw that LeCroix was no longer beside him.

He stopped and turned, casting a piercing gaze in LeCroix's direction. James was standing with arms akimbo and had a look on his ruddy face of a petulant child.

"I'm not going, Frazier."

"What the hell do you mean your not going? I thought we were on the same side."

"We are, but, I'd just get in the way."

Stanton looked up and blew a frustrated rush of air through his lips. "What is it, Jimbo? You want I should tell you that I need you, that I need your help? Will that do it? How 'bout I ask you real nice, and promise we'll stop on the way for some fucking ice cream!"

"Now you're just being an asshole. You don't under--"

From between several cars at their sides, six members of a squad stood up and fired their suppressed

H&K MP-5's at both men. Three slugs managed to take the top of Stanton Frazier's head off and another two penetrated his heart. He died instantly.

James LeCroix was not so lucky. A projectile found its way through a lens of his wire-framed glasses, ricocheted off of his cheekbone and exited through his jaw. The mandible shattered and left him slack-jawed with blood pouring out of his mouth. Two other shots pieced his neck, but he was so fat that the bullets missed all vital structures and exited cleanly through the front and side of his throat. LeCroix fell to the ground, struggling to breathe, his hands grasping at his neck.

A man dressed head to toe in black, only the whites of his eyes showing, walked up to LeCroix and calmly shot him in the head.

While the others started to clean up and prepare to pull out, another Special Forces commando standing near Frazier's Chrysler held an encrypted, digital radio to his face. "Brass Hat, come in, Brass Hat. This is Anaconda-One. Mission accomplished. Out."

LeCroix and Frazier were loaded into the gray Chrysler and strapped in as if going for a ride. A commando with big blue eyes pulled the pins on two thermite grenades, tossed them onto the laps of the corpses, and slammed the door shut. He made the sign of the cross, turned, and disappeared into the darkness of the parking garage. Seconds later, the car burst into flames and would not stop burning until there was nothing left but the shell of a warped, partially melted automobile.

*****

With so much going on at once, Fort Bragg in North Carolina was hopping with activity. To General Smythe, the swelling of the ranks could not have come at a more opportune time. He had the pick of more than a million personnel to recruit from to fill positions in his operation. With the ratification vote for the new constitution coming up, and the election of an entirely new government to follow, he was going to need a lot more manpower to guarantee a relatively smooth transition.

Over the prior weeks, the Rapid Response Team's Executive Staff had multiplied by the hundreds and quickly became unwieldy. With the command structure of a division, too much micromanagement was required by the division commander and executive officer. Since they had grown well beyond the strength of one division, a reorganization was ordered. With the consent of Andrew Stevens, Smythe divided the one division in three.

Special Master Stevens had also bequeathed Adam Smythe with a field promotion to the rank of Lieutenant General. Granted absolute authority over his personnel choices, he appointed a general staff of 24 career officers he knew would be loyal to him and him alone. Those Smythe selected to the top positions were officers he had known practically his entire life. They, in turn, populated their own staffs with people they had known or worked with for years--individuals they could trust with their lives.

The method used to fill out the command structure was not simply cronyism. There was more to it than that. To be chosen as one of the members of the Executive Staff was much closer to paternalism. The upper levels of the military were an insular group and heritage mattered. Having the right name or connection was the only gateway to be considered for positions under Smythe. However, the sigil that would guarantee entry into the exclusive club was a class ring from one of the military academies or VMI.

The three new divisions were placed under the command of brigadier generals who would oversee the multiple functions within each division. Other functions, not typically part of a regular detachment, fell to other close associates of Smythe. They would supervise the

189

continued militarization of the civilian forces, manage the computer networks, and maintain control of the massive internment camps spread all around the country.

The biggest change in the command structure was that the men selected for the Executive Staff would not be reporting directly to Smythe. Instead, they would report to the new Commander of the rechristened Rapid Response Command, Major General James Farthing. Smythe himself would continue to liaison with the newly appointed heads of the civilian intelligence agencies. The spooks and special agents were so intricately intertwined in the mission, he did not want there to be any gaps in communication.

Passing off the day-to-day responsibilities of the Rapid Response Command to General Farthing gave Smythe the ability see the big picture, to have more time to think strategically, and make sure they were in the perfect position to handle any and every eventuality. Up until that point, managing the national crisis had been like playing a game of whack-a-mole, forcing him to react to situations as they popped up. Although turning the table and taking the fight to the protesters instead of reacting to them had changed the dynamic of the conflict, there was still a lot to do.

When the team assigned to take out LeCroix and Frazier reported back, General Smythe felt relieved. He knew the two dead DOJ employees had not contacted anyone else with the information they gathered. By eliminating them, he had guaranteed their silence. Smythe would go to any length to make sure Andrew Stevens did not find out what they knew, at least not yet.

Having his computer experts continually monitoring the networks so closely was paying dividends. Snaring LeCroix, someone who was on their watch list, was like swatting a mosquito. As soon as he landed and started to probe, he was a squashed. Smythe knew real intelligence work was not about water boarding or stress positions.

Instead, it took a smooth hand to find out the truth about what other people really knew. By sitting back and waiting, the intelligence section received a windfall of information.

What they had learned by tracking LeCroix's activity on the MIN-OPS network was powerful information, knowledge that could be used to Smythe's advantage if handled in the right way. Not only had they discovered Sampson approximate location, they were also relative confidence that was where he'd be staying, Knowing exactly what he looked like with his surgically altered face would allow them to track him and monitor his movements.

Stanton Frazier and James LeCroix somehow knew enough to connect Sampson to Susan DiGiovanni, and that was the key. The necessary facts had been withheld from the system and that had made it impossible to track Sampson down. As the old saying went, garbage in, garbage out. The two dead men had been able to do what the computers couldn't, at least not yet, and that was to use their intuition to weigh the facts in order to reach conclusions. That Susan DiGiovanni, a relative nobody as far as MIN-OPS was concerned, stuck out in their minds was how they managed to discover so much.

The most important piece of intelligence, at least in Smythe's mind, was the connection discovered between Daniel Sampson and Andrew Stevens. Lots of manpower had been wasted looking for Daniel Sampson, and outside of Andrew Stevens's inner circle, no one really knew why. The fact that Stevens had not disclosed what he knew or explain why it was so important to hunt Sampson down made the relationship significant, a secret Stevens obviously did not want anyone else to know. But now they knew Maxwell York and Stevens, the two main men behind MYB, Ltd., were directly linked to Daniel Sampson, Cape Cod, and events in Greenwich. Without that knowledge, no one would have been able to figure out the rest.

Even though he could not be sure of exactly what had gone down, the evidence from Greenwich pointed to a hit by Sampson on Roland Troth. That presumption left a very bad taste in Smythe's mouth. It was as if people in that stratum would eat their own young if it served their purpose. It also made the general wonder, not for the first time, if he had chosen the wrong side. On top of that, Smythe had not forgotten that Sampson had sent a message by intentionally allowing his men to live instead of killing a bunch of them when he had the chance. What Smythe really needed to do was talk to Daniel Sampson and Susan DiGiovanni. When he did, he was sure they would be able to fill in the gaps. How Smythe was going to use the intelligence he garnered was something he had yet to figure out.

Chapter Sixteen

Several harried days passed after Sampson, Susan, and Liz made their way into the city and dropped in on the penthouse--taking Carlos, Michelle, and Darla completely by surprise. The days were filled with so many emotions and so much to do they seemed to pass much too quickly. Once Michelle, Carlos, and Darla were introduced to Sampson, they had a lot to catch up on with Susan and plans to make. At the same time, they were constantly put on edge by local developments and trying to make provisions for their own welfare.

Inside of the spacious Central Park West penthouse, if things had not been so hectic, so distracting, the level of tension would have made everyone uneasy. Most of the tension centered on the gruff, egotistical ex-Marine, Daniel Sampson. The situation could even have become highly explosive; but, lucky for the others, it never seemed like the right time to talk to Susan about her poor choice in men.

The more Liz observed Sampson, the more she disliked him. He moved stiffly like a robot, yet he was sneaky like a cat on the prowl. Despite his handsome face and great physique, the man was definitely not of Susan's caliber, not even close. He was bossy, rude, and domineering, all traits Susan usually detested. Seeing them together, a somehow unnatural coupling, caused Liz great distress. She was Susan's older sister, but it was not for her to say who she gave her heart, body, and soul too, even if the man was a creep.

For Michelle, the minute she laid eyes on Daniel Sampson, she knew something was wrong. It wasn't anything specific that put her on guard. Instead, his aura was just off in a way she couldn't identify. All she knew was that she was picking up on some unwholesome vibes. Yes, he seemed detached, as if he didn't know how to be among others, but her intuition told her it was something deeper than that, that he was somehow damaged.

Michelle was grateful Sampson had helped Susan and was getting them all food; yet her instincts screamed that the man was no good and it made her wonder why Susan did not sense what she sensed or see what she saw.

Unlike the others, Carlos took to Sampson the minute they met. The former Marine was, like him, a man of few words, direct, and to the point. Although he looked uncomfortable in his own skin, he was also very sharp intellectually and physically capable of just about anything. Besides Sampson's fastidious mannerisms, Carlos thought there was a lot about the man to admire.

At the same time, though, it was disturbing for Carlos to hear Sampson and Susan making love in the next room over. At first, he chalked it up to the loyalty he felt towards Donny, his best friend and the man who brought Susan DiGiovanni into their circle. It bothered him to see her with another man so soon, less than a year, after Donny had died. But, she was a grown woman, free to make her own choices and do whatever made her happy. Still...

Getting resupplied was high on their list of priorities. Since no one was willing to give up DNA to get an ID so they could get food, it was left to Sampson to provide provisions, enough to feed six. Asserting that he could move better on his own, none of the others argued with him. From their first night in Manhattan on, he went out by himself.

The ability to monitor the great lawns of Central Park and the activity from Harlem to Midtown gave Sampson a much better idea about the scope of the military maneuvers. Even though he had been able to snoop over the progress reports from the Joint Commission Task Force's Rapid Response Team, nothing prepared him for the magnitude of what he saw. It was still New York City, but it may as well have been East Germany at the height of

194

the Cold War.

With so much cargo being unloaded at the piers and then parceled out at night to the distribution centers, getting what they needed was child's play. But, Sampson was interested in obtaining much more than bread and rice. With the shortages of luxury items, black markets had sprung up all over the city. Steak, ham, and even eggs could all be had in trade for gems or precious metals.

Stealthily, he made his way around the city in the dark of night, locating the biggest dealers and choicest products. Every night, without failure, he was able to bring back choice delicacies no one in the penthouse had the right to expect. No matter how many times they asked, he would not disclose how or where he had obtained what he brought back to the penthouse. The luxurious food did serve to soften their opinion of him--but at the same time, it made them all quite suspicious.

There were things, Sampson knew, they would not understand and other things they did not want to know. Since it was early on in the association, he didn't trust them. As a rule, he probably never would. Although he believed Susan was on his side and would do him no harm, he didn't think it would be wise to disturb her with the fine details of what he'd been doing. In addition to the food and weapons he procured for the benefit of all, he had also taken the opportunity to dispossess street peddlers of as much gold and jewelry as he could safely hide.

Preparing for the unknown, Sampson did what he did to ensure not only his survival, but also a comfortable future. He took what he thought he would need if the day came where he set out on his own. The gold and jewels he stashed away, he knew, would serve him well. The bodies he left behind, stripped of all their valuables, would not be found for weeks.

Preying on the weak was one of many things he did and discovered while on the prowl and lurking in the shadows of the city. There was more to do and more to learn but to do it correctly, he had to work during the light of day.

"Come on, Susan, you're coming with me."

"Where are we going, and in broad daylight?"

"I need to do some more recon and I need you as a decoy."

"A decoy? Are you fucking kidding me?" Liz shouted, pushing her way between Susan and Sampson.

Intimidating as he was, it was not difficult for Daniel Sampson to impose his will on others. He glared at Liz with his steely eyes and then looked over her shoulder at Susan.

Feeling his gaze, she looked down and then stepped around her protective sister. "Don't worry, he won't let anything happen to me." Standing next to Sampson, she looked up and asked, "What do you mean?"

"While the others here are busy worrying about their fortunes, I need to get a better sense of the layout. That requires scouting over and above my forays at night."

Knowing he was not good with words--or at the social game--Susan prompted him for a rehabilitative response, "And you need me because?"

"You'll be good cover; a couple is more inconspicuous than a man traveling alone."

Michelle chimed in from behind them, "I don't want Susan going anywhere near the streets, Sampson!"

"Neither do I!" Liz added with conviction.

Susan raised her arms in disgust, "I am right here! You're talking about me like I'm some god damn little kid. I'm a grown woman and can make my own decisions, what the hell is wrong with you two?"

Seeing that the nasty, street-smart side of Susan's "Jersey Girl" routine was about to come out, both Liz and Michelle backed down. They were in no mood to encounter her wrath and, at the same time, piss off the maniac who was pulling her away from them."

"Fine, Susan. You do what you want--I'm staying out of it!"

"Good!"

Cherishing her victory, Susan quickly bundled up in a heavy jacket and headed toward the door with Sampson in tow.

Once outside the building, it took Sampson just seconds to notice the men observing their building and the clumsy young intelligence agents who were unskillfully shadowing him. Knowing Susan would immediately tell the others, he hid what he saw from her. What she was able to see with her own eyes was disturbing enough.

On every corner stood heavily armed N.Y.P.D. officers, but they were dressed head to toe in paramilitary gear. The streets were being patrolled by National Guard Humvees and other heavily armored vehicles. A constant whir of propellers from helicopters and UAV surveillance drones could be heard coming from above. The city had been pacified, but seeing things on the ground, it was clearly an imposed stillness. The conditions were no more peaceful than a city under siege waiting for the final assault.

Some people were walking around freely. On the streets, there was a constant stream of packed busses moving rapidly in every direction. However, almost everyone who was out had their heads down. The body language of the typically hardened New Yorkers was closed, more closed than usual, as if bundling up against the cold. In reality, the way people held themselves was an indication of their trepidation. They were clearly intimidated by the military's presence.

No one wanted to be stopped, patted down, and ordered to produce the DNA ID. If someone did not have a valid ID, they knew they were subject to being detained and questioned. Wanting to avoid the notice of authorities,

197

there was very little eye contact and no sudden moves that could possibly draw attention. Sampson wondered if what they were seeing was similar to how it was in the Jewish ghettos of Poland during World War II.

For hours, they did nothing but walk purposefully, seemingly on their way to some place important. All the while, they kept their eyes open, watching and noticing everything. Shortly after making their rounds and circling back to the penthouse, Sampson surveyed the watcher's sniper's nests and observation posts. In his mind, he had already mapped out several possible escape routes and ways he could get in and out of the building undetected.

Knowing he was being tracked did not disturb him. Instead, it gave Sampson a huge advantage and a sense of comfort. That they allowed him to move without trying to take him out on sight meant there was still time to formulate alternative strategies. And, due to his familiarity with the operatives' procedures, the teams assigned to monitor him would actually give away the exact moment they decided to make a move.

They were walking north on Amsterdam toward the intersection of West 79th Street, returning from midtown. On their last circuit, they had scoped out the headquarters of Hamilton Genomics, the facility where the man-made virus was created. Sealed up and protected from intruders by multiple levels of paramilitary security, they knew there was nothing more they could do or learn.

"They made the virus here and distributed it how?" She asked, her face turned sideways to look at Sampson as they walked and talked.

"The United States Postal Service."

"You're kidding me?"

"No, that's exactly how they sent it, in sealed vials."

"And then what?"

"And then the people who got the virus would mix it with some bacteria and grow it in some kind of witch's

198

brew."

Susan poked at Sampson, "Now don't go disparaging us witches-we had nothing to do with it."

"I said witches with a 'w'."

"Oh, you're such an ass!"

Susan leaned into Sampson's arm, taking his huge hand into hers. Although she did not like the way he ordered her around at times--and how he had to keep his little secrets--she was glad she had stuck with him. Never in her wildest dreams would she have believed she would have hooked up with a military man, or that she would start to catch feelings no less. But, times were tough and if he was able to keep her safe and fed, she could put up with his little quirks. At times, he could even be funny, sometimes cute, and occasionally he could even be romantic. It made Susan wonder why Liz and Michelle couldn't see those same qualities she saw and why they had come to dislike him so much.

"Is that the only thing Hamilton Genomics was doing at that building?"

"No. It's also a storehouse, a kind of repository."

"A storehouse, for what?"

"Sperm."

"What? Did you just say sperm? As in cum?"

Sampson could help but to snicker.

"What the hell for?"

"Do you remember when we were in the Ramapo Mountains how I told you I knew all about Maxwell York's plans?"

"Project Stasis: wiping out the economy, the virus, killing off the population and letting the rich take over as feudal lords? How could I forget, Sampson? We're living it."

"Yeah, I'm talking about Project Stasis and the feudal lord part."

"What about it?"

199

"Do you know who's going to be running things in thirty, forty, fifty years?"

"Besides the relatives of the Rockefellers and Rothschilds, no."

"Would you be surprised if I told you it was going to be none other than Maxwell York and people like him?"

"I'd think you're insane. From what you told me, the man is as old as dust and is dying from cancer. Were you wrong?"

"No, Susan, I wasn't wrong."

"Then how? How will York and his cronies still be here in forty years?"

"Well, he won't be here--not him exactly--"

"Sampson, knock it off! First, you're not making any sense; and second, you're talking in circles. What do you mean?"

"York and the super rich like him who have taken over won't be here, but their clones will."

"Get the fuck outta here! Now I know you're insane."

"No, I'm dead serious. They have vials of sperm locked up in a safe. As soon as York gives the order or dies, whatever comes first, they'll pull all the DNA material out of his sperm and implant it in an egg. All they have to do is zap it and the cell divides. An instant clone of Maxwell York or whoever else they want to duplicate. They implant the cells into a womb of a surrogate and nine months later..."

Susan saw a man walking toward her. She pushed her body closer to Sampson to try to avoid bumping into him, but it was too late. The man, unshaven and smelling like a brewery, slid his hand deftly into her pocket and dropped an object.

Sampson started to turn to confront the hobo but it was no use. He was gone, continuing to walk down the street as if nothing had happened.

"No! don't!" Susan spat out through gritted teeth. "I saw him, Samson, he winked at me and dropped a cell phone in my pocket." the last few words she spoke were little more than a whisper.

"Get rid of it!" he ordered. "They can track you--"

"No! He wants us to see it--he's trying to help us."

"How do you know?"

"I don't. It's just that--well--there was something familiar about him."

"Okay, okay, we'll see why he gave you a phone, but not at the penthouse."

"Then where?"

"Let's go shopping at Macy's. I need a new coat."

It was a major development they hadn't expected-- one that actually came out in their favor. Dr. Richard Clearmont, the man they were looking for and hoped to meet up with in the Bronx had searched for and located them.

It was not long after that first contact they received a cryptic e-mail somehow rerouted from Budapest. The message was a very specific set of instructions detailing what he wanted and how they could get information to him. They were commanded to dump the phone and pick up another he had hidden in the city. That would enable them to initiate several brief phone conversations.

To Susan and Sampson, it felt like they were acting out a lost episode of "Get Smart," and it seemed quite possible that Richard Clearmont was not playing with a full deck. If nothing else, the man always used an abundance of caution.

The good part, though, was that from a nondescript internet cafe in Soho, Sampson had been able to surreptitiously transfer gigabytes of Hamilton Genomics files to one of Richard's accounts in an anonymous file sharing network. The files were uploaded from a thumb drive Sampson had in his possession since being in York's mansion on Cape Cod. The files were then broken down into millions of data packets onto some sort of shadow net and streamed all over the world--only to be reconnected and put back together by a computer only Richard could remotely access.

Getting the data about the virus Hamilton Genomics had created to Richard would give him a chance to study the data before they met to discuss the ramifications. Once he had the details only a molecular biologist could love, they knew they'd have him hooked and he would help them. It was the best outcome they could think of.

Only moments after the files were successfully transferred, the response Sampson received was, "OMG! C-U L8R at zoo." It was all they needed to hear. To them, it meant that Richard Clearmont was not only able to read the files, but was also blown away by them; and, he would meet them at the appointed time at the Bronx Zoo.

Right after the last text message came through, Sampson grabbed the phone roughly out of Susan's hands.

"Hey! What'd ya do that for?"

He dropped the phone on the concrete of the sidewalk and stomped on it with his heel. "Like I told you before, no cell phones. I hate those god damn things--it's like having a neon sign flashing, 'Come get me, here I am!'"

"But you didn't have to pry it out of my hands! I would have given it to you."

"Listen, Susan, we've had a good day and I want to get back to the penthouse and celebrate."

"What does that have to do with you being an asshole and being all rough with me?"

"I thought you liked it rough."

Immediately, a wanton look came over her face. "Oh...is that what you mean by celebrating, huh?"

"Uh-hu."

"So what are we waiting for, cowboy?"

*****

The display of force in the cities and mass detention of activists had reduced the level of dynamic opposition, but the tactic had also generated the unintended consequence of driving insurrectionists further underground. That meant Smythe and his commanders had to simultaneously keep units patrolling the population centers while hunting down agitators through EL-INT, electronic intelligence. Having committed so many men to the cities left large swaths of territory exposed and ripe for rebellion.

There were two major trouble spots that concerned Smythe and his executive staff the most. A quadrant of land from Flagstaff, Arizona stretching across the Southern United States to the Florida Panhandle and up to South Carolina--the Bible Belt--had been relatively passive until the mandates concerning the Federal Identification Cards came out. In the big cities, Rapid Response Team units, supported by state and local authorities, were able to quell the disturbances the Bible-thumpers had caused. But, in the rural areas, the discontent was spreading and, as irrational as it seemed, it was all based on religious fanaticism.

From the reports Smythe was getting, many of the yahoos were unwilling to get what they were calling, "The Mark of the Beast," and refused to submit to any authority who wanted to obtain their genetic profile. The rural Bible Belt's civil disobedience had only started to become violent, and only mildly disruptive. However, the probability of escalation was growing by the hour as the people who did not obtain a valid ID could not buy anything and were quickly running out of food.

A much different type of civil disobedience was happening in the rural parts of the Mid Atlantic states. From Eastern Ohio, through Western Pennsylvania, and down into West Virginia, it seemed like no one was going along with the program. The area was not known for anarchist activities or paramilitary groups to rouse the population into an anti-government posture. The absence of dooms-day-like groups explained the complete lack of armed resistance they had seen and crushed in the Pacific Northwest. Also, unlike what the self-styled Minute Man groups along the Northeast corridor had staged, there had been no reports of sabotage along the major transportation arteries.

At the same time, the lack of compliance with ID mandates and the dearth of conversions from Federal Reserve Note-based assets to Amero Credits were quite disturbing. Oddly, even in the cities from Cleveland to Harrisburg and as far south as Wheeling, West Virginia, the people who were supposed to be in control had not requested Federal assistance. Only Pittsburgh, Cleveland, and Cincinnati had seen rioting and required several deliveries of food. But, since the early stages and initial strife, all three cities had been under control. The inactivity could not be explained by the sparse population, lack of financial interests, or even indifference. The people in that segment of the country were, in fact, engaged; just not in the type of activities anyone expected.

Instead of fighting amongst themselves, stealing from each other, or protesting what was happening to their country, they were busy making provisions for themselves. Entire communities had come together to make sure everyone would have enough food and fuel to last the winter. Even the politicians and civic leaders, some who were supposed to be in league with Stevens and his crowd, had joined in the passive resistance. They were no longer answering to the orders of compliance coming from D.C.

If it was a separatist movement, it was different from any movement Smythe had ever heard of, unannounced and emphatically peaceful. Even the agent provocateurs recruited to stir up several communities failed to garner any support and they were quickly routed out of the targeted towns. The people were somehow united in a common cause to keep the peace and find a way to survive on their own. If there was a model they were following, the closest Smythe could think of, ironically, were the Amish.

From what Smythe and the G-2 section could gather, the Rust Belt denizens, which included many dairy and crop farmers, were simply rejecting the new order and the concept of a nanny nation. They did not want the handouts, the gift of financial security in return for their compliance. The attitude seemed to be that if they went along with what the Stevens regime was offering, they would just be signing a deal with a different devil. Having just survived the assault on their jobs, homes, and prosperity from Roland Troth and the crooked banking sector, they were a lot more leery of the people who had taken executive control of Washington, D.C., and their bankers.

The hardy men and woman of the Rust Belt, offspring of steel workers, miners, farmers, and others who made a living off the sweat of their brow, were making due for themselves. They were actually doing a pretty good job of eliminate the need for external support. Leveraging the produce from dairy farms, vast stockpiles of grains, and a growing network of natural gas pipelines, the people of the region were trying to prove they could survive without the rest of the nation. A self-sustaining zone of resistance, to Smythe and his analysts, was the most dangerous development yet. If the idea spread and other areas of the country that could be self-sufficient actually did it, the only power anyone would have over them would be brutality, violence, or complete annihilation.

*****

Susan and Sampson took pains to establish a routine

so that watchers would be lulled into complacency. Each day, they went out and followed the same patterns, making it seem they were simply living their lives and not conducting counter-surveillance.

One day out, Sampson saw something he had no seen on their trip into Manhattan and on the other days of recon. Strange looking vehicles with military and police insignia were cruising the streets. The odd part was that each vehicle had a rack on the roof with antennae and other sensors. After watching them for only several minutes, their function became abundantly clear. Somehow, the cars were able to pick up on people who did not have a valid ID in their possession.

Avoiding the military and keeping away from the cars' obvious routes, Susan and Sampson observed how the roving patrols operated. Sampson figured the new ID cards must have an imbedded RFID chip the patrol cars could read. An uneven count between warm bodies and radio frequency signals would trigger some sort of alarm and entire groups would be rounded up for questioning. The people caught in the net would be detained until agents, cops, or MPs figured out who did not have an ID and why.

With so many boots on the ground, and technology to track possible dissenters, Sampson knew it was time to acquire a valid, federal DNA ID. It was not a responsibility he was willing to let the others have because he simply did not trust them. Unlike them, he had the ability to get a valid ID without using his own name, his old face, and, most importantly, not using his own DNA.

With no difficulty, he was able to fool the machine and get a valid identification. Because Roland Troth had arranged for the surgery to change his fingerprints, and a cadaver's flesh covered his hands up to the wrists, it was simply a matter of making sure one of the ID vans took a sample of the skin from his hand and no further up his arm.

Susan did not like the thought of being tracked no

matter where she went so she refused to give up her genetic profile. The fact she was dead-set against getting an ID was a huge relief to Sampson. Feeling much more secure with a valid DNA ID, Sampson was able to move relatively freely around the city. Nevertheless, because they had to contend with the roving patrols it meant that when he traveled with Susan, or any of the others, they would all have to be extra careful.

If the others decided to go out on their own and were taken away, oh well, he thought, that was not his problem. But, for them to bring him down just so they could move around less stressfully was not going to happen. He suspected that once they were able to get a valid lock on Susan or any one of the others in their group, whoever was tagged would lead the authorities right to him-- willingly or not.

Chapter Seventeen

The jet was cruising at 20,000 feet heading north-northeast toward Atlantic City International Airport. In one of the older casinos, a private suite served as a CIA safe house, where York and his detail would be staying. The aircraft they were in was something the public didn't even know existed, a private jet made of a special radar absorbing graphine shell and fitted with the latest stealth technology.

Five heavily armed, casually dressed men sat in different locations in the spacious cabin. Two were at the fore of Maxwell York and another man, three were aft of them. York and Chris Carlton, one of York's most trusted lieutenants, sat across from each other at a table near the middle of the plane.

Carlton was tall, fit, heavily muscled from years of activity. A thin black beard covered pockmarks on his dark skin and contrasted attractively with his bald head. York wore a white Oxford shirt and blue designer slacks. His typically combed white hair was in disarray, thinning so much in places that his scalp was visible. He looked ancient sitting next to the abundantly healthy operative. For York, the level of activity right after chemotherapy treatment was taking its toll. He was thin, gaunt, and even weaker than he looked. In front of them, there were glasses of single-malt scotch, neat, and neither one of them had touched a drop.

A man stepped out of the cockpit and cleared his throat, getting everyone's attention. "Chris, NORAD isn't tracking us and the civilian towers are all but blind. We're good to go."

"Thanks, Tony." Carlton turned back to face York. "Stevens is back in New York, we've got him pegged at the HQ on West 97th.

You know, Maxwell, we could take him out now, shit,

we could've had him taken him out weeks ago--all you have to do is give the order."

"I know, Chris, I know. You and your men have done a fantastic job thus far, but, in all actuality, Andrew is doing us a wonderful service."

"How do you mean? I thought you hated how things were going."

"Yes, it's tragic, so many lost lives, so much pain and suffering--and it didn't have to be this way. I did give Andrew the authority to act in my name when all of this started, but the second he thought I was dead, he strayed. I was upset he opted to do things his way and ended up creating a mess, but, Chris, there's a good side--what we had planned to take ten, fifteen years he has been able to accomplish in several weeks."

"What did he do different than you had planned?"

"That's not important now, we have to look forward. There's another thing Andrew has accomplished for me and that is to force the others to demonstrate their commitment to our objectives. For example, we didn't know if the Chinese Central Committee could be convinced to do what we needed them to do. Would they follow the path laid out to them by our people, the insiders we worked so hard to get in those positions? Could they be talked into intentionally causing a worldwide panic and devaluing the dollar? We didn't know, we couldn't possibly know for sure, but they did it."

"So, now you know who's with the program and how everything has shaken out, but how will your partners react when they learn that you're still alive? Andrew's been acting like you're dead, pushing his agenda down everyone's throats, and you haven't done a thing to contradict him. I don't know how you're planning on breaking the news that you're still alive and kickin', but when you do, there may be some hurt feelings."

Maxwell chuckled lightly and then started to cough.

He took a sip of the scotch and was able to compose himself. "That's neither here nor there, Chris. I'm not the only one who knows what to do when the dust settles."

Chris smiled. "I know. You've been very aware of your own mortality for a while. What I don't know is what you want us to do. We've been working in the background for years, helping you get things done that no one else could do. You've got your virus unleashed, Mr. Yoo is cranking out your drones, and most of the rest of the world is under the control of people you put into place. What I'd like to know is what you want for my teams, from me?"

"It's quite simple, my friend. Whether I live or die, there are several more tasks you're going to have to accomplish. If I'm correct, Andrew will follow through with the next few stages and as soon as he does, it will be time to cull the herd."

Completely engrossed in what York was saying, and not wanting to miss one single word of the weak, breathless voice, Chris leaned forward and fixed his eyes on Maxwell's pale, waxy lips.

"A lot of what's been taking place was part of my plan. Stevens had the entire strategy laid out for him. The only thing is, he's been trying to pull it off at the speed of light instead of taking baby steps. That may or may not be his downfall, time will tell. I do believe, though, he knows it will be disastrous if he deviates much more from the course."

Like an eager student given unfettered access to a highly respected professor, Chris prodded, "What's he going to do next?"

Maxwell York sat silent for a second and thought. He rested his elbow on the tabletop, cupped his chin in the palm of his hand and looked up with narrowed eyes. Finally, his eyes returned to Chris.

"He has to restore confidence and he's going to do that by introducing a new constitution. It was written not long ago and makes the old scheme of governance seem anachronistic. New freedoms, new rights, and a guarantee of prosperity, It will be a Pax Americana."

York had to stop, take a few deep breaths and another sip of alcohol before he could continue. Just thinking about how close he had come to getting everything he wanted made him ache. "You'll see it all and see it soon, Chris. He'll get the new constitution ratified and continue to run things, heading a North American Council of Seven of his own choosing. Once everything settles down, he'll act to make it seem like he's the Second Coming who's returned to make everyone rich and comfortable. The only thing he won't touch are the property and commerce laws."

"Why wouldn't he change those laws; so that everyone sees how great of a man he is?" Carlton asked. "He'd come off like a benevolent dictator that way, right?"

"No, he needs those laws because of what he's already accomplished. Under the laws in existence before the panic, Andrew Stevens and our compatriots already own, well, everything."

"Everything?"

"Yes. The people have been signing away their property rights without even knowing what they're doing. What we didn't own, for the most part, we have control of now. The panic, the market crashes, the credit crisis, all of that was intentional."

Chris looked confused. "How did something like that help the cause?"

York smiled at his smart but naive protector's ignorance. "It was like us hitting the reset button on the financial system and our people were the only ones in position to take advantage. When the stock market crashed and everyone else was selling their shares, it was Andrew and our other partners who were the only ones buying. No, they probably didn't get all the shares of every company, but I know they managed to acquire at least a controlling

211

percentage of every company in the Fortune 500."

Chris commented, "To enforce our ownership, they need the legal structure in place?"

"Yes, exactly, and that's very astute of you. When the fed flooded the market with dollars, they were disintegrating the value while at the same time other currencies were rising. What happened is that with the panic, we cut the market value of these companies to shreds and bought them up with cheap dollars--a double discount."

"And you don't care that others got the currency and are going to convert it to Ameros?"

York smiled hauntingly, his wicked streak on full display. "The senior partners control the means of production and the land, everyone else has to come to us to spend whatever money they have."

Getting the complete picture, Chris wanted to hear more about what was to come. "Then what? What does he do after he gets a constitution ratified?"

"As far as Andrew is concerned, he thinks all he has to do is sit back and use his power to get the world to settle down. He'll have some small issues to overcome, like getting people to submit their DNA samples to get their identification cards, and snuffing out any resistance, but he'll manage. He'll do it by bestowing some kindness on those who comply. For those who don't go along with the program, well, they won't fare so well."

"Is that it?" Carlton asked, completely surprised at the simplicity.

"No, there are minor details, such as getting the rest of the country wired up for observation."

"Why?"

"To be on guard for a counter-revolution and to be able to make sure we know everything. The future we are fighting for depends on being able to do almost everything with two-thirds less people. To replace manual labor with robotics and technology, a lot of data has to be collected.

We have to record and decipher everything everyone does so it can be replicated by machines--but more efficiently. In a few decades, most of what people do now will be done by machines, robots. The technology to do that now exists. You should know though, Chris, as close as Andrew and I were, there were things I never told him. There are other, let's just say, elements that will eventually take care of the rest."

Without asking, Chris Carlton knew Maxwell was talking about him and the rest of the Clandestine Service who were already on board. "What does that mean for us, Maxwell, for my teams?"

"What that means, my friend, is that everything we've worked for will fail as long as the political class survives. They will be the ones who get in the way, who try to stymie what we're trying to do. They will be the ones who rebel, who fight back, who try to stop us and make things go back to the corrupt meaningless drudgery they have locked everyone into for way too long."

"What you're saying is that you want us to kill off all the politicians?" Chris had no reservations about getting to the heart of a matter.

It was York's turn to smile. He loved the man's directness. "Yes, that is exactly what I want you to do."

"Why--"

York cut him of. "Because Andrew Stevens doesn't have the balls to do it! Sure, he's got no problems killing off the innocents, the less fortunate, people who are not of his ilk, but when it comes to people who are his friends, his kin." York allowed the statement to hang in the air for a few seconds before finishing his thought. "The people he can relate to, he'll be willing to beat them out of their wealth but not willing to kill them. What Andrew doesn't recognize is that those same individuals are the most dangerous people in the world to him."

Chris turned his head sideways like a smart, but

confused puppy, seeking an understandable answer from his master.

"Yes, Chris, even amongst the rich and powerful, there are strata, tiers of consequence, if you will. Some of us, as well as our offspring, have known all along that we would eventually have to cut the strings of the puppets. You and your caste, my friend, are no threat to us. Instead, you're the ones who'll cut the strings. Andrew Stevens and his kind are endlessly ambitious and would eventually eat each other alive before all was said and done and we would have gained nothing. Now that Andrew has tasted the power, and has felt the essence of unquestioned authority, he has to be eliminated, as will many of the second-tier partners. Who lives and who dies will be something me and my closest friends will have to decide over the next few weeks, if I live long enough to do it."

"And if you don't?"

"Don't worry, the others know how to reach you and they will let you know what to do. Is there anything else you need to know?"

"Yeah, why is it so important to get the UAV's, the drones, produced so quickly and off the ground?"

"Ah, a very good question, Chris. It's because you and your men are going to use those drones to put the final piece in place-- or, maybe I should say, take the biggest, most dangerous pieces off the board. You and men like you around the world are going to wipe out the nuclear capacity of every nation on earth. It will be your job to deal with the nuclear arsenal of the United States. You and your teams will be given the locations to wipe out the only real nuclear weapons this country has left."

"I don't understand, Maxwell. I thought there were thousands of missiles, atomic weapons on submarines, things like that."

"At one time there was, but not anymore."

Once again, Chris looked at the old man sideways,

all but begging for a deeper explanation.

"Years ago, we came to a decision that it made no sense to build more weapons. Being able to blow up the world ten times over was more than was enough. The strategic arms treaties were signed, as you know, but they went a lot further and cut a lot deeper than the public was led to believe. The United States, Russia, and China still possess multi-kiloton weapons, but they are all concentrated at a few sites in their respective nations."

"What about the rest? Those thousands of silos, all the submarines?"

"Dummies, all for show."

"I'll be damned!"

"Chris, we know where every single nuclear weapon on the planet is and how to get them. The FORTE satellites launched over the past few years can track even small amounts of weapons grade uranium and plutonium with unbelievable accuracy. That information will be provided to you when the time is right."

"We're going to use drones to take out these sites? That's all?"

"That's all you'll need. Some of the drones were made specifically for such a purpose, to take out the known bunkers and silos."

"How could you possibly know that?" Chris asked with a look of amazement on his face.

"Who do you think built the sites?"

"What about the rest of the world? Russia? China? Israel?"

"Do you think it was an accident that Putin, the former head of the KGB, was reelected as President of Russia? Did you know that the Prime Ministers of Canada and Australia were recruited and trained by MI-6, Britain's intelligence service? The Chinese military leadership has been with us all along, they can't wait to give up their nukes and take the weapons out of the hands of North Korea,

215

India, and Pakistan. You and your men are not the only operatives in the game. You've been working together with other spooks around the globe toward a common goal, you just didn't know it. And, in this instance, nothing has changed. Focus your teams at the targets you're given."

Chris tried to push the discussion for more specific details. "Maxwell, how the hell do you expect the few teams we have to coordinate and run so many missions? If you think we need to control the air, to ground the entire military, and hunt targets all over the United States, we won't have enough manpower to pilot the drones!"

"I guess you're not aware of the capabilities of this new generation of UAV's, are you? As soon as the squadrons are ready, all your men have to do is point and click and the human pilots won't stand a chance." York took another sip from his glass and reached for the bottle to pour another three fingers worth of scotch. He replaced the bottle and went on, "Once we take the threat of annihilation off the table, your job will be complete. Now, I know you and your people have been briefed about the virus."

"Yes, Maxwell." The look on Carlton's face made it clear that he was uneasy talking about the subject. He checked over his shoulder to see if his men were listing.

Maxwell continued, "When the changes in DNA start to effect the population over the next few decades, the ones who have been selected to remain, to procreate, will have one less thing to worry about."

Chapter Eighteen

Walking toward the main entrance of the building where they were staying, Sampson surreptitiously scrutinized the men who were watching him from the top of the building across the street as well as the men assigned to follow him. Everything was the same as it had been, which allowed him to breathe a little easier. A change in their routine would have been a warning sign that something had changed and maybe the watchers were ready to make a move. Satisfied they had not altered their routine, he knew it was safe to go in.

When moving about, Sampson dressed casually and traveled light. If on a mission to obtain something he or the others needed, he would only take along the tools of his trade: a satchel containing a weapon, ammunition clips, and assorted jewelry. Hidden away, strapped to his calf, was his favorite toy; the ever-present commando dagger. In close combat with the need for stealth and silence, he believed there wasn't a more dependable weapon in the world.

Since it was a return trip, he was also burdened with the goods he had to bring back. As he rode the elevator up to the penthouse suite, a large duffel bag stuffed with military fatigues sat on the floor beside him.

Carrying his goods, Sampson cautiously walked along the long Persian carpets that served as runners down the wide hallway. If the world had not gone to hell, he might have been impressed at the fine wood floors, ancient furnishings, and luxurious adornments of the pre-war structure.

When he reached the penthouse, before he even had a chance to knock and signal to Susan he was back, the door started to open. In the blink of an eye, Sampson was out of sight with his back against the wall and the 9mm automatic at the ready position.

He saw the shadow on the floor before he saw the person's head, which was hidden around the corner of the narrow alcove. Immediately, he recognized the high hair as Susan's--and he allowed himself to exhale. There was no danger, but still, Sampson wanted to teach her a lesson about being careful. He crouched low, ducked his shoulder and did a perfectly executed leg sweep with his left arm.

Undercutting Susan's legs so severely made her start to fall to her side and backwards. Before anyone with normal human reflexes could have reacted, she found herself draped over Sampson's shoulder, completely helpless. It happened so fast, she didn't have time to react or scream. She didn't know how close she had come to slamming her head on the floor before he had caught her in his arms and swung her over his shoulder.

As her sense of orientation reset and she realized the predicament she was in, Susan felt the blood rush to her cheeks. She inhaled deeply, preparing herself to scream like a Banshee in heat. It was then that the knot in her calf muscle from Sampson's initial blow registered in her brain.

"Uhhhhgghh!" she moaned as the muscle cramped up and locked her foot into an unbreakable, unnatural curl.

"Yeah, that's gonna leave a bruise. What'd I tell ya about walking out the door without looking first?"

"I was going to, you fucker, but you hit me before I had a chance!"

What followed was a tirade of curses and a vicious assault on Sampson's lower back and buttocks. Susan used her tiny, balled-up fists to launch the counter-attack, but she was unable to do any meaningful damage.

Whenever Susan went into her hardened, street-smart, Jersey Girl routine, it made Sampson chuckle--and this was no exception. He knew of her upbringing in a well-to-do, strict Catholic family, which perfectly matched her nature and appearance. But, she had also told him of her rebellious side. Playing the bad girl from the wrong side of

218

the tracks was something she had brought with her into adulthood. Not only did it give her the capacity to be tough when push came to shove, but she could also shamelessly swear like a sailor when the need presented itself or it served her purpose.

While she continued her futile assault, he carried her into the penthouse and set her down gently on the carpeted floor. Sampson looked around, expecting the others to appear. He was surprised no one else had come to see what the ruckus was. After he shut and secured the door, he grabbed Susan's leg and started to rub her injured calf while simultaneously forcing her toes toward her shin to release the cramp he had caused.

"Where is everyone?"

Susan winced as he rubbed, feeling the exact spot where his forearm had hit her. "I would've told you if you didn't fuckin' attack me. Damn it, Sampson, what the hell were you thinking?"

"I was thinking you should be more careful. I'll ask you again, where the hell is everyone?"

"There're out looking for Darla."

"Looking for Darla? What do you mean?"

"I mean she's snuck out--she's gone, took off and didn't say a damn thing to anyone."

"And the others went out to find her?"

"Isn't that what I just said?" Her ego also bruised, Susan's voice was filled with anger-laced sarcasm.

"Susan, that has to be the dumbest move--"

"Well, what did you want them to do? You know Darla's not well. They have to try and find her."

Sampson stopped rubbing Susan's leg and let her foot rest on his thigh as he continued his rant, "Yeah, I knew that lady was fucked in the head the first time I laid eyes on her--shit, I've never seen anyone pamper two Berettas like they were babies, have you?" Not waiting for an answer, he asked, "Did she take the guns with her?"

"Yeah, so?"

"So, she can take care of herself. Your sister and your friends can't--and I don't give a shit what you say, if they get caught, I'm not going to risk my ass to save them."

"Save them from what?" Susan asked, knowing the answer the second she spat out the question.

The roving patrols would nail them in a heartbeat if they went down the wrong road that would put them into close proximity. After that, Susan could only assume they would be tagged and given new IDs. Launching a rescue attempt for Liz, Carlos, and Michelle was not something she had thought about when they discovered Darla had gone missing. Now that Susan thought about it, she knew Sampson was right--partially. The others should have stayed put.

Even though they couldn't be sure, they had collectively reached the conclusion that Michelle was a person of interest the military and the police wanted to capture. If they wanted the exact location of the secret, high-yielding Canadian gold mine where they found the huge vein, or the technology used to reach the gold, Michelle was the one who had it. And, she had been the one to show her hand before the crisis, when she was working so hard and so fast to take the trusts public.

Now that the world had moved on and because she was not one of the elite few, the valuables she and the others possessed were in play. They all knew that authorities would do just about anything to get what they wanted--and that put Michelle at great risk.

Sampson didn't even bother to respond to her question. Instead, he just glared at her with fire in his eyes.

It was the first time Susan had seen Sampson so angry. It was also the first time he was so curt with her. She didn't know if it was because the others had gone out into the dangerous streets or because she had come down so hard on him. Whatever the case, she didn't like the way he was acting or the way he was looking at her. For the first time since they hooked up, Susan was actually afraid of him.

There was a knock at the door that startled them both. Sampson let Susan's leg drop to the floor as her turned and raised his weapon to chest level.

Before he had a chance to speak or open the door, they heard a man's voice.

"It's me Carlos--open the door."

"Anyone with you?" Sampson asked.

"Liz, Michelle, and King Kong, who do you think?" The last part was the signal, letting Sampson know they were alone and the coast was clear. No mention of King Kong meant trouble.

Sampson opened the door and, using the weapon in his right hand, motioned hastily for the others to come in. "Move it! Move it! Let's go! Let's go!" He crouched down, moved quickly along the floor to the alcove, and checked around the corner: left, right, and then left again. Seeing everything was clear, he stood up, backed up, and started to secure the door. Behind him, the others were talking and he picked up on their conversation.

"...there was no sign of her."

"Do you think we should go back out and try again? Maybe search the park?" Liz asked, her tone gave away how worried she was.

"No!" Sampson responded from behind the others. His voice was loud, deep, and commanding as he projected his authority. "If she's gone, she's gone, and she'll have to take care of herself."

"How can you say that?" Liz was incredulous. "The woman is helpless we just can't--"

"Yes, we can, and no, she's not helpless. She's got her 'babies' with her, doesn't she?" Sampson turned and picked up his belongings, making it clear there was no point in arguing.

So stunned by how callous the ex-Marine was being, the others were initially unable to react or respond.

Finally, Carlos was able to loose his tongue, "Is that what they teach you in the military, is that what they mean by duty, loyalty, and honor?"

"Duty to who? Some crazy woman who can't get over her husband being killed? She's loyal to him, good, it doesn't mean I have to be loyal to her."

"That's real brave, Major Dan," Liz spat out with malice.

Sampson's eyes moved from Liz to Carlos and then to Susan. His steely, unblinking stare was disturbing. After a long pause, he decided to leave no doubt in their mind where he stood. "No, letting her go out on her own is the smart thing to do. She would have been dead weight to us."

The pronouncement made Michelle gasp.

Not paying any attention to her, Sampson continued, "You're all gonna learn, to be brave, you have to be stupid and it's the stupid ones who get killed. It's only the smart ones who survive to fight another day. If you want to live to fight another day, leave it be, let Darla go. If you do go after her, as far as I'm concerned, you're on your own."

"And you're an asshole..." Susan said under her breath, barely loud enough for everyone to hear.

*****

It was the day Sampson was to meet up with Richard Clearmont at the zoo. But first, before he took the D Train up to the Bronx, he wanted to see if there were any changes at Andrew Steven's headquarters. After he extracted all of the useful intel Carlos has gathered, he had seen for himself where the new leaders of North America had established a New York base of operations. As he had done his entire career, on every mission behind enemy lines, Sampson made it a point to sniff out and establish the weaknesses at the enemy's headquarters. He knew the intelligence he gathered may be of no use, but he had to check--just in case a target of opportunity presented itself. This was his chance to go out for one final reconnoiter.

Carlos lobbied heavily so that Sampson would let him go along. As an inducement, he claimed he knew of a propitious vantage point that would allow them to safely scope out the area around the West 97th Street building. Because of the security on the ground, Sampson had not been able to get close, so he hoped taking Carlos along would provide him with the first opportunity to observe the layout around the building where Andrew Stevens was running the world.

Another factor weighing on Sampson's decision to take a guide was the fact that Carlos had graduated from Fordham University, right across Southern Boulevard from the zoo. Not only was he familiar with the territory, but he also knew what Richard Clearmont looked like. Carlos argued to Sampson that having an extra set of eyes could only help.

Although the information Carlos provided had been helpful, Sampson was reluctant to let anyone come along besides Susan. At least she knew how he operated and was careful not to get in his way. With much hesitation, he relented and, for the second time, he broke his own rules and allowed Carlos to join him.

It was early in the morning when they left the penthouse. Flakes of wet, fluffy snow were falling, the second early storm of the season, and the city was coated in white. On foot, Susan, Carlos, and Sampson walked several blocks to the west before turning north and making their way to a building that was still under construction. All three were dressed like they were going to work and did he best they could to blend in with the pedestrians on the sidewalks. At that time of the day, the streets should have been packed with traffic but even at the West 96th Street intersections of Broadway and Amsterdam, the only vehicles on the road were busses and military patrols. It was strange to witness, but the lack of traffic allowed them to pick out the roving patrols with electronic sensors.

Although the structure Carlos led them to was only partially completed, they were able to make their way in and up to the top floor. Standing behind mirrored windows above and to the southeast of MYB's headquarters, the three looked down from their perch and analyzed the view below.

The building Stevens was using as a headquarters sat back from the street, even further back from the wide sidewalk than the other buildings. Looking around, Sampson took note of how only a few modern structures in the area towered above the target and how all of the older buildings were limited to the maximum height allowed by the building codes of the past. There was simply no way to go in from above.

The activity outside of MYB's New York office made the area seem more like a military compound than a city street. An entire block of West 97th Street between Broadway and Amsterdam Avenue had been cordoned off by armored personnel carriers. Soldiers were posted at both ends of the street and patrols walked back and forth from end to end beside a Humvee that was on a continuous circuit.

The small bank and upscale boutique occupying the lots beside the headquarters had been commandeered and were converted into facilities more useful for the military. On the roofs of several strategic buildings on the block, snipers were posted and were actively scanning the perimeter for threats with infrared scopes. Cameras and motion detection sensors had been wired up at strategic locations in both directions from the headquarters. As good as Sampson was at black bag operations, with so much security and hardware, getting into Steven's building from ground level would have been impossible.

It was not a decision that came in haste but was grounded on decades of an experience as an assassin. He would not go in to get Andrew Stevens. Instead, in order to liquidate the Special Master, a man he should have killed months before, he'd simply have to wait for him to come out.

"Was it like this the last time you saw the building, Carlos?" Sampson nodded toward the glass structure less than 150 feet in front of them.

"No. There weren't nearly as many soldiers and the block wasn't completely sealed off."

Susan stood quietly, peering out of the same large glass panel as the men. After they started talking about the need to chop off the head of the snake in order to change the tide, she tuned out on what they were saying. The strategy and tactics they were talking about dealt with all topics that were not all that different from what the politicians said every election cycle: freedom, security, and the right to do this or that. It was all macho bullshit to her and she was at the point of not really caring who ran the world or what condition it was in. All she really cared about was that her kids were safe and that they were able to live a full, normal life.

Because of the threat of the virus Maxwell York and Andrew Stevens had unleashed on the world--she could not help but feel disturbed about what had been taken away from them all--their peace of mind. Unlike the way she used to be, Susan felt absolutely no sympathy or compassion for the likes of Andrew Stevens and what they planned to do to him. The situation she found herself in, she knew, had changed her. For unleashing what amounted to a biological weapon on her and her kids, Stevens and everyone he was associated with had to pay and pay with their lives.

Looking down at the beautiful white-coated city, everything seemed so eerily calm, which was so strange, so surreal, and, not for the first time, it made her wonder briefly what it would mean if what she was observing was really the new normal. Thoughts of Orwell's 1984 and Huxley's Brave New World immediately came to mind.

Casting one last glance at the building where Andrew Stevens was holed up, Sampson knew it was unlikely he would ever get a chance to snuff out the man who called himself "Special Master". The entire block was a modern day fortress and, barring some sort of disaster, getting in would be all but impossible.

"Come on," Sampson announced to the others. Let's change and get ourselves up to the Bronx. I'm itchin' to hear what Richard Clearmont has to say about the virus."

Chapter Nineteen

"I don't care what you think, soldier! If anyone tries to get onto this block or even tries to sneak a peek at Andrew Stevens, you have your orders--shoot first, ask questions later. Do I have to remind you, there's an assassin on the loose and if he wanted to, he could shoot your tiny little pecker off at a thousand meters? No one gets in these gates without proper authorization. Do you hear me, son?"

"Yes, sir!"

Colonel Turney was livid. The legendary retied Marine Major Daniel Sampson was in the area, on the prowl, and the Special Master had to be protected at all costs. His job, as ordered by Lieutenant General Smythe, was to protect the civilian puke, and here it was, the soldiers assigned to sentry duty were letting people walk right onto the block without authorization. The boys seemed to be more interested in the rich widows and beautiful young daughters who habituated the area than security. No wonder they never stood a chance in Afghanistan, the kids sent over there had absolutely no sense of duty or responsibility, the colonel mused. They were not like his generation.

Hearing a noise drew his attention to the perimeter. Colonel Turney watched the gates open and a black limousine slowly crawled past the men stationed at the guard shack.

"Holy mother of Christ! What the hell are you doing letting that car in here without checking it for explosives? Sergeant Burke!"

"Yes, Colonel?"

"Get on that." Shaking his head in disappointment, Turney spun on his heel and walked toward the gold-shaded glass and steel building he was supposed to protect.

"Yes, sir," Burke responded to the colonel's back.

Striding purposefully toward his squad and the limo, he yelled in a deep voice loud enough to rattle bones, "Who the hell is in that car and what the hell is it doing on my street?"

"Sarge, that's Senator O'Connell. He's got an appointment with Mr. Stevens, and--"

"I don't give a god-damn who he is or what he's doing here, son. What I wanna know is why the hell aren't you on your hands and knees looking for explosives? That man's not special, now hop to it!"

"Yes, Sergeant!"

Butch O'Connell, a one-time respected United States Senator, was livid. Not only did he have to endure the indignity of a pat-search before the soldiers let him into the building, but they also refused to let his security detail come into the building with him.

Sitting in a glass and chrome lobby decorated with modern, pretentious works of art, white leather sofas and a feminine peach carpet, Big Butch felt naked. It had been a long time since he felt so small, so weak, and so out of control. He had been the syndicate's point man in the Senate and was the one who had worked so hard for so many years getting everything in place. Yet, here it was with all of his work paying dividends and the big man in charge was treating him like a commoner, a criminal even.

Raymond Behn walked into the room and extended a hand. "Sorry to keep you waiting, Senator--"

"Yeah, I bet you are. Where the hell's Stevens? I've been waiting here for a gosh-darn eternity!"

Ray knew only several minutes had passed and the former Senator's outburst quickly reminded him why he couldn't stand the man. "So, Butch, what have you got for us."

O'Connell was holding several leather document binders under his left arm. His briefcase had been searched and left behind, by orders of the armed agents, near the door. "I'm not about to give it to you, I want to give it to Stevens myself." As he spoke, his arm perceptibly squeezed a little tighter on the binders.

"Come, come now, Butch," Raymond said in a conciliating tone, "we're both grownups here and you'll get the credit you deserve."

"You're god-damn right I'm gonna get the credit I deserve. None of you would have been able to do shit if it wasn't for me. Now that you've got your grubby little fingers busy pushing all the buttons, you think you can just push me aside?"

"No one's pushing you aside, Senator."

"That's right, I am a Senator and how dare you address me so casually. You don't know me, son, you may not have any idea who you're dealing with."

Raymond knew exactly who he was dealing with and he knew exactly why O'Connell was there. Butch had been able to convince almost the entire House and Senate to voluntarily resign at the end of their terms. He was carrying the formal, endorsed documents proclaiming as much. He was also in possession of the President's and Vice President's immediate abdication.

It was just a formality, to keep things nice and tidy for public consumption, but public relations demanded that a majority of the people stay convinced that everything they were doing was on the up and up. Yes, as a Senator, O'Connell had been a valuable tool, but that was all he had been; an instrument that had outlasted his usefulness. Losing his patience, Raymond let his tact fall to the wayside and unleashed his true disposition.

"The fact that there no longer is a senate seems to have slipped your mind, Butch. You have no more power or sway than I say you do." Much like the others, the newfound power and authority had quickly gone to Raymond's head. It was not hard to get caught up in a God-complex when one had almost absolute authority over the

Americas. "Now, just give me what you came here to give me and be on your way."

O'Connell's fat, pasty face immediately flashed a blazing hot red. "Be on my way? Are you fuckin' kidding me, Behn? You think you can just dismiss me like some sort of houseboy running your errands? I've got a mind to--"

Raymond turned away from Butch and looked at one of the agents standing near the glass double-doors. With nothing more than a nod and gesture with his chin, the agent stepped forward and grasped the former senator by the arm.

"What the fuck do you think you're doing? Get your goddamn hands off of me!"

As the bulky agent with arms that strained the fabric of his jacket gathered up Big Butch in a hold that made him howl in pain and wheeze as he gasped for breath, Raymond snatched the leather binders out from O'Connell's arm. He secured the documents and stepped back, watching two other men come in and shove the obese, gasping senator to the floor.

Behind the agents, who were busy trying to cuff O'Connell behind the back, Colonel Turney sauntered into the room. He didn't look the least bit surprised to see three men all but ripping the fat man's arms out of their sockets in an attempt to link the man's much too short arms behind his back. Turney liked and trusted Raymond Behn a lot more than he liked Stevens, but still, that wasn't saying much. For a civilian, at least Behn had enough common sense to treat the men holding the guns, and all of the other cards, with a touch of deference.

"Do you want him killed?" Colonel Turney asked nonchalantly. "No, just take him to the Bloomsburg internment camp. I want that pompous, self-righteous ass to experience how the other half lives."

Shortly after Butch O'Connell was escorted out of

the building, Raymond made his way to the residential section of the executive penthouse. He walked calmly down the wide hallway and knocked gently. Turning the knob, he found the door unlocked and poked his head through the opening he created pushing the door open.

"Andrew, you up?"

The sound of a yelp in a high-pitched voice burst through the air at the same time as a flash of white sheet could be seen as the woman next to Andrew quickly pulled the covers up over her head.

"Don't sweat it, Becky, it's just me," Raymond commented while sporting a Cheshire cat smile.

"Get out of here you creep, don't you know how to knock!" she yelled, knowing her outburst was pointless.

Andrew sat up, ignoring her. "What time is it?"

"Nine-thirty a.m., you just missed your appointment with Butch and he was quite upset."

"I don't give a shit. Did he bring you the letters of resignation?"

Raymond tapped the leather binders as he stepped through the door, casting a bright beam of light into the once darkened room. "They're right here. I'll put them on the dresser."

Without waiting for approval, Behn walked into the room and sat the binders down, looking around as if seeing the room for the first time. Seeing Becky's ripped thong lying on the floor, he bent over, picked them up and held them up to the light. "Victoria's Secret, very nice."

Becky poked her head out from under the silk sheet. Her usually perfect hair was mussed and the lack of foundation and rouge gave away a few years, making her look a little closer to her true age. "Give me those, you asshole! What the hell is wrong with you?"

"Hey, I was just saying--"

Andrew interrupted them, "What, are you two still in high school?" Again ignoring Becky, Andrew yawned

231

and directed his attention to Raymond. "So what did you do with Butch?"

"I did what you said you were going to do, I let him down easily."

"You mean to tell me he didn't put up a fuss after all he did for us?"

"I didn't say he didn't put up a fuss. Don't worry about it, though, I have a feeling the next time you see him, Big Butch will be a changed man."

"Whatever. Listen, I don't have time to go over those documents. Why don't you take 'em down to the media center and have scanned copies sent to the networks."

"Are you going to release a statement?" Raymond asked with an eyebrow raised.

"You do it, you're the head honcho here in North America, aren't you?" Stevens smiled and stretched his arms to the sides. "Better get used to facing the public, Raymond--you know the election is coming up and I have a feeling you're gonna win big."

Raymond couldn't help but smile, knowing without a doubt he would win a seat on the North American Regional Council. Since they owned and operated the election apparatus, they knew the fix was in. As they had planned, Andrew would step out of the limelight and focus on fostering good relations between the seven regions. He would take the position as a type of world ambassador and judge that Maxwell York meant to take.

Raymond, along with the six other chairmen of the seven regions, would run their domains as they saw fit but with an avowed respect for the dictates and opinion of Stevens--who would retain the power to negotiate and settle disputes between the seven councils. The goal was peace and prosperity for all regions and the compact they were preparing to sign after the election would solidify the establishment of the one-world government.

Shortly after Andrew gave his opinion on how the press release should sound, and they discussed several other pertinent topics, Raymond left the room, closing the door behind him.

The second she felt it was safe to reveal herself, Becky threw the sheet off her naked body and kicked her legs over the side of the king-sized bed. Standing on the plush, ruby carpeting, she stood up to her full height, raising her head high, pulling her stomach in, and arching her back for the short walk to the master bathroom. It was as if the shame and embarrassment she felt just seconds before had never happened.

"Are you going to take a shower with me or not?" she asked.

"I wasn't the one who was such a dirty little girl last night, now was I?"

"No, you weren't, but do you really want to go to your meeting with Adam Smythe smelling like you just spent the entire night having sex?"

"Maybe," he quipped, then under his breath, "It'd probably be the first time the old man smelled pussy in ages."

Still naked, Becky stepped off the marble of the bathroom floor back into the bedroom. Putting a hand on her ample hip, she asked, "What did you just say?"

"Never mind. Are you going to join us at the meeting?"

"As much as I'd love to listen to our boys talk about war games and all of those interesting tactical details, I'm sorry, Andrew, but I'll have to miss it."

He sensed the condescension in her tone but did not snap back at her obvious sarcasm. If there was one person in the world who could control him, it was Becky. The more power he gained, the more they had openly spent time together, and the more he was falling in love with her. As he looked at her curvaceous body and watched her run her

233

long, thin fingers through her hair, teasing out tangles, a strange thought popped into his head. He would give up everything for her, give her anything she wanted. She was in his blood, she possessed him, and in turn, he was starting to have a burning desire to possess her. Never in his life had he let his passions control him--but this time it was different. Having so much power was intoxicating, but he didn't want to have it all to himself. That would be like throwing the world's biggest party and only inviting himself. He wanted to share the wealth, share everything with Becky.

Ignoring the fact that she was just patronizing him, he asked, "So, what do you have to do that's so important, Beck?"

She turned and walked back into the bathroom. With the water running, she shouted, "I have a conference call with Sir Philip and his Swiss counterpart in charge of the International Bank of Exchange."

"What are you expecting?"

Becky poked her head out of the bathroom door, pulling a toothbrush out of her mouth. "I expect he's gonna tell me the good Queen Mother has pledged the gold reserves of the British Empire to back the new Euros."

"And if she doesn't?" Andrew asked, sincerely interested.

"Well, Sir Philip and the rest of the European Council are going to have a lot of explaining to do."

"Hmm. That's not too comforting."

"Don't worry, I've got it under control. You trust me, don't you, Andrew?"

"Of course I do,"

"Good. Now get your ass in this shower and wash my back."

Andrew whispered, "I love you, Becky," knowing fully well she could not hear him and had already stepped into the shower.

It was less than an hour later when a convoy of Humvees and armored personnel carriers drove onto West 97th Street. Expecting the arrival the of Lieutenant General, Colonel Turney had been walking the beat all morning, making sure his units were on point. Besides, he wanted to make sure he would not miss the opportunity to get a private audience with the man who had become the most powerful military commander in the world--if not by rank, at least by association.

Colonel Turney had gone to school with Smythe, and they had run the same career-driven gauntlets in order to reach the ranks they had reached. Gruffer and certainly less political than Adam, James Turney had been passed up several times for promotion to Brigadier General. It ate him up almost as much as watching the men he had trained and led so valiantly waste their skills and ammunition on American soil, spilling American blood. He knew if he was able to get into Smythe's head, they could reverse what was taking place--or better yet--subvert that candy-assed wanna-be, Andrew Stevens.

The convoy came to a stop with the center vehicle properly positioned so that it would be the shortest walk possible from the APC to the headquarters of MYB, Ltd. The relatively new building had, by default, become the new Capitol of the Americas. Everyone stationed on that block knew several floor housed vast computer networks. And, everyone working at the major midtown banks all the way to Wall Street knew all commercial activity was now being routed through the basement and sub-basement computer systems of that same building. The boutique owners, restaurateurs, and even the hookers seemed to be aware of the fact that any business they transacted using the new Federal IDs somehow led to the building with the gold-shaded windows and brass handled doors.

Smythe stepped out of the front seat of a Humvee and instinctively slowed to look around and take in his surroundings. He immediately noticed the snipers and electronic sensors strategically placed around the neighborhood. Knowing his escorts were getting antsy and wanted him to keep moving, the general started walking faster, heading for the carved marble steps leading up to the building.

As Smythe strode forward, Colonel Turney fell into step beside him, not bothering to salute the man he had known since before they grew in their short hairs. He extended a hand as they walked, "Here, one of those fake Cuban cigars that you like."

Grabbing the tube from his friend's hand and smiling, Smythe questioned, "I thought smoking inside of New York City Buildings was illegal?"

"Fuck the rules, this is our world."

Smythe couldn't help but chuckle. He stopped and gripped his friend in a congenial embrace. "It's good to see you, Jimmy. How are things going up here?"

Turney leaned in and whispered, "I'm not persuaded we're under the best leadership." He stepped back and looked long and hard at Smythe's face, trying to take a measure of his reaction. The colonel did not sense any negative vibes, so he continued. "We've gotta talk, Adam, in private."

Without completely giving away how he felt about the situation, Smythe smiled grimly. In a loud, lighthearted voice that was clearly out of sync with his emotions, he replied, "Well, what are you waiting for, lead the way."

*****

The chilly breeze off of the ocean kept the Atlantic City Boardwalk deserted, which was just the way Maxwell York and his adjutants wanted it. Seven floors above the beach, looking out over the white-capped breakers coming onto shore, York was in a foul mood. He could not distract himself from the pervasive thoughts that dominated his mind.

The waves coming in on the choppy ocean reminded him of the view from his Cape Cod estate, the only home he had ever known. He had lost everything when Sampson took it upon himself to turn the manor into a pile of rubble. However, the sense of betrayal he felt was not even close to the treachery brought on by Andrew Steven. As far as Andrew was concerned, there was absolutely no excuse for what he had done.

Maxwell had taken the young, ambitious scion of the Rockefeller clan under his wing, given him an education no one else in the world could have give him, and established the boy as his heir-apparent. It had to have been the lust for power that drove Stevens to want more than what he already had; and that made about as much sense as an alcoholic swimming in a vat of Jack Daniels. The fact his protégé could not patiently wait his turn to take the reins of power demonstrated a flaw in his character, a flaw that had been hidden for years.

Because of the severity of the personal affront, Maxwell York felt that redress for the betrayal had to be something worse than death--because death would be much too easy. Instead, he felt he would only be vindicated only if Stevens suffered a grave indignity --and that would be to strip him of everything.

York had sent Chris Carlton back to Utah so he could prepare to take control of the drones. At the NSA's Data Center, the war room was already set up for teams of operatives to program in the UAV's sorties. All that was needed to obtain proficiency in programming the drones was as much training as went into learning how to play a video game.

The extremely deadly, self-directed warplanes would be launched and follow the entered command parameters autonomously. And, for the first time in history, each drone would have the capability and authority to select its own targets and launch its own weapons. After the initial programming, the only thing Chris Carlton and his crew had to do was monitor the situation and, if necessary, change or override the mission parameters.

Left behind in Atlantic City were several of the most trusted former agents who, no matter what occurred, would not leave York unguarded for a single second. They were all masters with various weapons, experts in hand-to-hand combat, and qualified in every form of electronic communications. Maxwell felt absolutely secure, knowing he was in good hands.

York turned away from the window and looked at the image of a newscaster on a large screen television. She was going over the same details she had already reported for the hundredth time. Ti Kwai Fong, the Chairman of the China Domain's Council of Seven, had been executed. Fong, a dear friend and one of York's closest allies, had been targeted and taken out in what was obviously a sanctioned hit. Seeing him fall victim to an assassination, and, as a result, witnessing all of the nations in the Chinese sphere of influence return to a state of chaos, was disheartening. There was no doubt in York's mind, the assassination of Fong was orchestrated by Andrew Stevens. Hearing about Fong's death was all it took to push York to act.

Maxwell no longer had a choice he had to get back in the game before he lost more of his staunchest allies.

"George, is the secure connection to Utah established?" Maxwell was well aware of the built in capabilities of MIN-OPS because his company had been in charge of creating it. Since he knew the scope of the monitoring programs, he was leery of using any form of communication unless it was specifically designed to elude the agents and computers monitoring everything. To maintain communication with all of his most important contacts, he had been forced to activate a back-channel system one of his other companies had helped design.

George, a wiry, middle-aged man with all the hallmarks of Irish ancestry, handed him a satellite phone-- one that piggybacked on the signals to and from the latest generation of spy satellite. As per its design specifications, it maintained an encrypted NSA link to the Utah Data Center.

"Here you are, sir. Just press the send button and you'll be patched right through to Carlton."

"Thank you, George."

York did as instructed and held the somewhat bulky phone to his ear. "Hello, Chris. Yes, yes, I can hear you perfectly. Listen, this is what I want you to do; get however many squadrons of drones Mr. Yoo has ready and start getting them into position." He paused and listened for a second before responding, "I know, I know, but we have to move now or it may be too late. The refueling takers will take off from Scott Air force Base in Illinois in exactly four hours. Don't worry, the tankers' crews are with us, just coordinate the rendezvous with General Stark and make sure you get those drones to the Titusville, Pennsylvania airport."

The three men standing around York watched him nod and then tell Carlton that the munitions and fuel would be ready at the civilian airport, and once the UAV's were armed and refueled they had to be made ready for re-launch as soon as possible. York went on to stress that once the UAV's preparedness was established the drones should be ready to be set loose with no delay.

"What are the targets?" Maxwell asked into the phone, as if surprised by the question. He let out a quick snort of derision, revealing his innermost emotions about what he was about to do. "There will be two targets; one is to be protected, the other destroyed. The Pittsfield Foundry holding the stockpile of gold is to be protected from the ground forces of General Smythe. The target to be destroyed is my Headquarters on West 97th Street in New York City. I want you to commit whatever forces you deem necessary to destroy that building when I give the command, do we understand each other?"

After another brief exchange with Chris, York severed the connection, laid the large phone on the table, and turned to face George. With no hesitation or trepidation about what may come, he barked out, "Get the helicopter ready, we're going to New York."

Chapter Twenty

It hadn't been that long ago, several years, but it felt like yesterday when his wife, Rachel, and Donny's wife, Angela, became sick and died under some very curious circumstances. Now, Donny, his younger brother, was gone as well and the entire world had gone to hell.

Richard had spent millions of dollars and countless hours trying to figure out how a spirochete bacterium could kill some people so quickly and be transmitted sexually so easily with others. He had spent every penny he could get his hands on and even set up his own research facility to collect data to try and prove Lyme Disease was killing people. That, he knew, had the capacity to cause a national crisis--and why he believed the politicians and corporations had worked so hard to silence him. But now, ironically, now that he had the proof and the understanding of what was really going on, there was no one to turn to for help.

Walking along the wide footpath leading from Hughes Hall along the edge of the grassy quadrangle to Keating Hall on the campus of Fordham University, Richard Clearmont paused and looked over to Jack Coffee Stadium and the barren football field. Memories of a past life flashed before his eyes. He remembered watching his younger brother playing on that field, the cheering crowds, the tailgate parties in the parking lot, and the unruly crowds at the local bars on Homecoming weekend.

Those were fond memories, but the memories no longer made him smile. Since that time, he had lost so much that the good times seemed trite and meaningless. He had planned to stop off at Fordham as a tribute to his brother ever since being asked to rendezvous in the Bronx. After that, just like everything else he had loved, he would let Donny go.

After so many battles with the insurance companies,

Department of Health administrators, and the CDC, Richard was conditioned to take any risks necessary to learn as much as could about his singular obsession, finding out what had killed his wife. Because of that conditioning, he was unfazed by the prospects of yet another adventure, even if it meant leaving his comfortable, safe lab in Upstate New York to meet a stranger in the Belly of the Beast.

With so much going on in the world, and the realization he was completely alone, Richard no longer feared being ensnared by the people who had been trying to silence him for years. In fact, despite the incredible changes taking place, he felt apathetic as far as his life was concerned. Yet, he remained more cautious and vigilant than ever in order to do what he believed he was destined to do--find out what had killed his precious Rachel.

The trip from Rochester to the Bronx had been relatively uneventful and now all he had to do get to the designated meeting spot and wait for a guy named Dan. Although coming into the city on an overcrowded train had been suffocating, it was not what he had expected. Actually, he was too distracted to care; the anxiety about finally meeting the people who had helped him so much was compulsively dominating his thoughts.

From the time Richard read that first message and the offer to meet outside of the Bronx Zoo, talking to whoever had the information about his wife's illness, and finding out exactly what they knew, became new obsession. Teased with information about the puzzle he had been trying to solve for years, he had not been able to wait for some blind meeting at the Bronx Zoo with some stranger. Instead, he became so intrigued by the mysterious messages sent to him, he had taken the initiative, and the risk, to seek out the person who claimed to know how and why his wife had died.

It had not been hard for a man like him, a man with an extremely analytical brain, to figure out where the messages had come from. Whoever had reached out to him had to have been involved with Donny and his friends. That much was for sure. There was no other way to explain how the person who contacted him knew exactly who he was, that he was a molecular biologist, and that he was looking for answers to such specific questions. On top of that, how else would they have known both he and Donny had been infected by the bacterium that causes Lyme disease, even though they weren't bitten by ticks--and neither one of them got sick?

He quickly concluded everything sent to him via e-mail pointed to the Seven Rams, or people who associated with Donny. Since that was the path of least resistance, it was the first avenue of inquiry he pursued. It took him just one phone call to track down the most knowledgeable source of information about his brother, and that was to Donny's old friend, Michelle Rivera-Alvarez.

As soon as he was able to get in contact with her in Manhattan, Richard knew for sure he found the source. Being as cryptic as possible, because they knew they were being monitored, they were able to communicate on a very basic level. Using coded language, Michelle had been able to tip him off that she was with the man he was seeking. However, even that vacuous dialogue led to Richard acquiring the information that would, once again, change his life forever.

Once the voluminous data files about the virus were sent to him, a whole new world had opened up. The information about the virus contained in the files from Hamilton Genomics had blown Richard's mind. The details of the perverse genetic manipulation that firm was involved in--and what had been unleashed on an unsuspecting public was nothing short of astonishing.

Richard turned and started walking again, following the sidewalk out toward Southern Boulevard. Once outside of the university's gates, he turned right and walked past the

New York Botanical Garden. Soon, he would have to traverse Fordham Road and the cross over to the other side of Southern Boulevard so he would be in front of the Bronx Zoo. The people he expected to meet would be coming soon, and he did not want to be late. Yet, he took his time. He needed to think, to clear his mind, and try to figure out what he was going to do with what he knew.

When he was alive, Donny used to laugh at him when Richard would talk about a conspiracy to cover up the disease that killed their wives. Richard thought wistfully, if Donny was still alive, seeing how everything had shaken out, his brother wouldn't think the conspiracy theories were so funny. Now that he finally knew the truth, a truth so frightening that it made him ill when he first figured it out the magnitude of what had been unleashed. Deciding on a simple, cogent way to explain what he knew to a troubled, distrustful world was something he had been unable to figure out. Getting the word out, and warning others about what was infecting them all, was all that really mattered. That, he knew, was the way Rachel would have wanted it.

As far as Richard was concerned, there were no more authorities he could go to and no more justice to be had. Some of the same insurance company CEOs who he had been going after were now in control of, well, everything. Just like so many other executives from the drug industry, HMO's, and state insurance regulators, their names had been popping up as part of local, regional, state, and even national ruling councils. The world had become the playground of the rich and powerful--and they were not even bothering to hide the fact that they had no one to answer to for what they were doing.

The unelected executives taking the reins of power had not hesitated to project their influence and demonstrate their authority. Just looking at the streets devoid of cars, yet still heavily patrolled by armed military men in all-black uniforms, revealed how dire the situation had become. The Bronx looked like a post-apocalyptic world without the apocalypse.

Through the media outlets, he had also seen the round-ups and mass detentions, the modern day internment camps and reeducation centers reportedly built as facilities to hold the people who were being called dangerous revolutionaries. But, Richard knew better. He knew some of the people who had been taken away and locked up in Bloomsburg or other internment camps and they were anything but revolutionaries. It was a frightening time for everyone and, although it was not even close to the worst-case scenario he had envisioned for America, it still felt eerily familiar to him.

Coping with a strange new world with its undefined boundaries and shifting sands had left Richard Clearmont with only one choice. He was determined to hook up with Michelle Rivera-Alvarez and the curious man who had sent him the Hamilton Genomics files. They knew the truth, and Richard just hoped that the path they were taking was the right one.

Just as Richard set foot on the sidewalk in front of the zoo, an odd-looking vehicle came crawling down the street in his direction. The strange car had both military and police insignia and a rack on the roof with numerous electronic sensors.

From what people on the train into New York had told him, he knew exactly what that type of car was meant for: to find people who had yet to get a valid ID. Because he did not have a new federal, genetically encoded identification card, Richard started to sweat. At any second, he knew the car could pull over and they would detain him. Zeroing in on warm bodies without valid ID's was what those cars were built to do--and they had him dead to rights. As hard as Richard tried, he could not avert his eyes. All he could do was watch as the vehicle approached him.

245

There were three Marines in the car, two men and a woman. The woman was sitting behind the wheel and had her hair tucked up under a hat. As the vehicle neared, Richard could not help but focus on the woman's big brown eyes and pouty lips. Observing how beautiful she was, and how out-of-place she looked, was not what froze him in his tracks. What caused him to stop and hold his breath was that he recognized her as the woman Donny was seeing when he died--the woman he was staring at had inherited the bulk of his brother's estate.

The black sedan came to a hard stop right in front of Richard Clearmont and the two men jumped out of the car, leaving the woman behind, seemingly ready to speed away.

"Get down on the ground!"

"Put your hands over your head."

"Don't move!"

The loud shouts coming from the men rushing toward him were more disorienting than anything. Richard was unable to decipher exactly what they were commanding him to do. Instinctively, he raised his arms and covered his head, pressing his elbows against his ears. Before he knew what was happening, the Marines had all but picked him up and carried him to the vehicle. After shoving him in the back and slamming the door, the car peeled out and took off down the street with sirens wailing and lights flashing.

When Richard regained the nerve to open his eyes and look up, the man sitting beside him had taken his hat off and was smiling. The much bigger Marine sitting in the front passenger seat was in a half-turn, arching his neck to glare at him. The woman who was driving had adjusted her mirror so she could sneak peeks at him while she drove. Oddly, her lips were parted and she looked even more startled than he did.

The thin man sitting beside him extended a hand. "Hi, I'm Carlos." Gesturing toward Sampson, he added, "and that's Major Dan."

Sampson grimaced at the appellation.

Richard reached out and took Carlos's hand. At the same time, he looked back up at the rearview mirror and caught another glimpse of the stunned woman.

Noticing the look, Carlos added, "That's Susan."

Smiling at her, Richard cleared his throat and finally found his voice. Hoarsely, all he could manage to say was, "I know."

Susan audibly gasped. It could not be him, it just simply could not be... "Donny? Donny, is that you?"

The sound of glass crashing into the windshield silenced Richard Clearmont's response.

*****

Sequestered in a private office on the ground floor of the MYB, Ltd., headquarters, General Smythe and Colonel Turney spoke in hushed tones. The room had been swept for bugs twice, yet they proceeded with an abundance of caution.

"So, what are you proposing, Jimmy?"

"What I'm suggesting is that we take out these yahoos and take over this whole damn country. This isn't the America I want, this isn't the America our fathers fought and died for. Besides, Adam, they don't respect us, they don't respect you--to them you're just a means of control."

"Come on, now, Stevens has given me free reign over the taskforce--and that's nothing to sneeze at. At this point it'd take the whole damn Marine Corps to bring us down--and they'd have one hell of a fight on their hands."

Despite his objection, it was clear Adam had been planning the coup in his head for some time, so Turney pushed forward, "Ya know, you just made my point for me. Who's there to stop us? All you'd have to do is send out word and half of the generals in the Army, along with all of their men, would be standing right behind you. You're that respected. The problem is, though, as soon as Stevens figures out your influence extends well beyond the Rapid Response Team and Special Forces, you're as good as dead."

Colonel Turney's words made the general take pause. In a world with no checks and balances, with power concentrated in a few hands, he really didn't have any protection beyond the loyalty of his comrades in arms. The civilian side had not yet consolidated their power and the country was still on edge. If there was a time to act, to protect himself, Jimmy was right; the time was ripe.

Smythe did not agree with the way things had transpired, not in the least. He tried to convince himself everything he had done up to that point was things he was ordered to do. And, like the Nazis during the Nuremberg trials, he believed that absolved him of responsibility. However, deep down, he knew there was a lot of blood on his hands, thousands upon thousands of people had been killed or detained because of his orders. That fact was eating him up from the inside out. On top of it all, he felt sickened by the fact that hardly anyone at the top had suffered even the slightest bit of hardship.

Smythe knew from personal experience and from what his men told him, pretty much everyone else in the country had been devastated in one way or another. Even those who were upper-middle class or wealthy had been financially wrecked. The result of the money games Stevens and his confederates had played was to throw everyone, except for the extremely wealthy, into privation. Because of what Stevens had told him during their last meeting, Smythe was painfully aware of that the contracts everyone was signing were a scam. The Americans, Canadians, and Mexicans participating in the required dollar-Amero swap and so-called debt consolidation were either oblivious to what was really going on or they didn't care.

No one seemed to realize was that in return for what seemed to be better terms on their loans, people were forfeiting all of their rights. Smythe wished more people recognized what Stevens was offering had one big string attached to it. Unfortunately, that string was a noose to tie around their own necks. The lack of insight, or apathy, whatever the case may be, was rather disturbing.

What the people did not know--the part Stevens had kept hidden--was that before long, there would be no jobs, no way to make a living, and no way to pay back the loans. Wherever possible, robots, drones, droids, whatever one chose to call them, would be doing the labor humans once did. When the people failed to repay their debts, everything would revert back to the Corporation of the United States of America, an entity fully owned and operated by Andrew Stevens and his partners. While the people used the Amero credits and ran up new debts to survive, they did not know that, eventually, the contracts everyone was being hoodwinked into signing would then bind them into a modern form of indentured servitude. Smythe hated himself for letting it happen so easily and taking part in the rape of his own country.

Andrew Stevens, the so-called, "Special Master," was nothing but a crooked banker who had caused, and was collecting on, the world's biggest bankruptcy. It was so distasteful to even consider, but it was the truth. The people, Smythe's soldiers included, were already gorging on the same capitalistic poison; they were swallowing the rotten bait hook, line, and sinker. With each new development, he regretted allowing himself to be pulled into the conspiracy.

"What do you think--how do we do this as painlessly as possible?"

"Painlessly as possible!" Turney shouted,

disregarding the need to be inconspicuous. "What have you turned into, Adam? I'm talking balls-to-the wall, all-out warfare. We leave no doubt who's in control and we take out any and all opposition. No more pussy-footing around and we do what we've been trained to do, we take the fight to them!"

Smythe could not help but laugh and he clapped his old school chum on the shoulder. He loved the old boy's fighting spirit, but, on this one, Turney had completely missed the boat. "What are we gonna do, Jimmy? Invade Martha's Vineyard? Firebomb Greenwich? We'll hunt down all the rich folks like they're Al-Qaeda and raid their compounds until every one-percenter on the planet hands over the keys to their Bentley!"

Turney was not used to being mocked and he bit his lip to stop himself from saying something he would regret. Instead, he let the scowl on his face and his eyes express everything he was thinking.

Seeing the look on Jimmy's face, Smythe let up on the laughter. "Look, Jimmy, I agree with you, and I wouldn't even have entertained this conversation if I didn't feel exactly the same." Raising his voice for the benefit of anyone who may have had their ear pressed to a wall, he went on, "Don't worry, Colonel, we'll take down the protesters and any opposition using any means necessary. Now, this is what we've got to do..."

Reverting back to hushed tones, and leaning close to Turney's ear, the general whispered, "We've got several primary targets that have to be taken down simultaneously. We've got to secure and maintain full control of the nuclear arsenal; we've got to commandeer the gold reserves At Fort Knox, West Point, the New York Federal Reserve, and that foundry in Pittsfield, Pennsylvania--"

"Why that foundry? What is it about that place?" Turney asked, lifting a skeptical eyebrow.

Smythe didn't have the time or the inclination to

reveal what he knew about the people involved with the two mining trusts. The gold stored at the facility was a drop in the bucket compared to the find they had made in the Canadian wilderness. What Smythe wanted more than anything were the exact coordinates of that mine and the technology to get at the gold they had found.

Instead of going into detail, Smythe responded curtly, "Because they're hoarding a shitload of gold there-- and don't interrupt me. Where was I?"

Even though he had been thinking about taking such a drastic step for some time, under the strain of actually committing to a coup, Smythe felt the panic starting to rise. No amount of training could have prepared him to make a play to take over the world.

Turney prodded him, "We have to corral the nukes, grab the gold, and what else?"

"Oh, yeah, right," Smythe shook his head and grimaced. "This building, it's wired into everything, it has to be taken out--and, of course, we've got to knock off Andrew Stevens and the others at the top."

"Sir, it would be my honor to cut off the head of that snake!"

"Shhh!"

"Sorry, Adam."

"Just shut up and listen. Do you have enough men to gain and hold control of the New York Fed? If not, let me know now and I'll send up another regiment."

Not wanting to be chastised again, Turney kept his response brief. "No, I've got enough men."

"Good. You already have this place under control, just wire it to blow and take out these motherfuckers in one shot. They won't even see it coming."

Jimmy Turney was dying to protest, to make the argument that blowing Andrew Stevens to Kingdom Come was letting him off the hook. He wanted to argue that a few hundred sessions of water boarding and stress positions would be more appropriate, but he did not dare. Instead, he just nodded.

Smythe went on, "You leave it up to me to get as many base commanders on board with us and taking out the other sites. I know the top five men at the nuclear stockpile and the commander of the detachment at Livermore. Once I absolutely, positively get them on our side and secure the nukes, then we'll make our move. But, Jimmy?"

"Yeah, Adam?"

"Don't you dare make a move until I tell you--because if you do and my men aren't in position, you're not just gonna be hanging us both, but you're going to set the world on fire. Do you understand me?"

"Yeah, Adam, I read you loud and clear. Just let me ask you one thing."

"What's that?"

"How are you going to keep Stevens from finding out what you're up to? You know he's got his own moles inside of your camp."

"Yeah, I know...but I'm going to distract him with something of a personal nature."

"What do you mean?"

Smythe couldn't help but smile. He leaned back away from the colonel and raised his voice, "Whatever Mr. Stevens orders you to do about Major Daniel Sampson, just do it!"

Colonel James Turney smiled a knowing smile and watched as Lieutenant General Smythe turned and walked toward the door. He was late for his meeting in the private penthouse suite. "Keep your ear to the ground, do you hear me?"

"Yes, Sir!" Turney stood erect and snapped off a smart salute.

Chapter Twenty- One

Lucky for everyone in the car, the bottle that slammed into the windshield was not a Molotov Cocktail. Unlucky for them, when Susan crashed into a city bus, the noise and panic resulted in a significant amount of unwanted attention.

Before anyone else knew what was happening, Sampson jumped out of the vehicle and started barking orders at the soldiers and paramilitary units who were converging at the scene. His many years of military service came to the forefront and not only did his voice change, but also his demeanor took on an entirely different countenance. His presence announced that he was the man in charge.

Pointing in the direction of Fordham Road, he started yelling that the people who attacked their vehicle were getting away, demonstrating the direction they took, and commanding the soldiers to go get them. That had the immediate effect of several groups of men taking off in the direction he was pointing.

Turning to one straggler who was simply looking to see if anyone was hurt or if he could offer any assistance, Sampson hollered, "Why are you still standing here, soldier? Who's your squad leader?"

Inside the car, Susan could not hear the boy's response, but she saw him pointing in the direction of an older man donning sergeant stripes. As Sampson walked toward the sergeant, who immediately stood at attention and saluted, his loud, authoritative voice faded. Because of the sirens and other vehicles racing around, she could not hear what he was saying. Sampson gestured, pointed, and she could tell he was barking at the men who had gathered around him for orders. It was obvious that the gold oak leaf cluster made him the highest-ranking officer on the scene.

A lieutenant and then a captain came rushing into view, double-time, and that brought a quick resolution to the situation. Susan saw the captain turn and yell at another soldier, who started to speak into a radio-like device. She then witnessed Sampson once again pointing off in the direction of Fordham Road. Seconds later, the soldiers loaded back into their patrol vehicles and a heavily armed convoy raced away to chase a ghost.

Sampson started walking back to the car with the captain in tow. As they neared, Susan heard the tail end of the discussion that had set off what was nothing more than a wild goose chase.

"So, Major, that's your high-value civie, huh?"

"Yeah, I didn't want to say any more to your men for security purposes, you understand?"

"Yes, sir, I sure do. Who is he?"

"I'm not supposed to say, Captain, that's classified; but just this one time--"

Susan watched carefully and she was shocked at how smoothly Sampson lied--how he was able to act like he had known the captain all his life and even co-opted his loyalty by seemingly bringing him into a confidence. Sampson was so suave that, for a second, she even found herself believing what he was saying.

"That there's Andrew Steven's brother. We were supposed to sneak him down to the HQ on the QT, but those terrorists must have got a whiff of what we were doing. Now, Captain, I am leaving it to you to track down the people who did this and bring them to justice." Sampson put his hand on the shoulder of the captain and looked at him sternly. "This is a Level One priority and has to be done with discretion, do you catch what I'm telling you?"

"Yes, sir!"

"As a matter of fact, Captain, you never met me and you never saw this accident happen, understood?"

"Affirmative, sir."

As Sampson dismissed his subordinate and got back into the car, it was like the accident never happened. The bus had been undamaged and went on its way. In the distance, they could hear the sirens of some major action taking place several blocks away. Besides a few pedestrians, the streets were clear.

Still feeling shaken, Susan asked nervously, "How did you do that?"

Sampson merely looked at her and grinned. Then, he reached up and tapped the gold oak leaf and told her in his most affected voice, "Membership has its privileges."

Coming from his lips, the quip sounded stale and completely phony. Susan didn't know why, but for the first time since she became intimate with Daniel Sampson, the blinders that had prevented her from seeing him for who he really was started to slip.

After the near-disaster, they rode in silence for several minutes. Once they were far enough away from the scene to relax, Susan's mind returned to Richard and what had distracted her so much in the first place.

Drawn like a fly to sugar, she couldn't help turning and looking back at Richard Clearmont. Peering deeply into his sparkling brown eyes that reminded her of Donny, her true soul mate who was forever lost to her, she took a deep breath and addressed him as if no one in the world existed, "I'm sorry, Richard, in person, you look a lot different than the pictures I've seen. Thin as you are now, you look a lot more like my Donny."

The usually unemotional Sampson found his face glow red and bile rise in his throat. He had never experienced jealousy before, but hearing Susan claim the dead Donald as her own made him feel a different, more radical kind of anger than he had ever known.

Richard responded. "Yeah, sometimes our mother had a hard time telling us apart, even though I'm older. By the way, Donny told me a lot about you before he passed. You look a lot different in person as well--the picture I saw of you didn't do you justice."

Susan blushed and unable to focus on the road. Hearing a voice so similar in tone and timbre made her look back again to make sure Donny was not in the car with her. Staring at the eerily familiar face of Richard didn't help.

Finally able to get her eyes and mind off of the man who reminded her so much of her lost love, she asked no one in particular, "By the way, which way are we going?"

Gruffly, Sampson answered, "If you were paying attention, you'd know the only way in is via the Whitestone and then into Manhattan through the Midtown Tunnel--dumb ass." Although not holding back his ire, the insult came out as a barely perceptible, seething aside.

Not only did Susan hear the slur, but she also felt his piecing tone and responded indignantly, "If I was paying attention? What the hell is wrong with you?"

Carlos did not realize how dangerous of a man Daniel Sampson was, so he teased in his Spanglish-effected accent, "Looks like my man can't handle a lil' bit of competition, eh?"

"Shut the fuck up, Carlos!" Susan snapped. She, of all people, knew a little of what Sampson was capable of; and she also knew he lacked a sense of humor. Biting her own tongue, she knew the last thing she needed was the men who she was counting on to help her survive going at each other's throats.

Carlos was taken aback by the chastisement. "What? What'd I say?"

Sampson responded, "Just keep your mouth shut!"

Reaching behind her seat with her left hand, Susan was able to feel and then grasp onto Carlos's pant leg. She slyly tugged, making him look up at the rearview mirror. Her eyes were plaintive and she lipped the word, "Stop."

Carlos looked over to Sampson in the front passenger seat and noticed the eerie glare on the man's face. Feeling chagrined and a little scared, he sat back, crossed his arms, and started to stare out of the window. His lips were sealed, but in his mind he realized that there was something terribly wrong with Daniel Sampson. The vibe he was picking up from the former Marine was nothing less than caustic.

Sampson turned further in his seat and looked squarely at Richard. In a cold, emotionless voice, he asked, "So what can you tell me about this virus? Are we all going to die or what?"

*****

Usually, it would have been impossible for the helicopter Maxwell York was traveling in to fly into Manhattan airspace, let alone land at a heliport, without attracting attention. However, since they were flying in a Ghosthawk, a bird that was painted all black with no insignia, just like the other covert and special-ops equipment being utilized by the national forces, there was no need to try and sneak in. They were also employing the proper beacons that announced someone of some importance was on board. Because the super-wealthy and the military had asserted proprietorship over the airspace and landing facilities, no one paid any mind to just another rich guy or general in a stealth helicopter going into Manhattan to carve up another piece of the country.

At one of the few heliports in the city along the Hudson River hidden away from prying eyes, a black May Bach with mirrored windows was waiting. As soon as York, squeezed between his three escorts, was safely seated in the back, the armor-plated, yet unescorted, vehicle slowly pulled away.

There was little time to observe how much the city

257

had changed, or how much different it felt with no privately owned cars clogging the streets and a armed militia guarding every street corner from what had been labeled "terrorist attacks" against the new regime. Instead, with nothing but line after line of city buses hauling people to and from their destination, York knew the trip to the United Nations would be a quick one. Several of his affiliates were waiting for him in the underground parking garage. From there, he would execute the plan to both depose Andrew Stevens and reclaim the seat of power.

Ever since Maxwell made the decision to stop being a spectator and put things back to where they should be, he had been invigorated. He no longer felt the effects of the chemotherapy and he felt his mind clicking like it had when he was sixty. Having a formidable enemy and a battle to fight made him feel alive. Ever since the collapse of the Soviet Union, he had been spoiling for a fight. Even at that moment, he never recognized his need for a challenge, nor realized how powerful acting instead of reacting made him feel.

York reached for the discretely hidden phone secreted in the soft leather padding of the rear seat.

Gently, George also reached out and touched York's arm, shaking his head "no" as soon as he got the man's attention. "Sorry, Boss, it wouldn't be wise to use that phone."

York smiled wryly. "Sorry, George, I almost forgot. That wouldn't have been very smart of me, now would it?"

The former CIA operative did not respond. Instead, he handed York the encrypted satellite phone and sat back, turning away as if to give York some privacy.

York dialed and put the phone to his ear. "Chris, how are things going?"

Secured in the war room bunker of the NSA's Data Center in Utah, Chris Carlton was standing behind a glass partition, watching as casually dressed men worked furious at a series of computer terminals. Each screen was covered with detailed maps of the Northeastern United States with vector lines representing flight paths, menus of battle parameters, and graphical representations of weapons systems, fuel consumption, and proximity to other drones. Many of the men were clicking from one UAV to another, manually checking the flight status and making sure none of many previously programmed birds had strayed off course, even though the action was unnecessary. The planes were all programmed to act autonomously and human intervention would have been superfluous.

"Everything's hunky-dory, Mr. York. Just like you said, the learning curve wasn't very steep. Once we programmed in what we wanted, the birds took over everything without a hitch; and several squadrons in route as we speak."

York smiled. "Good. I want you and your men to authenticate the attack on the Manhattan headquarters building and shadow the action. Oh, and Chris, I want you to leave no doubt."

"No doubt as to what, Mr. York?"

"Not one computer, not one data storage device-- hell, not one goddamn rodent--survives. I don't want a building on that block to be standing when you're done."

Carlton put his hand up to his face and griped his chin in as if in deep thought. "Are you sure that's what you want, Maxwell? I mean, a lot of innocents--"

"I know, I know, but we have to take out that nerve center no matter what the cost. Now, you have the schematics of the MYB building, don't you?"

"I'm looking at it right now, sir." A three-dimensional wire-frame image of the structure pivoted and rotated in space on the screen in front of him.

"Take note of the two sub-basements. I had those designed to survive a nuclear attack. The computer storage facility on that site is protected by three feet of reinforced concrete and sits between two subway tunnels. Do you see it?"

"Yeah, can't miss it."

"Do you see any other way of getting to those servers other than by using bunker-busting munitions and taking out the entire block?"

Carlton was a quick study. He knew from work he did in Iraq, trying to track down and destroy Saddaam's WMD program, and from planning on the destruction of Iran's nuclear facilities, that the ability to paralyze an opponent's nerve center usually required collateral damage. To an enemy hoping to destroy such an important target, it would be a much greater cost, and risk, than simply taking out a few buildings and machines. It was specifically planned so that the political expense attached to destroying an important site included killing innocents.

"You're right, Mr. York. Consider it done."

Knowing Chris was would do what he was told; York disconnected the call and placed another to his own headquarters, the golden-mirrored building on West 97th Street. "Raymond? It's me. Yes, it's time. I don't care what it takes, you have less than two hours to get yourself and Andrew out of that place. Just do what I tell you and follow the plan..."

Raymond Behn disconnected and slid the miniature phone into the inside pocket of his tailored Armani jacket. Standing in his office off of the MYB, Ltd. trading floor, he looked across the room and saw Becky pacing back and forth. He thought to himself that she must still be on the line with Sir Philip; and judging by the look on her face, she was having a hard time finalizing the details needed to secure the New Euro with gold.

Behn remembered, just like Maxwell York had predicted, moving too fast had led to a level of disorder they were unable to manage. When Andrew took over, they had expedited the process, painfully aware that if things went wrong, all could be lost.

Even though the major cities seemed subdued, everyone involved in their plans knew trouble was brewing right underneath the surface and it wouldn't take much to set off another wave of revolutionary violence. The fact they had made it so far, so fast--without being strung up by their necks by the people they had destroyed--had been an amazing feat. However, based on the intelligence coming from the Bible Belt and the old Rust Belt, they had not accomplished all they needed to secure their future. Whether they cared to admit it or not, the territory of the United States was still in play.

In addition to the trouble in the states, there were big issues brewing all over the globe. In North America alone, Mexico City had become like a tinderbox and, on the eve of the Canadian people casting their vote to nationalize all of their natural resources, new protests had broken out. The Canadian people, many of them participants in royalty trusts from natural resources, were up in arms about turning over the rights to the new Canadian Governing Council.

The same type of popular uprising in Russia and Australia, the other two nations they were counting on to anchor the system, was highly likely. But, by far, the biggest mistake they had made was ordering the assassination of Ti Kwei Fong, the Chairman for China Realm's counsel. He had been personally selected by Maxwell Yolk, not because he was one of the elites, but because of the influence he had over the Chinese Military leaders. As soon as he was assassinated, the entire China region had been in the midst of numerous power plays. Chaos had ensured.

Unfortunately, Raymond thought, Andrew Stevens had his head up his own ass and refused to acknowledge what was going on; and that was probably because either he had no idea what to do or he was pussy-whipped by Becky.

261

In either case, the situation was rapidly spinning out of control.

Raymond was grateful Maxwell York had decided to come out of hiding and retake the reins. Only under the mature, guiding hand of the man who had done nothing but plan the New World Order for years would they be able to correct their course. At the same time, though, he wished he did not have to leave Becky behind. She had been a good friend and a close ally for many years. But then, Raymond remembered, ever since she had tossed her hat in with Andrew and made her way into his bed, she had changed. Maybe it would be for the best when she fell victim to her own avarice and went down with what had become the commercial center of the world.

Taking long strides, Raymond walked between the rows of desks where traders and brokers worked to consolidate the positions of the senior partners and angled to take over whatever remained of the world that they did not already control. The traders were euphoric, able to make deals with outsiders who had no choice but to deal with them and who were fully aware they held all the cards--in the form of Amero Credits. The brokers and traders were living in a deal making heaven and their excitement made the air around them crackle with exhilaration.

After working his way past the trading floor, Raymond finally reached to the cubicle where Becky and several associates were staring at a screen. On the display, they were looking at Sir Philip's back and at the faces of the Prime Minister and a representative from the Royal family. They were sitting on the opposite side of the large, dark desk and engaged in some sort of heated debate. It was apparent that the people facing the camera had no idea the negotiations were being monitored and the live feed was being sent to New York City for Becky and her assistants to observe.

"What's happening?" Raymond asked in a hushed whisper.

"Shhh!" Becky responded. "The House of Windsor is balking at passing on the family jewels."

"You mean they're not going to turn over their gold reserves?"

"No, I mean they're negotiating for better positions, more status for the Princes."

"Oh?"

Becky turned and looked at Steven. Noticing the worried expression on his face, she touched his arm and smiled. "Don't worry, Ray, I've got this--it's under control and I'm going to seal this deal before lunch."

"I know you will." He patted her hand in a sign of confidence and then asked, "Where's Andrew? I have to talk to him and it's really important."

"He's up in the penthouse meeting with General Smythe, but I don't think you should bother them."

"Why's that?"

"Security sent down word that they've heard some shouting and wanted to know if they should intervene."

"What'd you tell them?" he asked, intensely interested in her response.

"I told 'em the same thing I'm telling you--leave them alone."

Ray Behn shook his head, blinked, and started walking toward the elevator.

Calling behind him, Becky asked, "Where are you going? Didn't you just hear what I said?"

"I heard you--but I have to, it's really important."

"Okay, but don't say I didn't warn you."

As soon as Raymond stepped on the elevator, Becky turned her attention back to the negotiation between Sir Philip and the British Royal family.

*****

263

General Smythe was not backing down, but neither was Andrew Stevens. When Raymond walked into the room, they were almost chest-to-chest with fingers pointing at each other's face.

"You do what I tell you to do!"

"You can't talk to me that way, after everything I've done!"

"I don't give a shit what you think you've done!"

"Who the hell do you think you are--you'd still have rioting in the streets if it wasn't for me!"

"What, you don't think some other cowboy could've done just as well--maybe even better?"

"I don't just think it, Stevens, I know it!"

Raymond had no idea what had set off the argument, but it looked like the gray-haired, stone-faced, old general was about to rip the head off the younger, but much smaller man. Although Stevens had his fists balled up and was ready to fight, he was obviously no match for Smythe, whose physique and posture was that of a seasoned veteran of the martial arts.

"Whoa, whoa, whoa! What the hell's going on here?" Raymond shouted the question as he forced his way in between the two combatants.

"This son-of-a-bitch knows where Sampson is-- sounds like he's known all along?"

"So?" Raymond asked.

"So?" Andrew repeated mockingly, "This incompetent asshole let an assassin hide out just blocks from here and never told me."

General Smythe started regaining his composure. He backed off and walked over to the wet bar. After pouring himself a drink, he strode calmly, in exact, measured paces, over to the plate glass windows looking over 97th Street.

Recognizing the other men were awaiting his

264

rejoinder, he turned calmly toward them. "I apologize, Andrew, for losing my temper, but you didn't give me a chance to explain." Smythe took a sip of whisky, further composing himself, and continued, "I assure you, sir, at all times you were safe and you were never in jeopardy."

Andrew let out a snort, "You realize you're betting your career on the fact you can prove that?"

Smythe ignored the threat but prefaced his response, "Mr. Stevens, not even the President of the United States talks to me the way you do, there are certain protocols--"

Stevens sneered, "I'm not the President."

"I'm coming to realize that. I assure you, moving forward, I'll conduct myself accordingly. Now, as for this Sampson character, the reason my men didn't say anything sooner was that we had to be sure it was him."

"What do you mean, you had to be sure?" Raymond asked.

"I mean, sir, that the retired Major Daniel Sampson no longer looks the same as he did when he was in the service. He's had his face surgically altered, and he's managed to alter his fingerprints and DNA."

Even though Andrew knew everything, the general was saying was true, because of the bugs that were in Troth's mansion when the surgery was done, he did not want to let on how far back they were connected. "Oh, come on, now--that's impossible!" Stevens shouted.

"How the hell could you possibly know that?" Raymond asked in chorus.

Without bothering to explain how they were able to gather the intelligence, or that it fortuitously fell into their lap when on the trail of Stanton Frazier and James LeCroix, General Smythe laid out the details of what he knew; where Sampson had been, what they believed he had done, and where he was staying. He left both Andrew Stevens and Raymond Behn standing agape when he told them about the major hiding out only blocks away with Michelle

Alvarez-Rivera, Susan DiGiovanni, and several others. He even recounted some of the assassin's exploits within the city they were able to trace back to the major, including the murders of black-market food dealers.

Smythe then went on to describe how they had been trailing Sampson the best they could until they confirmed his identity. Finally, he detailed how they were able to pick up Sampson's new DNA signature and fingerprints when he obtained a verified federal Identification card.

"Oh, my God," was all Stevens was able to say. He was well aware of how dangerous Sampson was, but it never occurred to him the man was capable of going on killing sprees simply to gather food and accumulate wealth in the form of gold. If Sampson was capable of such plebeian acts, there would be no limit to what he would do to obtain real power and real wealth. Just thinking about the man's penchant for meaningless violence made Andrew shiver.

"How was he able to do all of that, I mean, changing his DNA?" Raymond asked.

Smiling, General Smythe finally explained the mystery, "Well, he had help, help from one of your very powerful friends, Roland Troth."

That was a fact Stevens was well aware of since he was the one who ordered the hit on Troth, but, with everything else going on in the world, he couldn't believe anyone had been able to put the pieces together.

The general continued, "We know Sampson had reconstructive surgery and a cadaver's skin transplanted over his hands. These facts would have helped us locate him sooner, or at least verify his whereabouts." Facing Stevens directly with an accusatory stare, Smythe went on, "That you didn't tell me you had dealings with Major Sampson and knew what he looked like is the reason why this has taken so long."

Stepping closer to Andrew, the general's voice went

deeper, "Mr. Stevens, now that I've told you everything I know--and this information cost us many man-hours and several lives--is there anything more you want to tell me?"

"Such as?"

"Such as why we've been after this man, what does he mean to you, and why are the two of you so interested in killing each other?"

Stevens opened his mouth to respond, but nothing came out. All he could do was look back and forth between the general and Raymond."

"Don't look at me," Raymond uttered, "he already knows most of it, so you may as well tell him the rest."

Reaching up and touching the scar on his ear where Sampson had cut off a slice, Andrew finally responded, "Yes, I've had encounters with Daniel Sampson--but it's none of your concern why I want him dead. As far as him wanting to kill me, why do you think? It's because of my position, my status--he wants what I have, and it's your job to protect me. That's all you need to know."

"Okay," Smythe agreed, "you don't have to tell me why you put a hit out on him in the first place; but, the reason he wants you dead is personal, I already figured that much out."

Stevens cringed. He was extra sensitive about that glaring error and the trouble it had caused, allowing Sampson's escape so he could blow up the Cape Cod estate.

General Smythe went on, trying to further his advantage, "I also know you want to get at Sampson so that you can avenge the death of Maxwell York."

That caused Stevens to shoot a piercing look at the general.

"Yes, I know about that, too. My men tell me everything, and when you had them hunting for that ship, the Hellbender, and tracking the movements of several foreign businessmen, I had to wonder why. Mr. Stevens, the name Maxwell York is not completely alien to me. He was an advocate for the military long before you were born, son. I was just surprised to hear he is still alive."

"Still alive?" Andrew shouted. "What do you know, where is he?"

General Smythe smiled and took the tube of the ersatz Cuban cigar out of his pocket. Pulling the cigar out of the tube with his teeth, he bit the end off and spit the tobacco plug onto the shag carpet. Looking away from the others, he couldn't help but smile.

Chapter Twenty- Two

"I read those files and this sounds like a crock," Sampson snorted. "If this is some kind of biological warfare program, I should've heard about it before York gave me those files."

"Three, maybe five years ago, you'd be right. It would have been top secret, hush-hush military stuff you may have been privy to--but now the technology exists so people can buy cheap PCR machines on the internet and make other equipment from spare computer parts." Richard's words were coming out fast. The excitement from orating about his specialty was obvious. "You can even order samples of deadly viral DNA through the mail and the CDC will ship it right to your doorstep." He concluded in a haughty, rushed tone, "This is private work, not some government financed program. You get a few good scientists in a room and pay them enough, you don't think they can recombine DNA at will? Man, you people are behind the times."

The lack of tolls and traffic enabled them to make good time despite the indirect route they were forced to take. As soon as they crossed the Whitestone Bridge into Flushing, Queens, they drove down Francis Lewis Boulevard until it branched off onto 35th Street. Then, they quickly made their way east down Northern Boulevard and then onto the Grand Central. Still donning the camouflage Marine fatigues Sampson had obtained for them, Susan, Carlos, and Sampson listened with rapt attention to Richard Clearmont.

Because the topic was molecular biology, at first they had little to add to the conversation, but they had lots of questions. Occasionally, they had to interrupt Richard in order to get him to speak English instead of some scientific gibberish only a doctoral candidate could understand.

Susan was still driving, but she was very distracted. Her cheeks were flush from the anger she felt at Sampson and his rudeness. As hard as she tried to put what she was feeling out of her head, the nastiness he had displayed kept on popping back up as intrusive thoughts. Nevertheless, she forced herself to keep her cool and listen to what Richard was telling them about the virus.

The implications were more than profound, they were disturbing. They had already discussed the statistics, if two people could only procreate once, over time the population would be cut in half. Along with that, other population groups lacking the precise genes wouldn't be able to procreate at all--if they survived the initial infection. All told, within a generation, they could expect the population to shrink significantly.

"Okay, Richard," Susan asked, maintaining the pretense that she was not upset, "explain to me again how they got this virus to spread."

"In its primordial phase, the virus itself is too weak to pass from human to human through the air or from physical contact. A human's mucous would kill it."

"Why didn't they make it stronger like the rhino virus or the flu?" Carlos asked.

"Oh, they could have, but I'm guessing they didn't want to make it so robust that they couldn't control it--and I suppose they're just keeping their fingers crossed that evolution doesn't make that happen on it's own." Richard's hyper-articulated lecture sounded as if his words were racing to get out of his mouth. Quickly answering the aside, he went on, "So what they did is design this virus and reprogram a strain of the spirochete bacteria to be a carrier. Bacteria is a lot hardier than the virus but can also be controlled a lot easier. Also, the virus acquires some genes from the spirochete bacteria that flourishes in the reproductive system."

"Like syphilis?" Susan asked, remembering

exposure to syphilis caused stillbirths. It also made her remember how careful Donny had been when they made love, knowing he was infected with something no one could identify.

"Yes, exactly like syphilis, which is also in the spirochete family. But, there's more; the virus itself initially needs the bacteria to survive until it gets into the human bloodstream. After that, whoever's infected can infect others."

"I thought you said the virus was too weak to survive." Sampson commented skeptically.

"It is until it becomes active, combines with DNA most of us already have, and mutates. When the secondary permutation evolves, it becomes its own vector."

Sampson shot out another question, seemingly not satisfied with what he was being told. "That place, Hamilton Genomics is where they made the virus and the bacteria, but I never saw who militarized it or how they did it."

"I don't know that either, but it was pretty ingenious how they included the bacteria in pesticides and sprayed the formula all over the place--there was no way to avoid picking it up: ticks, bedbugs, mosquitoes, they're all carriers. Anyone who ever was bit was infected by the virus, a primary source, and some of them, like my wife, died."

Susan looked back at him again using the rearview mirror. In a concerned voice, she asked, "Were you able to figure out why she died while you and Donny didn't even get sick?"

Richard squinted his eyes as if trying to see through a thick fog. Taking on the detached tone of a professor, he responded, "Humans evolved differently all over the planet. A long time ago, humans mated with Neanderthals; or, I should say, some populations did, and our DNA combined. Over thousands of years, those Neanderthal genes were weakened and became less important. I guess you can say most went dormant, but they still existed in a large segment of the population."

Carlos asked, "If they went dormant, why are the Neanderthal genes relevant?"

"There are still some differences between the populations as a result of the combination. For example, those who didn't get certain nucleotide polymorphisms are lactose intolerant as adults."

"Nucleo-what?" Susan asked.

"Just think of it as genetic variations."

"Oh, okay, go on."

"My wife was southern Italian. Somewhere along the ancestral line, her parents' ancestors mixed with others who didn't have these particular genes. When she inherited her two X-chromosomes, neither one of them had the target genetic variant."

"So, what happened?" Susan was still driving but she couldn't help herself from continually looking back at Richard as he described how the virus killed his wife--and Donny's wife.

"What happens when the virus invades a cell is this: it seeks to insert itself into particular segments of human DNA. By the way, 8% of the human genome already comes from viruses, so this isn't some kind of magic trick; it's just how things work. Anyway, this virus invades the cell and alters that segment. If the virus invades someone lacking the right genes, it inserts itself randomly and disrupts the functions of the cell. Since it's so good at replicating, it takes no time at all for every cell to be infected.

"With a random change in someone's DNA, eventually the immune system recognizes a damaged cell and attacks. That's what happened to Rachel and Angela. Their own immune system caused a mass necrosis in their brains and there was no way to stop it--"

"Because you were fighting the Lyme Disease

bacteria and not the virus."

"Yup." Richard answered dryly. "The powerful antibiotics we used only helped to kill her."

As if not recognizing how the atmosphere inside the car had become melancholy, Sampson turned to Richard and asked, "So that's what all of those population studies were about? They figured out how many people would live and how many would die from the infection?"

Thinking about his wife--and really in no mood to continue talking--Richard simply nodded.

Sampson shot out another question, "Aren't the odds of those women both lacking the same genes and dying pretty slim? That means something went wrong and lots of people should have died, but that didn't happen, did it?" His voice was accusatory, as if the information Richard was giving them didn't add up, as if he was lying to them.

"I guess you don't understand what I'm saying." Richard shot back testily. "Protein coding genes randomly inserted into chromosomes can wreak havoc on a body in lots of different ways. What you're not recognizing is that lots of people did die, but it was called other things, SARS, bird flu, swine flu, H1N1, cancer, even pneumonia, because no one knew to look for a genetically altered retrovirus. It's the same thing that happened with HIV. Thousands died until someone figured out a virus was involved. Not only have lots of people died from this, a lot of kids got sick; didn't you ever wonder why so many children are being born with Autism?"

Susan interjected, "I thought that was from vaccination?"

"No, some people had the right idea but they focused on the wrong source. Lots of disorders that never existed exist now and the people at Hamilton Genomics felt it was just an unintended consequence of what they call 'creative destruction.'"

"No, that's not what they called it, that's what

273

Maxwell York called it." Sampson's tone was still severe. He realized Richard had nailed it and had been right all along, but he was becoming impatient with what he felt was irrelevant conversation.

Carlos added in, "So, this is his way of weeding out the weak and making room for a generation of the strong."

"I guess you can say that, Carlos, a type of reverse eugenics; instead of improving on humans through genetics, this is an attempt to speed up evolution with a man-made agent. But, if by 'weak' you mean lacking certain genetic traits handed down by Neanderthals? No," Richard replied. "It has more to do with statistical probability of a certain populations having those genes than the actual genes themselves. It's not really about race or ethnicity, it's more about finding a target that can make procreation selective. The rest is collateral damage that'll take the world's population down to about a third of where it's now."

For clarification, Susan asked, "So, the virus infects everyone but kills those who have no Neanderthal DNA. Those it doesn't kill it changes and stops them from having more than one child?"

*****

Smythe finished lighting his cigar and took a few long pulls. "Don't be so surprised, Andrew, of everyone, you should know the capabilities of the tools you've provided me; you know about most of the assets we possess, but you don't know about all of them."

"I'm going to ask you one more time, General Smythe, where is Maxwell York? Are you sure he's still alive?" The fact that there had been no contact from Maxwell, no attempt to disrupt what was going on, had allowed Andrew to let his guard down. If York was still alive, he had been in hiding and had kept silent. Hearing

Smythe knew Maxwell was still alive--and that he may have a bead on the big man himself--caused Andrew to go into a near panic. Beads of sweat started to form on his forehead and above his lip.

"I don't know where he is, but what my operatives are telling me is that something's going on and he's been on the move."

"What do you mean?"

The general went on to explain the radar blackouts in Utah, the trouble they were having maintaining contact with Air Force bases and radar installations all across the nation, and how former members of the covert intelligence apparatus were simply disappearing off of the face of the earth.

Raymond had to force himself not to react. Since he had been Maxwell York's inside man--and had been made aware of what was going on behind the scenes--it was shocking to hear how much General Smythe knew. He was itching to dig deeper and find out more, specifically if Smythe and his team were privy to the coming attacks so he could pass the information onto York, but he didn't dare tip his hand.

"So, what you're telling me is that York has activated one of his old networks and he's coming after me?"

"No, I'm not saying that. What I'm saying is that it's highly probable the man's still alive and he's working behind the scenes to do something. Only he and his partners can move like that, using technology to block surveillance. At this point, we have no evidence he's planning to do anything against you and we don't yet know exactly where he is."

"Then what do you know?" Andrew shouted. "What am I supposed to do?"

"My advice is to sit tight. You're safe here. Besides, you'll have Colonel Turney at your disposal to hunt down this Sampson character and take care of your personal business. I'll put Turney on notice to keep you posted on all developments and make sure he redoubles your security. You'll have some of the best shooters in the world crawling all over this building to make sure you're safe. Just trust me, Andrew, I'm on your side."

The words, and especially the general's advice, made Raymond cringe. His orders from York were to get Stevens out of there as quickly as possible because the building was going to be destroyed. Now, this asshole was advising them to stay put, which would make his job that much more difficult.

Unable to think of any other way to change the dynamics of the situation, Raymond spat out the first thing that came to mind, "You mentioned Michelle Alvarez-Rivera was the one hiding Sampson."

"So?"

"She's important to us, you know. Right before everything happened, she was about to announce a major gold find in Canada and we need to know where it is."

That they were aware of the Seven Rams Trust and the gold was no big surprise, but that Smythe forgot the Rivera woman was connected made him want to kick himself. Recovering quickly, he answered, "Yeah, according to what Colonel Turney told me, we can bring her in right now and you can interrogate her right here."

Signaling the end of the meeting, Smythe turned and starting making his way to the door, speaking as he passed the other men. "Listen, whatever you need, just tell Colonel Turney--I'll bet you all come up with a way to use that Rivera woman as bait and lure in Sampson. That's real smart of you, Mr. Behn, figuring out a way to kill two birds with one stone. As a matter of fact, let me take care of setting this up right now."

"No, wait, General!" Raymond's words were of no use, the general kept walking away.

"I'd love to stay and chat, gentlemen, but I've got a war to run." He stopped at the door and turned. "Good luck, men, and I'll let you know when we learn more about Maxwell York and what he's up to."

Andrew's face was pale and he felt sick to his stomach, but he somehow managed to speak. "Yeah, you do that."

There was just too much going on, too many things happening at once, and Andrew Stevens could not think clearly. All he wanted to do was grab Becky and fly off into the sunset, leaving Daniel Sampson, Maxwell York, and General Smythe to fight it out amongst themselves. Just by the way the meeting had gone and the tone Smythe had used, Stevens knew General was setting up some sort of power play; another man vying to become the most powerful man in the world was no big surprise.

Instead of doing what he wanted to do, what he should have done, Stevens grabbed Raymond by the arm and led him toward the door. "Come on, let's go down to the command center and simplify my life."

"What do you mean, Andrew? I think we should get the hell out of here before it's too late. I don't trust the general."

"I don't trust him either, but what choice do we have? Let's just get rid of this Sampson character once and for all and we'll worry about the general later."

Raymond was on the edge of his own panic attack. "But Andrew, I don't--"

"I know, Ray, I know...let's just set this trap for Sampson and then we'll get out of here, okay?"

The words should have put Raymond at ease, knowing he would be able to get Stevens out of the building, but the statement raised even more questions, what exactly did Andrew Stevens know, and why the hell had he agreed to leave without even an argument?

In the upper echelons of power, the paranoia was

starting to run rampant.

No one responded to what was obviously a rhetorical question posed by Susan and were left in an eerie, intense silence. The fact a virus had been unleashed that selectively narrowed down who could and who could not procreate, that had the capacity to kill, and that caused debilitating conditions for those who had the wrong genetics, was overwhelming. Without even saying it, they all realized the world as they knew it was gone forever because the likes of Maxwell York thought it would be okay to play God and mess with the evolutionary process.

Even though caught up in the bigger picture, Susan's focus quickly flashed back to her two young children. She was thankful they survived and were both healthy--meaning they had the right genes--but she wondered about their future and what kind of life they would have. As was her way, Susan pushed her desire to know to the forefront and asked, "Richard, so, a woman gets infected with this virus, then what happens to her?"

Richard sighed and paused, trying to think of a way to explain things more clearly than he had the first time. He looked up at the rearview mirror and saw Susan flash a concerned look at him before she looked back at the road.

Sampson scowled at Susan, angry at the way she kept on cutting into the conversation before he secured what he felt was much more relevant information. To him, there were many more important details to gather. Her ways, her independent streak, and lack of respect, were no longer cute. As a matter of fact, her personality had started to rub him the wrong way. Plus, the more attention she paid to Richard Clearmont, the less attractive she seemed in his eyes.

Having never experienced this level of jealously,

278

the emotions he felt made him feel off balance. Sampson knew the time was rapidly approaching where he'd have to make some major life changes--meaning he did not like what he had become. Because of his feelings for Susan, he was getting soft, lax, and it was long past the point where he should have reverted back to his old ways. The old ways, he told himself, were better--and that would be the last time he'd let Susan's impudence pass. It was either that or get sucked into a life he never wanted.

At that moment, he decided to allow his Alpha-male instincts, which had been lying dormant, to start to reemerge. The next time Susan stepped out of line, she'd learn the hard way to let the men talk and to keep her stupid mouth shut. But, more importantly, he decided he was going to have to start getting rid of the other people around them who commanded Susan's attention. Then, and only then, would things be better for him, and he believed, for her.

Richard replied to the question, "Let me put it this way, Susan, when a woman gets pregnant, when the merged egg and sperm cells divide, they form a cluster of cells called a blastoma. Those cells contain foreign DNA from the father and there is an immuno-response from the mother's body. Of course, that usually causes a cascade of events that prepares the body for the fetus. I guess the best way to put it is, as far as the body is concerned, that cluster of cells is a parasite; and, naturally, a woman's body would initially fight that.

"Sometimes the immune system can't adjust to a first pregnancy and the fetus is expelled; but the fact that a woman became pregnant changes her in significant ways--especially if the child was a male."

Sampson cut in, his voice tight and curt, "Can you speed this up, Doc, this isn't Biology 101."

Richard was a bit taken aback, but he went on, "Okay, well, in any case, once a pregnant woman's DNA actually changes and certain, lets say 'switches', are turned off and on to deactivate or activate genes--that allows her to take a pregnancy to term. This particular virus was engineered to interfere with those mechanisms and suppresses the woman's ability to endure the new cells' foreign DNA. After being infected, and after having one child, any other blastomae are attacked and usually won't survive to develop."

There was another long, heavy silence in the car. Susan continued driving, keeping her thoughts to herself.

The traffic orders and other directives for the military, paramilitary, and civilian forces were conveniently posted on an easily accessible heads-up display on the dashboard. The NYC Transportation Order of the Day directed non-essential military vehicles entering Manhattan had to use the Midtown Tunnel.

Everyone remained silent as they passed the eastern checkpoint and slowly made their way through the tunnel with their eyes wide open. As Sampson had explained, if they were going to be trapped, the ambush would be set up in a place where there was little to no chance of escape. Moving slowly through the darkened concrete tube under the East River, they remained extra vigilant with side arms at the ready.

Susan's mind wondered back to more than ten years before, and how she and other women she knew had such a difficult time getting pregnant, as well as the many women she remembered having miscarriages. If it weren't for the fertility treatments, she never would have had Chris and Lisa. Without even being told, she instinctively knew that some form of the virus had been unleashed long before-- and that was why she couldn't get pregnant.

Exiting the tunnel into the eerily calm city streets, they breathed a collective sigh of relief.

Wondering if he could confirm her suspicions, Susan asked, "Richard, how long ago did this program start?"

"Unbelievably, it got off the ground in 1990, when they knew enough about genetics to clone Dolly."

"The sheep?"

"Yeah, after that, the funding for genetic research took off and according to what I read, this other company, MYB, Ltd. spent hundreds of millions on trying to learn how to manipulate genes for cloning soldiers, altering human physiology, and creating biological weapons. That's the stuff you were speaking of, Mr. Sampson. This virus and other strains before it are the result of that work."

Susan felt like she had been let off the hook. All those years ago, she blamed herself for the inability to get pregnant or carry to term, now she knew for sure it hadn't been her fault. But, that raised new questions in her mind.

"So, how do people know if they're infected?"

"That was in the files, too. They have a microchip assay that can test blood, or skin, and they know almost instantly if you've been exposed. You know those identification tags everyone is being forced to get?""

"Yeah."

"That's what they're using to determine how deeply into every population the virus has spread. If there are too few, they can always come back and reintroduce the bacteria. Do you really think it's a coincidence how a few years ago bedbugs started infesting the city's hotels after a hundred years without them? The city folks hadn't been traipsing around in the woods enough, and not having enough sex with people who do--so these people brought in the bedbugs and, viola, all of a sudden the people in the cities get infected, too."

Finding an opportunity to interject, Carlos asked, "Richard, you never told us if the documents revealed a way to combat the virus. Is there a cure?"

"Yeah, is there a cure?" Susan repeated, again thinking of her kids.

The question also interested Sampson because even though he had read the Hamilton Genomics files, he had been unable to do more than scan the scientific jargon. More than anything else, he wanted to figure out a way he could capitalize on a cure.

"Well, yeah. It's actually pretty simple. All you have to do is introduce one of several harmless parasitic worms into a woman's intestines and they will suppress the immune system enough to let a woman who wants to have children carry to term."

"Worms? That's it?" Susan asked, "You're kidding me, right?"

Richard smiled, "You'd be surprised at how many parasites, bacteria, and viruses we carry around with us all the time. As a matter of fact up until the 1900's almost everyone had worms in--"

"Stop the car!" Sampson shouted.

Susan slammed on the brakes and brought the vehicle to a squealing halt. They sat idling on Central Park West, only a block away from the penthouse.

Susan looked at Sampson and glared at him. "What the hell is wrong with you? You scared the shit out of me!"

Not bothering to explain his sudden outburst, Sampson curtly commanded, "Turn left here and ditch the car on Amsterdam. Change clothes, come back here, and just wait for me."

When he reached for the door handle to make quick exit, Susan grabbed his arm, "What? What's going on, Sampson?"

"The soldiers who were watching the penthouse, they're gone. I'm gonna go and see what's going on, if that's okay with you." His face was of stone and his tone was severe, all business.

Barely recognizing the man, but very afraid of his hostile temperament, Susan didn't say a word. She let go of his arm and watched as he trotted over to the sidewalk, taking cover by dodging into the shadows. Seconds later, he was gone.

*****

There was more than one secret parking garage under the United Nations building, and probably more than one hidden facility. Driving down a heavily guarded, restricted ramp on East 48th Street took the black May Bach underground and past several sub-basements. Access to a heavy-duty lift was restricted by steel spikes, which the driver brought down using a state-of-the-art laser pointer that conveyed the correctly encrypted password. After punching in twelve digits on a keypad, a set of steel doors parted and slowly gaped open.

Driving off of the elevator fifty more feet under the UN, the May Bach could only move forward twenty yards before the driver was forced to stop. Quickly, the former CIA operatives opened the rear door and ushered Maxwell York toward a steel bulkhead. Before they even reached the expanded metal plates that formed a platform leading into the chamber, several heavy metal clicks could be heard and the massive door swung open. Without delay, the escorts led York deep into the bowels of what was once a clandestine NSA listening post.

Judging by the darkened devices mounted to the walls, the technology dated back to the 1980's. Maxwell knew the site had been abandoned and all but forgotten, but at one time the entire UN had been wired, with every audio and visual lead hooked up to the dusty old control room. Through the many feet of bedrock under Manhattan, and only one closely watched telephone connection leading out, there was no way Soviet spies could find them, monitor their activities, or intercept their messages.

When the Soviet Union fell, they no longer had much use for the facility and it had fallen into disrepair.

However, there was no safer place on the East Coast to hide out in case of a natural or man-made disaster. There was only one way in and one way out and they had enough food, water, and fuel for the generators to stay down there for a year if necessary. Not knowing how everything was going to shake out, York had decided to play it safe and wait out whatever may come.

George cleaned off and offered a seat to York, who dismissed him with a wave.

Standing before the five men around him, Maxwell took on the carriage of an emperor or dictator addressing his subjects. "Okay, men, it's for real this time. Make sure you establish secure contact with Chris Carlton in Utah as soon as possible. I want to keep track of how well the drones are doing."

"Already done, sir," George replied dutifully.

"Very well. Now, as soon as Raymond shows up with Andrew, I want you to bring them here, to me, so we can talk. I have a few things I have to say to my former pupil."

Maxwell York was finished speaking, so he sat down on the clean chair. Putting his elbows up on the dust-covered desk, he folded his hands under his chin and rested his head as if in deep thought. At the same time, the men who were standing in the room left, scurrying about to take care of other duties and responsibilities.

"Andrew, Andrew, Andrew, what am I going to do with you?"

Chapter Twenty- Three

There was no subtle way to get into the building and make it up to the penthouse. One elevator in the lobby was dedicated to the top floor and it could only be accessed with a special key. The fire escapes were in plain sight, so Sampson had no choice but to play it safe.

Before he went in the building, he took the precaution of checking out every approach and angle where a sniper would have a clean shot at him. Oddly, the snipers were gone--as were the men who had been stationed, around the clock, to try and monitor his movements. Sampson, whose keen sense of sight and sixth sense about being watched, had never fallen victim to an ambush--and there was no way in the world he was going to let it happen on his home turf. After the quick reconnoiter, he was not put on guard by anything he saw or felt. Still, before even going near the entrance of the building, he waited patiently for thirty minutes to try and detect anything suspicious.

Because he was still in uniform, he did not stand out at all. The city was filled with soldiers of all stripes and, relaxed as he made himself out to be, he looked like just another officer taking a break. Stuffing a discarded newspaper casually under his arm and strolling up and down the block gave him excellent vantage points of the building. He was able to see the windows of the penthouse and surreptitiously observe all of the entrances. Also, Sampson knew from experience, very few people could remain concealed without having to move--and giving themselves up in the process--for more than five or ten minutes. That was especially true with him strolling about as bait. If they were onto him, some hothead would make a move--and out in the open as he was, that would give him a chance to escape.

Not seeing or sensing anything out of the ordinary,

he simply walked into the lobby of the luxury building and directly to the elevator as if he had absolutely every reason to be there and nothing to fear.

When the doors of the elevator opened on the top floor, it was easy to discern that whatever had happened was over and whoever had raided the place was gone. There were no noises, no guards posted, and the hallway was clear. But, the people who had come did not hide the fact they had been there. The hallway was strewn with evidence of a raid; splinters of wood and shards of glass stuck to the disheveled carpets.

Sampson pulled the standard issue Marine Beretta 92F out of its holster and held it up in the air as he inched forward toward the penthouse door. As he neared the entrance to the penthouse, he could clearly smell the smoke of a cheap cigar. The door was propped open but no discernible noises came from the inside. Sampson crouched down into a low squat and darted his head around the doorjamb for a fraction of a second. Relying on his peripheral vision's motion-detecting cells, he did not perceive any human presence, nor did he see any movement. The second time he looked down the long hallway of the penthouse, he did not pull away immediately and gave his eyes enough time to focus. No one was there-- but his exceptionally sensitive ears did pick up some subtle reverberations, something akin to the sound of ice in a glass. The smell of the cigar was getting stronger, yet it was fresh, and he knew someone was in the apartment, someone he did not know.

Remaining in the crouch, he turned the corner and pulled the weapon down from the ready position, training it down the length of the hallway. Just like a low-slung wolverine, he quickly skittered his way down the hall and took up a defensive position in the kitchen with his back pressed against cabinets and his head below the counter. Unless someone had the place wired with motion detectors, they wouldn't have known he was there. He had successfully entered the penthouse without making a sound.

Moving furtively, Sampson crawled on the floor to obtain a better position so he could see into the living room and dining room without being seen. It helped that the lights were off and where he eventually stood to peer out was in the shadow of a kitchen corner. Holding the gun up with his arm bent, he leaned forward and exposed only a small fraction of his head so he could look down the hallway toward the bedrooms. Since there was no visual contact, he knew, for at least a few seconds, it was safe to come out into plain sight and make his way deeper into the penthouse.

Two silent steps down the hallway and Sampson heard a noise that made him come to a complete stop--a cough came from the master suite and there had been no attempt to stifle the sound. Whoever was in the room was not in hiding and it was obvious by the lack of ambient noise that an ambush was not waiting for him across the threshold.

Aiming the Beretta in front of him, Sampson took several long strides and all but dove into a prone position at the entrance of the bedroom. Besides the dampened sound of his elbows hitting the floor, he gained access to the room with his weapon aiming forward and his finger extended along the trigger guard. Someone waiting to shoot him would have only seen the barrel and little else.

Lying on the bed was Liz, Susan's sister, who was not moving. Standing by the dressing table, holding a sweating glass of scotch on the rocks, was Major General Adam Smythe. There was no one else in the room.

Turning toward and the door, the general was briefly startled to see a 9mm pointed in his direction by a man lying on the floor. Quickly recovering, Smythe lifted the highball glass and put it to his lips. After taking a long swallow, he lowered the glass and nonchalantly walked over to the end of the king-sized bed. After unbuttoning his jacket, the general sat down heavily on the mattress, causing Liz to stir, groan, and partially roll over.

"Come in, Major. I've been waiting for you."

*****

Susan, Carlos, and Richard did what they were told. They parked the car they had stolen in the Bronx on Amsterdam Avenue and walked several blocks east back to Central Park. Taking turns, Susan and Carlos went deeper into the park and stripped off the baggy extra layer of military clothing and left the stolen fatigues in the trees.

"What are we supposed to do now?" Susan asked, looking at Carlos and then Richard.

Richard had a dour look on his face and asked, "I don't know, but I don't trust the major."

"I used to," Carlos chimed in, "but today he showed a side of himself I did not recognize or like." As usual, when he was upset, Carlos's speech was more formal and his Spanish accent more pronounced. It was clear he had not let go of being chastised and ordered to shut up. Despite the diplomatic words, the contempt he felt was written all over his face.

"Yeah, I know what you mean, Carlos, that man's got his panties in a bunch about something--"

"Don't you mean someone?" As he asked this, Carlos tilted his head toward Richard Clearmont, the only man who had been competition for Susan's attention since they made it into Manhattan. "I believe Sampson has a jealous streak a mile wide."

"Yeah, I noticed that too, and what a turn-off. The way he was acting, I honestly have no clue what I saw in him. It's like he's a chameleon--sometimes I don't even know who he is."

Taking both Richard and Carlos by the hand, she

288

looked at them in turn, casting her big brown eyes at one and then the other. "Listen, guys, I know Sampson better than you, and I promise you, I'll have a talk with him when the time is right. But, for now, let's just deal with this and make it through the day so we can decide what to do."

"Why not ditch that asshole now and go back to Jersey?" Richard asked plaintively. "We can even go back to my lab in Rochester-- at least there we'll be safe from all these jack-booted thugs." As he said this, a roving patrol was walking in their direction, eyeing them suspiciously as they passed. Once the heavily armed soldiers passed, Richard finished his statement, "It's not that hard of a trip."

Susan looked at Carlos as if she was considering it and Carlos nodded back, silently encouraging her to agree.

"No. We've got to stick it out. I've got a feeling we're going to need Sampson to get out of here safely.

*****

The UAV's attack parameters were modeled after thousands of sorties flow by actual pilots or from the records of human guided drones. Each plane's internal computer system was networked with the other drones in the squadron and with other squadrons in each wing. There was nothing human pilots could do that the drones couldn't do faster, better, and with more precision. Every action they took was based on the records of the best fliers minus the few human mistakes that detracted from perfection.

One wing was circling high above Pittsfield, Pennsylvania, seeking out anything that resembled an American military force or hardware. There were hunter-fighters protecting seeker-bombers from aerial attack; electronic surveillance and jamming drones; and, fuel tankers all arrayed for maximum destruction. An imaginary circle had been drawn around the perimeter of the Pittsfield Foundry and any soldier carrying a weapon or armored

289

vehicle approaching the boundary would be electronically tagged and met with what could only be described as something akin to the biblical hellfire and brimstone.

A similarly configured wing was heading towards New York City. If a civilian or military radar station had been able to pick up the armada heading east, every military jet on the East Coast would have been scrambled to try and stop what was to be the biggest air raid on American soil since Pearl Harbor. But, because the drones were using next-generation stealth technology that was thought to be only theoretical by the Pentagon, all of the radar sites across America were completely blind to what was coming.

There was actually very little for Chris Carlton and his crew of former agents to do. After they had either subdued or turned the NSA agents in the Utah Data Center and programmed in the battle missions into the squadrons of drones, he himself could have gone on autopilot.

Over a hundred times a second, each plane automatically adjusted its flight path while sending logistical information to the other members of the swarm. All the drones were also designed to make constant threat assessments and protect against an attack. If anything but an F-22 Raptor came close, its gyroscopes and computerized fly-by-wire controls would be electro-magnetically engaged and put out of commission. The drones were capable of making that happen before the pilot would have a chance to arm his systems. Then, the fighter jet would be shot down. If one of the few mission-ready Raptors did appear, the one jet they could not disable before attacking, entire swarms of drones would engage it and seek to take it out of the sky using any means necessary, including mid-air collision. Against the hunter-fighters, human pilots did not stand a chance.

When it came time to fulfill the pre-programmed attacks, no human intervention would be necessary. The drones did not need any further targeting information or authorization to launch the GPS guided munitions. In no time at all, the MYB, Ltd. building on West 97th Street, and one square block around it, would be nothing but a pile of rubble.

The only thing Chris Carlton and his subordinates could do was override the mission and stop the birds from attacking. Based on the orders from Maxwell York, that was something that would never happen.

*****

Sampson stood up still aiming his sidearm at the general. He looked around to make sure no one was hiding in the bathroom or walk-in closet.

"Don't worry, Major, we're alone, but I assure you if you do me any harm, you won't leave this building alive."

Without being told, Sampson concluded several Special Forces units must have taken up ready positions in the adjoining penthouse suites and were waiting for some sort of signal to either attack or move out. Knowing the only way out of the trap was through the window and down the fire escape, Sampson mentally kicked himself not being more careful. In essence, his life depended on the survival of the general who was sitting on the bed sipping on scotch.

Walking towards Smythe, Sampson addressed him curtly, "Don't call me Major, I'm not in the military anymore. Who the fuck are you?"

"I'm not surprised you don't know me, or remember our brief encounter, that was many years ago--"

"And, who the fuck are you?" Sampson asked again, casting his voice as if he was talking to a child.

"I'm Adam Smythe, the de facto head of the Armed Forces under Special Master Andrew Stevens."

"So, you've moved up in the world, huh? The last time I read about you on the MIN-OPS network, all you

291

had going for you was that Fort Bragg gig hunting down unarmed civvies--real challenging."

"Pacifying three hundred-plus million Americans is much more challenging than you can imagine. As you know, the round-ups, the internment camps, that was all psych-ops to get the masses to cower and cave--and they did."

"For now." Sampson took a few steps over to Liz and looked down at her. He could see that she was breathing deeply and must have been sedated. Her hands were bound with zip-ties, but she looked none the worse for wear. "So, General, what do you want from me? If you wanted me dead, we wouldn't be talking right now."

""Right to the point, I like that. Okay, this is the thing, Dan--"

"Call me Sampson."

"Okay, Sampson, I appreciate what you did--you spared my men in New Jersey. When you wired that house to blow, you could've killed entire squads of my men if that's what you wanted to do, am I right?"

"Yeah, but I wasn't being as charitable as you think. I was sending a message to back off because the next time I wouldn't have been so nice. I guess you didn't figure that out."

"Well, in any case, now I'd like to pay back the favor. Andrew Stevens is onto you. He already has your friend Michelle Rivera Alvarez in custody and is interrogating her as we speak."

"Hmm, what do you want from her?" Sampson knew exactly what the general was after because Susan had told him about the huge gold mine they had discovered in the Canadian wilderness. When he was hired by Roland Troth, it was initially to find out the exact location of the mine--but what he had learned he had kept to himself.

Sampson knew at that moment Stevens was going to make a play for the Canadian mine and the foundry in

Pennsylvania--and, as a good judge of character, he knew Michelle would give it all up in a heartbeat. She was a strong-willed woman, but she wasn't built for the type of interrogation any second rate G-2 could give her. Without being told any more, Sampson also knew the General was planning on getting the gold for himself. Smythe wouldn't have shared the information about Michelle unless he thought it would be a distraction, as if Sampson would drop everything to rescue her--and that would draw Andrew Steven's attention away from whatever designs General Adam Smythe had.

"That's not important," the general responded, "but I suggest you hightail it outta here, go to deep cover, and get in touch with me at Ft. Bragg when the dust settles. I have the perfect position for you."

"You'll have a position for me? What about that uptight prick, Stevens? Won't he have something to say about that?"

Smythe couldn't help himself. The grin of a cat that just swallowed a canary crossed his face. "He won't be around to care."

Sampson was intrigued. "So, what do you have in mind?"

✶✶✶✶✶

Raymond couldn't bring himself to watch. Michelle Alvarez was an attractive woman who obviously took good care of herself. The only thing that gave away her true age, probably the late 40's or early 50's, were the gray roots that had started to show under her raven black hair. Seeing Andrew Stevens hover over her pressing her for answers while a couple of military thugs backed him up was not a pretty sight to see.

They were in the basement where the soldiers had transformed a utility closet into a makeshift interrogation room. Every light except for the ones over the interrogation table had been shielded. The center of the room had been cleared of everything except for what one soldier referred to as a utility kit. The kit itself was nothing but a big, black leather case containing lots of ugly looking tools and implements on tiered, retractable shelves. The tools, needles, and knives looked to be set up for display and not any practical use.

Michelle was tied down to the table with lights glaring down on her. Although her shirt and jeans were still on, the buttons on her blouse had been torn off and her bra sliced in half. Hanging over the side of table, the right cup of her bra and the tail of her shirt shook back and forth as she cried and shuddered.

"Just tell me the exact coordinates of that mine and I'll tell these men to let you go."

"Which mine?" Michelle was able to gasp out for what seemed like the hundredth time.

"Oh, come on now, are we going to keep on playing this game? Don't you think I know about that meeting with the lawyers and bankers, about you planning to go public, about your claims of a significant find? Those men you met with at the penthouse before all hell broke loose, well, they work for me; so I know you know which mine I'm talking about. What are the coordinates?"

"I don't know!" Michelle was able to scream out her response between sobs.

She looked down at her own body and saw her large breasts exposed. Stevens had threatened to cut her tits off if she didn't talk, but the soldiers, the men who were with him had looked surprised when he said it. That hint of uncertainty gave her a measure of strength and the notion Andrew Stevens wouldn't really hurt her. Yet, being so vulnerable, tied down with men all around her, she was scared to death and she couldn't stop crying no matter how hard she tried.

"Go ahead and do it, soldier."

"Do what, sir?"

"Cut her nipple off!" Stevens shouted.

The soldier, First Lieutenant Eric Franklin was a G-2, trained in military intelligence and a veteran of two wars. He was not used to taking orders from civilians, and knew what Andrew Stevens was doing would amount to nothing. He had seen and done worse himself, but had found such actions to be ineffective. Franklin knew that treating a detainee so roughly was not only beyond the pale, but the woman would end up telling them lies just to get them to stop. To be successful, interrogations had to be subtle and psychological, not physical and psychotic.

When he and his partner had prepped the room for the interrogation, they had set up the minicamera and microphone above the table so they could record any information gleaned from the detainee. From the minute Andrew Stevens burst onto the scene, it was clear he either did not know everything was being recorded or he did not care--but the lieutenant himself sure did.

Both stalling for time and attempting to absolve himself from what looked like was about to go down, Franklin lowered his voice and responded with determination, "Sir, that's not the way we do things and I refuse to comply!"

"You refuse to comply? What the fuck does that mean, do you know who I am?"

Raymond was stunned. He had never seen Andrew so out of control--and so out of touch with right and wrong. Without saying a word, he ducked out of the utility closet and headed toward the stairs to find Colonel Turney.

From behind, he could still hear Andrew shouting, "You're a goddamn coward! Give me the scalpel, I'll do it myself!"

The sound of Michelle's screams was the last thing Raymond heard as he started taking the stairs two at a time.

Chapter Twenty- Four

Under the slate gray skies that were quickly turning dark, a caravan that had been waiting in a nearby parking garage pulled up to the building on Central Park West. General Smythe was quickly escorted out of the front door by three squads of Special Forces troops. It took only seconds for the men to load into the vehicles and be on their way.

Smythe was satisfied with the meeting he had with Sampson. He had provided the major with enough information and promises about the future to secure his loyalty, at least the general believed he had. Also, he had hung out enough bait to keep both Sampson and Stevens occupied with each other so the rest of the plan could be put into action.

The second the convoy started to move south down Central Park West, Smythe was handed a satellite phone with the highest level of military encryption. He selected several pre-programmed options and activated the phone for a conference call. There was still more work to be done.

He had moved quickly to try and get the necessary partners on board with him and was relying on their love of country to get them to agree to a junta. The selling point had been that for future generations, they would all be considered the ones who delivered America from the grips of tyranny. What he had promised them, and Sampson, was a return to a truly democratic society where they would all be hailed as saviors of the republic and a new generation of the Sons of Liberty.

The other commanders he had enlisted were powerful people in their own right, and the last thing he wanted them to think was that he was trying to grab the power for himself. To maintain that posture and not come across as a dictator, he reminded himself to assume the proper decorum.

After greeting them individually, he simultaneously addressed the four other generals and one Admiral--four men and one woman who controlled other sections of the military's most critical elements. Smythe's tone was much less severe than usual, yet, he left little doubt how serious the situation was, "Gentleman, Madam, this is the last chance we have to back out. If we're going to do this, we have to do this together, as a team. If anyone has any doubts or reservations, the time to speak up is now."

No one responded.

"I'll accept your silence as an affirmation that we are all united. Now, there's one last thing before we commence--we all have to vow that no matter what happens, on our honor as Americans, we will return power to civilian authorities once we have restored the Constitution. Is that agreed?"

Five energetic voices could be heard, almost in unison, "Agreed."

General Smythe asked gruffly, "Any dissent?"

Again, there was silence.

"Good. Now, as far as New York goes, you can consider Andrew Stevens dead. If Colonel Turney's men don't blow him to hell, Daniel Sampson will get him. General McCartney, is the raid on the Pittsfield Foundry ready?"

"Yeah, Adam, we've got three platoons in place and air support is on the way. They're just waiting for confirmation of the orders."

"We'll, give it to 'em Sam, let's get this thing started."

*****

Raymond made it to the landing on the ground floor with a sense of urgency he had never felt before. The screams of the woman being abused in the basement had crystallized everything in his mind--what they were doing was not what he had signed on for. It was one thing to go to war and bomb an enemy, but it was something else all together to torture an innocent woman for information.

What he had witnessed had sickened him and Raymond's intent was to hunt down Colonel Turney and demand that he put an end to what was happening in the basement. If that meant clipping Andrew's wings by force, than so be it. Things had gone way too far and Andrew had to be stopped.

After taking a quick right turn off of the landing and pushing through the access door to the basement, Raymond ran smack into two soldiers. They were placing what looked like an electrical box with a digital face and wires protruding out of the sides on one of the load-bearing support columns just outside of the lobby.

"What the hell are you doing?"

The young soldiers stopped working, looked at each other with confused expressions, and let their arms drop to their sides.

The older of the two, a sergeant, spoke up, "I thought you knew, sir. These here are motion detectors. We've been ordered to secure this place and--"

Raymond was incredulous. "That's not a motion detector! What, do you think I'm stupid?"

He didn't hear the officer walk up behind him, nor was he able to protect himself from the blow to his skull. When the butt of the Beretta 9mm automatic landed with a loud, wet thunking sound, Raymond Behn crumpled to the floor unconscious.

"Take him out of sight and secure him." Colonel Turney's words were flat and unemotional. "Then, finish rounding up the rest of these civilian pukes and liquidate 'em all, they're enemies of the state."

"What about Mr. Stevens?"

298

Remembering how disrespectful the Special Master had been, and not wanting him to get off so easily, a small grin cracked across Turney's face. "Go downstairs, get our boys out of there and lock Stevens in the closet. Let's let the 'master' be on the receiving end of some real power."

"Aye, sir," the Marines saluted stiffly and bent over to grab Behn by the heels.

Dragging Raymond by his feet, the Marines started to head toward the basement stairs. The sound of two muffled gunshots echoed up from the basement stairs into the lobby. There was no question where the noises came from and the Marines let go of their load and started to run to the stairs.

*****

Sampson's "automatic bullshit detector," did not sound off when General Smythe was laying out the scenario. Although the conversation was brief, the general had said quite a bit. It all sounded well and good to restore the Constitution and bring the United States back to what it had been--but none of that interested Sampson in the least. Instead, the offer of complete immunity and an appointment to head a new security apparatus was what intrigued him. To secure a future for himself, and Susan, all he had to do was take care of two more tasks.

The first mission was to make sure Andrew Stevens did not survive the destruction of the MYB, Ltd, headquarters building. Since a very capable colonel and his men were in charge of the demolition, Sampson believed they'd get the job done. That made his first assignment out to be little more than acting as an observer. The second commission would be much more challenging--to hunt down and kill Maxwell York.

The intel General Smythe had provided on York was startlingly precise. The MIN-OPS computer network had captured video and pictures of men who had once been in the CIA or NSA escorting a man in a car to the UN, where it had disappeared. Using artificial intelligence, the computers had figured out who he was and where he was hiding. It was the same person who had been in the stealth helicopter and was driven in a May Bach to 48th Street.

The name and face of that person would have been unknown to the network--since York's companies had built it and eliminated any images of or references to their reclusive boss. However, prior to the latest searches, there had been additional human intervention. Earlier in the year, Daniel Sampson had entered some critical data and search parameters to find out more about the rich man with the big ideas who had been holed up on an estate in Cape Cod. What he had turned up were court records from more than fifty-years before. The court records had been sealed, but not tagged as top-secret, and the programmers who tried to erase all traces of Maxwell York had missed them.

Once that connection was made, the computer did not forget and the MIN-OPS network did what it did best, it electronically rebuilt the clandestine history of Maxwell York. With the help of Smythe's intelligence section, ironically, York's own computers and surveillance networks had figured out exactly where he was.

Sampson did not have to ask why they were blowing up the new center of government and the business center of the world, nor did he care about York being killed. It all made perfect sense. Because Stevens had overplayed his hand and lost control of Smythe, hence, control of the military, he was all but powerless--except for the fact that MYB's computers were in control of commerce. If Maxwell York was able to step back in, straighten out the ship, and use his contacts to establish his own military force, things could get ugly. It was obvious that in order to kill this particular snake, they had to chop off more than one head. With Stevens and his staff gone

300

and York eliminated, there would be a power vacuum General Smythe and his confederates would quickly fill.

It was a nice plan, Sampson thought, but short sighted. After all, who in their right mind would trust a bunch of generals who just whacked the man who had given them economic freedom? At least Andrew Stevens had given them the appearance of it and that allowed people to hope for a better future. Offing the so-called Special Master before a legitimate election would not sit well with anyone.

It was easy for Sampson to let go of that train of thought because none of it mattered much to him. It wasn't like him to think that far ahead. Like many other sociopaths, he took each day as it came with little regard for the future and focused on the things he needed to get done--and what he had to get done after making sure Andrew Stevens was dead entailed hunting down Maxwell York, his biological sperm donor.

Sampson always did love wet work, but killing Maxwell York would give him more pleasure and a different sense of accomplishment than usual. The orphanages, the foster homes, the poverty, and the scars of an abusive childhood were timeless.

Before Sampson could take care of the two tasks assigned to him by General Smythe, he had some personal business to tend to. He knew when he went back and joined the others; they would have lots of questions for him--many more than he cared to answer. To prevent what he thought of as unwelcome, unnecessary conversation, he knew what had to be done.

There was not one second of doubt or indecision. To stop the needless tears and conversation, and to eliminate lots of extra baggage, it would take only one second of work. Unsheathing the commando dagger, Sampson looked down at Liz, smiled, and slit her throat.

She never moved, struggled, or felt a thing. Seconds

later, the blood stopped pouring out of the gash in her throat and Liz was dead--silenced forever.

*****

A lot of time had passed, too much, in Susan's opinion. Sampson should have been back and they shouldn't have been standing out in the open for so long. Richard and Carlos had pretended to take turns walking back and forth to several park benches, acting out meaningful activities, just in case they were being watched. But they only keep that up for several minutes. Their nervousness then exploded into pure fear when they saw a large caravan of military vehicles heading right toward them. To their relief, the armored personnel carriers and Humvees passed without incident.

More time elapsed after the convoy continued south without paying them any mind, but the scare had been enough to make all of them even more skittish. Having long since tired of the charade of looking like they belonged, the trio had stopped walking around and were simply standing silently, looking up and down the sidewalk next to Central Park. They knew it wasn't safe, yet they had little choice but to stand there until Sampson showed up.

Susan was worried about Liz, Michelle, and she found herself starting to worry about Sampson. It wasn't like him to be irresponsible; and leaving them exposed for so long was nothing short of reckless.

No longer willing to wait, Susan whistled and nodded her head to get Carlos and Richard's attention, "Come on, let's get out of here--this is stupid."

"Where are we going?"

"What about Sampson?" the men asked at almost the exact same time.

"I think we should go to the penthouse and find out what the hell is going on. For all we know, Sampson's been captured."

"You mean, if we're lucky," Carlos quipped

"If we're really lucky, the bastard's been killed," Richard chimed in."

"You two are assholes, you know that!"

Despite her growing distaste and distrust of Sampson, Susan didn't appreciate the negative commentary. Their words stung her because if they were right about his character, like she suspected they were, that meant she had been wrong and made a stupid choice by letting a maniac into her life. It was something she wasn't yet willing to admit--but she was getting there.

Coming to Sampson's defense, and her own by defending the choices she had made, she added, "You both know we're gonna need him, so knock it off. Come on, let's go."

They had only traveled ten steps north along Central Park West, when they heard an engine revving and roaring in front of them and to their right. Looking into the quickly darkening Central Park, they saw headlights and roof-mounted spotlights of a Humvee racing toward them, tearing up large patches of grass between the stately oak trees.

"Holy shit! What the hell is that guy doing?" Richard yelled.

"They're coming right for us, what do we do?" Carlos asked.

Susan didn't manage to say a word. She simply stood like a statue and waited. She had no doubt whatsoever that the driver was heading right for them.

The Humvee did not slow until it was about fifty feet away. The wheels turned sharply right and spun, kicking up huge divots of sod as the vehicle went into a power-slide. The bottoms of the locked front wheels plowed through the turf and left huge gouges in the lawn as the rear wheels continued spinning and getting closer to

303

where they stood. The Humvee's velocity quickly started to decline at a rate that almost made it tip over onto its side.

When the massive vehicle came to a complete stop, it was just five feet away from Susan, who had not moved an inch. Carlos and Richard had both taken several steps back. The driver's door opened and a large man wearing a hat and wrap-around sunglasses stepped out onto the running board.

Still donning the uniform, Sampson extended himself to his full height and turned his body to face the others. "Come on, get in! What the hell are you waiting for?"

*****

As the elevator car made its way slowly up to the first floor, the smell of sulfur was thick in air. Smoke continued to seep out of the end of the barrel of the snub-nosed .38, which Andrew gripped much too firmly in his left hand. When the elevator door closed in the basement, he had not seen the two Marines all but fly past him toward the utility closet. If he had, he may have sent a few shots in their direction. A couple more hits would have meant a few less soldiers coming after him.

Ever since the encounter with Daniel Sampson several months before, Andrew never went anywhere without a sidearm. The fact that the lieutenant had put his hands on him wasn't enough to justify shooting him, or the other soldier in the room, but it happened and there was nothing he could do about it.

Andrew knew the stress of witnessing how quickly everything seemed to be falling apart was getting to him in ways he never expected. Nevertheless, the fact he was just about to slice off a woman's nipple was something he himself could not comprehend. It had all felt like a dream and the fact he had so much power and control over another human being caused him to go over the edge.

That had to be it, he told himself, and that also had to be the reason why he killed two men at point-blank range without blinking an eye. Sure, he was the most powerful man in the world and he could do whatever he wanted--but he had gone too far and was still trying to figure out what the hell had gone wrong when the elevator doors opened.

Andrew looked out and did not see anyone standing on the first floor, but he did see the limp body of a man who was dressed in a very expensive suit. Immediately, he knew it was Raymond and he ran up to his friend.

When he got close enough to get a good look, it appeared as if Raymond Behn was already dead. There was a thick trail of blood behind him leading up to the back of his head and it looked like he had been gurgling blood. Whoever hit him must have crushed his skull. Andrew figured it was too late to help, so he stepped over the man he had known ever since they were boys and moved stealthily into the lobby.

Judging by the sounds coming from the trading room above, there was something dramatic going on, but it was impossible to tell what. The sounds echoing off of the lobby walls were a mixture of yells, screams, and some dull, thudding noises. Whatever was happening in the trading room, it was frightening to hear and added to the sense of terror. He no longer felt like the most powerful man in the world--but like a deer caught in the headlights.

It was not just pure gut instinct that caused Andrew to have a burning desire to get the hell away from that place--although his autonomic flight response was already in high gear. Somehow his brain perceived new boxes that looked like timers on the walls, and he thought of his partner behind him lying in a pool of blood. Then, his mind added in the muffled cries and screams coming down from above. Taken together, he felt a pending sense of doom that was overwhelming.

Completely out of the nowhere, he suddenly realized what was troubling him so much. The soldiers who were supposed to be guarding the building were gone. They were not standing sentry at the door, nor could he see the patrols cruising up and down the street as they should have been. The place seemed like it had been evacuated or abandoned by the same men who he was counting on to protect him--and that raised Andrew's sense of panic to a whole new level. The implication behind the absence of soldiers made Andrew want to vomit.

What he had been thinking and sensing when meeting with General Smythe jumped to the forefront of his consciousness and his worst fears were coming to fruition. Andrew knew the general must have turned on him and, at that very moment, was making a grab for power. There could be no other reason for what he was witnessing.

He heard footsteps either coming up the basement stairs or coming down from the loft above. He couldn't tell which, but he knew it was the last possible chance for him to get away. For only a brief second, he thought of Becky, of her beauty, kindness, strength, and for a nanosecond he ached to be with her. But, those feelings evaporated into thin air as he sprinted past the reception desk up to the heavy glass doors leading out to West 97th Street.

Andrew slowed only long enough to grab the large brass handles and tug the doors open. Twisting his narrow frame and pressing against the glass wall to the left of the marble staircase, he hunched his shoulders and slipped away heading east under the cover of night.

*****

The aerial cover for the forces surrounding Pittsfield never made it to its destination. Six pilots flying modified F-16 Fighting Falcons and eight pilots coming in

306

at nearly the speed of sound in their F/A-18 Hornets were sent into nosedives and tailspins before they were within twenty miles of the target.

Maxwell York's squadrons of Unmanned Aerial Vehicles were armed with advanced electronics that not only blinded the older military jets by jamming their avionics, but also sent out electromagnetic pulses that caused the jet's computers to fail. With no on-board computers to activate the fly-by-wire controls and no instrumentation to tell the pilots where they were in space, every jet sent to cover General Smythe's platoons' advance toward the Foundry crashed into the mountains and forests of Northwestern Pennsylvania.

*****

Smythe was sitting in a helicopter flying south towards Philadelphia when the emergency call was patched through.

"Who is it?" Smythe asked the Com operator, yelling over the drumming sound of the rotors.

"Admiral Dugan, CO of Cent-COM."

"I know who the hell she is!" Smythe barked as he grabbed the headsets off of his head and replaced them with another set linked into the secure network from the cockpit. "Smythe here, go ahead."

"General, this is Lydia Dugan, down at Mac Dill-- we've got ourselves a problem."

"What kind of problem, Lydia?"

The admiral hesitated before responding. "We figured out what all those radar blackouts were across the country."

"And?"

"And, well, they were caused by unregistered UAV's flying over our airspace."

"Unregistered? What the hell does that mean?"

307

"It means that we don't know who they belong to--but they're not ours."

"Say again!?"

Although the rest of the men in the helicopter could not hear one end of the conversation at all, and only snippets of what the general was yelling back, they were able to get the gist that whatever news General Smythe was getting, and it was not good. Smythe's assistants watched his face go pale, and then red, and then they saw his jaw drop. Unable to hear enough to completely comprehend, they were left to speculate until he was done.

Admiral Lydia Dugan had no choice but to bite the bullet. They were her planes, her pilots, it was her mission under her command. She knew she should have led with the news about the fourteen planes going down and all of the pilots either dead or unaccounted for--but she was hedging her bet that General Smythe would be glad to know they had already figured out what they were up against. She was wrong.

After telling him where the drones were and where they believed they came from, then, she dropped the big one on him--telling him about the loss of the planes. When Smythe recovered from the initial shock and pressed her for more information, all she could think to do was apologize. There was little more to say. When she explained that they were still working on it and getting details on the fly, General Smythe had cut her off.

Using his access codes and classifying his orders as top priority signal traffic, General Smythe send out only one set of orders--the platoons preparing to take the foundry outside of Pittsfield were to fall back and take defensive positions. He knew they were heading right into a trap and he hoped he had reached them in time.

When the general finally disconnected the secure link and put the chopper's internal headset back on, he did not disclose to his men what he knew. He only made had one stern command, "I don't care how you do it, get me to Bragg as soon as possible."

*****

Unfortunately, what the general did not know was that his orders for a retreat had come too late. In the fields and forests around Pittsfield, the drones were using ultraviolet scopes, laser guided systems, and computer-aided search patters to hunt down every soldier and American-made military vehicle within a twenty-mile radius.

The American troops were located using their own electronic signature, weapons systems, and communications gear--and stalked unyieldingly. The drones had no mercy and no compassion; they were simply fulfilling the mission as programmed in by Chris Carlton's crew in the Utah Data Center. In less than an hour, when the fireworks were over, not one man from the three Special Forces platoons was left standing.

It was the people from the city of Pittsfield who went out into the woods and fields and found the wounded soldiers. The citizens of the free territory extended every ounce of energy to bring the warriors back to safety. Behind the thick concrete walls of the foundry, stripped of their weapons and electronics, the soldiers were made as comfortable as possible until help could arrive.

No one was sure, though, what help would arrive. It was obvious by the dead soldiers and body parts strewn around the county that a war had started--but no one knew whose side they were on.

Chapter Twenty- Five

It was obvious that the military units assigned to protect the area around the MYB headquarters had bugged out. Guiding the Humvee between the raised, abandoned crossbars of the eastern checkpoint, Sampson figured they were probably too late. If security was gone, so was anyone of any import.

"There's no one here," he told the others, "what do you wanna do?" His tone was flat and his demeanor casual, as if their task was one of several chores on a daily to-do list.

"How do you know no one's here?" Carlos asked indignantly. "We have to go inside--maybe we can figure out where they took them."

For the first time since being picked up and told of what happened, Susan looked up, rubbed her eyes turned to face Sampson. After picking them up in Central Park, he had explained what went down at the penthouse, leaving out the details about his meeting with Smythe--and the fact that Liz was still alive when he got there. When Susan heard that her sister and Michelle were gone, and the penthouse ransacked, she simply blacked out.

It had taken the short drive from Central Park to West 97th Street before she had been able to regain some semblance of composure, but it was obvious she was still not herself. Not fully believing what Sampson told them, Susan was very interested to hear how he would respond to Carlos's suggestion about finding Michelle and Liz inside of what appeared to be the abandoned headquarters of Andrew Stevens. If he wasn't willing to help them that would tell her everything she needed to know about the man she thought she could trust.

Sampson responded with a shrug, "Okay, I'll go in-- but all of you stay here. I don't like the feel of this place."

After he opened the driver's door and stepped out, he looked back into the vehicle and commanded, "Carlos, you drive. Keep your eyes pealed and be ready to hightail it outta here. You follow me?"

Resentful of the commanding tone Sampson was using with him, but fully aware that their lives may be on the line, Carlos nodded and moved up to take the position behind the wheel.

Richard and Susan watched from the passenger-side window as Sampson hustled up the elegant stairs to the mirrored glass doors of the MYB, Ltd. building. Once he opened the door and disappeared inside, Richard turned and started scanning over the interior of the Humvee. He got out of his seat and began poking around the storage compartment.

Speaking to himself more than anything, Richard asked, "Where the hell did you find that guy, and how come it's so easy for him to steal these trucks?"

Neither Susan nor Carlos responded.

"Well, if he's so damn smart and so good at survival, you'd think he'd remember to grab some water-- maybe some food."

As he talked, Richard continued to search, poking and prodding two canvas army bags lying in the back. The one on the bottom was very heavy and made a metallic clinking sound when he pushed at it with his hand. Curious as to what could be in the large canvas bags, he asked, "What's in these?"

This time, Susan looked back to see what Richard was talking about. Taking a deep breath and trying to get out of the paralyzing funk she was in, she replied, "That's our stuff, extra clothes, weapons."

"I don't think so," Richard responded. He squeezed open the heavy clip attached to the strap and pulled it off of the steel hook. Tugging the brass grommets up and over the hook, the canvas bag fell open and piles of tangled gold

311

chains and assorted jewelry toppled onto the floor of the Humvee. "What the hell is all of this? Did you two knock off a jewelry store?"

Hearing the sound of metal against metal, both Susan and Carlos turned to see what Richard had done. He picked up several heavy gold chains and held them up in the air.

"Are you sure this is your bag?"

Susan squeezed her way to the back of the Humvee to inspect the Army surplus canvas bag. Looking at it, she knew from a few tears and discolored spots that the bag was the same one they had with them since being in Cape Cod. "I'll be damned!"

She poked at the other, closed bag and ran her hand down the side. Susan recognized the curved stock of the sniper rifle and decided that Sampson must have switched bags, or got another one to stow a boatload of gold-- something he never told her he was doing. Looking closely at the chains in Richard's hand, she could see dark brown and rust-colored stains. It was dried blood. At, that moment, she knew she had to get away from Sampson as soon as possible.

"Hurry up! Put that stuff away and get back up here--he's coming and he's got Michelle with him!"

Carlos put the Humvee in reverse and spun the wheel. He pressed on the gas and went backwards for thirty feet before turning the wheel toward the marble steps of the building and accelerating toward where Sampson and Michelle stood waiting for him. When Carlos pulled up and over the curb, Sampson's displeasure was written all over his face. The hasty maneuver had given Susan and Richard a few extra seconds to make their way back up to the front of the Humvee.

Inside the building, Sampson had immediately recognized the explosive charges and knew the place was wired to be brought down in a controlled demolition. That was something General Smythe said was going to happen. He had also seen Raymond Behn dead, laying on the floor and that made him absolutely sure Smythe had been good to his word. The coup had already started.

Coming out of the building, it pissed him off to no end to see that idiot Carlos wasting time with his smart-ass antics--as if he was really helping. Trying to bring the hummer in close had actually wasted more time than the move had been worth. Sampson shook his head in disgust and mused to himself that he couldn't wait to put a bullet in the back of the man's head.

When Carlos brought the Humvee to a complete stop, Sampson all but ripped the passenger door off its hinges as he opened it, pushing Michelle into the vehicle in front of him. She looked disheveled and battered, but the fiery, intense spark was clearly visible in her dark eyes.

"Step on it, son!" Sampson yelled as he jumped in the back and landed on the floor. "The place is wired to blow!"

Susan latched onto Michelle's arm and pulled her close, "Are you okay, Michelle?"

"I am now, Honey."

*****

"What we've done, Chris, is achieve proof of concept. The idea of eliminating humans from the equation of warfare has been around for decades. What you and your men have done is show that machines, drones, whatever you want to call them, are superior to man when it comes to battle. Now, get back in there and make sure you get your drones rearmed and ready to repel a counter attack. I want to let this General Smythe know we are not playing--and if he wants a war, we'll take it to him."

York was talking into the encrypted satellite phone, pacing back and forth in the steel and concrete enclosure of

313

the listening post under the U.N. The update Chris Carlton had provided him about the defense of the Pittsfield foundry was terrific news. Things had gone better than they hoped.

In the NSA's Utah Data Center, Carlton was not so happy. Viewing the action through the cameras on the UAV's, he had watched some of the best warriors the world had ever created being shredded to pieces. Even though he knew what they were doing was supposed to be for the greater good, he was still having a hard time swallowing the fact that the men the drones were killing were American soldiers.

"Whatever you say, Maxwell. I'm already knee deep in this shit, I may as well go all the way in, huh?"

"Oh, come on, Chris, I know you don't like the idea of killing your fellow Americans, good, loyal soldiers--but think of the big picture. For those who die now, there will be a better life for their children, their progeny, and yours."

Carlton felt little comfort, but he knew York was right. They had to take the battle to Smythe with overwhelming force-- before Smythe even knew what hit him--and that way they'd be able to come to a quick resolution with minimal loss of life. A protracted battle for power would end up killing millions, and no one wanted that.

"You're right, Mr. York. Like always, you're right." Carlton decided to change the subject, signaling the he had truly conceded the point, "So, what are you going to do about Andrew?"

"Raymond Behn was supposed to bring him in, but there seems to have been some sort of problem. We've been trying to reach Raymond by phone but there's been no response."

"You want me to track them down electronically?"

"No, I already sent George out to determine Andrew's whereabouts, he'll bring them in cleanly."

314

"Then what?"

York chuckled. "What is it with you today, Chris? Are you bucking for a promotion?"

"No, Mr. York, it's just that the drones are approaching Manhattan and if George can't get his hands on Andrew, well..."

"Yes, he might be lost, and that's perfectly okay with me."

The smile on Chris's face was conveyed as exhilaration in the tone of voice, "That's all I needed to hear."

*****

Carlos mashed on the accelerator and sped off toward the intersection. The wheels screeched around the turn as he headed north on Amsterdam. Watching the Humvee race past, several civilian patrols got on their radios to try and find out who was driving the Humvee and why they were in such a rush. Before a response could come, Carlos took a few more quick turns onto some of the narrower streets of Uptown Manhattan to lose any potential pursuers in the city's labyrinth.

Susan was relieved to see Michelle alive, and seemingly well; but, at the same time, she was very concerned. One look at Michelle and Susan could tell the woman had gone through hell. Her makeup was smeared from her tears and her blouse had obviously been ripped open. With no time to ask what happened, Susan simply held Michelle in her arms as they sped away from the building on 97th Street. As they left the immediate danger behind, she tried to comfort Michelle by hushing her sobs and stroking the woman's gray-streaked black hair.

For her part, Michelle barely had the strength to wrap her arms around Susan, and could do little more than bury her face in her breast, holding on for dear life. Still

315

trying to get her bearings after such a harrowing ordeal, she did not want to talk, and it was clear that she did not want to move from that immediate cocoon of safety.

When Susan tried to take Michelle's hand into her own, Michelle was able to give up a secret she instinctively knew she had to keep from Sampson. As she looked up into Susan's eyes, she said everything she had to say with her expression at the same time as she palmed off the small phone she had taken from the dead man's jacket pocket. Even though some minutes had passed since it all went down, Michelle's body was reacting as if everything was still happening. She could see it all in her mind's eye clear as day.

It all happened in the building where she was being held and prepared for torture. After Andrew Stevens shot the two soldiers and took off, other men had come into the room where she was tied to the table. Seeing the carnage and blood all over the room, the soldiers had not bothered to check if she was alive. Half-covered by the body of one of the dead men, Michelle had remained still and waited until the others left before she made her move.

Lucky for her, the man lying on top of her had a utility belt and a knife she was able to reach. As soon as she had cut herself free from the zip-ties, Michelle looked around the basement to try and find a better place to hide-- but, because she took one of the soldier's radios with her, she was able to hear when the rest of the men were ordered to leave the building.

It shocked her to learn that they soldiers were going to blow up the building, because she knew the infrastructure had become the center of commerce and the center of power. But she didn't have time to think of the implications. Instead, she focused her mind on the most important task--she had to get out before it was too late.

Slowly and cautiously, she had made her way up the

stairs toward the lobby. Several times she was forced to stop when she heard gunshots coming down from above or ringing phones. She knew she was taking a chance being on the stairs but she figured being out in the open and on the move was better than standing still locked in an elevator.

Only after most of the radio traffic stopped did she feel safe enough to peek her head around the corner of the basement stairs and look into the lobby. That was where she saw the man lying on the floor. Just by looking at him, and the drying pool of blood around his head, she knew he was dead. Seconds after Michelle had walked up to the body and looked down to see if she recognized him, the small phone inside of his jacket pocket started to ring.

At first, the chirping phone almost scared her to death. Then, because she recognized Raymond Behn's face from all the news reports as one of Andrew Steven's associates, she decided to take the phone. Only minutes later, Sampson had come barging into the lobby and all but dragged her out of the building.

Silent and scared in the back of the Hummer, no words had to pass between them. Susan recognized the look Michelle had given her as she passed off the tiny phone and also felt the strong squeeze of her hand. Slyly, Susan took the phone and slid it into the pocket of her well-worn jeans.

Once Carlos felt safe enough to slow down, he looked in the rear view mirror at Sampson. "Where do we go now?"

Hearing the question, Michelle let go of Susan's waist and looked up. At the same time, Susan and Richard turned to face Sampson. Since he had taken control, and because he was supposed to be the survival expert, they all looked to him to make the decision, hoping he would know what to do.

"They're going to blow that place, and that means this whole city is gonna go up in smoke. We've got to get

317

out of here ASAP. Carlos, get to the GWB and get on 80 West--then we'll decide what to do."

With no hesitation, Susan barked out, "What about Liz? We can't leave her here!" Placing her hand on Michelle's cheek and guiding her face around so they were eye to eye, Susan asked, "Did you see my sister? Do you know where she is?"

Michelle's face went pale. She wet her dry lips with her tongue and a sad expression passed over her cheeks. "I'm sorry, Honey, I think she's dead."

Susan's face took on a questioning expression.

Michelle continued in as tender of a voice as she could muster, "She saw the Army guys come into the penthouse and one of them shot her with some kind of dart gun after she hit the floor, so I...I'm, don't know...I'm sorry honey."

Susan had no more tears to cry. Her emotions were so overwhelmed by everything that had happened that the only way her mind could cope was by disconnecting. Like hitting a light switch, all of the feelings of grief, anxiety, fear, and pain went away and were instantly turned off. Her friends and family would think of her in such a state as having a complete emotional breakdown--but a Military Instructor would see her transformation in a completely different way. Someone like Sampson could look at Susan DiGiovanni and know she was conditioned for war. The blank stare in her eyes displayed the fact that she was mission ready.

Things could not have gone any smoother for Daniel Sampson. Without having to say a word, Michelle had provided him with cover as far as Liz was concerned. How she really died was no longer relevant, nor was the fact that he had killed her. In addition, by stumbling across the stunned Michelle in the lobby of the MYB headquarters, he believed he looked like some kind of hero in the eyes of the only other person who mattered, Susan.

The only thing left for him to do was to get himself and Susan out of the city and lay low until the dust settled.

As surprising as a lighting strike and a clap of thunder on an otherwise clear night, the initial flash from the explosion caught everyone in the Humvee off guard. From behind them, the first bunker buster bomb exploded deep within the bowels of the building on West 97th Street. Seconds later, the concussion from the blast and the sonic wave made it seem like the entire city was shaking.

*****

"Fire for effect! Fire for effect!"

The night lit up with tracers and the streaks of rocket exhaust flaring behind shoulder-fired missiles. But, it was no use. The planes kept on coming, the bombs kept on falling, and there wasn't a damn thing they could do to stop the onslaught.

The planes the men were shooting at did not resemble any flying machines they had seen before, and none of the soldiers witnessing the display could believe what was happening. Try as they might, neither the civil air defense units nor the well trained, armed forces specialists were able to bring down a drone. Somehow, the UAV's were immune to SAM's, able to out-maneuver Sidewinder missiles; and shooting mini-guns at them was like trying to hit a humming bird with a spitball. The attacking birds were simply too fast, too precise, and too aggressive at lighting up and taking out every radar installation.

Word spread quickly amongst the defenders that what they were facing were drones put into play by some unknown enemy force. However, because the men in the air-defense units were expecting to maintain complete air superiority--they had left most of their plane-puncturing toys at home.

As the soldiers on the ground continuously fired and

painted the sky red with ineffective anti-aircraft fire, the men were all waiting for the fast movers from Norfolk and New London to swoop in and take out the drones. Unfortunately for them, it was something that would never happened. They had no way of knowing the national air-defense assets had all been taken out of the game without firing a shot. Even if the upper-tiered commanders did know the drones had wiped out the aircraft sent to defend the city that would be the last piece of information they'd tell the troops.

Within twenty minutes after the first squadron of Ova's appeared, not one building was left standing on West 97th Street between Amsterdam and Broadway. Not one of Andrew Steven's associates was left alive. Not one computer system or data storage device remained operable. In one fell swoop, the entire financial system of North America based on Ameros came to a screeching halt.

*****

Andrew had no idea where he was going or what he was going to do. When the attacks started, there was no doubt in his mind his facility was the primary target. He was also sure that General Smythe wanted him dead--but that didn't explain the aerial attacks on Manhattan. If they wanted to take him out, there was no need to go to such extremes. Why not just go with the demolition they had planned--the explosives being put into place Stevens himself had seen? Either something had gone terribly wrong or someone else had jumped in the game and was making a move to take over America. Stevens knew there was only one person who had those kinds of ambitions and that kind of capability--Maxwell York.

Skulking his way south through the nearly deserted streets of Uptown and then Midtown, it was easy to go unrecognized. No one was interested in a man walking the streets while the city was being bombed from above. Cars and trucks of military men, fire engines, and all manner of emergency service vehicles were all but flying through the streets, heading north to where the attacks were concentrated. With so much confusion, the only idea that came to Steven's was to get as far away from the explosions and destruction as he could.

A black Mercedes pulled up to the curb right next to where Andrew was walking. The only private car on the streets of Manhattan pulling up beside him, Andrew realized, was an impossible coincidence. Moreover, trying to blend into the environment, or be invisible was impractical since he was only one of very few people on the sidewalk. At first, Andrew did not turn to see who got out of the car, but he did hear the car door slam. He wished whoever was walking behind him was a stranger and wanted nothing to do with him. But, that's all it was, wishful thinking. He knew whoever was looking for him had found him.

Having no choice but to confront his pursuer, Andrew stopped and turned. A thin man wearing casual clothes stepped out of the shadows and slowed his pace as he got closer.

"George? George is that you?" Andrew knew the man to be one of Maxwell's old sycophants; one of many old-school lackeys who did what he was told when he was told. He also knew George had worked with York over the years to dislodge dictators and corrupt foreign dignitaries; it was no surprise then that after the world had fallen apart, he would crawl out from whatever rock he was hiding under and be there to prop up the likes of Maxwell York.

"Yes, Mr. Stevens. Mr. York is waiting for you. I need you to come with me right now before it's too late."

"Too late?" Andrew held his hands out, palms up as if he was feeling for rain, "I think it's already too late. I screwed up, George, and I did it at Maxwell's expense--so what do you think he's going to do to me?"

"All he wants to do, Andrew, is talk to you. It's not safe out her--so let's go, now."

George had been a top spook in Clandestine Services for decades and then acted as a handler for some of the best sources in the Middle East. No matter what he was up to, though, he always tried to maintain his tradecraft and make sure not to lose the edge a spy needed to sustain his livelihood and his life. Included in that was a sixth sense to know when one was being watched or followed.

At that moment, the hair on the back of George's neck stood at attention. "Come on, Andrew let's get the hell out of here! I give you my word, we'll be safe."

The roar of jets buzzing the city, and the explosions from the bombs they dropped, had ended. Besides the sounds of sirens and the roaring engines of passing emergency vehicles, there was an eerie silence. Looking up and down the block, the few pedestrians who had been visible were gone. It was as if the others knew something was about to happen and they did not want to be around to see it.

The sound of high heels clicking on the blacktop and echoing between the buildings broke the silence. George felt relieved, thinking what he had sensed was the person who had been standing on the other side of the street watching them.

A tall, black woman wearing a skin-tight black dress and three-inch black pumps sashayed over to where George and Andrew were talking. There was no way she was a prostitute, George thought. Looking at her clear skin, bright eyes, and manicured hands, he could tell she was a woman of means--which made it even stranger to see her out at night and alone.

As she approached, the woman pulled the spangled Gucci bag from under her arm, opened it, and started to reach inside. Instinctively, George reached for his piece and pushed back against the nearest building.

"Do either of you gentlemen have a light? It's great to be able to smoke in the city again, don't you think?"

Stunned by the woman's casual mannerisms, Andrew started to pat down his jacket and pants looking for a lighter, as if one would magically appear in one of his pockets. "Sorry, Miss, I don't smoke."

George hesitated, looking back and forth between the woman and Andrew. Realizing they did not know each other, and she was not some sort of decoy, he let his guard down. As soon as he started to reach into his pants pocket for his trusty Zippo, he knew he had made the biggest mistake of his life. The woman raised a Beretta 9mm and pulled the trigger.

George's head snapped back and hit the wall behind him as the bullet passed through. As if moving in slow motion, with his back against the wall, he slid down further and further until his legs buckled and he tumbled to the sidewalk.

Andrew's eyes burned and his ears were ringing. His mind could not absorb what he had just witnessed and it felt like he had gone blind. While blinking his eyes, the vision of old George with a big, gaping hole in his forehead came into focus. Then, as the ringing in his ears receded and his normal vision returned, Andrew realized the woman was pointing the big black gun directly at his face.

If he had his wits about him, Andrew would have remembered to reach for his .38 and at least try to fight for his life. But, at that moment, planning anything was well beyond his capacity to think. He could still feel the slick mist of blood from George's head drying on his face.

The woman did not shoot him where he stood. Instead, she wanted him to know who she was, why she was there, and why she was taking his life. In full control of the situation, and as smooth as a martial arts master practicing a move for the thousandth time, she turned her body, twisted her hip, and lifted her leg as she kneed Stevens in the balls.

Andrew saw stars and felt the rush of pain traveling from his groin into his gut. The next thing he remembered, he gagged, turned his head, and dry-heaved until it felt like was going to blow his esophagus out of his mouth. When he finally came back to his senses, the beautiful black woman was sitting on his chest, straddling him, pointing the barrel of the handgun into his nostril.

Focusing his eyes on hers, he just knew the woman was insane and he was a dead man. All he could do was try to buy some time and hope someone would come along and save him.

"Do you know who I am?" the woman asked, smiling smugly.

Andrew tried to shake his head, "no" but she was pushing the gun too tightly against his nose.

"Answer me!"

"No."

"Well, let me tell you. My name is Darla Jones. Darla Jones. Does that name ring a bell?"

"Uh-uh," was all Andrew managed to get out. He wasn't even trying to link the name and the face. Knowing he was going to die, it didn't seem to matter if he knew who the woman was.

"Tommy Jones was my husband, and you had him killed. Do you remember now?"

"I don't know who the fuck you are and I don't care! Just do what you're gonna do or get the fuck off of me!"

It was as if Darla did not hear him. She pushed the gun into his nostril even deeper and pressed on, "Are you are the one who ordered my husband killed at Roland Troth's estate in Greenwich, yes or no?"

Thinking it may be the only way to save his own skin, Andrew replied meekly, "Okay, lady, yeah. I knew about your husband being killed, but I didn't do it."

"Then who did?"

"Ask Daniel Sampson, he was the one who did it!"

Funny, it was Sampson and Susan DiGiovanni who told me it was you. This is for Tommy."

Those were the final words he ever heard. Darla squeezed the trigger and blew the top of Andrew's head off.

Confident she had avenged the death of her husband, Darla let the Beretta fall from her hand. She wouldn't need it anymore.

Standing up and looking over at George, she saw the keyless remote laying on the sidewalk beside his hand. With no prior consideration or planning, she walked over to the black sedan, started it up and drove off.

Darla didn't know where she was going to go or what she was going to do. After days following, trailing, hiding, and playing crazy cat and mouse games with the military men guarding Stevens, it was all finally over. Without even thinking about it, she found herself on the George Washington Bridge heading west. The first conscious, considered thought that came to mind was getting on Interstate 80 and driving all the way across the state of Pennsylvania until she was in Pittsfield. At least there she'd be safe.

*****

York's men had been able to take control of the Long Endurance Multi-Intelligence Vehicles hovering over the city. Hacking into the blimps' computers and accessing the array of cameras was especially easy since firms owned or financed by one of York's subsidiaries had built the top-secret blimps. With almost limitless perspectives from 5,000 feet over the city, streaming, real-time images were being beamed down to the bunker hidden deep below the United Nations.

Once the Mercedes George had been driving came

to a stop, Maxwell York and his men had monitored the situation. They had witnessed the beautiful, tall, black woman approach and methodically assassinate both George and Andrew. It had happened so fast there was nothing they could have done to intervene.

Jackson, the senior man remaining on York's detail had not hesitated to step in and take charge. Before Maxwell even had the chance to speak, UAV's and other assets were being directed to locate and eliminate the assassin getting away in the Mercedes.

"Sir we have the woman on target, what do you want us to do?" Jackson's voice was deep and commanding, but his sense of duty and loyalty led him to defer to the old man.

York looked even older, sicker, saddened by the turn of events. Things were not going as he had hoped or planned. What made him sad wasn't so much that Andrew was dead. Instead, he was upset because he never had the chance to ask him Why.

Maxwell hated New York with every fiber of his being. More than anything, he loathed the residents; the foreigners, the blacks, and the homosexuals. In his mind, there was nothing in the city worth saving and he saw the situation as an opportunity to do something he had wished to do for as long as he could remember.

"No, Jackson, leave the woman alone...I don't care what she does."

"So, what do you want us to do?"

"I want you to use whatever firepower you have left and destroy this god damn city and everyone in it."

Chapter Twenty Six

A matter of seconds after the computer networks in New York stopped responding, the contagion, a new wave of financial calamity and confusion, spread across the globe. Within hours, the streets of London, Paris, Berlin, Moscow, as well as Tokyo, Beijing, Mexico City and Montreal were alive with wave after wave of undulating crowds. That all took place simultaneously with the rioting from New York to Los Angeles.

Despite the promises of safety and security for their funds, and most everyone switching over to an electronic, gold-backed system, the inability to use their gold credit cards to buy anything brought on a level of remonstration the world had ever seen.

The old governments had failed and elitists, business moguls, and bankers who were allowed to come in and fix things seemed to have failed as well. Only a few short months had passed and, once again, the world was falling apart. Feeling they were out of options, and with nothing left to lose, most of the people in the civilized world started to riot.

*****

It was well after midnight when the Humvee reached the Delaware Water Gap. At that hour, even if the world had not fallen apart, the multiple lanes of Interstate 80 connecting New Jersey to Pennsylvania would have been clear. With no reason for any sane trucker to go near New York City, even the tractor-trailers used to haul merchandise to and from the East Coast's megalopolis had abandoned the highways.

Carlos drove the heavily armored vehicle cautiously, not pushing the engine to conserve fuel. Even at a modest pace, the rumbling noise inside the steel-shielded cabin would have drowned out routine conversation. Michelle sat behind him in a jump seat. She was still very much on edge from the ordeal she had been through, and because her nervous system had been tweaked to such an extreme, she found it impossible to sleep. At the same time, she was in no mood to talk. That would have required her to shout over the drone of the tires, something she did not have the vigor to do.

Susan sat in the seat beside Michelle. She had her eyes closed but, instead of resting, she was deep in thought. Despite their narrow escape from the attack on Manhattan, and unimpeded trip through New Jersey, there was no way in the world she could let her guard down. Losing Liz, along with the unmasking of Sampson, the man she had shared her bed with, made her feel an overwhelming amount of distress intermingled with disgust.

The man she was focusing on was sitting right in front of her, and if he could sense the wrath of her stare, he would have felt her eyes burning holes in the back of his head. The strange part about everything, Susan thought, was that Sampson had not been all that deceptive. More than anything, he'd simply been illusive.

She knew the basics about his past--he was not just a former a Marine but also that kind of government hit man. He had told her as much and his survival skills were what initially made him so attractive. Yet, all along, he had been acting, pretending to be some kind of decent human being while successfully concealing the true ugliness and evil inside. Sampson had successfully presented himself as a caring, yet socially awkward, man with a pure heart. In her time of need, she had fallen for the facade--and that was what made her angry.

All along there had been clues, hints about his true nature--but she had ignored them. The minute she saw the blood-covered gold, obviously a private stash he had collected while trawling the streets of Manhattan, the veneer came crashing down. The gold could have been some kind of insurance policy, a reserve of hard currency just in case they needed it. The fact he had kept the stockpile from her meant he never intended to tell her about it.

The possibility of him being a monster had hit her like a sledgehammer. How many people had he robbed? How many people had he killed to accumulate that treasure? It was unusual for her not to intuitively sense the masquerade before having the truth thrust in her face and it made her mad at herself for being so easily drawn in. Sure, Sampson had made it very easy for her to fall into his web of deception. The man was obviously very good at what he did, and he was a master manipulator. Of that she had no doubt. Still, looking back at the way things had evolved with him, that she had spread her legs for him, made her feel sick to her stomach.

Sampson was seemingly sound asleep in the front passenger seat of the Humvee. Even though Manhattan had been lit up like a Roman candle, and world starting to collapse around them, the man had been able to slouch down, lower his chin to his chest, and doze off as if everything was just peachy. He hadn't even bothered to give them orders, as was his way. Instead, Major Daniel Sampson, USMC (Ret.), was acting as if he did not have a care in the world.

The chirping of the small cell phone stuffed in Susan's pocket was of a high enough pitch to cut through the humming ruble produced by the tire's treads.

At the exact same time Susan swatted her hand down to cover the ringing of the phone, Sampson's eyes snapped open. "What the fuck was that?" His tone was more than accusatory, it was downright chilling.

Susan looked pleading at Michelle with her eyes wide open, unsure what to say.

329

Unlike Susan, Michelle was not as attuned to Sampson's wrath and did not have first-hand knowledge of his capacity for violence. She responded with confidence, "I took it off of one of Stevens's men, I thought we could use it."

"I told you no fucking cell phones!" As he said this, Sampson got out of the front passenger seat and moved to the back of the Humvee. Even hunched over in a crouch, he still presented an imposing, threatening figure as he hovered over the women.

"You told me no such thing!" Michelle retorted defensively.

"Give it to me," he ordered, extending his hand out in Susan's direction.

Susan had managed to slip the unusually small phone into her palm where she had squeezed it to try and silence the continuous chirping noises as it rang.

In her anger, Susan couldn't resist poking at Sampson's distaste for not being in full control. With a disrespectful, slanted grin, she handed him the device. "Everyone knows where we are by now, what are you gonna do?"

He snatched the phone out of her hands and looked at it. It was not a commercial model and he immediately recognized the tiny fractal antennae package as military satellite communications gear--although it was a device he had never seen before. It didn't surprise him that one of Steven's men had such a device on him.

They all knew Raymond Behn, Andrew Steven's number-two man, was dead. Both Michelle and Sampson had seen him splayed out on the floor of the MYB headquarters before it was turned into a pile of debris. They also knew from following the news that Behn was favored to win in the upcoming election of the North American Ruling Counsel, one of the most powerful positions in the world. Since he was dead, and the world's new center of commerce was obliterated, something the power brokers had to have known, they should also have known it was impossible to reach Behn. That fact made the ringing phone, and who was on the other end of the call, into an irresistible enigma. They all wondered who would be trying to reach the dead man on an ultra-secure link.

Unable to resist the impulse himself, Sampson pushed a button and held the phone to the side of his face. "Speak!"

"Ah, Daniel, is that you? I knew you were with the others, but I didn't think you'd answer."

The old man's voice on the other end of the call struck a chord with Sampson, but initially he was not exactly sure of the source. "Who the hell is this?" he asked grimly, shocked that whoever was calling knew him.

"I think you've already figured that out. This is Maxwell York."

"York? You've had some powerful people looking for you these past few weeks."

Sampson looked up and noticed the women staring at him, startled to hear that the illusive man behind the rest of the elites was on the line.

"Yes, quite strange, wasn't it." York replied smugly. "But I was never lost, they were."

"Is that why you decided to take out your protégé?"

"And my headquarters, yes. They had made a mess of everything by moving so fast so I decided to start out fresh--a clean slate if you will."

York sat back in the old, sturdy padded captain's chair at the head of the conference room table inside of the bunker. Although the generator was on, casing a pale yellow light across Maxwell's face, the pallid tone of his skin made him look less than alive.

The computer terminals and monitors mounted in the walls of the bunker where nothing but relics of the cold war. However, the big metal desks and Formica counters provided plenty of space for modern gear to be set up. The men attending to York had needed only minutes to set up the equipment needed to communicate with their partners and monitor the situation on the ground. The laptops and tablets arrayed around York and his men even had the capacity to display the video feeds from whatever drones they chose. At that very moment, York was looking at the infrared image of a Humvee moving at a moderate pace crossing a bridge over the Delaware River.

"Why are you trying to reach Raymond Behn? You know the man's dead, don't you?"

"Oh, come on now, Daniel, you continue to underestimate me. You must know I'm talking to exactly who I want to be talking to."

"So you know he's dead?"

"And so is Andrew," York added, not a hint of sorrow in his voice. "Don't you know the technology these days is quite amazing? I've seen more than you can imagine--in real-time no less."

"Geez, you're worse than a crocodile, you'd eat your own damn young if you could, wouldn't you?"

Ignoring the barb, Maxwell went on, "I'm surprised you didn't try to locate me. Isn't that what Smythe ordered you to do?"

Sampson pulled the phone away from his mouth and covered it in his palm. Addressing Carlos, he ordered sharply, "Pull over, we've got to get rid of this phone and switch vehicles."

"Switch to what?" Carlos asked, shrugging his shoulders and looking around to empty lanes beside him.

"Just shut up and do it before a drone puts a missile up our tailpipe."

"You better do it," Richard chimed in from the back, "If they've got a hook into that phone, they already have a bead on us."

Carlos pulled the Humvee over and brought it to a

complete stop right next to the guardrail overlooking the roiled waters of the Delaware River. Just as Sampson pulled the door open and stepped out onto the concrete surface, heavy flakes of snow started to fall.

Replacing the phone, Sampson started speaking as he walked away from the vehicle, "So that's it? You bombed Manhattan because you wanted to send a message to Smythe, huh?"

"That, yes, and I also wanted to get your attention as well."

"My attention? Why the hell would you care about me? Didn't you give up on that decades ago?" The bitterness in Sampson's voice was a surprise, even to himself. The years of abuse and neglect still stung him and talking to the man who had subjected him to such a cruel life was not so easily forgotten.

"Don't be so sentimental, Sampson. It's just an accident of history that has you in possession of what I need."

Chagrined, Sampson felt his face go red. He immediately thought of going back to New York, hunting the fucker down, and poking York full of holes so that every drop of the man's arrogance would ooze out of him-- then and only then would he kill the bastard. "What do you want, York?"

"I want access to the Seven Rams' gold mine in the Yukon,"

"Well, that's your first mistake--it's not really in the Yukon, it's in the Northwest Territories--"

Walking up behind him, Susan heard the last words out of Sampson's mouth and knew he was talking about the mine--the one reason, she knew, the people who had taken over had let them live. No only did the men in charge need the coordinates for the lode of gold, but they also needed access to the technology used to get to such a beautifully hidden vein.

333

Susan knew it was her fault Sampson knew it all--
and she knew at that moment he would trade what he knew
for his own future. That was something she could not let
happen.

Without listening to another word, Susan turned and
took purposeful, determined strides toward the back of the
Humvee.

When she nudged past Richard without even
looking at him, he asked her quietly, "What's up? Where
are you going?"

"I've got some shit to take care of," was all she said.

Seeing the determination in her face, Richard
simply stepped back and let her go. He turned and looked
west, watching Sampson walk further and further down the
bridge.

"So," Sampson asked into the small phone, "what's
in it for me?"

*****

General Smythe looked over the statistics again, not
believing the information his eyes conveyed to his brain.
He had lost several brigades to the drones and his entire
battalion in Pennsylvania had been disabled. On top of that,
the civil air defense system on the east coast had been
completely helpless against just a few squadrons of the
mysterious UAV's.

By the time the general had reached Fort Bragg, the
Intelligence Group had figured out where the drones had
come from and who was behind them. But, that was way
too little way too late. The acquired knowledge did not help
matters any--instead, knowing Maxwell York and his
network of old spooks had such a devastating capacity
under their control was infuriating. Without air superiority,
the capabilities of the rest of the armed forces under
Smythe's command were immeasurably attenuated.

There were staff members standing and sitting all around Smythe in his office. Some of them looked anxious, as if awaiting orders; while others tried to hide their faces, hoping they wouldn't be confronted. The silence in the room of senior, executive officers was so abnormal that it was distracting.

Finally breaking the silence, Smythe barked out, "Get on the MIN-OPS system and figure out what York is doing. I don't care how you do it--but get in touch with him and let him know we want to negotiate."

Immediately after he barked out the orders, several officers took off in a jog toward their posts.

"What's the situation with the nukes?"

"They're under our control, General, as are the boomers and carrier groups. Any orders?"

"Yeah, tell 'em all to sit tight until the dust settles. No use losing any more men than we have to and blowing up the world a couple hundred times over won't do us any good, now will it?"

The fact that Smythe had not lost his mind and had decidedly taken the nuclear option off the table made everyone in the room breathe a sigh of relief.

"Listen up, and listen good," Smythe commanded with a resolve that lifted the spirits of everyone in the room. "I need you all to get to work and get to work right now consolidating our forces and getting everyone up to speed on what we're facing. We have to warn everyone about these drones and their capabilities so we don't let a few wings of machines wipe us the hell out. Second, I want you to assemble the best men we've got and figure out how to bring those suckers down. Finally, get your psych-ops people out and about--we've got to get the support of the people and let them know what we're facing. If it's a war Maxwell York wants, we'll give it to him--and we'll get Dixie to rise again to kick his Yankee ass all the way back to Cape Cod."

"Sir, I got a man named Chris Carlton on the horn. He's at the NSA's Utah Data Center and says he can get us in touch with York."

"Sir!" Another officer came running into Smythe's office, waving an iPad in her hand.

"What is it Colonel?"

"We just got word from London, the Queen just ordered the execution of Sir Philip Gross and his staff!"

"Sir Gross? Who the hell is that?"

"I don't know, but she's also asking us for military assistance to take on enemies of The Crown and the common people of Europe."

"The common people of Europe? You mean to tell me she's taking sides against her own?"

"Looks that way," the colonel answered with a shrug, her face red with a mixture of excitement and confusion. "But what we do know for sure is that the people of London have taken to the streets and the city is burning..."

Speaking to no one in particular, General Adam Smythe shrugged in response and said in a low, morose tone, "Oh, God. This is about to get real messy."

*****

When Sampson finished the conversation, he switched off the phone and started to slide the small devise into his front pocket. Before he started to turn around, he knew the others were watching him--and they were standing relatively close to where he was. When he did turn to face them, he was surprised to see Susan standing in front of Michelle and Carlos holding his fully assembled sniper's rifle.

"What the hell are you doing with that?"

Gesturing with the barrel of the weapon, Susan asked, "What are you doing with that phone? I thought you

336

said you had to get rid of it."

"I changed my mind. Now, are you going to answer me, you stupid bitch? What are you doing with that weapon? Put it on the deck and step away from it before you do something you're gonna regret. Do I make myself fairly clear?"

"I already regret what I've done." As she spoke the words, Susan raised the weapon and flicked off the safety. When she pointed it directly at Sampson's chest, she put her finger on the trigger.

Sampson looked around for a route of escape and could only come up with one possibility. "Hold it, hold it!" What's this about, Susan? Why are you doing this?" As he spoke, he moved backwards toward the bridge's side. Even though he knew she could pull the trigger before he could react, he had no choice but to try and to keep moving. "Susan! Susan! Look at me! Stop it--put the gun down!" With each word, he moved closer and closer to the guardrail.

Carlos and Michelle were so caught up in the drama unfolding in front of them, they didn't hear the engine of the Mercedes or notice the headlights as the car approached. Richard saw the car coming but was too stunned by its appearance to react. Instead, he pressed his body against the Hummer and let his jaw drop open in a paralytic gape.

Locked in a death-stare, Susan sensed nothing but the beating of her own heart. It was only when the tires squealed and the headlights of the big sedan blinded them all that they became conscious of the Mercedes barreling down on them.

Carlos grabbed Michelle and pulled her out of the way. Together, they ran toward the safety of the hummer. Susan was a little slower to react and she was forced to dive out of the way as the tires screeched and smoked when the big Benz hit and bounced over the high curb.

It looked like Sampson did not stand a chance. The car was heading right at him and there was nowhere for him to go. As the driver of the Mercedes pressed the car forward, the gap between the front grille and the side railing of the bridge disappeared. Sampson, who had been standing in that gap jumped, spun, and pushed off the hood of the car with one foot. As the car crashed into the guardrail, he was launched several feet into the air and took flight in the direction of the river.

The last thing Susan saw of Daniel Sampson was the bottom of his military boots. Then, gravity took over and he started to take the long, cold drop into the raging waters below.

When the Mercedes hit the steel rails, the crunching sound of metal and sound of breaking glass overwhelmed the senses. It took several seconds for everyone to regain their composure and fully realize what had happened.

Susan was the first one to her feet. Unconsciously, she secured the sniper rifle and pointed it toward the Mercedes as she took several tentative steps toward the driver's door. From behind her, Carlos and Michelle walked up in support, both anxious to find out who the person driving the car was and why they crashed the way they did.

Richard was compelled to run over to the rail and look over the side. He wanted to see if he could see or hear Sampson swimming or struggling below. In the pitch black of night, he neither heard nor saw a thing.

Everyone came to a stop when the driver's door popped open. A lithe, caramel-skinned leg of a woman extended out and a bare foot was placed hesitantly on the cold concrete. Susan saw the hem of the black dress as the tall black woman stepped out of the car and came to her full height.

"Darla! Oh, my God! What are you doing?"

After Darla Jones had disappeared and none of them thought they would ever see her again. Susan, Carlos, and

Michelle all ran up together and gathered her in their arms, holding her up and hugging her.

Ignoring their questions about where she had been and what had happened, Darla continued to focus on the job she knew she had left undone. Struggling against Susan's grip, she finally managed to get their attention. "Sampson--he, he killed Tommy. We have to get him, he got away!"

"No, honey, no! He didn't get away, you hit him didn't you? If that didn't kill him, the fall to the water did." Susan's voice was shaking and she wasn't nearly as confident as her words sounded.

"No! He jumped," Darla gasped. "We have to get him, he killed my Tommy."

Susan did not know why she did it or what drew her to the side of the bridge. It was pitch black and there was no way to see down into the water. Yet, she walked over to the railing and looked down. The sound of the water roiling over the rocks could be heard but little else and, at the moment, she believed what she was doing was pointless-- until she remembered what she was holding in her hands.

She raised the rifle and looked down at the water using the scope that was specifically designed to display the heat signature of a potential target. She intuitively guided the infrared lens toward the near bank and scanned first north and then south along the woods bordering the water. The green and red outline of a man appeared like a glowing ghost against an ebony background. He was crawling out of the water and struggling to find his way through the thick brush next to the river.

Looking at Susan DiGiovanni, her beautiful brown hair tied back in a pony-tail, her cheeks glowing red from the cold, her big brown eyes, and the grin that came across her face, there was no way one could tell she was about to kill a man. For a split second, she did think it was ironic that the man she was about to kill was the one who taught

339

her how to shoot. Then, she realized, in some strange way, Sampson being gunned down the same way he had killed so many others was nothing less than poetic justice. Raising the barrel only slightly, Susan took aim, put her finger on the trigger, exhaled and squeezed.

The other three jumped at the roar of the gun and ran over to where Susan remained standing, using the scope to detect the pattern of remains splattered around the body and the eerie green glow of the body itself. Sampson was not moving.

"It's over," she said calmly. "I got the son-of-a-bitch."

—

Epilogue

Unbelievably, it had only taken weeks for the vast majority of the world's population--voluntarily or otherwise--to come under the control of new regimes. Governments had been toppled and replaced by administrators or governors who took whatever measures they deemed necessary to quell all disturbances. Most nations were easily subdued, while a handful still faced critical situations or all out war. The difference between the conflicts and others that had come before was that every nation in the region, and on the planet, had agreed to come together as one.

However, as quickly as it had come together, it had all fallen apart. What had been promised had not been enough and the citizens of the world rebelled.

The world had been partitioned by the neofeudalists into seven regions of influence: North America, Central and South America, Europe, Africa, Middle East, Asia, and Northeast Asia. They had appointed seven Councils of Seven, executive boards to administer each region and a master board of seven to resolve differences and disputes between them all. Since the new leaders all belonged to the same elite group as Maxwell York, and had the same ambitions, they were committed to crush the resistance, wherever it occurred, at any cost. Even though things were happening faster and different from the way York and his inner circle had planned it, the men and women in charge were smart, highly adaptable, and had every resource in the world at their disposal.

The governing counsels that had taken over were being propped up and supported by powerful forces, forces that had either been co-opted or infiltrated over the years by the rich and powerful. Supporting what was necessary to bring the world under their dominion were most of the world's CEOs, a vast majority of the military leadership, and, most importantly, the media moguls who had the power to sway opinion. Using combined international resources, it was not hard for the exceptionally, but unusually, generous governing councils to prevail in the under-developed world. Provided with free housing, food, and medical care if they conformed, many people all over the world were once again pacified.

It was all a show, a parade of manufactured evidence that everything was going to be okay. What the people of the world didn't know was that the power brokers who had taken over were slowly but surely replacing everyone who did physical labor. Once the computers, drones, robots, and machines could provide the things the elitists needed, the lower casts would be systematically replaced and eliminated. Until that happened, in most of the world, the people would live in ease and comfort until the day they died.

Unfortunately for most, only a select few would be allowed to procreate. The virus had taken hold and was doing exactly what it had been programmed to do. The lineages of the rich, successful, smart, connected, talented, and powerful would continue on. For everyone else, in less than fifty years, their hereditary line would come to an end.

There was, however, one part of the world where things were not so simple and the transition to a New World Order not so smooth. In North America, across the land that was once the United States, Canada, and Mexico, the wars and battles for supremacy continued. There were people who would not give up the fight to have liberty and control their own destiny armed with the facts about the virus and the truth about what the neofeudalists planned, they fought on.

*****

The sun was in its full glory, lighting up the valley and casting few shadows in the chasms and crevices of the surrounding mountains. Looking down from the top of the northeastern mountains, the tree-lined streets, and neat rows of single-family homes revealed an unlikely serenity in the town below. Only in the distance, where the highway bypass ran parallel to the Susquehanna River, did the activity of the busy world become apparent. Semis, most of them hauling liquid or compressed natural gas containers, sped along the elevated roadway.

The rapid transformation to a completely natural gas economy had been a necessity. Because of the war, the people in the Mid Atlantic had learned to make due with what they had. They had become one of several self-sustaining territories carved out of North America.

Outside of the Rust Belt, no one could know or predict what would be operational, where it would be safe to go, or who was in control of what. The uncertainties of war had torn the nation to pieces. But, inside the zone that called itself Free America, there was some stability and the people worked hard to maintain that peace; at least away from the front lines.

The Deep South was firmly in the hands of General Smythe and a large majority of the former American armed forces. The eastern seaboard, along with everything west of the Rockies, was the domain of Maxwell York and his associates--mostly former spies supported by the patriarchs of the New World Order. Because the people in the Rust Belt were surrounded, they could neither rely on Smythe nor York's for peace, let alone fair trade. Thus the inhabitants from Pennsylvania to Michigan and into Canada had quickly transformed their way of life, ably fighting off invaders on several fronts.

Much like the rest of the world, there were many pockets of territory unaffiliated with the three main factions that had divided the continent and had gone to war. At the

343

same time, there were very few areas protected from infiltration. Just east of the relative freedom offered in the territory run by the foursome of Charles "Carlos" Rivera-Ortez, Michelle Alvarez-Rivera, Darla Jones, and Susan DiGiovanni, was an active battlefield. From Upstate New York through New Jersey to the suburbs of Philadelphia, hardly a building was left standing. New Jersey was the Eastern Front and most cities closely resembled the post 1944 firebombed Berlin. South of the Mason-Dixon line to the border of Virginia, due west all the way to Denver was also no-man's land. The shale beds of the Dakotas and Wyoming were constantly changing hands as the warring parties battled endlessly for access to the valuable natural resources. Most of Texas was barren, inhabited by only the brave and the foolish who risked life and limb to secure what was left of the oil fields.

There were no more tankers shipping crude oil overseas. The pipelines from Canada or Alaska and from the Gulf of Mexico north into Texas and Louisiana had long been destroyed. Because both Smythe's and York's armies were heavily dependent on oil, wherever the black gold could be found, those were the most frequent targets and that was where the heaviest battles would occur. Also, because those two warring factions were so busy trying to destroy each other, that allowed the people of Free America to further build up their defenses and better prepare for their future.

Unlike many other parts of the country that were constantly under siege, the rural areas of Central Pennsylvania had remained relatively unscathed. Not only was there stability, but the people were actually prospering. Part of that had to do with the readily available natural gas right under their feet but the other reason for their strength was due to an alliance with Queen Elizabeth and her subjects in Canada. Through their alliances, Michelle had secured the gold and gave free America the one thing the

344

others in North America did not have, a stable means of commerce.

The governors of Free America were able to offer anyone willing to work, live, and fight for their freedom something the other warring parties couldn't--a currency backed by something real, something tangible--and that made all the difference. Having the right combination of local commodities, labor, and the proper motivation made everything else come together.

The steel workers, miners, and heavy-industry professionals provided the labor and expertise to produce the hardware. Robotics and computer experts from the universities provided the expertise needed for the software. In addition, many soldiers, sailors and others adept at the art of war who defected from the other sides joined in the fight and provided the experience for the armed forces to defend them from the attacks of Smythe's armies and York's drones. Led ably by Carlos, Free America had survived the prior months of onslaughts and had come out of it stronger than ever.

*****

The black Ford pickup pulled up to the mansion and slid to a stop on the sand and loose gravel. The engine cut off and the last of the vehicle's energy released as the tires rolled a final inch. Both doors of the elevated cabin opened and the two passengers eased out. A small woman first stepped down on the running board and then down to the stone-covered ground. Then, a small, wiry man exited slowly and carefully from the driver's side.

Michelle Alvarez-Rivera watched Carlos and Susan walk towards her from the drive to the walkway that overlooked the valley below. Carlos was walking rapidly as tiny Susan took quick little steps in her high heels to try and keep up. Long gone were the combat boots and, instead,

345

Susan was dressed as if ready to attend a diplomatic function.

The three of them had all taken up important roles in the governance of Free America. Michelle was responsible for the economy and commerce, Carlos led the national defense, and Susan was the one designated to be overseeing it all. She, along with Darla Jones as her lieutenant, was the head of the new nation; the public face of the government who conveyed to the people what their intentions were.

Susan herself would have laughed if someone had told her that she, a typical Jersey-girl--would be in any sort of political position, let alone the head of one of the most stable nations on earth. Although she had a lot of power and influence, she also knew she was primarily a talking head and the number one cheerleader for Free America. She thought to herself, if what she was doing helped, then so be it.

"Hey, girl! You're looking mighty fine."

"You don't look so bad yourself, Hon." Susan responded, greeting Michelle with a hug and a kiss on the cheek.

"How are the kids, Susan?"

"They're great! It's hard to believe how resilient they are; it's like the only thing that changed was the size of their clothes."

"And, don't forget," Carlos added, "with their Aunt Helena hovering over them at every second, they have become very spoiled." He was more than proud at how his wife had handled things in Costa Rica and how quickly she had arrived in America with Susan's kids.

Now that everyone was together, it brought an entirely new sense of urgency. They knew they had to secure their part of the world as quickly as possible so they and the future generations would have a safe, stable environment that would allow them to grow and prosper.

346

"Where's Richard?" Susan asked, looking behind them toward the mirrored windows of the house.

"He's still at the lab, working on the vaccination. I think he said he'd be here after the fireworks."

"Too bad he's going to miss the show."

Michelle looked at her watch and pointed toward the east. Off in the distance, they could see plumes of smoke starting to rise. "Look, it's time."

Susan stepped forward and took both Michelle and Carlos by the hand. Facing what they knew to be the launch pads for their newly developed ballistic missiles, a tear started to fall down her cheek as she saw first one, and then another, and then a third nose-cone rise up over the tree line and start to accelerate toward the clouds.

"Are you sure this is necessary, Carlos?" she asked, her face giving away the horror she felt at unleashing weapons of mass destruction.

"Chairman Smythe hasn't given us a choice. Either we take out his computer networks at Fort Bragg or his people keep on hijacking our systems."

"But these bombs?"

"It's the only way we can make sure Smythe's troops are both blind and deaf." Carlos answered.

"And how's that going to affect us?" Michelle asked, tilting her chin up to see the first three missiles break past the clouds and arc south.

"I don't know yet," he admitted, "we'll just have to wait and see. If that MIN-OPS system is wired into everything like Samp--"

Carlos stopped himself before he said the name no one dared to pronounce around Susan. After catching himself, he went on, "like we were told it was, we all may get hit, Smythe, York, and us."

Susan watched the second wave of missiles come up above the tree line. "And what about York? What's the purpose of bombing him and his men back into the Stone

Age?"

"Two reasons, Prime Minister," Carlos said in a serious tone, addressing Susan with her formal title. "First, we have to make sure the drone facility in Utah stays off-line so his men can't make anymore UAV's."

"And the second reason...the reason for hitting his bunker in New York City?"

"To show him we can."

Susan was surprised to see that it was Michelle who had answered. Not only was Michelle seemingly unparsed by the launch of some horrifying weapons, Susan noticed she seemed to relish the thought of raining hellfire down on York and his associates. The callousness was frightening and Susan knew she'd have to keep her eyes on her friend to make sure the power she wielded did not go to her head. As she knew all too well, the power of life and death, the power to control the lives of others could be intoxicating.

A Note From The Author

Writing a trilogy about a dystrophic future was not my intent when I first came up with the idea behind Money Games. Although it has been a wonderful journey, the writing process has also taken me to places I never thought I would go.

I have to give credit to many individuals, corporations, and governments for turning what was supposed to be a story about a common woman finding her way through a treacherous world into a commentary about the world we live in. Being so effected by the news, there was no way I could leave out traces of what is happening to all of us, right here, right now.

During the course of writing all three books, the news has been filled with items I'd shake my head at in wonder. The banking crisis, wars, killer drones, computers, and systems that know everything about us; not to mention politicians bending over backwards to help the very few at the expense of the many. These events, topics I've discussed with my friends and family, are what molded and guided the evolution of this story.

Some people may feel disappointed at the ending, or feel the story is incomplete with too many threads left unresolved. Please, let me assure you, the end of this little tale has been written--just not by me. If you are anxious to see where the world of Susan, Carlos, Michelle, Darla, and Richard goes, all you have to do is read Orwell's, "1984" or Huxley's, "Brave New World". For another possible outcome, you can even flash back to the 1980's and watch the film, "The Terminator" to get a sense where the world I wrote about is going. The classic novels were my reference points. Unfortunately, it seems as if that is exactly where "the powers that be" (whomever they be may be) are taking us.

For me, the most difficult part of writing this

adventure had to do with the military. Again, I have to thank my friends for talking me through so many aspects and allowing me to use artistic license when dealing with the elements I adopted from our conversations. Thankfully, they were kind enough to accommodate me and my list of unending questions.

Finally, my readers should know that I have spent countless hours writing, reading, and revising these books and the reason I have done it is for you. The positive feedback I have received has made every second spent on this endeavor worthwhile. Soon, I'll be working on other projects; and, as an author, what will motivate me and carry me along through other journeys is the thought of allowing my readers to travel with me.

Susan DiGiovanni, widowed, with two young children, thinks she has met the man of her dreams, Don Clearmont, a technology aficionado and programmer for hedge funds. When he is indicted and killed in jail, her entire life changes.

Fearing for her life, she connects with several of Don's friends, scions from gold mining families who call themselves the "Seven Rams". As a group, they try to discover who killed Don and why. What they find is a financial world gone mad with a conspiracy to devalue the American dollar, create monopolies, and destroy the American dream.

Using all of their resource, including a stockpile of gold bullion-- along with a few programming tricks left behind by Don--they take on a powerful man they believe is responsible for having Don killed and destroying the economy, Roland Troth.

Troth, however, uses former members of the Special Forces to get what he wants, using any means necessary. Troth wants to eliminate all threats against him and get his hands on a cache of gold stashed in a small town; his team of mercenaries leaving a trail of murders from Wall Street to Pennsylvania. It is up to Susan, a once-typical Jersey girl, and her two new friends, Mario and Tommy, to stop Roland Troth from destroying the American economy and get revenge.

　　　In Part two of this Trilogy, Susan DiGiovanni has come into a fortune worth billions as well as ownership of a massive gold mine. Unfortunately, it cost her the love of her life and made her the target of a cabal trying to take control of the world. Roland Troth is the man Susan has to take down so she can excerpt her revenge.

　　　Troth, a member of a secret society, has reached out for help from a man even richer and more powerful than himself, Maxwell York. York is interested in one thing, establishing a neofeudalistic society with him and his associates controlling the world. To Clean up Troth's mess he hires Daniel Sampson, an ex- Special Forces operative. In a strange twist, Sampson falls in love with Susan and convinces her to team up with him to take down the entire cabal of elitists. When the most powerful of men in the world's secret societies start to fall, a power-play to fill the void draws entire nations into the fray and puts the United States in a state of panic.

　　　Susan and Sampson, the indirect cause of international collapse, looks for a way to escape and survive to fight another day.

Urban House Publishing Order Form

Money Games I, By Kimberly Barnes -
$15.00/ $3.50 shipping_____copies
Money Games II, By Kimberly Barnes -
$15.00/ $3.50 shipping_____copies
Money Games III, By Kimberly Barnes
$15.00/ $3.50 shipping_____copies
 Cross Artist, By R. Jacobs
_$15.00/ $3.50 shipping___copies
Prime Time, By R. Jacobs
$15.00/ $3.50 shipping____copies
My Life as a Certified Clapper, Br R.Jacobs
$15.00/ $3.50 shipping____copies
Dip City Wetland, By R. Jacobs
$15.00/ $3.50 shipping____copies

Send checks or Money Orders to:
Urban House Publishing
P.O. Box 1826
Montclair, N.J. 07042

*Books available at Amazon.com,
CreateSpace.com, and
UrbanHousePublishing.com. Also available as
an E-Book.

Urban House Publishing Order Form

Money Games I, By Kimberly Barnes -
$15.00/ $3.50 shipping_____copies

Money Games II, By Kimberly Barnes -
$15.00/ $3.50 shipping_____copies

Money Games III, By Kimberly Barnes
$15.00/ $3.50 shipping_____copies

Cross Artist, By R. Jacobs
_$15.00/ $3.50 shipping___copies

Prime Time, By R. Jacobs
$15.00/ $3.50 shipping___copies

My Life as a Certified Clapper, Br R.Jacobs
$15.00/ $3.50 shipping___copies

Dip City Wetland, By R. Jacobs
$15.00/ $3.50 shipping____copies

Send checks or Money Orders to:
Urban House Publishing
P.O. Box 1826
Montclair, N.J. 07042

*Books available at Amazon.com,
CreateSpace.com, and
UrbanHousePublishing.com. Also available as
an E-Book.

www.ingramcontent.com/pod-product-compliance
Lightning Source LLC
Chambersburg PA
CBHW070159260626
47160CB00002B/396